NOCTURNE

ANDREA RANDALL

CHARLES SHEEHAN-MILES

Books by Andrea Randall

November Blue
Ten Days of Perfect
Reckless Abandon
Sweet Forty-Two (coming December 2013)

In The Stillness
Something's Come Up
(with Michelle Pace, coming November 2013)

Books by Charles Sheehan-Miles

Thompson Sisters
A Song for Julia
Falling Stars
Just Remember to Breathe
The Last Hour
Rachel's Peril (coming December 2013)

America's Future
Republic
Insurgent

Prayer at Rumayla
A Novel of the Gulf War

Saving the World on Thirty Dollars a Day:
An Activist's Guide to Starting, Organiz-
ing and Running a Non-Profit Organization

NOCTURNE

ANDREA RANDALL

CHARLES SHEEHAN-MILES

IF YOU ENJOYED THIS BOOK, PLEASE SHARE IT
WITH A FRIEND, WRITE A REVIEW ONLINE, OR SEND
FEEDBACK TO THE AUTHORS!

www.sheehanmiles.com
www.andrearandall.com

ISBN-13: 978-0-9898688-2-2

Printed in the United States of America
Cincinnatus Press
www.cincinnatuspress.com

v1I012013

for Maggi

ACKNOWLEDGEMENTS

OUR THANKS GO to our amazing friend Maggi Myers, who was the first to support our collaboration and who read the earliest drafts of the book. Maggi, your support and friendship went well beyond the pages of our books and will have a lasting and wonderful impact on our lives. Friends, always.

We'd also like to thank our amazing Beta Readers. They are, in no particular order: Melissa Brown, Michelle Pace, Pamela Carrion, Kelly Moorhouse, Laura Wilson, Beth Suit, Kirsten Papi, Erin Roth and Kirsty Lander.

Finally, thanks go to our amazing cover designer, Sarah Hansen of Okay Creations and our inestimable editor, Lori Sabin.

Prelude

GREGORY

LOOKING UP AT the next candidate to enter the room, I immediately found myself subtracting points. Her dirty blonde hair was long and flew all over the place in ungroomed waves. She wore a sleeveless blue sweater and a grey skirt that was inappropriately short, well above the knee, with high black leather boots. She looked as if she were going out on a date. A young woman so attractive my breath caught a little as she positioned her sheet music on a stand and stood facing us with a confident expression.

James slid a folder across the table to me and spoke quietly. "Savannah Marshall. She's got a somewhat unconventional background."

I raised my eyebrows. He had an unreadable expression on his face.

I opened the folder, pointedly ignoring the girl who stood in front of us. I glanced over her application. Like most of the students auditioning this morning, she was in her senior year of high school. She listed an impressive number of performance credits on the application, but some of them were... odd. Venues I'd never heard of, and a wide variety of music, not all classical. That was unusual for prospective students at the Conservatory. In particular, she listed a summer spent *touring with a rock band*, probably in barns and warehouses since she was under twenty-one and wouldn't be able to play in the dive bars that such bands frequented. I snapped the folder closed. This one was an unlikely prospect. I had no intention of admitting students who were not serious about their music.

I'd been through auditions often enough, though it had been a number of years. I could see the yearning in her eyes, but her composure was impressive. Most of the auditions that morning had been nervous affairs. Sweaty palms, dropped instruments, feet shifting, heavy breathing, the typical nervous terror of teenagers facing a life-changing audition. So many young people came here every year dreaming of music. So many failed. This one was different. Her confidence implied that failure simply wasn't an option. Or that she simply didn't care, which seemed more likely given her dress. *We'll see*, I thought.

I waved a hand, beckoning her toward us. "Please proceed."

She raised her arms, bringing the flute to her mouth. Her sweater rode up slightly, exposing perhaps half an inch of skin above her skirt. Highly inappropriate. However, her form was precise. She nodded her upper body slightly toward the accompanist, who began playing.

The piece was a Paul Jeanjean etude, a fairly advanced and difficult piece. I leaned forward, my elbow on the table, chin cupped between my thumb and fingers, idly pulling at my beard. Her execution was meticulous. James, sitting next to me, also inclined forward in his seat, his eyes focused. He heard the same thing I did. This one was something. By far the best audition we'd heard, and she was only a few bars into her first piece.

James leaned toward me as if to say something. I didn't shift position. "She's good," he murmured.

"Shhhhhh." I wanted to hear the music, not his commentary.

It was rare to hear an audition this well-rounded. Her sound was technically flawless, and the timing and tone were nearly perfect. As she wrapped up her first piece, I waved my hand again and said, "Continue."

She began the second piece, a Mozart Concerto in D Major. I wrote some notes in the margin of her application then scanned it again. Good grades in high school thus far, though we didn't have her senior year transcript. I looked through her recommendations. They were glowing. One of them caught my eye. The recommendation was from a private music tutor in Philadelphia who I knew and respected.

I closed the folder again, and just listened. Savannah was beginning her final piece, the Dutilleux Sonatine. An ambitious piece, but one students often attempted. Beautiful when played correctly. A disaster when not.

As the piano accompaniment began, she took a slow breath, composing herself. Then she brought the flute to her lips. Her sound was exquisite, and she had a level of confidence that made it seem as if she wasn't even aware we were in the room. Her upper body moved with the music, and as she reached the most difficult, demanding portion, she closed her eyes, ignored the sheet music and just played.

I found myself holding my breath. Savannah was an extremely gifted musician. I closed my eyes, listening, delighting in the rich tone, the speed and beauty of it. I would never tell a student this, but she was nearly good enough to audition for the symphony *now*. We had to have her at the Conservatory. We had to watch over her career, preserve it.

I opened the folder again, made some notes, and then leaned close to James. "We must have this one. If she can't afford it, get her a scholarship. Whatever it takes."

He nodded his agreement.

Savannah finished. I met her eyes for a brief second. She had an exalted expression on her face, a tremendous smile. Not the panic and fear I was accustomed to seeing on a student during and after an audition. She knew. Which was dangerous, because too much confidence could lead to being lazy.

I knew how to deal with that. I lifted my hand in a dismissive wave. "We'll be in touch," I said, my voice as cold as I could make it. Then turned away, not waiting to see her deflate.

SAVANNAH

EIGHT MINUTES AND forty-nine seconds.

I saved my major contemporary work for last, and that's all that separated me from the end of the audition. It wasn't that I always *wanted* to go to the New England Conservatory; it's that I knew I would be going. It was the only option for me. I couldn't help the instant connection I felt with the sound the minute I first picked up a flute when I was nine. I was meant to play it. Now, almost nine years later, I stood before the most pivotal panel I'd ever faced, taking a breath before starting Dutilleux Sonatine. I'd played every second of this composition, in pieces and at once, so many times that I could hear it in my sleep. I knew it cold. All eight minutes and forty-nine seconds of it. I wasn't nervous at all. I'd prepared more than half my life for this.

That's a lie. I was scared shitless.

I only had eight minutes and forty-nine seconds left to seal my next four years, which would, in turn, seal the rest of my life. I had nailed the previous three pieces, and it was all down to this.

I took one last look at my judges before starting. I watched someone from the admissions office slide my folder to *him* again. Gregory Fitzgerald. While the identities of the judging committee aren't released ahead of time for a number of reasons, I knew all of the professors and musicians at the school. I was certain Gregory Fitzgerald was put on the panel solely to intimidate. He was a cellist. *The* cellist. He played for the Boston Symphony Orchestra and taught at the Conservatory. His reputation as a musician was undisputed. He was one of the youngest musicians, let alone cellists, to be granted a seat with the BSO. If the rumors Nathan told me were true, they nearly begged him to audition.

His reputation as a person, however, was less impressive. He had a knack for belittling students, making them feel like they knew nothing. No one needs that kind of harsh negativity in their lives. He could be a dark, broody, reclusive musical stereotype on his own time for all I cared.

He was hard to look away from, however. I'd give him that much. The pretense that surrounded him like a cloud vanished for a split second as he said something to the person sitting next to him and gave a slight half smile. Small creases that formed at the edges of his eyes proved he *did* smile from time to time, and it looked good on him.

Not wanting to give away that I might have been staring at him for a second too long between pieces, I nodded to the pianist and started. The song starts on a very low note, which is easy to completely screw up when playing a high-pitched instrument. But, that's just throat stuff. Nothing big. My biggest anxiety in the piece came just before three minutes in. When staring at the notes on the page for that section, it looked like a set of rapidly ascending and descending stairs. If I wasn't careful, it would sound like I was falling down them. It's easy to let your fingers get ahead of your eyes, especially with the fast stuff, and that would ruin it. Everything. So, as I approached that measure, I did something I'd only done once before and still can't believe I did in the middle of the most important audition of my life. I closed my eyes.

The notes came easily; they were woven through the fibers of every muscle in my body. My fingers floated across the keys and my tongue felt light as I executed the challenging note runs. The freedom that comes from playing rock and jazz is exciting and invigorating. Spending last summer on tour with The Howling Toddlers around the Tri-state area allowed me to dig into new creative spaces with my instrument. But, the comfort, structure, and pure beauty of classical music felt grounding. Like home. For the remaining five minutes, I sank myself into the piece, into the notes, into the sound. If I could have smiled without screwing everything up, I would have. I wanted to cry. Goosebumps sprang across my skin as I finished the last string of notes and opened my eyes.

I nailed it.

Gregory Fitzgerald met my eyes as I held my flute low in front of me, feeling shockingly nude under his scrutiny. Adrenaline I thought I'd depleted during my last song resurged through my veins. His right eyebrow twitched up before he looked back down at my folder, the rest of his face unchanged. He gave the requisite arrogant, dismissive wave before saying, "We'll be in touch." I tried not to let my shoulders sink, but his tone felt like a kick in the gut.

Still, I smiled, nodded, and walked backstage.

Asshole. He knows I nailed it.

As I walked through the backstage door to the hallway, Nathan greeted me with a huge smile.

"So?" he exclaimed, holding out his arms.

Nathan was already a student here, but I'd known him for years. We seemed to follow each other around to various musical summer camps across New England since I was ten and he was eleven. He plays the flute, too, and encouraged me as I prepared for this audition.

Finally away from the stage, and the music, and the opportunity to screw anything up, I let some nervous tears fill my eyes as I smiled. "I killed it!"

"Yes!" he shouted, wrapping his arms around my waist and spinning me around once before kissing my forehead as he set me down. "I'm so proud of you, Savannah."

I playfully smacked his shoulder as I started taking apart my flute. "What the hell was Gregory *Fitzgerald* doing in there? Doesn't he have some first years to harass or something?"

Nathan's playful hazel eyes widened. "What? He was?"

"Oh, of course he was. Why wouldn't I have one of the strictest judges ever for the most important day of my life?" I rolled my eyes and placed my music inside my bag before zipping it, still feeling the effects of his crystal blue eyes as he studied my carefully chosen clothing. "I'm just hoping I don't end up in an ensemble he organizes. He didn't seem too impressed with me."

"Ouch," Nathan sighed, "did he thank you for your time, or anything?" He already had a conciliatory look on his face.

"No, he said *we'll be in touch.*"

Nathan's smile returned as he grabbed my shoulders and looked me square in the eyes. "Are you sure that's what he said?"

"Um...yeah. That's what he said, with his little asshole wave." I mimicked the hand movement as my stomach sank. Maybe I didn't sound as great as I thought I did. Maybe that was all in my head and I really blew it.

Nathan squeezed my shoulders and smiled bigger than I'd ever seen him smile. "You're in, baby. You're in!"

Part One

Three Years

Later

Chapter 1

SAVANNAH

"I'M GLAD WE were able to put off this class until Madeline was teaching it." Nathan stretched his arm across the back of my chair as we settled into one of our last required Music Theory classes.

It was spring semester of my junior year—his senior year—and while there was still a light covering of snow on the ground, since it was late January, I was thrilled to be taking a class with Madeline White. She was a flutist who I'd had the pleasure of working with off and on for the last few years, and she'd been my private instructor since I entered the Conservatory. Most importantly, she shared some of the same liberal music theories we did.

"I totally agree. Our last two classes were painfully boring. At least we have a chance of staying awake this semester." I chuckled and rested my head on his shoulder for a second.

Nathan and I are both natural flutists. That's not bragging—it's a damn relief. We were able to tackle harder note runs and the highest and lowest octaves before most of our peers, opening a wide range of opportunities for us when we got here on campus.

While our technical abilities might lead some to assume that we would spend our days digging through the vast historical music library to conquer pieces written before the founding of America, sometimes we did just the opposite. We played with the music. We took the gift we were each given and tried to make it fun, alive. I love the classical pieces, don't get me wrong. There's something chilling about playing pieces written during the middle of a plague when the world was falling to total shit. However, being able to take notes invented before certain cultures and languages, and turn them into something fresh and new was invigorating. White, we knew, felt the same way. While I knew we'd have to cover a lot of the nuts and bolts of music and scales and the way pieces were written, I was happy to work through the tedious material with someone as bright as Madeline. She always told us to call her Madeline while we were at camp, and I wondered if it would be the same in class.

"It's ten after." Nathan shifted in his seat. He can't sit still for long. Which, by the way, is hilarious to watch him try to control during a performance. "Where the hell is she?"

Just then the door opened, and the class sighed in a mix of disappointment at having to stay in the class, and relief that it would get under way.

"What the hell?" I groaned as Nathan pulled his pencil out of his bag.

He sat up and looked to the door. "What's he doing in here?"

It was Gregory Fitzgerald, smugness wrapped in a cello, from my audition three years prior. I had, obviously, gotten into the Conservatory. Not only did I get in, I'd received glowing accolades from the judging committee upon my first few months here. From everyone except him, that is.

Whatever.

I hadn't seen much of him around campus since getting in, but, three years later, he was walking into Madeline White's Music Theory class. With his cello case. He still had the same beard, though it was slightly shorter. It was well-groomed but made him look a bit older than the thirty-one years I knew he was. That was probably what he was going for. I read an interview with him once, in the BSO newsletter that was sent to my grandparents' house every quarter, along with newsletters from the other four Big Five orchestras. The reporter asked him what he thought about being one of the youngest first-section cellists for the Pops. He shrugged it off, arguing that age and experience were trumped by hard work. His dark hair didn't seem to have any grey in it, though I assumed that would change quickly if he never wiped the scowl off his face.

"Ladies and gentlemen," he announced unapologetically. "Unfortunately, Madeline White has had a personal emergency and will be out for the whole semester."

Nathan leaned over and whispered in my ear, "And they couldn't find someone else to fill in for her today but him?"

I shrugged. "We should call Madeline after class and see if she's okay," I whispered.

"I know. I really don't want to have to find another instructor. I've worked with her forever."

"Compassionate." I smacked Nathan's arm and shifted in my seat before I turned my eyes back to our new, attractive professor.

"So," Fitzgerald continued, "I'll be taking over this class." A cacophony of complaints and cheers filled the class.

Christ.

Gregory Fitzgerald was a surprisingly divisive topic amongst students, given how little time he spent with the actual student body. Most of the population was in agreement about his ability; there was little you could do to argue that he was at the top of his field. And, most of the females seemed to be in agreement about his looks. As the guys around us began to frown at not getting to have class with the beautiful Madeline White this semester, the girls took on blushing grins, suddenly looking much more interested in music theory. His allure didn't come exclusively from the clear blue of his eyes, but from the way they sought me out. Like prey, as he surveyed the field of students and targeted in on me.

Breathe.

The disagreements, however, began when we all tried to break down how it was he got there. He was known to spend twenty hours a day practicing before he made it to the Pops. Sure, that's fairly typical, I guess. But, what wasn't typical, were the rigorous hours he put in on a regular basis. Ten, fifteen hours every single day was the rumor, and it was only slightly less on performance days. Work, work, and more work was definitely his reputation, and my excitement about music theory this semester bottomed out in an instant.

"If you're all quite finished and ready to act like the adults the government insists that you are, let's get started." He set his cello case on the floor by the podium and began the driest introduction to an upper level music theory class in the history of humanity. He didn't even introduce himself. He didn't have to, but that he knew he didn't have to really got under my skin.

Nathan wrapped his arm around my shoulder once again. "Get comfortable, beautiful. It's going to be a long-ass semester."

By the end of the lecture I was watching the seconds tick by on the clock, certain it was slowing down on purpose. I bounced my knee anxiously as Gregory spent the lecture discussing why musicians should learn certain scales in certain orders, and how that translated into certain classical pieces. He stepped away from the podium and the class began to shift in their seats, collecting their bags, and some standing up. He grabbed his cello case and headed for a seat in front of the podium, sitting down and opening it up. I looked up at Nathan, and he just shrugged his lean shoulders and turned back to Gregory. Without addressing the class, without asking anyone to sit back down or be quiet, he started playing.

It was Bach's Cello Suite, No. 1 in G major. Everyone knows it. Even people who aren't musically inclined would recognize the piece within the first measure, if they didn't already know it by name. I scrunched my forehead, trying to figure out why he would be playing such an easy piece, given what I knew he could play. Hell, if I had a little bit of time with a cello, I could probably play it.

By the third measure, it was shockingly clear. Suddenly there weren't any other students in the class, and I could barely register that Nathan was standing, unmoving, next to me. I was locked on Gregory's hands. His face. The way his body swayed each time his bow moved seductively across the strings. Inside ten seconds, he was a musician. Just like the rest of us. Screw that—he was nothing like the rest of us. He was perfect. It was perfect. His eyes were closed, and as the song slowed before the last twelve seconds, or so, he hung onto the pause with his eyebrows pulled together. I held my breath, my throat tight with anticipation, and with tears stinging my eyes at the absolute beauty of this seemingly elementary song he'd just taken to a level I didn't know existed.

Exhaling only when he carefully ran through the end of the song, I cleared my throat and looked up at Nathan, who was still standing and completely slack-jawed. It wasn't that we just watched some groundbreaking performance, and that was the cause of the dead silence in the room. It was that we just watched a musician with one of the sternest reputations live up to it in a classroom full of students who could only dream to play with a fraction of the greatness he possessed. Right before our eyes.

Resting his bow against the top of his thigh, he opened his clear blue eyes. "Class dismissed."

GREGORY

JUST ONE SEMESTER. That was all I had to deal with...one semester of dealing with arrogant, disruptive teenagers bent on wasting my time in a class I didn't want to teach in the first place. I was hoping Madeline would be able to pick the class back up before the end of the semester, but given the extent of her wrist surgery, it didn't seem likely. She would be spending her free time in physical therapy to get back to playing. *That* I could understand. Turning the corner to walk down the long hallway of practice rooms, I shuddered at the thought of not being able to play for a few months, as was going to be the case with Madeline.

The practice rooms are mostly soundproof, so it took me off guard to hear the high-pitched melody of a flute floating through the hall. The tone was solid, the sound itself was beautiful, but the notes were disorganized. It didn't sound like jazz—which I could appreciate on a technical level, if not a sound and composition level—it sounded like rock music of some sort. Suddenly the notes stopped and the hypnotizing melody of Entr'acte from Carmen took over my senses. While this was a fairly simple song, note and rhythm-wise, to be able to play it beautifully was the challenge. It was largely in the upper octave and played between piano and mezzo-forte—especially challenging for under-trained throats that tend to lean toward blaring through the upper-most octaves as though they're in a marching band.

As I made my way toward the end of the hallway, the song started again as soon as it was finished, sounding even more beautiful than the time before. I knew it wasn't Madeline, even though it sounded keenly like her. It had to be one of her students. Madeline was thorough and demanding in the physical instruction of her students—coaching their throats to stay open and strong. While that was good practice for all flutists to learn, Madeline was able to train her students in such a way that gave them great endurance. Approaching the room, drawn by a curiosity that didn't usually strike me with woodwinds, I began to think maybe it was another instructor. The sound, though, was too familiar to be someone I didn't know. When the second run of Entr'acte ended, that unfamiliar rock song started again.

Normally, it's poor form to spy on someone as they are practicing, but their sheer inability to stay on task irritated me. How could one jump from classic opera, to that uncultured noise, and back again? I raised my eyebrows when I saw Savannah Marshall, her back to me, playing as she stood in front of an empty music stand. Her control over the notes is what held my ears captive. Despite her playing music I had no use for, I couldn't look away. While I remembered her audition nearly three years ago like it was yesterday, since I'd never heard a seventeen-year-old flutist with such skill in all of my years, I chalked some of it up to her ability to audition.

Some people get stage fright. This is why, increasingly over the years, musicians have turned to anti-anxiety medications and beta-blockers to calm their nerves. Some musicians, however, do their best work in an audition, and can't ever maintain that level of skill. I'd assumed the latter was the case with Savannah. I still remembered her almost cocky attitude for her audition, and her constant chatter during my lectures led me to believe she simply did not take music seriously.

The young woman before me, however, was certainly a musician. Her posture was perfect, and she swayed just enough to show she felt the music, but not so much that it looked forced. Suddenly, as if she sensed someone looking in, she dropped her flute from her lips and turned around. She didn't seem startled as she took me in with large brown eyes that seemed to be misting over.

"You really should close the door, Ms. Marshall." I bit the inside of my cheek to keep any praise off of my face as I placed my hand on the handle.

She cleared her throat and shook her head. "Sorry, Mr. Fitzgerald. You can leave it open, though. I'm finished."

I dropped my hand as she walked toward the chair by the door and started taking apart her flute, cleaning the inside of each piece before putting it back in the case. The instrument was gorgeous. It had a rose gold body with silver keys, and a gold mouthpiece that was engraved with scrolling designs. Quite a high-end piece for a student—even one in Conservatory. Someone certainly believed in her a great deal, as this professional-grade flute was easily ten to fifteen thousand dollars.

"That's a beautiful instrument you have there." I tried to keep my tone ambivalent, not wanting to let on that I was most interested in how she acquired such a piece. I'd mortgaged my late grandmother's home in the most expensive neighborhood in Boston to buy my cello. Because when you play an instrument at this level, you gave it whatever it took. Your entire life.

"Thank you," she replied. "My father gave it to me over winter break. I'm still getting used to it, but I love it." Her face brightened as she spoke.

"Well, he must think a lot of your ability, Savannah."

Her eyes flickered straight to mine, and her brow furrowed as she seemed to process my statement.

"I'm here at the Conservatory, aren't I?" she shot back. "This isn't just a hobby of mine, Mr. Fitzgerald." She chuckled to herself as she snapped her case shut and placed it in her instrument bag.

"That piece you were playing..." I started.

"The Entr'acte? What about it?" She shrugged on her green wool peacoat and matching scarf.

"It's a bit of a simple piece for you, isn't it?" I held the door open as she walked through and met me in the hallway.

She turned on her heel to face me once again. "So was the Bach suite you played in class last week."

Inexplicably, I followed. She was wearing some kind of floral perfume. It wasn't overwhelming, but for a brief moment it lingered in each step she took.

"Yes, but that was the piece that made the cello worth playing, for me. It was the first real classical piece I tackled that made it all worthwhile." I cleared my throat, shocked at my own honesty with a student. "I certainly didn't waste my time, though, on rock music." I arched my eyebrow in her direction.

Savannah stopped in her tracks. "And the Entr'acte is mine. It was the first piece of substance I mastered. I was ten..." Her gaze trailed off with her voice as she ignored my jab at her other musical selection.

"Ten?" I questioned. "It has a pretty ambitious octave for a young flutist."

"My mother was in Carmen at the time. I heard the song and wanted to learn how to play it immediately. So, I learned it. It was like I was playing along with her." Her voice sounded distant, still.

Ah, so her mother was a flutist. It certainly made sense, of course. Most students here had at least one parent who was a musician—or who tried to be.

"So your mother plays for the opera? Which one?" I asked as we reached the door. I loved the opera.

Savannah's eyebrows pulled in a bit before she gave a relaxed smile. "I have to get back to my dorm. Sorry about the door, Mr. Fitzgerald. I'll remember to close them from now on." A blast of frigid cold air hit me as she quickly exited the building.

"It's quite all right, Miss Marshall," I mumbled to the closing door. She hadn't answered the question about her mother.

Two years before, I'd been in Washington, DC for a concert at the National Arboretum. I vividly recalled the sun shining in through the glass at an angle, the slight sound of water from a fountain, the beauty of the music as we played. Most of all, I remembered the faint smell of lilies drifting over me, almost intoxicating, as I played.

That's when it hit me, the perfume that I couldn't identify before. I've never been an aficionado of gardens or flowers, but I remembered that scent. That's what she wore.

The faint smell of lilies lingered in the air behind her as the door latched closed and I stood alone in the hallway.

Chapter 2

SAVANNAH

I SLID INTO MY seat in music theory and leaned toward Nathan. "Feeling better?"

He looked at me with bleary eyes. Hung over, and it served him right.

"Not really," he mumbled, his voice only as loud as I assumed his headache would let him speak.

We'd gone out the night before, intending to have dinner and a couple of drinks, and he'd had more than just a couple. That led to a strange moment late in the evening as we were walking back toward the school. He'd stopped, his feet skidding on the snow, and looked at me.

"Savannah?" He slurred his words.

I raised my eyebrows, turning back toward him. I met his eyes, and he met mine. He looked as lost as I'd ever seen him. I felt like I should say something—he looked angry, sad, and confused all at once. Before I could open my mouth, he shook his head.

"Never mind," he finished.

I didn't press. We had walked on, returning to the dorms.

This morning, he looked a little better, but just a little. His skin was washed out, pale looking beneath the freckles scattered across his nose and cheeks, and his eyes were red-rimmed. It was out of character for Nathan to drink that much.

The door to the classroom burst open, and in marched Fitzgerald. He carefully leaned his cello case against the wall, then shook off his jacket and ran a hand through his hair. A few snowflakes evaded his effort to brush them away.

Ignoring all of us, he walked to the white board and began writing on it. Contrary Motion. Mirror. Proportional. Spiral. Accompanied.

He turned around. His blue eyes slid right past me, fixing on Nathan for a few seconds, then to the other students in the class. His face was set in a rigid frown, and his posture highlighted tension, restrained motion, intensity.

"Mr. Connors. Please remind the class what are the three requirements for a musical composition to qualify as a strict canon?"

My eyes darted to Nathan. This morning he was lucky to remember his own name. He was so obviously hung over; I could only think Fitzgerald had singled him out deliberately.

Nathan shifted in his seat, and his face actually managed to go a little bit whiter. He coughed. "Um...the second voice... can't vary from the first...or its um...contrapuntal variations... um...the second voice enters later...except for..."

Nathan's voice trailed off and he closed his eyes.

"Mr. Connors, I explained during the first week of class that I expect you to show up for class prepared. This is material we reviewed on Friday, and you had the entire weekend to review it. How are you supposed to understand today's lesson?"

I raised my hand. Fitzgerald ignored it.

Nathan kept his eyes closed and took a deep breath. "Sir, my apologies, I am not feeling well this morning."

Fitzgerald continued to glare at Nathan, and so I finally spoke up, hoping to distract his attention from the too obviously suffering Nathan. "The three requirements are: the second voice must be an exact repetition of the first, or a contrapuntal variation. The second voice enters later than the first, except in proportional or retrograde. The riposta is generated by the proposta."

Gregory's gaze shot to me, and for three long seconds he stared, causing my stomach to flip as I stared back. Swallowing once, he pursed his lips dismissively. "That's very good, Miss Marshall. Or it would have been if I had called upon you, which I did not."

I breathed a sigh of relief when he waved toward the board, then picked up a stack of paper and began handing the sheets out.

"This week we're going to talk about some of the more unusual forms of the canon. Your assignment for the week is to compose your own brief form of canon. You'll work in groups of two, choosing whichever instrument you wish. Each composition must be no longer than four minutes, it must strictly follow one of the forms of canon we have gone over, and you will perform it two weeks from today."

He paused when he got to my desk, placing the assignment sheet on it, then his startling blue eyes met mine as his hand remained on my desk. "Miss Marshall, when I say I want strict adherence to the assigned structure, I mean it. If you wish to get away with breaking the rules, you must first understand them thoroughly. Am I clear?"

I nodded, but he hadn't waited around for an answer, moving on to the rest of the class. I scanned the paper, which contained a detailed list of the criteria he intended to use to grade the assignment. It had been a challenge. Writing a canon, any canon, and making it sound good, was difficult, and beyond the scope of what most musicians could accomplish. I closed my eyes, the beginning of an idea forming in my head.

He didn't want us to break the rules. We were required to adhere to the formal, stultified rules of strict canon, rules which were in place four hundred years ago. That was fine.

But he didn't say we couldn't combine rules. Bach had done it more than once, as had a very few other composers. I tuned out the classroom, letting a melody form in my mind, visualizing it, then adding layers, one on top of the other, until I felt a loud tap against my desk.

My eyes flew open. Fitzgerald stood there. His eyebrows were squeezed together in irritation, a furrow running right down the center of his forehead. I could feel the heat coming from his body he stood so close.

"Are you still with us, Miss Marshall?"

I blinked a few times, my heart racing as I stared into his eyes. "Yes. I was thinking about the assignment. Sorry."

He turned and walked away, returning to the lecture as I once again found myself needing a cleansing breath.

Thank God his attitude sucked, or I could have been in real trouble.

GREGORY

It grated on me how Savannah continuously challenged me in class. I would never have tolerated it from any other student. Ever. But I'd watched her for the previous two years, and she was an accomplished musician and incredible student. That required some special consideration, but my patience only went so far.

Not to mention that her behavior encouraged others to do the same. Nathan hung onto her every word, apparently enamored with her radiance, and he'd followed her into challenging me in class earlier this week.

Nathan was unlikely to question me again. He left defeated at the end of class, tight-lipped and angry after showing up to our intellectual gunfight with a knife. But the fact was, they were both in for much tougher challenges than me if they intended to be successful. It was my job to help them prepare. I wasn't enthusiastic about teaching this course, but I'd agreed to it, and I intended to do my best.

Savannah though...she was impressive. Two weeks ago I had assigned the class a difficult challenge: to compose a four-minute strict canon. She had followed the assignment to the letter, but then turned it completely upside down, by composing an accompanied canon in contrary motion. Complex. Layered. Exquisite. One of my cello students, Marcia, accompanied her, a flute and cello duet which captured all the complexity of some of the best Baroque music, but also expressed a longing, and a depth of emotion I rarely felt hearing students play.

Her music, even her movements, were imbued with an inherent grace, a beauty I'd seen a hint of during her audition, but had pushed to the back of my mind. I'd never encountered an undergraduate with such depth of skill. I closed my eyes, trying to shut out the music blaring from the speakers in the restaurant, instead focusing on the string of notes she'd played.

"Are you even listening to me?"

My eyes flew open. Karin—my date—stared across the table at me, her face twisted in annoyance.

"I'm so sorry," I said. "I was just thinking about something that happened in class."

I spotted our waiter, a poorly shaven young man. He had a tiny brown spot on his shirt. I waved him down. "Excuse me. Perhaps someone could shut off the ghastly noise coming from the speakers?"

The waiter stood there, dumbstruck. I jerked a finger at the speaker for emphasis, and he said, "I'll, uh...talk to the manager."

Karin said in a teasing voice, "The girls at the office are right...you really are insufferable sometimes."

I shrugged. "Hardly. This noise is awful."

She shook her head, a grin on her face. "You think any music written since the 18th century is awful."

"No, that is not true. There are a number of 20th-century symphonies I absolutely love. But this?" I mock shuddered.

Karin went back to her story. And the truth was, I wasn't terribly interested. James had insisted on setting us up for this date, sure that Karin and I would hit it off. She was attractive enough. Blonde hair, and an attractive body. But she knew little about music. How she could possibly work for the Conservatory and not actually care about music? She might as well be a heathen who just happened to work in a cathedral. She went on for quite some time about the politics of the school administration, something that I cared exactly nothing about.

But I knew I was expected to say something. "That sounds...terrible."

She gave me a look as if she knew my words weren't sincere. Then she gave up.

"What about you?" she asked. "When you aren't busy with the orchestra, or teaching, what do you like to do?"

I felt my eyebrows move toward each other. "Practice. Or go to the symphony, or the occasional ballet. I'd love to see the Bolshoi someday."

She leaned back in her chair. "Movies? Do you golf?"

I flexed my hand defensively. "Sports don't interest me. Especially any that could injure my hands."

She shook her head. "So really...it's all about the music with you?"

I gave her a long look. "It is...all about the music."

I studied her. It seemed I already knew an inordinate amount about her, because she'd talked quite a lot so far during dinner. She graduated with a BA in Economics from Tufts, somehow ending up at the New England Conservatory, managing, among other things, the sizeable endowment for the school. Of course I was fully aware the endowment was essential to the functioning of the school, and that financial matters must be attended to. But in truth, I'd rarely paid any attention to such things. My focus was always the music. Other things were of limited importance by comparison.

At least my student, Savannah, understood that. While her opinions were often maddening, there was no question in my mind that she got it. When she talked about music her face glowed, highlighting excited brown eyes. Although, in truth, I was concerned she might be prone to flights of fancy, and I worried far too much about her future.

Frankly, it disturbed me that I thought about her at all once class ended for the day. Never in my career had a student antagonized me as much as she did. For one crazy second, though, I wished it were her sitting across from me at the table. I wanted to hear the sweet pitch of her voice as she argued her ridiculous opinions about musical freedom, so I could argue back. That would be far more interesting than a dissertation on office politics and who on the faculty was sleeping with whom.

It was intriguing. I hadn't intended to teach music theory at all this semester, instead concentrating on cello students exclusively. But Madeline White was injured and personally asked me to take the class. A decade ago, we'd attended the Conservatory together, and had been friends ever since. She often said I was too rigid. And I, in turn, often told her she was far too freewheeling. But the respect between friends was important to me. So I took on the class. And the very first day I walked in, I didn't miss the expression on Savannah Marshall's face, nor that of her hyperactive boyfriend, Nathan. Both of them—the entire class, in fact—appeared horrified to see me.

I wasn't concerned with being liked. Only respected. As long as I was teaching that course, they would get the most rigorous education possible.

Karin reached across the table and touched my hand. Her expression was a little incredulous. "Are you still there?"

I gave her a tight smile. "Please forgive me. I'm afraid I'm not quite well. It's not your fault. Perhaps another evening?"

She looked disappointed. There was little I could do about that, and to be fair, it wasn't her fault. I was just...preoccupied.

Karin collected her things, and the two of us walked out of the restaurant after I paid the bill. I prided myself on being a gentleman, and this evening, I'd been no such thing, and that made me uncomfortable. I took her arm as we waited for a taxi.

"I truly am sorry. Perhaps we can meet again. I have tickets for the Boston Opera. Would you care to join me?"

Mollified, she smiled. "Yes. I'd like that very much."

"I'm glad. I'll call you later this week."

She nodded as the cab rolled up. When it pulled away, I ambled down the street. I was only a few blocks from my townhouse on Pinckney Street, and I took the route that led me past a residential garden. My thoughts on a different woman than the one I'd just said goodbye to.

Chapter 3

GREGORY

A BEAD OF SWEAT rolled down my forehead to my chin, where it nestled somewhere in my beard. My body was tense, my right arm beginning to tire, the left cramping. I refused to give in. It was nearly nine o'clock at night. I'd been practicing since four in the morning. The music demanded a devotion that required every bit of attention I could muster, no matter how painful it might be, no matter how much time it took. I'd devoted my life to music, letting it take priority over family, women. It took priority over everything.

I ignored the doorbell when it rang, merely frowning. There wasn't time for interruptions. I was working on the prelude for Bach's Suite for Solo Cello No. 3 in C Major. A beautiful piece. In fact it was *the* composition that had turned my interest in music from simply interest to absolute obsession. The music swept over me in waves, my eyes closed, ears turned toward the instrument, wincing every time I thought I was close to missing a beat.

The doorbell rang again, and I cursed under my breath. I couldn't imagine who would show up at my house at nine o'clock on a Sunday evening. Whoever it was, they were infuriating.

I continued to play and ignore the doorbell. Until it rang again. And again.

Finally, I halted at the end of the movement.

Carefully, I leaned my Domenico Montagnana cello in its stand. The instrument once belonged to Pablo Casals, and I bought it at auction two years ago for seven hundred fifty thousand dollars. This, in turn, raised the ire of my entire family against me. I'd inherited the house on Pinckney Street from my maternal grandmother. Valued at just over a million dollars, a new mortgage on a property, which had been in my family for two centuries, was just enough to get my hands on an instrument without parallel; an instrument produced by one of the finest master luthiers in history, when Boston was merely a trade outpost of the British empire.

Once my instrument was in place, I walked toward the door. Immediately my legs cramped. I'd been sitting in the same position for many hours. I stood still, ignoring the now continuous doorbell. The sweat, which had rained off my body, stained the carpet for four feet around where I'd been playing, and my body was slick with perspiration.

A good practice.

I found James sagged against the doorframe as I opened it.

"It's about time." He rolled his eyes and scratched his head.

"You should have called ahead."

"I did. Your phone is off, Gregory."

I shrugged and walked back into the house, leaving the door open. James followed, his nose crinkling a little, probably at the stink of sweat I was giving off. "That's usually a hint that I don't wish to answer the phone."

I walked into the kitchen and pulled a bottle of water out of the refrigerator. "Drink?" I asked. I already knew he wouldn't accept; there was nothing in the refrigerator but water.

"No, thanks." He stood there, staring at me.

"Is something bothering you?"

James sighed. "I'm worried about you. What are you putting in right now? Eighteen hours a day? More?"

I shrugged. "I do what it takes."

"Have you seen Karin lately?"

"We date occasionally. But she understands my music comes first and always will."

He shook his head slightly. "I'm sure everyone who ever comes into contact with you knows that. But you need to get out a little. There's such a thing as having a life."

I finished gulping back the water and tossed the bottle in the trash.

"We've had this discussion, James."

"I want you to go get a shower and get dressed. Let's go get a drink."

I gave him a long, level look. Then I shrugged. "Fine."

My muscles were tired, aching, and irritated with me as I climbed the stairs. James and I had been friends since both of us were students at the New England Conservatory. He was my only friend really, apart from Madeline, and certainly the only person on earth who could pull me away from practice. I'd learned to let him do it. When he decided I'd had enough, he would call and bang on the door and interrupt until I finally gave in. Generally, I found it cumbersome to have people in my life, but James's friendship was oddly gratifying, perhaps because we'd known each other so many years. He was correct on one point. I hadn't realized I was famished. I thought back, trying to remember when I'd last eaten, and came up with an unsatisfactory answer. It was sometime yesterday afternoon. Now that I'd stopped playing, my entire body was shaking like the vibrato I put into the strings.

Clean now, I stepped out of the shower and dried off, then changed into plain black pants and a white shirt, then slid on a jacket and walked back downstairs.

"Wherever it is that we're going, they need to have food," I announced when I got to the bottom of the stairs.

James obliged. A few minutes later we walked into Murphy's Pizza on the Common and sat down facing each other. A wave of exhaustion washed over me as we sat down, and James gave me a concerned look.

"Stop that," I said. "Another lecture about how I work too hard would be tiresome."

He shook his head and shrugged. "How long have we known each other?"

Thank God the waitress appeared at that moment. I ignored his question and looked at the menu, then placed my order. James did the same, and then he looked at me.

"Damn it, I'm not going to lecture you, but look at yourself. You've lost too much weight. Your clothes hang off of you. You've always been intense, but lately it's seemed a little much. Even for you."

I didn't dignify his micro-lecture with a response. Instead I pointedly looked at the waitress, who had paused to talk to another server instead of bringing our drinks. She saw the look and started moving again, bringing us our beers.

I tasted mine. It was swill, but it would do for now.

James shook his head. "Anyway, that's not what I came over to talk to you about. Have you thought at all about the email I sent you Thursday?"

I shifted through my mind. I had received an email from James, I recalled looking at it. I couldn't for the life of me remember what it was about.

"Refresh my memory," I replied.

"Jesus, Gregory. It's amazing we've stayed friends all these years."

I stared across the table at him. "We have a series of shows coming up starting next week, James. I've had a lot on my mind."

He frowned. "This is about the boy."

Right. The *blind* boy.

"Yes, I do recall, now that you mention it. Something about a blind boy who wishes to learn cello."

James sighed. "Don't sound so callous. His name is Robert Donovan. From what I understand he has considerable natural talent."

That infuriating phrase again. "Music isn't about talent, it's about hard work and dedication to your craft."

"Fine, then. Whatever it is...this boy deserves a break in life."

"How did you encounter him?"

"I met his adoptive parents a few weeks ago at a dinner party."

"Adoptive?"

James nodded. "Robby was severely abused when he was younger. His birth parents are in prison. They actually thought he was autistic, but that...seems to be trauma. He's brilliant."

"And what exactly does this have to do with me? Surely you can find some..." I waved my hand in the air, trying to find a phrase that wouldn't sound as arrogant as I knew this was going to sound. After flailing uselessly for a moment, I said what I had on my mind. "Surely you can find some second-rate cello instructor to help this boy with his playing."

Our meals arrived as we spoke, so we paused for a few moments. Once the waitress was gone, James spoke. "This boy has a remarkable ear, Gregory. We're talking a couple of hours a week."

"I don't do private lessons outside of the Conservatory. You know that."

"I want you to consider an exception. Just meet the boy and listen to him play. I know you're not busy next week—it's spring break."

I sighed and very slightly shook my head, then took a sip of the swill. "Fine, James. I'll meet him. I'll consider it. I'm not promising anything. It's one thing teaching students at the Conservatory...but it's another thing entirely to teach someone entirely new to music."

Especially someone who's blind.

I had no idea how I'd stand a chance teaching a young child how to play notes he couldn't read on a page, or see the location of my fingers on the strings. I'd figure something out.

James grinned. "Tuesday? 4 p.m.?"

"Certainly. Whatever you require. Just tell me where to be and leave me alone about it."

James's voice trailed off in my head as the bells on the door directed my eyes upward, where I saw Savannah Marshall and a group of her girlfriends. I was slightly annoyed, at first, that the waitress sat them at the booth diagonal from ours, given all their high-pitched giggling and incessant talking. The irritation lasted only as long as it took for Savannah to remove her oversized white winter jacket, revealing a snug red sweater underneath it.

Any time I'd seen her in class or on stage, she mostly dressed professionally. Apart from her wildly inappropriate audition clothing three years ago, of course. That aside, I respected that she never seemed to put herself on display the way so many of her female classmates did. This sweater, however, clung to the severe curve of her waist in a way that made my lips part and take in an extra breath.

She was stunning. Absolutely stunning.

Prying myself away from staring inappropriately, I peered up to her face. Just as she turned to sit, Savannah caught my eye, seemingly startled to see me. Her already wind-blushed cheeks deepened in color as she took a visible breath.

"Hi Mr. Fitzgerald," she said sweetly, melodically almost, as she politely waved.

Gregory, please. Call me Gregory.

I didn't say that. I did, however, return her greeting with a grin and a wave of my own. "Savannah," I replied, nodding once.

"Wh—were you even listening to me?" James held out his hands, exasperated.

"Calm down, James. A student said *hi*. I was trying to *have a life*, as you suggested earlier."

James turned to the gaggle of laughing girls and shook his head, looking back at me.

"What?" I asked as his face turned suspicious.

He shook his head, grinning as he took a sip of his beer. "Nothing. Just watch your ass, Greg."

Rolling my eyes, I sipped my beer, too. "Must you be so crass, James?"

"Yes," he chuckled, mocking me, "I *must*."

SAVANNAH

Assobio a Jato.

My senior recital wasn't for over a year, but I knew I'd be playing this piece as part of my program the second I heard it. It's a piece for flute and cello, and I planned on asking my friend and roommate, Marcia, to accompany me. I was lucky Gregory Fitzgerald hadn't overheard me practicing this piece when he saw me the other day in the practice rooms. I'm sure he would have given me an earful about how I was "doing it wrong," since he didn't seem to like me very much. At first I assumed his gruffness toward me was because of my mother, but he didn't seem to have an idea of who she was. Well, he probably knew *who* she was, but not that she was my mother. I chuckled a little, recalling that I'd put my mother's married name any place on the application that asked for my parents' names. I'd wanted to get in on my own.

Each year there was always a fresh batch of rumors about who got in and why. Some people were accused of bribing members of the pre-audition committee in various ways, but others, reportedly, took it all the way to the top and went for the jugular. Paying off the school.

I knew there were enough people at the Conservatory that knew who my mother was, but the fact that Gregory Fitzgerald didn't calmed me somehow.

Marcia rolled her eyes when I told her Fitzgerald was the new instructor for my music theory class. Luckily, Madeline was able to set me up with a trusted colleague of hers to provide my private instruction for the remainder of the semester. Marcia actually had Gregory, as he requested she call him—which shocked the hell out of me for some reason—for her private instruction. She was thrilled to learn from the best cellist at the Conservatory, and, really, in the country, but she found his style a bit militant.

I shook my head, lifted my chin, and resumed practicing.

Open throat. Don't let your fingers get ahead of your eyes.

I don't know why the hell Gregory Fitzgerald got under my skin.

Yes, I do. He was an arrogant, snobby musical stereotype of the worst kind. He barely looked out into the class when he was talking, and when he did, his clear blue eyes shot through me like ice. He was only ten years or so older than me. His thick, black hair and fairly tight physique spoke to that. But the grim, smug expression he plastered on his face aged him another ten. Easily.

Seeing him at Murphy's with James Mahone the other day caught me off guard. I wanted to blow him off, ignore him the way he ignores all of us when we're out in public. But, he wasn't ignoring me. I'd caught him staring at me, and it didn't infuriate me. It excited me. I felt his eyes on me as I took off my coat, and when I turned toward him, those blue eyes pulled a juvenile *hi* from me before I could filter it. He grinned back, returned the greeting, and I wanted to melt. *He might be human after all*, I thought.

Before I knew it, I stumbled across a string of notes that should have been an easy run.

Shit, see what happens? Focus. He's still awful, even if his smile did that to your insides.

I took a deep breath, exhaling all thoughts of the annoying, lifeless professor, and started the piece over again. This time, it was good. Not ideal—I had to slow down a few times over some of the runs, and my throat was definitely going to be sore in the morning, but it was good. I groaned at the thought of the exercises I'd have to get back into doing to pull off this, and other pieces, with solid tone.

"You know," Nathan startled me as he walked into my dorm room, "they have soundproof practice rooms so you can grumble in private." He sat next to me on my bed as I put my flute away.

"I know, jerk," I teased, "I just wanted to get one last go at this piece before quiet hours. How many pieces are you playing for your recital?"

Nathan ran a hand through his thick, dark curls as he sighed. "Three."

"Don't sound too excited, or anything," I toned out sarcastically. He didn't laugh. "Hey," I put my case away and placed my hand on his leg, "you okay?"

He stared at my hand for a second before shaking his head. "Yeah, I'm fine. You ready to go out?" He stood and held out his hand for me. I took it.

"Absolutely. Just don't drink as much as you did last time. You got all weird."

Nathan stopped at the door, dropping his hand from mine. "What do you mean?"

I shrugged. "You just drank a ton and then got all...I don't know...sad." I shrugged again, indicating I had no idea what he was going to say that night.

"Sorry..." he trailed off, running both hands through his hair.

"Don't be. Just don't drink *all* the liquor at the bar tonight." I giggled and took his hand again. An easy smile spread across his face as he followed me down the hall.

"So," he seemed eager to change the subject, "that piece you were playing when I walked in requires a cellist."

"Uh-huh, I'm going to ask Marcia to do it, I think."

"What?" Nathan asked as he held the main door open for me. "You don't want the dashing professor to do it?"

I let out a full-throated laugh. "Yeah, can you imagine? I'm going to have a hard enough time passing the most recent composition he gave us to write. I'm excited about it, because I think I can turn the piece into something really exciting. But—"

"He'll fail it," Nathan cut in.

I nodded. "I'm sure of it," I said with a smile.

I knew what Fitzgerald was looking for when he gave us those assignments. He wanted us to play by all the rules that held his brain in his head. Rules that would make our compositions indistinguishable from the composer at hand. As much fun as that sounded, I was determined to breathe new life into old music. To keep it alive and fluid and moving. Snobby professor-be-damned.

Nathan chuckled. "I wish I could play along in your effort to make his head explode, Savannah, I really do. But, I put off this class for the last minute so I could take it with you, and if I fail it, I'm screwed."

"I appreciate the sentiment." Idly, I found myself wanting to see what my latest composition looked like through those gorgeous blue eyes that belonged to Gregory Fitzgerald.

"Whatchya thinking about?" Nathan asked as he wrapped his long arm around my shoulders.

"Oh," I sighed, "just what a fucking long semester this would be if I didn't have you to sit next to in that theory class."

He smiled and kissed the top of my head. "Anything for you, doll."

I tilted my chin to meet his eyes. "I might hold you to that if I end up in jail for strangling him. He's so boxed in it drives me crazy."

Nathan just laughed and kissed my head again. "Please do your best not to end up in jail, Savannah."

"I'll try," I smiled, "promise."

Chapter 4

SAVANNAH

A COUPLE OF WEEKS later, I stared at my perfectly polished lips in the mirror one last time before meeting Nathan in the entrance of the dorm.

It's going to be fine, Savannah. Just...it's going to be fine.

"Happy birthday, Savannah." Nathan linked arms with me and we headed down the stairs to go meet my dad.

"Thank you, gorgeous." I smiled, playfully messing up his short, dark curls. I was definitely excited to enjoy my night with the people I loved.

Twenty-one.

I guess that would mean something to someone who did things in an ordinary fashion. While I'd moved back to the States with my dad when I was eight, spending summers in Europe led to me having my first drink out in a tiny restaurant in Italy when I was sixteen. It was a vintage Pinot Noir my mother had ordered for the table. I was worried that I'd disappoint her, somehow, if I hated it. I didn't. It was the best thing I'd ever tasted. Smooth and smoky, it sucked me in, and now I'll rarely order anything else if an Italian Pinot Noir is on the menu.

"Hey Dad!"

My dad, Stephen, leaned against the entrance to the opera house. He wore a black tux underneath a grey cashmere and wool overcoat. The plaid scarf I'd purchased for him on holiday in Scotland when I was twelve made me smile almost as much as his warm brown eyes.

My mother was prima donna at *Teatro Alla Scala* for the last fifteen years, and my parents and I lived together in Italy, traveling Europe as her schedule permitted. My dad moved me back to Philadelphia with him right before eighth grade, and we lived with my grandparents so I could go to school like a "normal kid." As normal as could be expected when your mother is a world-renowned opera singer.

Of course, middle school isn't the ideal time to relocate countries and be normal. One of the reasons I think Nathan and I became so close was because he was one of the few people I met then who really understood me.

"Happy birthday, sweetheart." My dad gave me a tight squeeze and then reached out to shake Nathan's hand. "Good to see you again, son."

"Great to see you, Mr. Marshall." Nathan quickly brushed his hand off on his pants, even though both of them were wearing gloves, and he shook my dad's hand.

My dad grinned and ran his hand over his increasingly thinning hair. "Oh for God's sake, Nathan, for more than ten years I've been insisting that you call me Steve." He chuckled.

Before heading up the stairs, I smoothed my hands over my floor-length emerald gown. In my everyday life, I found it a major facade to have to "dress a certain way." Just to make a point, I had underdressed for my audition to the Conservatory. You could say that my point was made, since I got in, but Madeline White softly scolded me about it later. However, tonight wasn't my everyday life. Yes, it was my birthday, but tonight my mother was performing as a special guest in Tosca. I'd never seen her sing this particular opera, and I was anxious and excited. I was thrilled to see her, and respected every bit of pomp and circumstance that went along with the opera.

"Is it lame that I'm really excited to see your mom sing?" Nathan whispered as we made our way to our excellent, "special guest" seats.

"No," I whispered back, "I'm super excited too. It's been a long time for me." The anticipation alone gave me goosebumps.

While Nathan and I have been friends for more than ten years, my mom worked so much—and most of it overseas—that he's never seen her perform live. And it's always better live.

As we settled into our seats, I couldn't help but wonder what Gregory would think of all of this. While his class was proving to be thoroughly more irritating than I could have even imagined, the image of him playing that Bach piece on our first day of class was still seared in my brain. The man was a walking contradiction. He spent the last several weeks trying to prove to us that music was all science and math. His point of doing that Bach piece, he told us the next day, was to illustrate that if you study how music is written, you could, in theory, start a piece and finish it on your own, even if sight reading, because everything is a formula. He said the trick, however, was to still be able to put feeling into it, which, in his mind, came from more practice.

That was an incredible lie I really think he believed. What was going on with his body and on his face while he was playing that piece was anything but practiced. I wondered, idly, if he'd ever seen himself play. Surely he has recordings of his Pops performances? Whatever his reason for insisting that practice really does make perfect, natural talent or not, he was hell bent on teaching the class his way.

Still, thoughts of his eyes scanning over my body a few days ago in Murphy's had me silently wishing he was sitting next to me, watching me more. My stomach flipped the way it did when he grinned at me, and I shifted in my seat, trying to ignore my thoughts.

Sitting between my dad and Nathan, I pulled out the program. As always, I was filled with pride to see her name. I saved every program of hers I could get my hands on. She'd send me some, and her agent would send me the rest when she was on a whirlwind tour.

"Dad," I whispered, "Mom says she gets a break for a while after this?" I spoke to my mother earlier in the week, and she said she would have a few months off before deciding if she wanted to continue. That's the longest break I can remember her having, and the first time she alluded to possible retirement.

He nodded, with a strange, tight look passing over his face. "That's the word."

Before I could respond, the lights dimmed, the orchestra tuned, the show was on, and I was lost in it. My mom's stage presence really was something to covet. She was gorgeous. Tall, my height, but deep, rich black hair that accented her Italian olive skin. Her face was made even more impossibly beautiful by enticing blue eyes—eyes that were in such stark contrast to the rest of her dark features that they almost looked fake. She wasn't born in Italy, but her grandparents were, and Italian was always spoken in her house growing up—it was the natural place for her to want to carry out her career.

By the time the second act was underway, I pried my eyes away from the stage and looked at my dad. As my mother's voice reached nearly every octave possible, his eyes widened and glistened. The reverence beaming from his face highlighted the deep love and admiration he's always had for her. And she was in love with the opera. It wasn't that she didn't love my dad. It's just that opera was her first love, and you can't come between first loves—people or not. She was singing long before she met him, and he took on the role of supporting that, no matter what it meant for him. They met when he played in the pit for one of her shows. He's a French horn player. Or was.

I gave his hand a slight squeeze, which seemed to startle him, and he took an exaggerated breath before looking at me. Something on his face had changed. I'd never seen that lonely look in his eyes before. I cautiously glanced back to my mom on stage before returning to his face. He nodded, as if to tell me everything was fine, but I started to wonder if twenty years of success in a certain kind of marriage would translate into the same success when the structure changed.

By the end of the show, I was emotionally exhausted. In order to be a great opera singer, you have to also be a great actress. That's how it works. My mother took both to heights that made people's jaws drop. That was her job. Her facial expressions, the movement of her body, and the pairing of that with her voice was something to behold. Nathan was still and silent through the entire show, and was buzzing with excitement by the end. On the rare occasions I saw her perform, I was fascinated by all the emotion my mother projected.

"That was amazing!" Nathan yelled as we stepped outside onto the cold March air. Puffs of frozen breath swirled around us as we laughed.

"It was certainly one of the best I've seen from her in a long time." My dad nodded and shoved his hands in his coat pockets as we hurried to the Hyatt Regency, where my parents were staying.

We were going to meet my mom there for dinner and drinks. I hated the backstage scene after a show and always felt kind of crowded out anyway, so I always waited until an hour, or so, after a show to meet up with her. That way she was focused, and I could have her to myself for a little while. In the meantime, my two favorite men and I would sip drinks at the bar. A half hour later, my dad got a text from my mom that she was on her way over, when Nathan elbowed me and nodded to the far end of the bar.

"Look who it is."

Leaning forward so I could see what he was looking at, I instinctively rolled my eyes. Gregory...Mr. Fitzgerald...whatever, was sitting at the bar having drinks with a woman I think I'd seen once or twice at the financial aid office on campus. She was turned toward him, resting her chin on her hand, staring at him like he was a prize. He, however, seemed to be having trouble figuring out where to look. His eyes darted between the bottom of his glass and the woman's more-than-approving gaze.

"How about that, he has a social life." Shrugging, I turned back to my conversation with my dad, but found myself watching the gruff recluse from the corner of my eye. Annoyed at the twinge of jealousy I felt toward the pleasant looking woman with hair and eyes almost the same color as mine, I hastily finished my drink and ordered another.

GREGORY

"ANOTHER DRINK, SIR?" The bartender at the Hyatt Regency placed his hand on the bar in front of my drink.

"Please." I nodded. "Another gin and tonic." As he walked away to mix my drink, I turned to Karin. "That show was excellent, wasn't it?" I asked. I knew it was.

Thankfully, Karin smiled. "It was spectacular. I haven't been to the opera in ages, thank you for inviting me." She gently placed her hand on my forearm.

I cleared my throat, thankful when the bartender returned with my drink. "I wouldn't have missed this one for the world. Vita Carulli's performance was exquisite. We're lucky to have caught a show of hers, I understand she's going to be retiring soon."

While I typically favor instrumental-only performances, it is difficult to deny the pull of the opera. The way a person can use their voice and body as an instrument is something to be respected. I found it surprising that Vita was considering retirement. I'm certain years of singing is taxing on the voice, and all the traveling wears a person down. But, I couldn't imagine what she would do after that. What does one do when they stop doing their life's passion? The question made no sense in my brain. I didn't follow her career well enough to know anything about her personal life. I don't have time for those kinds of details. What I did know was there wasn't anyone currently in the circuit who could sing like her.

"So why did you decide to take on teaching Madeline's class?" Karin interrupted my thoughts.

I waved my hand dismissively. "She and James and I went through the Conservatory together. She's always been very kind to me, and she asked me to take over. I agreed."

Honestly, it annoyed me when Madeline asked me if I would take over her upper-level theory class. Foundations are important, don't get me wrong. They're everything. But, early on I found myself getting extremely frustrated with the students who lacked the self-discipline to do the necessary work. I was much better off helping talented students reach the next level, rather than helping them get off the ground in the first place.

"How's it going so far?"

"It's going well, I suppose. I have a few students who seem to want to challenge every word that comes out of my mouth. I'm not really sure what it is they think they're challenging. Notes are notes, scales are scales. What is there to discuss?"

I sipped the cool gin, letting it calm my insides. It's not that I was nervous or uncomfortable around Karin, she was a lovely woman. It was, however, sometimes a struggle to think of anything other than my music. James was right, I needed a break sometimes. If Karin was really interested in me, she deserved better than the cold shoulder I was unintentionally offering her.

"What about you?" I asked, hoping to turn the attention off of me for a few minutes. "How's work going?"

Karin beamed. "The endowment has actually stabilized really well. You know, given the state of arts in public schools nowadays, the alumnae are even more willing to give to the school so we can help run programs at public schools in the area."

Her brown eyes lit up as she talked and, I'll admit, I was impressed. I hadn't given much thought to her job, but when I had, I assumed she was less involved with actual music than that. I was appreciative of her knowledge of the state of affairs in the arts world. In the middle of Karin telling me about a new fundraising initiative, a high-pitched giggle drew my eyes to the far side of the bar. Throwing her head back, in full laughter, was Savannah Marshall.

Her normally wild hair was twisted up elegantly away from her neck, held by a sparkling clip. She was wearing what appeared to be an expensive green silk dress that highlighted her long and lean frame. I wondered what sort of occasion garnered this kind of high fashion attire. She was stunning. She was with her boyfriend, Nathan, who never seemed to take his hands off of her, and another older man I didn't recognize.

Karin wrapped her fingers around my forearm. "What are you looking at?" She tilted her head, trying to find my line of vision.

I took a deep breath. "Just another student who thinks they know everything already." That wasn't entirely true of Savannah. She really did have an incredible knowledge of music;

it was her constant readiness to challenge me that I found infuriating.

"Savannah Marshall?" Karin asked, looking back to me.

"Yes, you know her?" I sat up straight, suddenly more interested in Karin's knowledge of Savannah than her knowledge of the Conservatory's endowment.

Karin's tone brightened. "Of course I know her...or of her. She has a reputation as a real natural. I heard she played her final piece for her audition with her eyes closed. Weren't you on that panel?"

Of course I was. "So, what, does that mean she doesn't practice as hard as the rest of her peers? Does she have license to slack off because people tell her she's a natural?" I scoffed.

"I didn't say that, Gregory. In fact, I'm not sure anyone's ever told her she's a natural. I do know she does happen to work very hard, but she doesn't kill herself doing it."

Karin arched her eyebrow, intending to direct the last part of her sentence to me. Then she said something completely inexplicable. "Of course, how hard she worked really wouldn't have mattered, in her case."

Before I could form a rebuttal and ask how exactly she knew anything about Savannah's abilities, Savannah squealed in delight again. Shifting my gaze back to her end of the bar, my jaw dropped at the sight of Vita Carulli entering the bar and walking straight toward Savannah with a beaming smile on her face. How in the world do those two know each other? I knew nothing of Savannah other than what I could remember from her application to the school, but nothing that I recalled mentioned her studying with Vita Carulli.

I stared openly, pulling my eyebrows together to watch the interaction unfold. Without reverence, but maintaining her ever-present grace, Savannah nearly ran over to Vita and threw her arms around her neck, planting a kiss on her cheek before squeezing her close. Vita returned the gesture.

"What the hell?" I muttered, just under my breath.

"What?" Karin asked, seeming slightly agitated.

"How does Savannah Marshall know Vita Carulli?" I slid off my stool and absentmindedly made my way toward them.

"Gregory, that's..." I lost Karin's voice as I weaved through the now tightly packed bar, distracted by this out of place interaction.

As I approached Savannah, my pulse raced. I had to meet Vita.

"It's so good to see you, darling," I heard Vita say as I got closer. While I was excited at the prospect of meeting one of the best opera singers in the world within a few seconds, I was now completely invested in how Savannah was close enough to Vita Carulli to have her calling her "darling."

Before Savannah could respond, she caught me standing there out of the corner of her eye. "Oh, Mr. Fitzgerald...hi." She seemed caught off guard as she bit her lip and looked between me and Vita.

"Hello, Ms. Marshall." I nodded my head once. "I don't meant to interrupt here, but, Ms. Carulli, I wanted to tell you that I was at your performance tonight and, truly, it was one of your finest." I took her hand and kissed it once, catching Savannah as she scrunched her forehead and rolled her eyes. I didn't know what I had done to elicit such a reaction from her.

"How kind of you...Mr. Fitzgerald, is it?" Vita's speaking voice was just as gorgeous as her singing voice, which I didn't consider was even possible.

"Yes. Gregory Fitzgerald." I looked between Savannah and Vita for a moment, a sense of familiarity rising through my chest.

Savannah let out a slight sigh. "Mom, this is Gregory Fitzgerald, cellist for the BSO, and teacher of my music theory class."

Did she just say Mom?

"Mr. Fitzgerald," Savannah continued, somewhat hesitantly, "this is my mother, Vita Carulli."

What? My eyes moved to Karin, who gave a pointed nod toward Vita Carulli, as if to say, See? Musical royalty. I returned my focus to Vita and then Savannah, whose normally soft features seemed cold and stringent.

"It was a pleasure meeting you, Ms. Carulli. See you in class, Savannah."

Savannah held her head high as she gave a curt nod and a poor excuse for a smile.

I wandered back to the table impressed that Savannah hadn't spent the last few years, to my knowledge, throwing her mother's name around in the game of Who has better genes that the students insisted on playing with each other. Those students, though, needed that game. Their talent didn't stand up to that which Savannah possessed. Whether through hard work or the genetic lottery, Savannah Marshall could be remarkably successful given the proper attention.

When I reached the bar and picked up my gin and tonic, now watered down with melting ice, I took one last look over my shoulder. As Nathan's hand rested on the small of Savannah's back, my jaw tensed. That was not the kind of attention Savannah needed to produce the results she was capable of.

She needed someone who took her career seriously.

Someone who took her seriously.

Chapter 5

SAVANNAH

"**A**REN'T YOU FREEZING, Savannah?" Nathan pulled me close as we walked quickly down the sidewalk to the dance club.

I stopped and twirled once on my tiptoes, allowing the skirt on my bright red dress to flare up around me. "Hell yes." I laughed. "But, at least there's no snow on the ground, so my feet won't get wet." I kicked up a heel of my silver strappy heels before maintaining our stride.

"You've been a little quiet in Fitzgerald's class the last two weeks," Nathan said out of nowhere.

"Nothing to say, I guess." I shrugged.

Nathan stopped half a block from the club and turned me toward him. "Nothing to say? Come on, Savannah, I know you better than that. What gives? Yesterday he said something more archaic than usual and looked *right* at you, and you didn't even bat an eyelash." The dimple in his left cheek deepened as he grinned mockingly at me.

"Come on," I sighed, "you saw how he looked at me when he met my mom..." I wrapped my arms around me as the wind whipped down the alley.

"Not this again, Savannah." Nathan sighed and looked to the sky.

"Yes, this again. This always. People know who my mom is and they get this look on their face, like by knowing me, they've somehow touched the greatness that is Vita Carulli." I was a little heavy-handed in my sarcasm, but this situation called for just that.

"Has he said anything to you?" Nathan shrugged and furrowed his brow.

"No, but the way his eyes lit up—"

Nathan cut me off. "What the hell do you care *what* he thinks?"

"I don't..."

Did I? Shit. I did.

"Fuck it, then. You'll be done with him after this semester, and it won't matter what he thinks of you...or your mom." He wrapped his arm around my shoulders again and chuckled as we finally made our way to the club door.

"I guess you're right," I admitted.

Still, I felt I had enough of a hard time getting Fitzgerald to take my thoughts seriously without him knowing who my family was. And, I couldn't decide if his knowing about my mom would work in my favor or not. Either way, I didn't want it to have any bearing on my success in his class. Though, as the semester wore on, I was caring less about what grade I received, and more about my point being received by him. His ideas were so fixed, so rigid, I couldn't imagine ever having to put up with him as an instructor. He was at the top of his field, no question, but I would bet good money on his students developing serious OCD. Even as a classroom student of his, I found myself wanting to impress him. But I wasn't willing to change my opinions to accomplish that.

As soon as I stepped through the door of the club, I was swallowed by heat and music. The sounds of the live band, filled with trumpets, drums, flutes, and everything else needed to make Spanish music work, was shocking the atmosphere with excitement.

"*This* gets me in the mood for spring break!" I hollered into Nathan's ear as he led me straight to the dance floor.

Tomorrow was our last day of classes before spring break, and even though I wasn't going anywhere tropical, music got me in the mood to relax for a week. We had a pretty important composition due in Fitzgerald's class in the morning, but I wrote mine a week ago. I don't think he really paid attention to my words, though. If he did, I'd certainly have been getting a better grade than I was. Given the grades in the rest of my classes, it didn't really matter *what* I got in his theory class. But I was determined to prove that his word was *not* gospel. He disagreed every Monday, Wednesday and Friday, any chance he got.

"What's with the look on your face, doll?" Nathan leaned down and planted a soft kiss on my cheek. "You're not still thinking about...him...are you?"

"No." I shook my head, smiling up at the curly-haired hottie. Nathan was a few inches taller than me, muscular but lanky. But he had this gorgeous hair and that adorable dimple that made me smile whenever it appeared.

"Prove it," Nathan teased as he spun me around before pulling me so close I could easily smell the Ivory soap he used.

"I'm so sad you're graduating this year." I gave an exaggerated pout as we waited for the band to set up their next song.

"Ah, come on..." He grabbed my waist and kissed my forehead.

"I'm serious, Nathan. You've been a huge part of my life since I was ten, for God's sake. Now I'll have one more year here while you are...where?" I hadn't asked about his plans after graduation, since he was highly superstitious about the whole application and audition process.

"We'll be fine, Savannah. You went years only seeing me in the summer." He sighed, spinning me in another circle as the band started up again.

"I know, but I've been spoiled the last three, getting to see you every day. I like that. Come on, spill it: tell me where you're auditioning." I set my hands on his broad shoulders as we moved in time with the salsa coming from the stage.

Nathan shook his head. "You know I won't, Savannah. Just...trust me, okay?"

Before the song was over, I caught a shockingly out of place figure at the bar, causing me to stop and stare.

"What?" Nathan asked, turning around.

"He dances?" I gestured to Gregory Fitzgerald, who was sitting next to the same blonde woman he'd been with at my mother's opera. Since the opera I'd seen her on campus once, coming out of the endowment offices.

He was dressed more casually than I was used to seeing him, but just slightly so. Black was definitely his color. I often mocked his monochromatic color palette in my head while staring at him during our lectures, but in the club tonight it looked just right. While the snug black t-shirt almost made him invisible in the shadows of the bar, his eyes commanded my attention. In the classroom they sometimes felt like icicles, sending nausea over anyone they came across because you really didn't want to be on the other end of a debate with him. Well, I did. It excited me to go back and forth with him. I wasn't usually one for classroom debates—especially on things that there wasn't much to debate about. But, with him I couldn't seem to help it. Before I knew it, my eyes were resting on his shoulders, tight from years of playing. They were usually hidden under the suit coats he wore to class. Not tonight.

Wow.

Nathan let out a full-throated laugh, apparently ignoring the fact that I was blatantly staring at our handsome professor. "What in God's name is he doing in here?"

"Let's go find out." I grabbed Nathan's hand and led him up the three stairs to the bar area.

"What are you going to say to him?" Nathan's lips grazed my ear as he talked.

"I'll figure it out on the walk."

When we got up to the bar, Nathan ordered me a cosmopolitan and himself a beer. My back was to the woman, but I couldn't hear what they were saying. There were words passing between them, though, which seemed to be a small miracle in itself. I drank the cosmopolitan in three sips, and Nathan downed his beer. He tilted his chin to the good professor behind me, and butterflies danced erratically in my stomach at the prospect of approaching him.

"Your cheeks are red..." Nathan raised an eyebrow.

"I just swallowed my drink whole, Nathan." I gestured with my empty glass to try to cover up what Gregory was doing to my body. "Gimme a minute."

I took a deep breath and turned around, blushing deeper when I saw that Gregory was already looking at me. Studying me. His eyes moved up the length of my body, hitching my breath as they slowed over my curves. As I stepped forward, his eyes shot to mine, maybe hoping he hadn't been caught.

He had.

"I've never seen you here before." I smiled as he shifted in his seat. He mumbled something absolutely unintelligible given the band was in the middle of a salsa number. I had to lean in so our faces were inches apart. "What?"

He sucked in a quick breath. So close to my ear it caused goosebumps down that side of my body. "I said, do you come here often, Miss Marshall?"

I laughed, causing him to furrow his brow.

"What?'

"It's Savannah. Please, call me Savannah, Greg—" I stopped short, covering my mouth and silently cursing the vodka for making me call him by his first name. It wasn't the vodka at all, but that was as good an alibi as any.

Mr. Fitzgerald grinned before taking a quick sip from a short glass filled with what I assumed was a *something* and tonic. "It's okay, Savannah..." He shrugged, not offering anymore.

His features were relaxed as I nodded, breathless at the way he pressed his lips together after sipping his drink. I'd forgotten about the woman he was with, until she cleared her throat.

"Savannah, this is Karin Briggs from the endowment office." Gregory spoke quickly, seeming flustered.

"Savannah," Karin spoke sweetly as she extended her hand, "it's a pleasure to meet you. I've heard a lot about you."

"Nice to meet you," I replied.

"If you'll excuse me, I must run to the ladies' room. I'll be back in a moment, Gregory." Karin stood as Gregory nodded in acknowledgement.

"You're quite good, Savannah," Gregory's tone was unmistakably seductive.

But, I *had* to be mistaken. He was my professor.

I opened my mouth to speak, but I was suddenly unsure how to respond. "I..."

"Where'd you learn to dance like that?"

Nathan, apparently growing impatient with my increasingly long conversation with Gregory, saddled up next to me as I sat in the seat Karin vacated.

I shrugged. "Spain, mostly," I said matter-of-factly. One summer spent literally dancing through the streets of Madrid will teach anyone all they need to know about dancing. And love.

Gregory's eyes widened in approving surprise. "Spain…" He shifted on the stool, his attention diverting expertly away from my legs as I crossed them.

"Yeah," I sighed, "when I would visit my mom in the summers we'd take lots of trips around Europe. It would last all summer until I was old enough for the Tanglewood Institute, then I'd spend the first part of the summer with her in Italy, and the second half at Tanglewood."

"Ah, Tanglewood." Gregory nodded in approval. "Excellent program. I attended through high school. It completely changed my life." He ran his index finger along the rim of his glass as he stared into the clear liquid. I was taken back by this bit of honesty from him, given it was a memory that caused him to pull his eyebrows together for a second before looking up again.

"So," I cleared my throat, circling the conversation back to his initial question, "*you* dance?"

"It seems so, given our setting, wouldn't you say?" Half his mouth quirked up as he arched his eyebrow and took another sip of his drink.

Damn.

"Do you want to dance?"

Nathan was engaged in loud conversation with a friend of his behind us. I had no one to stop me.

Gregory's eyes widened a little bit at the question, and he sat up straighter. "That's probably not a good idea."

Yes. His eyes said yes. The rapid rise and fall of his chest accepted my invitation. Why did he *say* no? "Why not?"

"Because…" He hesitated after the word. Out of character… Gregory didn't hesitate. But just as he was about to continue, Karin returned.

"It was nice to meet you, Karin." I smiled, extending my hand to shake hers one more time before turning to Gregory. "See you in class tomorrow."

Gregory eyed Nathan, his face returning to the rigid structure we'd come to expect from our time in his class. "Don't forget about your assignment."

Nathan laughed a little before hooking his arm around my waist and yanking me into his body. That caused me to let out a squeal and a laugh. I turned and saw Gregory's mouth open just a fraction, as if he was going to say something, but I just smiled and waved before letting Nathan lead me back to the dance floor.

GREGORY

MY EYES INVOLUNTARILY followed Savannah Marshall, as she and her boyfriend, Nathan, moved back to the dance floor. Savannah wore a form fitting red dress that flared at her hips, revealing shapely legs which were accentuated by matching heels. I took another too big sip of my gin and tonic, forcing myself to look away from her as she walked away. Looking away did nothing, however, to rid the sight of her skin glistening a mere foot from my face as we chatted.

"What is it?" Karin shouted over the extremely loud music. Good music, though. Full of rich undertones and an off-tempo Caribbean flair.

"What is *what*?" I asked.

"You looked startled!"

I brushed off the question. "It's nothing. Please continue."

"How about we dance instead?"

I suppose I knew that was coming. Karin and I had been out on several dates, virtually all of them venues I had selected. The Opera, the symphony on one of my rare nights off, elegant dinners. For this date, I'd asked her where she wanted to go, and she'd selected salsa dancing. Not something I normally did, but I suppose if one is dating, you must make some compromises. And, the music was good, after all.

We moved out to the dance floor. Thanks to my mother's insistence when I was a child, I'm not a bad dancer, though it's not something I particularly enjoy or seek out on my own. I put an arm on Karin's waist, took her left hand in my right, and we began to dance. I swung her around on the floor, and as she laughed, my eyes involuntarily fell on Savannah Marshall again, in that red dress, with her boyfriend's hands inappropriately sliding down her waist and too low on her back. It shouldn't have bothered me, but it did. Did that young man have no culture at all? I turned with Karin, so aggressively she almost stumbled, so that my back was to Savannah. But my thoughts lingered on the narrowness of her waist and the way the bodice of her dress hugged her breasts.

Annoying thoughts. Inappropriate thoughts, considering she was a student. A student who was out on a date with her boyfriend.

The band slowed down, and the couples on the floor moved closer together. Karin folded herself into my arms, nestling her chin against my shoulder. She was pressed fully against me, and we swayed slowly with the music.

"Gregory..." Her whisper was right in my ear. I squeezed my arms tighter around her, because that seemed all the response necessary.

I sighed a little as Savannah and Nathan swung into view again. They were appallingly close, and his hand was resting just on the top of the curve of her ass. She was truly a remarkable young woman. And probably deserved someone a lot better than Nathan, who was little more than an overgrown boy. I almost let my mind run to the thought of her in bed, and my body involuntarily responded.

I tried not to freeze, because Karin noticed. And pressed herself against me, tighter. "Gregory?" she said.

"Yes, Karin," I murmured.

"Let's go back to my place?"

Chapter 6

GREGORY

I CHECKED MY WATCH. 4 p.m. I was late. I hated tardiness. It showed a lack of respect. But today it was unavoidable. I'd spent the last three hours grading papers for music theory class, which I shouldn't have been teaching in the first place. Once I started something, it was difficult to quit. And it was my luck that at 3:30 I'd pulled the next paper off the stack.

Savannah Marshall.

I want to be clear. I'm a fair instructor. Some students think I'm too harsh, too demanding. But this isn't a liberal arts community college for those who desire to enter the fascinating world of cosmetology or small business finance. This is the premier Conservatory in the world, where we train musicians who will go on to the top of their fields. I would do my students no favors by coddling them and giving them false illusions, which would only be shattered by harsh reality when they left the confines of these walls.

That said, her paper presented a dilemma. On the one hand, it displayed a level of brilliance and sheer power that was rare in students her age. On the other hand, it was a muddle of ridiculous assertions. Instead of technique, she wrote about *feelings.* Instead of placing the music in its proper context as a work of sublime art, she wrote about its historical context and how it represented the people and relationships involved in its composition.

In short, she understood nothing I'd been teaching. Or worse, she understood it, and dismissed it.

At 4:01 p.m. I scrawled an F across the top half of the cover page. I knew as I wrote it that it was harsh. Heavy-handed, even. But, half-steps are best left to scales, and have no business in my classroom. She needed to be taught a lesson. Sighing, I stood, and hurried out of the office.

Thanks to Savannah Marshall's bizarre and irrelevant paper I was nearly four minutes late arriving at the practice rooms.

In the hall, I found a depressingly middle-classed young couple. At a glance, I could tell he was a computer something or other for some company on 128, and she was probably an elementary school teacher. Perhaps a *music* teacher, which I hoped to God not, because she would soon be attempting to tell me how to do my job. Between them stood a young boy, perhaps twelve years old, with what appeared to be an undersized cello case. It was beat up and marked with a rental agency's logo.

"Good afternoon, I'm Gregory Fitzgerald," I said.

The mother stepped forward. "Susan Donovan," she said. "This is my husband David, and our son, Robert."

Robert looked nothing like the couple. She prodded him forward. I felt unsure. Did one speak to a child that age as if they were simply a short adult? Or give orders? My father once told me that I'd never been twelve. Of course, as much as I loved my father, it became clear early on that he had no idea what to make of me.

Short adult then. I reached out a hand, not to the boy's mother or father, but to him. He couldn't see the hand of course, so I reached down and took his, gave him a not too firm handshake. I don't generally shake hands, because men like to engage in stupid games of who can grip harder. My hands were my music. They were my life.

The father spoke. "We'd like to thank you for meeting with us..."

I cocked my head. "I was under the impression your son was the student, not you?"

David Donovan looked somewhat shocked, and opened his mouth to speak, but his wife was the faster of the two, because she quickly said, "We thought we'd spend a few minutes explaining Robert's issues—"

"Unnecessary. Robert...come. The practice room is right over here."

I put a hand on his shoulder to guide him.

"He doesn't like to be touched..." his mother said.

I waved her off, and the boy came willingly enough.

"Have a seat," I said to him, setting my practice cello in its case against the wall. This was a relatively inexpensive instrument that I kept at the Conservatory. The Montagnana was only played for rehearsals and live shows for the symphony.

He put a hand out, and said, "Where's the chair?"

I was already unsnapping the case for my cello, but I turned and took his hand, then stretched it out so he was touching the back of the chair. Then I turned away.

Gently, I lifted my cello from its case, then took a seat. A moment later he'd found his own seat, and took his out. In the meantime, his irritating parents were pushing at each other, because only one of their heads at a time would fit in the small glass window in the door.

I studied the boy as he fumbled with his case. He had extensive scarring around his eyes. I couldn't tell if he'd been in a fire, or what, but he wasn't born blind. Something had happened to him. Whatever. It wasn't his eye that mattered. It was his hands, and his ears.

He was awkward with his instrument, a training instrument intended for smaller children. It was in terrible condition, obviously rented. The bow was caked with rosin, the screws and fittings oxidized, and the hair brittle and glazed. The cello itself had multiple scratches. It would take a magician to get a decent sound out of that instrument. I almost felt a fit of rage over the mistreatment of the instrument, as well as whatever shyster had rented it to the boy's parents. It was typical that a beginning musician would be given an instrument that would be most difficult to play.

"Why do you want to learn cello?" I asked.

The boy just looked confused by the question.

"You're blind, not mute, correct?"

At that, he recoiled a little. "I can talk."

"Then tell me why you're here."

"My mom...she...um..."

"Your mother wanted you to learn? Does she think because you are blind you'll be some sort of prodigy?"

The boy flinched. He nodded, just a little.

"And what do *you* want?"

His face turned away from me, his blank, scarred eyes moving around aimlessly. Then he said, "I want to stop feeling like I'm a freak."

I bit the inside of my cheek. All right, then.

"Then listen." I set the bow to my strings and began to play. The same beginner piece I'd played for my useless music theory class a few weeks before. Bach's Cello Suite No. 1 in G Major. The first music I'd learned on the cello. The music that had transformed my life.

As the notes rang out in that tiny practice room, I watched the boy. I watched his expression. I wanted to see inside his head. See his thoughts. See if he felt it. If he believed it.

And then something quite magical happened. He began to sway in his seat. He did feel it.

Finished, I said, "For you to learn to play like this, you'll practice until your fingertips feel like they'll split open. Day and night. You won't stop when you're hungry. You won't stop when you're tired. You have to want it enough to give up your entire life for the music. You have to be able to coax beauty out of nothing. Do you understand me?"

The boy nodded his head. Quickly. I thought about the difficulties of teaching this boy. I wasn't the instructor to get him started. But I would ensure he found someone.

I leaned forward until our faces were almost touching. "If you're willing to go that far, then I'll find someone to teach you."

I stood and put my instrument away in its case. Then I opened the door, and walked past his parents, who had to scatter in front of the swinging door. I paused for just a moment and turned back toward them. "You'll need to get him a decent instrument. That one isn't going to work if he's going to seriously learn. Call me on Thursday and I'll find you an instructor."

Without another word, I walked back up the hall to the stairs, back to my office.

SAVANNAH

I SQUINTED AGAIN AND took my pen out of my mouth. The top of it was thoroughly chewed. Bad habit, I knew, but sometimes when I was really concentrating I tended to chew on whatever was at hand.

I'd been sitting in the coffee shop for two hours, working on a composition. This wasn't an assignment, though it had been inspired by one. Just before spring break, I'd completed a paper in music theory on Claude Debussy's music and life. That led to some speculation on variations that might be possible with the Debussy's Claire de Lune. So I'd taken the original composition and begun to rework the beginning, which was all piano, into a cello and flute duet. For hours I'd worked on it, closing my eyes. Imagining the layers of notes, the point and counterpoint.

But now I was stuck. My legs were cramped, my tea was cold, and I needed a break.

So I shook my head, took my earbuds out, and stood. I hadn't actually been listening to music with the earbuds. But keeping them in served two purposes. First, it helped shut out some of the noise. Second, it deterred would-be conversationalists. I walked up to the counter and ordered another chai latte, then waited. And then it hit me.

I closed my eyes. And then I imagined...the Claire de Lune, but transposed with Debussy's *Nocturnes*. It would take a lot of adjustment in both pieces, but the end would be...a magnificent and beautiful contradiction. Haunting.

Someone tapped my arm, and my eyes jerked open. The barista stood there looking puzzled and tapping a foot in impatience. "Are you all right?" she asked.

"Yeah..." I was a little breathless. "Thank you."

I turned to hurry back to my seat and get to work, then came to a halt.

Gregory Fitzgerald sat at the counter diagonally opposite where I'd been sitting the last two hours.

He had a frown on his face as he paged through a stack of papers. Assignments, from the look of it. Sitting like that, his head bent over the papers, he looked younger than I usually thought of him. Less intimidating. More...approachable, perhaps because his frown merely represented concentration rather than his usual scowl.

I found myself walking back toward my seat along a path that would take me by him. I came to a stop, pausing only long enough to take a breath and reconsider, before sliding into the seat next to him.

He continued to study the paper he was reading, his blue eyes scanning through the lines of text. He paused, circled something with a red pen, and then continued on, his concentration so intense he didn't notice me staring at him, studying him.

I'd never been this close to him for more than a few seconds. This close, I could see that his right eyebrow rose slightly higher than the left, just by a fraction of a centimeter. He had a profound focus on his work, to the exclusion of everything else in the room. If I set fire to the place, would he even notice?

Then he reached out and touched his empty teacup and lifted it to his lips. His eyes shifted from the paper to the empty cup, breaking his concentration. He set the cup down, looked up and met my eyes, and I felt a sudden jagged thrill of fear.

"Hello." My voice wasn't exactly shaky, but I felt an edge to this entire encounter.

His eyes widened, and his lips curved up into the slightest smile. "Miss Marshall. A pleasant surprise."

"Savannah," I replied. "I'm on spring break."

"Gregory, then."

I shifted in my seat and licked my lips before speaking again. "Term papers?"

"This? No. I'm actually reviewing a list of instructors who might be willing to take on a disabled student. Blind." He struggled with his words, which I found unsettling.

"Differently abled." I chuckled.

"What?" He scrunched his eyebrows together, genuinely baffled by my statement.

I shook my head. "Never mind. How old is..."

"Oh, twelve. Him. He's twelve." Gregory sank down a little in his seat and rubbed the back of his neck.

"What instrument does he play?"

Gregory's eyes shifted away from me and toward the window. "Cello."

"Why aren't you doing it? You teach." I shrugged and rested my elbow on the table, facing him as I propped my cheek up on my hand.

Gregory took a deep breath and closed his eyes for a minute. When he opened them, he finally faced me. "I'm not...I just don't think I'm qualified to handle such a task."

"Certainly not, if you are referring to the student as a *task*. Seriously though," I continued when it looked like he was going to cut in, "you could totally teach him. Marcia Taylor is my roommate and she says you're a genius."

He chuckled a little. "As much as I appreciate the observation—"

"I'm serious," I cut in again, sitting straight in my chair. "I was nine when I grew tired of racing up and down the rows of chairs in an empty opera house during line rehearsals. I wanted to *do* something. I wanted to play something. The woodwind coordinator for the orchestra was a flute teacher, and my mother paid her to start teaching me. She resisted at first because she'd never taught a child."

"I can relate." Gregory nodded and crossed his arms in front of him, leaning back until he was resting against the window.

I did an unattractive half-laugh, half-moan at the memory. "She was awful. Seriously. She would teach me notes and would start out by doing the standard circle diagram of the flute keys, filling in the ones where our fingers needed to go. But, *then*," I reached forward and took hold of Gregory's hand, ignoring the shocked look on his face, "she'd take my fingers and manipulate them to solidify her point. I'd be holding the damn flute with her bossy hands all over me, as if it was appropriate for a nine-year-old to be playing an openhole flute to begin with."

Gregory's eyebrows shot up. "You *learned* to play on an open-hole flute?"

I smiled a little at his reaction to my starting with a flute many don't use until they've played for several years. "She may have had no finesse whatsoever in dealing with me, but she got the job done. I've never played anything but openhole, and I have her to thank for drilling me and training my hand muscles to reach far enough to cover the keys. My point? You can teach this kid, if you want to."

Gregory nodded slowly, looking at the table just past our hands.

Our hands.

I'd gotten so swept up in the story of Giada Barone that I'd left my hands on his...demonstrating a middle E-flat. Shifting slightly to try to pull my hands away without creating an awkward moment, my fingers slid in between his and from a distance it would have looked like we were holding hands.

All the sound in the room disappeared as I felt the fingers on his left hand tighten around mine. They were as strong as I'd imagined, but softer than I'd expected. His thumb skimmed over one of my knuckles, and I yanked my hand away. I shot my eyes to his face as my lips parted, my lungs begging me to take the breath they'd been waiting ten seconds to receive. Gregory's eyes came back from his contemplative stare into nowhere as I cleared my throat and wrapped both hands around my latte mug.

"Oh, Savannah..." He sounded rather panicked as he dug for something to say.

It was just an accident. A reaction. He wasn't thinking. This isn't about you.

I smiled as wide as I could in order to hide my surely flushed cheeks.

"You should give that kid a chance, Gregory. You could change his life." I shrugged, speaking too quickly. "I wouldn't be here if it wasn't for Giada. I know that for a fact. Enjoy the rest of your spring break."

I left my seat before he could tell me he hadn't meant what had just happened.

"You too, Miss Marshall." He ran his hand down his face and left it over his mouth as he continued scanning the papers in front of him.

I scrambled over to my cozy booth and regained control of my senses, looking around to see if any of my classmates may have witnessed that. As much as it could have screwed things up had someone seen it, I felt like I needed some sort of confirmation that it had happened at all.

I got all the confirmation I needed when I looked up, and Gregory's eyes met mine across the coffee shop. For the next twenty-two seconds, we were the only people in the coffee shop. Then he broke the spell, looking away, leaving me devoid of reason and racing for the door.

Chapter 7

GREGORY

I T WAS THE afternoon of the first day of classes after spring break, and technically my office hours, which I was required by the Conservatory to keep, though few students ever dared to interrupt me in here. I was sipping a cup of tea, leaning back in my chair, with my feet upon the desk. Rachmaninoff was playing, a new recording by the London Symphony. Not quietly. Such music is never meant to be played softly, as if it were background music. It demands attention. Several nagging papers from the Conservatory administration lay ignored on my desk. I wasn't prepared to deal with them, especially while wrapped in the sounds Rachmaninoff.

My eyes were closed, therefore I was completely unprepared for the disturbance when my office door flew open and banged into the doorframe with a loud thump. My eyes flew open, and I dropped my feet to the floor.

It was Savannah Marshall. She had bright spots of color in her cheeks, and her right fist was clenched at her side, her left gripping a paper that was now slightly crumpled. An angry line ran down the center of her forehead where her eyebrows pushed together.

I cleared my throat, unwilling to show her just how ruffled I was by her entrance. Or her appearance, which was shockingly fetching with that dark rose color highlighting her cheeks, a tight blue sweater over faded jeans that emphasized every single curve of her body.

"Miss Marshall. Perhaps you forgot to knock?"

She held up the paper. "I came here to discuss *this*."

I raised my eyebrows. This wasn't likely to go well, given her inclination to argue everything to death, so I took a sip of my tea in an effort to maintain my equilibrium. Then I mustered the coldest voice I could manage. "There's not really anything to discuss."

"An F? This paper did not warrant an F." Her cheeks were still flushed as she spoke, and I found it difficult to take my eyes off of them.

"Miss Marshall, your paper most certainly did. I took a considerable amount of time justifying your grade before putting it on the paper. I don't intend to justify it further. You are capable of much better work than this."

She smacked the paper on the desk—the large "F" scrawled across the top half.

"Mr. Fitzgerald." She took a deep breath. I suppose to calm herself, which seemed to be necessary. "Number one. You gave exactly no feedback. There is not a single mark in this paper. Nothing to indicate what is right or wrong. Simply a grade. Number two," she took another breath and her voice was much more even, "I very carefully met every single requirement of the assignment. You required a comparison of Debussy's compositions from early in his career and late. You required an analysis of the technical aspects of at least two of those compositions. You required that I address the differences in tempo, meter, pitch, harmony. I addressed each of those."

I frowned. Her tone rang with unattractive self-importance. She'd done the things I'd asked, true. But she'd also included nearly five pages of completely irrelevant material. "Hardly. Miss Marshall, the assignment was a comparison of the music and its elements. Not a biography. You have more than three pages in this paper about *his wife*. What possible relevance does she have to the assignment?"

Savannah shouted, her brown eyes nearly popping out of their sockets. "She shot herself in the chest days after he announced he was divorcing her! How could that not be relevant? How could that not affect his music?" The color in her cheeks deepened the louder her voice got.

I sat forward in my chair and against my better judgment, found myself arguing back, "It's completely irrelevant! The assignment was to compare the musical composition, not delve into the composer's personal life!"

She flipped the pages of the report and stabbed it with her index finger, leaning over my desk as she did so. "I *did* do that, if you'd actually bothered to read the paper. Yes, the music was changed, and I illustrated that in the paper. But his music was changed by his *life*. His music was changed by his experiences. But, this isn't about me at all, is it? This is about my mother! Are you simply punishing me because of her?"

At that, I stood. Her chain of logic made no sense at all. What did her mother have to do with anything? Of course, Savannah came from good musical stock, and that had to be respected on some level. But punishing her? No, I was pushing her. Pushing her to do better than the paper she'd turned in.

I did something I have never done in my entire career as an instructor. I shouted at a student, leaning forward over my desk, which had the effect of bringing us nearly face to face. "Miss Marshall, I don't care if your mother is a harlot selling herself in the street! This isn't about that. It's about you and your talent. You are too *good* for this!"

Her face went slack, reflecting shock at my words. I continued, inching closer to her face until we were almost nose-to-nose. "You have the ability to be one of the premier musicians this Conservatory has ever graduated. And yet you *waste* it. You waste it on your pointless musical experiments. You waste it on your weekends spent…*dancing*…and *drinking*… when you should be perfecting your craft. You waste it on the time you spend with that *boyfriend* of yours."

Her face scrunched up, a mixture of confusion and amusement on her face, and an oddly formed laugh forced itself out. "Who are you talking about? Nathan? Not that it's any of your business, *Mr. Fitzgerald*, but Nathan is *not* my boyfriend."

We maintained our stance inches from each other's faces. Inches from each other's lips. With only my desk separating us.

Not her boyfriend. What was he then? This boy who constantly had his hands on her, this boy who leaned over and whispered in her ear in class, who touched her intimately while dancing, who repeatedly made a fool of himself in my class. I'm not a sociologist, but if he wasn't her boyfriend, he certainly wished he was. I started to reply, but then clammed up. This wasn't about that anyway. I took a breath, attempting to calm myself.

Pulling back slightly, I spoke in calm, measured words that belied the tension roiling inside of me. "Miss Marshall, it matters to me not one bit whether or not the boy is your boyfriend. What matters to me is that you accomplish your best possible work."

"No." Her voice was low and bitter, if not a bit baiting. "This grade isn't because the work isn't good. This is because I disagree with you. You think music is this heartless engineering construct made of nothing but notes and rhythms pasted together by architects. It is not. Music is communication. It's emotion. It's passion and love and hate and expression."

As she continued she leaned even closer to me, anchoring her hands on my desk as her hot breath invaded the space between us.

"Mr. Fitzgerald, music was around long before there were theorists to talk about rules. Music is what makes us alive, and I feel sorry for you for not understanding that. If all you care about is mechanics and theory, then you're in the wrong field, no matter how talented you may be."

I recoiled. Since I was sixteen years old, when I won my early admission to the Conservatory and a full scholarship, not a single person had ever suggested that I might be choosing the wrong field. That this appallingly arrogant twenty-one-year-old thought she could do such a thing was infuriating.

She stuck out her red polished index finger and poked it on my chest. The same finger I'd instinctively traced with my thumb just last week. "I'm formally appealing this grade. Please reconsider it on its merits, and not your knee jerk emotional reaction to the idea that musicians might *feel* something. And if you don't change it, I intend to take it to the Dean."

With that, she backed up and walked out of my office, leaving a gaping hole of fury in her wake.

SAVANNAH

I TORE OUT OF Fitzgerald's office door in a flurry, breezing past Nathan, who I'd honestly forgotten was waiting for me.

"That...sounded intense." Nathan followed quickly behind me, stuffing his hands in his coat pockets as we neared the exit.

"You think?" I was still breathless from my face-to-face showdown. "Damn, he's a prick. Did you hear what he said? He had the audacity to say that his treatment of me has *nothing* to do with my mother."

Nathan shrugged and placed his hand on the exit door. "Maybe it doesn't, Savannah. You know how Fitzgerald is. And, he didn't even know who she was until a few weeks ago. He was on your case long before that." His tone had fallen flat as he spoke.

"Whatever." I pushed past him and out into the unseasonably warm late-March air. I was still worked up from my first-ever shouting match with a teacher, and I didn't bother to put on my coat. Looking back, I saw Nathan lagging a few steps behind, looking at the ground. "What?" I stopped, waiting for him to catch up.

"He thought I was your boyfriend?" Nathan gave a slight nervous chuckle and brought his eyes to mine.

I laughed and rolled my eyes. "No kidding, right?"

He shrugged, looking just past my shoulder for a second. "What's so funny?"

"Oh come on!" I rolled my eyes. "Gregory Fitzgerald is so damn out of touch with reality that he can't even decipher your sexual orientation? You don't find that the least bit humorous?"

Nathan's face paled for a split second before his nostrils flared and he pointed his eyes damn near through me. "I'm not gay, Savannah. Wait, you think *I'm gay*?"

I jumped as he shouted the end of his sentence.

Looking around the vacant sidewalk, I was knocked dizzy by his words. "Wait. Wait. What? Nathan. Wait." I was out of breath, my cheeks heating and feeling dizzier still. "Aren't you?"

"No!" He took a step back, running both hands through his hair before turning to the right and storming off.

What the hell?

"Nathan, wait!" I ran, nearly falling on the still-slick sidewalk before I caught up to him. I grabbed the fabric of his coat and pulled as hard as I could until he was forced to stop and turn to face me. I almost wish he hadn't. There were actual tears in his eyes. "What do you mean *no*?"

"Are you fucking kidding me, Savannah? We've been friends for ten years!" He couldn't even look me in the eye.

"Yes, I know!" I shouted, matching his volume. "And in ten years I never saw you date anyone—"

"We only saw each other during the summers at camp!"

"Stop yelling!" I took a breath and felt tears rising in my own eyes. In a much softer voice, I continued, my mind racing a thousand miles a minute. "You never once talked about any girls, not even when we talked during the school year."

"I never mentioned any *other* girls, Savannah."

"And that time at camp when I was fifteen, when you punched Jared Reese after he grabbed my boobs?" I felt anger at the slimy little saxophonist all over again.

"What'd you think that was?" he asked condescendingly.

My eyes bugged out. "Uh, sticking the fuck *up for me*, not you being pissed that someone else copped a feel!"

I felt bile rising through my body and felt my face flush.

Nathan grabbed my shoulders as I staggered back a step. "What? Are you okay? You look pale."

"I've told you everything, Nathan. *Everything*. Oh my god." My knees gave out and I collapsed, cross-legged in the snow-covered grass. Squeezing my eyes shut, I placed my head in my hands.

"What?" Nathan sounded irritated as he stood in front of me. "Get up, Savannah, you're going to get soaking wet."

"We hold hands, you kiss my head, I kiss yours...we dance..." I breathed for a few more seconds until I felt Nathan sit next to me. Looking over, I found his knees bent, arms resting on them as he looked ahead.

"I'm sorry..." He shook his head and looked at me from the corner of his eye.

"You're sorry? For not being gay? Wait. I'm confused. Why the hell didn't you ever tell me you weren't gay?"

Nathan scoffed. "I didn't realize it was an issue."

"You never talked about any girls, Nathan."

And then he said it again, the words that made me feel like I'd been punched in the gut. "No. I never talked about any *other* girls, Savannah."

Looking over at him, I found Nathan pinching the bridge of his nose. "What are you talking about?" My voice was barely a whisper.

When he finally opened his eyes to look at me, he didn't say anything as he stared at me, apparently waiting for something to sink in.

It did.

I squeezed my eyebrows together, certain I was misinterpreting.

Nathan shrugged and cocked his head to the side as he took a deep breath.

All of my dizziness and guilt I felt for assuming my best friend was gay for the last ten years was instantly replaced by anger.

"You're a bastard," I hissed as I stood up. Brushing snow from my jeans, I took off in the direction of my dorm.

"Excuse me?" Nathan shouted as he ran after me, catching up to me. "You've spent the last decade thinking I'm gay and *I'm* a bastard?"

"Jesus *Christ*, I've told you *everything!* You knew about my first kiss, when I got my fucking period, and...fuck! I told you about when I lost my virginity to that jackass of a trumpet player during our last summer at camp together! This whole time you liked me, or whatever, and you just let me spill my guts to you over and over again?" My mind played over every secret I'd told him, every tear I cried on his shoulder over every boy that had broken my heart.

"We're friends, Savannah, that's what friends do."

"It's different and you know it! Why didn't you ever say anything?" I wrapped my arms around myself, suddenly feeling exposed. "Were you hoping to learn all of my weaknesses, all of my insecurities, and play off of those in order to get me into bed, or something? Fuck, Nathan!" I covered my face with my hands as tears streamed down my cheeks.

"Do you honestly believe that about me, Savannah?" His tone turned about as vile as mine. "Why didn't you ever ask me if I was gay?"

"Oh, I don't know, Nathan, maybe because I have class? Damn it, you were my best friend at camp, I knew that if you wanted to tell me, you would. I figured you weren't ready. Why didn't you ever *say* anything to me if you've liked me this whole time." I placed my hands on my hips and took a cleansing breath, waiting for his response.

"I didn't *like* you." He sighed and ran a hand through his hair, looking a bit like he might pass out.

I opened and closed my mouth a few times, trying to find words to express the sheer confusion I was feeling, as ten years of assumptions just blew up in our faces. "You just said," I managed, trailing off.

"I didn't like you, Savannah. I don't *like* you." His nose crinkled as he strung out the word *like*. "I love you."

"You...you what?" My throat started to close around my words.

Nathan grabbed my shoulders, took a breath, and bent down so we were nearly nose-to-nose. "I love you, Savannah. I have from the moment I first heard you play at camp that summer, and fell harder when I heard you laugh three minutes after that. I know I was only twelve then, but, still, I knew. I knew that someday...I just knew. Each summer it only got worse. And I got nervous. You were so gorgeous, so carefree, and so fucking *nice* to me. The nicer you were, the more nervous I got. Then, you told me about how Danny Perkins kissed you behind the tree that summer we were thirteen. The look in your eyes...I knew you thought I was just your friend."

"You were fourteen, Nathan, what stopped you from saying something?" My chin quivered as I replayed even more memories over what I considered ten years of friendship.

He sighed. "I figured you'd get the hint eventually. I ignored all the other girls, and only hung around you."

"Yeah," I nodded, "you were fourteen, and one of two boys in the flute section, surrounded by gorgeous girls. You ignored all of them and you're pissed that I thought you were gay?"

Nathan shook his head, trying to come up with something to say.

"What about the last three years, then?" I asked. "You've dated...right?" I rose my eyebrow, trying to scan through all of our conversations and all the parties we went to, trying to pinpoint a moment, any moment, where I might have seen him with a girl, or heard him talk about one at least.

"Yeah, but..." He clenched his jaw.

"You never said anything to me, Nathan. How was I supposed to know? God, when I broke up with Mark last semester, you let me cry on your lap until I fell asleep! You've just hung around waiting for me to figure it out? That's total shit."

"No...I mean...there's never been anyone worth telling you about. You know how wrapped up I am in my coursework and practicing all the time. I've had dates and...whatever. But there was never anyone worth mentioning. And, by now I've resigned myself to being your friend. I love you, and I care about you, and...I don't fucking know anymore."

I shook my head, trying to backtrack to where this conversation derailed. Unfortunately, that was at the beginning. "So why are you telling me this now? Because I thought you were gay? Sorry about that, by the way." I tried to chuckle, but the noise came out all wrong and I ended up snorting.

"That, I guess...and it's been driving me insane watching you fall in love with someone else." His lips formed a straight line as I watched him swallow hard.

I looked around the empty space surrounding us, certain I was standing in the middle of a different conversation than the one I'd started in. "Is this about Mark? We broke up last year. You were there..."

"Oh come on, Savannah, I know you're in love with Fitzgerald, and it's fucking ridiculous!"

My mouth flew open as I tried to determine if he'd actually spoken those words. His face was stone cold serious, though.

Nathan continued before I could reply. "You blush every time he looks at you, and you spend more time watching him than the words he writes on the board. You challenge more things he says than you do in any of your other classes, and it's obvious that's so you can have more interaction with him."

"Wow," I spit out, "you're awfully sure of yourself, aren't you?" Dropping my arms I continued my trek toward the dorm, not wanting to give Nathan the satisfaction of engaging in the most ridiculous conversation that I've ever had.

"It's not just you, you know," Nathan called after me, stopping me, once again. "He feels something for you, too, Savannah. I can see it."

"You're delusional," I said as I walked back toward him, until we were standing toe-to-toe. "Just because I'm not with you, and just because you know my entire sexual history, doesn't mean you know anything about who I'm in love with. And, I promise you, it's not Gregory Fitzgerald."

"Whatever," he scoffed, looking quite self-righteous. "Keep telling yourself that. I tried that for ten years, Savannah. To tell myself I wasn't in love with someone. Let me tell you, it's fucking useless torture." His dark brown eyes lowered to mine, and they looked empty. Furious.

"I'm going back to my room."

"No, allow *me*." Nathan brushed past me, fuming.

"Nathan!" I called after him, but he didn't turn around.

For the first time in our friendship, he ignored me.

Chapter 8

SAVANNAH

I 'M NOT GAY.

Oh God, of *course* he isn't gay. It was glaringly clear to me as I tossed and turned that night. Marcia was out late practicing again. *Maybe I should do the same.* I was awful to him, I thought as I sat up, running a hand through my hair. Honestly, though, who is in love with someone for ten years and says *nothing?* Resigned to a sleepless night, I threw on sweats and my coat before grabbing my flute and heading to the twenty-four hour practice rooms. I needed to think. To process. I called Nathan two or three times, but he didn't answer

Trying to sort out the largest can of worms anyone had ever dumped on me, I began to tear up again. I'd trusted Nathan with every secret, every insecurity, every emotion. Okay, fine, it wasn't his fault that I thought he was gay. But...ugh. On top of not being gay, he was in love with me?

Sighing as I clumsily put my flute together and ran through a few scales, I tried to think about the situation rationally. Fact: Nathan and I had been friends for more than ten years. Fact: I never actually got the feeling from him that he was coming onto me, or the feeling that he was trying to get me to tell him things for his benefit. Fact: Nathan Connors was my friend and I'd hurt him yesterday in more ways than one.

As the threatening tears escaped, and rolled lazily down my cheeks, I had to look at some other facts, too. Nathan, who possessed more graceful confidence than most people I'd met, never bothered to mention in ten years that he had feelings for me, let alone that he loved me. Further, we had severely lax boundaries with each other. He always had his arm around me, sometimes we held hands, and for the love of God, his lips have been on my forehead and cheek more times than I could count. He wasn't gay this whole time, knew damn well I wasn't gay, and was pushing those boundaries with me. Where the hell did he think it would all lead? We would need to have a discussion about that…but not now.

Then, there were the accusations Nathan made about Gregory Fitzgerald and me. I stopped playing, incensed at the idea, and sat down, setting my flute on its stand.

I know you're in love with Fitzgerald.

I don't know what was more infuriating—that Nathan thought that, or that I found myself wondering what it was he saw. Nathan knew me well. He'd known about nearly every boyfriend I'd ever had, and spent summer upon summer watching me flirt and be flirted with. He wiped my tears when a boy broke my heart, or, worse, never liked me in the first place.

I huffed, placing my forehead in my hands. It was completely absurd that I was considering the possibility that I was in love with someone and I didn't know it. Of course I wasn't in love with Gregory. Mr. Fitzgerald. Not only was I not in love with him, I couldn't stand him. If emotional ideology around music could be placed in a straight line—which I'm sure would please Fitzgerald to no end—we would be at opposite ends of that line. I saw music as sights, sounds, colors, scents, lives, births, deaths, all rolled into a breathing, living thing that could be passed down through generations.

Music gave life beauty. Music spoke the language of the human spirit for all to hear and understand.

Gregory, on the other hand? Not only did he appear to view music as a thing, he seemed to have little regard for the effect his own music had on people. The first day of class when he'd played that simple Bach suite, I was swallowed by goosebumps. Tears stung my eyes as I'd watched his forehead scrunch at certain parts and relax at others. His body swayed and his tight shoulders moved against his breathing.

He was living music and didn't even know it. Tragic.

Lifting my head, I sat back with my arms crossed over my chest. I had no intentions of practicing at all. I just needed a change of scenery. What the hell was I supposed to do? About...everything? Nathan hadn't answered my calls, and it was just as well. The kind of conversation I needed to have with him would indeed be a lengthy one, and it would need to be done in person. It would surely chase the sunrise and be filled with yelling and crying. I didn't even know what I was going to say to him, or what I wanted to ask him. Certainly there would be things I didn't want to know, but I needed a few days—or more—to figure that out. I knew I didn't want to hurt him any further, no matter what it was I decided to say. He was my friend...right? Suddenly, I wasn't sure. I could almost feel him slipping away.

He feels something for you, too, Savannah. I can see it.

What the hell was that supposed to mean? I knew for a fact that Nathan had precisely zero interaction with Gregory outside of the classroom. Nathan had put off his last theory class so he could take it with me, and I knew he needed the grade to be decent. He wasn't in any ensembles that Gregory was involved with, so...what? What was it that he saw? Because, honestly, all I saw when I looked at Gregory Fitzgerald was a lonely, sad, angry man who lived alone with his cello. That was it.

No. That wasn't all.

When he sat behind his cello it was like he transformed into a different person altogether. A human, even. Not the monotone robot that directed us in the ways of music theory. About five minutes after our first music theory class with him ended, I found myself searching through the music library to find a flute transcription for that Bach cello suite. I had to learn it. Immediately. Because when he put his bow in hand and brought it to the strings, he transformed into something transcendent.

I can't explain what was going through my head as I'd thumbed through the files and files of transcriptions, not stopping until I found exactly what I was looking for. I guess...if that song, those notes, could pull emotion out of a man like Gregory and transfer it directly to the center of my gut...I wanted to feel it, too. The way he did. I wanted to get in his head, even if for only a minute, to feel what he felt from that side of the stand.

But...why?

"Ugh," I groaned, deciding to just pack up my flute and head back to the dorm to try to sleep.

"Savannah?" a voice from the other side of the door startled me. It was my roommate.

"You scared the shit out of me, Marcia!"

"Sorry. Girl, how many times do I have to tell you to shut these freaking doors? Lock them, too, when you're here by yourself this late at night." She shook a finger disapprovingly as I put my coat back on.

I sighed. "Sorry, Mom."

"Plus, didn't you say Gregory walked in on you practicing once? Do you really want to risk another run-in with him if you can avoid it?" She laughed, and I did, too.

"I guess not." I shrugged, but felt my heart rate pick up slightly when I realized the day he walked in on me was the day I stopped shutting the door all the way.

I ran a finger over the knuckle of my index finger, tracing the path Gregory's thumb had taken the week before. Taking a deep breath, I forced myself to get a hold of reality. And fast. He was my professor. I was his student.

But, reluctantly, I caught myself staring at my fingertips, and recalling how the muscles of his hands felt beneath them.

GREGORY

MUSIC IS COMMUNICATION. *It's emotion. It's passion and love and hate and expression.* Savannah's words rolled through my head all the way home, echoing, over and over again, as if she'd somehow punctured my very identity. *If all you care about is mechanics and theory, then you're in the wrong field.*

I was in a foul mood when I unlocked the door to my house and entered the living room. I marched into the kitchen and opened the refrigerator, opening a bottle of water and gulping it back.

How dare she. This was the reason I did not want to teach. Right here. In my rage, I found myself repeating myself. *How dare she.*

I paced back and forth. I needed to practice. I was supposed to be meeting Karin at eight for dinner. I needed to clear my head and get something done. But my mind kept circling around *that girl*, and it wouldn't stop. Not just her arguments, which had not only the ring of truth, but reflected very badly on me. My mind turned to her eyes. The graceful, almost ethereal way she moved. The sway of her body and the sound when she played the flute. *The music.*

I closed my eyes. Because I had no choice. I needed to get a grip on myself. She was a student, for Christ's sake. Incredibly gifted, yes. Passionate about her music. No question about that. But she was a *student*. A distraction.

I was a cellist with the Boston Symphony Orchestra. I was at the beginning of what promised to be a remarkable career, a career rivaling those of Casals or Rostropovich, and the last thing I needed was *distraction*. What I needed was relentless focus. On my music. And nothing else. That was the reason I had no personal life. That was the reason I'd shuffled the blind boy off to a different teacher.

I picked up my phone and sent a text message to Karin, cancelling our date for the evening. I turned the phone off before she could reply, tossed my jacket over the couch, and then unlocked the fireproof case for the Montagnana. As always, I opened the case in reverent silence. I took out the bow, tightening it then applying a fresh layer of rosin. And I began to play.

I began with Bach, the simple, yet beautiful piece which first brought me to my knees when I was a child. After I'd heard it, I'd begged the band director to let me try the cello. For two months, every day, I'd worked through lunch and after school, until I'd mastered just the beginning, using a cello I borrowed every day from the band room. I didn't tell my parents, because I knew my father would consider it a frivolous pursuit. When he found out, he'd brushed it off as unimportant, but by that time, I was obsessed.

But today. Today, when I played, the low mournful sound that defined the beginning, I saw *her*. Savannah. The first day of class, when she stood, eyes closed, mouth slightly open, her body slightly swaying, responding to the music.

Did I know even then? Did I know that I would become obsessed with her? That I would sometimes wake in the night and see her brown eyes, her waist, her lips on her flute as she formed magical, incredible music?

Savannah was correct about one thing. I *had* been too harsh with her. I'd shut her down in class. I'd given her shockingly bad grades when her performance deserved far better. I'd dismissed her ideas, her passions, her talent. Not because they were wrong. But because they disturbed me. Because they were hers. Because she was so much more talented and brilliant than her peers. Because in her, I saw me as I could have been. Living a life that sometimes went beyond the music. Caring about other people. Having friends, dating, and loving.

It was as I had told the boy, Robert. You must be willing to sacrifice *everything* for the music. This wasn't a hobby. This wasn't a nice job in an insurance company. This was an artistic calling that required the utmost passion, commitment and sacrifice.

My mind refocused on the music. The smooth movement of the bow, the change of strings, the melody, which picked up and wrapped my mind in the nearest thing to ecstasy I'd ever experienced. My vibrato was just slightly off, and I corrected. This was the worst I'd played in a long time. The sound seemed to me choppy and forced. I frowned in frustration.

Only once before had I allowed emotional and relationship considerations to affect my music. My sophomore year at the Conservatory, I'd become involved with a young lady, a violinist. Mariana Passos. Brazilian. Her English was poor, but the music…that was something else entirely. She'd come to the United States on a student visa strictly to attend the New England Conservatory. Lithe, graceful, beautiful. In far too many ways, Savannah reminded me of her. But such things rarely work out. We had a tempestuous breakup, messy beyond measure. I was heartbroken and nearly failed two of my classes that semester.

I'd promised myself I'd never let go again. Not like that. Not in a way that could endanger my career, my life.

As I played, my arms and body unconsciously moved through the measures, and my mind continued down this course to the only clear conclusion. I'd been wrong about Savannah's grade, and I would correct that. But I'd been right about something else. Savannah wasn't just a gifted musician. She wasn't just a beautiful girl. She wasn't just a brilliant mind. For me, she represented much more than those things. She represented a distraction. If I forced myself to be honest, I was…fascinated with her. Attracted beyond measure.

I wanted her.

Savannah Marshall was *dangerous*.

SAVANNAH

I WAS INTENTIONALLY ALMOST late to Music Theory on Wednesday, waiting until the last second, in hopes of avoiding an awkward discussion with either Nathan or Gregory. Mr. Fitzgerald. I couldn't look at Nathan right now—the silence between us was cumbersome and I couldn't stare it down just yet. And Gregory just…

I was tired from tossing and turning two nights in a row. I was cranky. And the last thing I wanted was a run-in with either one of them. I needed time to think. I needed time to *process*. I needed to be left alone.

Unfortunately, Tuesday I'd been full up. My academic classes are Monday, Wednesday, Friday. Tuesday and Thursday are reserved for one-on-one flute lessons, followed by hours of practice and rehearsals. On top of that, several of my professors, including Mr. Gregory Fitzgerald, had assigned a metric ton of crap on our first day back from Spring Break.

I checked my watch. One minute for class to start. Then I looked both ways up and down the hall to make sure Nathan wasn't lurking anywhere in order to avoid an awkward confrontation in front of our class. With any luck he was already in the classroom. I darted across the hall, through the door, and slammed right into Gregory, who was reaching for the door.

He grunted, and I gasped, nearly dropping my bag. I backed away a foot, then said, "Sorry," and darted around him, my eyes going to the floor.

Not-Gay Nathan was in the usual spot where we normally sat. I made my way to the opposite side of the room and slid into an unused seat.

Gregory slammed the door shut unnecessarily hard, then marched to the front of the room, immediately launching into the depths of a lecture on the mathematical relationship between different keys. Which was interesting if you were building a bridge, I guess, but only served to irritate me now. It's not that I didn't care about or love the fundamentals of music. It's that I was tired of his implication that this was all there was to it.

Usually I was fully engaged in this class. Combative even. But today my attention drifted. My eyes on Gregory Fitzgerald. My professor. I didn't like his attitude. I didn't like his haughty superiority, his snobbishness, or his insistence that music was nothing more than an engineering construct. I mean, sure, he was incredible with his cello. I could still close my eyes and hear him playing. I'd been to the symphony twice this semester. I'd told myself I was just soaking in more music. But I was disturbed, then and now, by just how much attention I'd paid during Gregory's impassioned, tension-filled solos.

What kind of man produced such incredibly emotional music, then denied that emotion had anything to do with it?

It didn't hurt that he was incredibly attractive.

When he walked in front of the classroom, his motions were economical, but filled with an inner tension that arrested the eyes of everyone in the room. Watching him, I thought that whatever his protestations, inside there was tremendous passion and emotion. Locked away, hidden, only released through the contact of bow and string.

I blinked when I realized, first, that I'd been staring at him, and second, that the entire class had gone silent.

"Miss Marshall?"

"Gregory?"

I said the word. Then I froze. *Oh, crap.* He'd called on me. For something. And I had no idea what. And then I'd called him by his first name. What the hell was wrong with me? Casting a glance to the side, I noticed the wide-eyes of my classmates judging my error.

"I'm sorry. *Mr. Fitzgerald.* I got lost in pondering all the wonders of mathematical relationships." I was trying for sarcastic, but my words came out in a rush, one word stumbling over the next.

His eyebrows moved close together, his face forming into a frown. But his gaze lingered over me for just a second, and for that second I felt like I was under a microscope.

"Something on your mind, Miss Marshall? Is your personal life distracting you, perhaps?" Meaningfully, he looked between me in my new seat, and Nathan, across the room from me.

In a tight voice, I said, "My personal life doesn't really belong in this room."

He raised a finger. "Exactly my point. To all of you." He turned his back to us, walking to the front of the room. Every eye in the room swiveled between Nathan, Mr. Fitzgerald, and me. Wondering. Questioning.

Fitzgerald spun around, then pronounced, "If you wish to succeed as a musician. If you wish to be among the best.

If you wish to count yourself as one of the greats, then there are sacrifices you must make. All of you. You've selected one of the most difficult, demanding career choices anyone can make. And if you want to find yourself seated amidst the Boston Symphony, or the New York, or London, or the other greats, then you'll make great sacrifices. You'll practice until your fingers are numb. You'll turn down your *dates* and give up a private life. And even then, only a few of you have the capacity to succeed."

His eyes fell on me again. Examining me until I felt almost naked—as if he were staring into my soul, my courage, and seeing all the doubts I had. The questions. The doubts I had that I even wanted to pursue music. Because that was the truth. Sometimes I thought I'd chosen this path only to please my mother. My mother, the world-renowned opera singer. My mother, who I rarely saw, except in between engagements.

I looked away from him, swallowing back emotions I couldn't even identify. I didn't need his hassle right now. I didn't need *any of this.*

"Class is dismissed. Miss Marshall, please stay behind for just a moment."

I closed my eyes. Leaned my head back. And in my mind, I told Gregory Fitzgerald to just shut the hell up.

I heard, but didn't see, as the rest of the class filed out. Finally I opened my eyes, just in time to see Nathan looking toward me from near the door. His face was oddly fixed, as if he were trying to restrain emotions too big to express.

"Mr. Connors, is there something you need?" Fitzgerald asked.

Nathan looked at him, anger washing over his face. "No. Nothing. Sir." His limbs tense, he turned and walked out of the room. I sighed a little. I couldn't put off talking with Nathan for too long. Because my refusal to talk now was hurting my best friend.

I wiped thoughts of Nathan from my mind. I could only deal with one crisis at a time, and at the moment, Mr. Fitzgerald appeared to demand my attention. He was approaching me now, with what appeared to be my paper in his hands.

"Miss Marshall. I've been considering our discussion from Monday." He looked uncomfortable. Tense. His eyes swept over me, then away, then back to me again. Then he said, "You are correct. Perhaps I've been too hard on you. I see a great deal of talent in you, the potential for...for greatness. I see now that I've pushed too hard. Your paper, in fact, met all of the requirements which were assigned."

He set the paper down in front of me. The F was crossed out, replaced with a B+. I narrowed my eyes. It was an A paper. I waited, not saying anything, wondering if he intended to explain himself.

It seemed that he did. "I told you the first week of class that before you break the rules, you must thoroughly understand them. Therefore I'm still counting off one letter grade for the extraneous material in your paper. That said," he took a deep breath and looked away from me, "it was quite brilliant."

Brilliant? My head was swimming. I went from an F to brilliant? I stood up and tucked the paper in my bag. Unaccountably, I wanted to cry. I wanted to shout. I wanted to tell him to shove the paper up his ass. I didn't even know *what* I felt.

He gave me a questioning look. What? Did he want me to thank him? For backing down on being an ass? Being *wrong*? Did he expect me to fall to my knees in gratitude? What the hell did he want from me?

"Miss Marshall..." he said. His eyes were on me as he said the word, his expression unreadable, his eyes tightly focused. "Savannah..."

I stepped back, putting another foot of distance between us. He sighed, his expression suddenly hardening. He said in a much softer voice than usual, "I'll see you in class Friday. Please have your personal affairs in enough order that you can pay attention in class."

Adjusting the straps of my backpack on my shoulders, I turned for the exit. In the next breath I was facing him again.

"Gregory?" My voice shook, but I did my best to ignore it.

He looked up from his papers, waiting for me to continue, uncertainty on his face. "Yes?" he asked after my silence ran over "normal."

"I...never mind. Thank you for fixing the grade." I sighed and left the room in a hurry, stopping just outside the door to rest against the wall for a minute.

Just go back to your room, Savannah.

Chapter 9

GREGORY

I LEFT CLASS THAT day angry with myself. Angry at my lack of self-control. Angry that I'd almost said something to her, which I would surely have regretted. Angry that I couldn't stop thinking about her, that when I sat down to draw music out of my cello, it was her that I thought of. Angry that when I woke up, I thought of her. Angry that for the two days after our confrontation in my office, I'd found myself continually returning to the argument. Angry at myself that I'd graded her unfairly, and angry that my thoughts kept returning to her reaction.

Angry that I cared about her reaction.

For the next three weeks, I mechanically went to teach my classes, to rehearsals, to performances. I met with Robert and his parents twice more, and introduced them to a young cellist, a former student, who agreed to take on teaching the boy. At Karin's insistence, we went out twice for dinner, and both times she became angry at my inability to pay attention. Because I kept circling around the same thought. The same formless, overwhelming emotion. The same question. Because somehow, despite all my protective armor, despite

all my focus on the music and the music alone, I'd become...
infatuated. Obsessed. With Savannah Marshall.

I kept a professional, distant relationship with her. Anything else would have been a tremendous mistake. But sometimes, when she wasn't looking, my eyes would fall upon her
in class. I examined the curve of her cheeks, the arch of her
eyebrows, the flow of her hair, the curve of her hips and calves.
It was disturbing, on far too many levels. She was my *student*.
She was volatile and emotional. She was a disaster waiting to
happen. And all of that aside, even if I wanted to throw cau-
tion to the wind, even if I was willing to throw away my hard
earned discipline, the fact was, she wanted absolutely nothing
to do with me.

Arrogant, I'd heard her mumble. On more than one occasion, especially after we'd gone back and forth in class.

I found myself inappropriately curious about what had
passed between her and Nathan Connors. On the Wednesday
after our confrontation, she'd come in the class at the last second, and sat as far away from him as possible. Then, when
he left the class, he gave her a look of such longing, such naked devotion, that I was stopped cold for a moment, unable
to react. Since then, the two of them continued to sit apart,
not speaking, not interacting in any way. The other students
noticed, and I'd overheard two of them talking in the hall,
just outside the classroom, about a lover's spat. My stomach
clenched at the thought. I wanted to believe her protests that
Nathan wasn't her boyfriend. Even though it was none of my
business.

Two weeks after spring break, I was packing up my things
in the office to go home for the day when James knocked on
the doorframe.

"Got time to go grab a drink?"

I didn't really. I had planned to go home and play, all night. But the BSO's season was over, and James wasn't one to be put off by excuses.

"Yes," I replied.

A few minutes later we slipped into a corner bar several blocks away from the Conservatory. James had chosen this bar when we were undergraduates, and we'd been coming here off and on ever since. Dark, smelly, and mostly catering to local residents, it was a place we were highly unlikely to run into faculty or students. He ordered a beer, and I got a gin and tonic, and we sat down in a tiny booth. The table was a little sticky, so I carefully kept my arms away from it.

For a few minutes, we discussed random happenings from the Conservatory, then Robert and his parents. When I told him I'd passed Robert off to a different instructor, James frowned briefly, but then moved on. His look disturbed me. I didn't understand his expectations. I was in no way equipped to teach any child, much less one who couldn't see.

We sat in silence for a few moments, and he gave me a long, serious look. "Talk to me, Gregory."

I raised an eyebrow. "About?"

He took a sip of his beer. "About Savannah Marshall."

Very carefully, I kept control of my expression as I took a sip of my drink. "Why is she the topic of the day? She's in one of my classes. Gifted musician, but undisciplined."

"Then why did you freeze in place the moment I mentioned her name?"

"You're imagining things, James."

James raised one eyebrow as he stared at me. "I'm not imagining that you've become the subject of rumors."

Rumors. One thing I'd never been was the subject of the gossip that inevitably flowed out of being part of a tiny community like the Conservatory. I intentionally kept my personal life, what there was of it, far away from the school. The only concession I'd made on that front in years was dating Karin, which to an extent I only did to keep up appearances.

"What sort of...rumors?" I tried to keep the warning out of my voice. But I think some of it slipped through, because he sat back in his seat, giving me a wary look. He sighed then leaned forward again.

"Here's what I'm hearing, Gregory. You can take it for what it's worth, but I'm concerned about you. What the rumors say is: the two of you have been consistently combative in class. Constantly disagreeing, constantly sparring. Two weeks ago you two had a shouting match in your office. The same day, she suddenly stopped hanging out with her longtime boyfriend, and the two of them aren't even speaking. Since then you've cancelled three dates with Karin, who has been quite vocal about it. The *rumors* say that she stared at you openly in class. And that you've been doing plenty of staring of your own. Roughly half of the school thinks she and Nathan split up because you slept with her. Luckily the other half is too wrapped up in their own lives to care."

Without thinking, I blurted out, "Nathan Connors was not her boyfriend."

James closed his eyes and winced. "That, my friend, was not what I wanted to hear from you."

I coughed and took another drink. "I assure you, I would never sleep with a student. The whole idea is distasteful."

"She's attractive...gifted...it's not a hard sell."

"She's a disruption to the entire class. Undercuts me any chance she gets. I can barely stand her presence in my classroom." That wasn't true though. In fact, all I could think about on the way to class was her being there.

James rolled his eyes. "It's not your classroom that concerns me."

I leaned forward. I could feel my heart beating in my temples. Anger? Tension? Anxiety? I had no idea. "James. Listen to me. You're all too aware of my feelings about relationships, about getting involved with someone that might interfere with my music."

James leaned forward, keeping his volume low. "If she wasn't a student, I'd tell you to go for it. She's a good match from what little I know of her. And...that concerns me."

"You're out of your mind." I sat back and ran a hand through my hair.

He grimaced. "Gregory. Be honest with me. We've been friends for more than a decade."

I gave a large sigh, tossed back the rest of my drink, and waved at the waitress, pointing at the empty glass. Then I leaned forward again and said, "James...I...she...nothing has happened. Nothing will. The subject is closed."

"Can I suggest, then, that you become a little more circumspect? If these rumors get back to the Dean, you're going to find yourself answering questions for the administration. And while the Conservatory is lucky to have you, I think you know there are plenty on the faculty who are either jealous of your talent or resentful of your attitude. They won't hesitate to throw you under the bus."

I grimaced. "You're well aware I avoid office politics of any kind."

"I know that. You're above all of it. But don't think it can't drag you down into the mud."

I sighed. "James, thank you for bringing this to my attention. But in all seriousness, the subject is closed. I refuse to discuss it any more."

James shook his head and ordered another beer.

SAVANNAH

I STOOD AT THE base of the steps to Nathan's apartment for a long while, debating whether or not I would actually press the buzzer. Rain falling in cold, fat drops rolled down my forehead and balanced on the ends of my eyelashes while I stared at his name next to his doorbell. The last three weeks had been awkward. No, they were awful. After three days of dealing with him ignoring my calls, I stopped calling. I'm sure he was further irritated by my avoiding him in class. Not my finest moment of maturity, sure. But, I was confused. I was reliving our whole friendship in the framework of an entirely different paradigm than the one I'd been operating.

Buzz.

I pressed the buzzer, waiting nervously. What if he wouldn't let me in?

"Who is it?" Nathan's tired voice nearly knocked me off balance.

"Nate, it's me..." No one ever called him Nate. Not since we were about thirteen and he deemed it to be childish. But, that's how I was feeling. Like the thirteen-year-old girl that had a boy best friend who meant the absolute world to her.

"What do you want, Savannah?" His tone would have seemed cold if I didn't hear his voice shaking a little.

"We need to talk."

There was a dreadful silence before a sigh.

I rolled my eyes, annoyed to be having this conversation through a speaker. "Please, Nathan. I...look, it's cold and raining out here, are you gonna let me in or not?"

"Shit, sorry," he mumbled before I heard another buzz, and the door click, allowing me access.

Shaking raindrops from my coat as I walked to his second floor apartment, I saw his door pop open. Walking through, I found Nathan leaning back against his kitchen counter with his arms crossed over his chest. I tossed my coat on the table by the door and ran my fingers through my hair a few times, trying to dry it out a bit.

"Oh for Christ's sake, Savannah, you're all wet," Nathan huffed, walking toward his bathroom. He returned with a towel that he held out in front of him.

I felt his eyes on me as I ran the towel over my hair. "Thank you." I sighed as I set the towel on top of my jacket and made my way to the couch.

"So," he shrugged, "what do you want to talk about?"

Tilting my head to the side, I spoke gently. "Come on, Nathan, sit."

He stared at the space next to me for several seconds, a battle playing across his eyes, before he sighed and sank next to me.

"Look," I started before he could, "we've been friends for ten years. You've always made me feel safe, protected..." I trailed off, watching his face.

He swallowed hard but didn't quite look at me.

"Anyway," I continued, "I need you to understand that I'm not upset that you're not gay. That's ridiculous. I just... it's just that I shared some things with you that, honestly, I wouldn't have told you if I thought—"

"If you thought I was straight?" His tone was clipped. Irritated.

"It's not just that, Nathan." I wrapped my hand around his, but he didn't respond. It sat flat in my palm. "If I thought that you liked me...I wouldn't have ever gone on about the boys, the kisses, the breakups."

"But I wanted you to, Savannah." Nathan grumbled a little as he ran his hand over his face.

"Okay, but if you liked me..."

"I still wanted to be your friend, okay? I figured out pretty quickly that you didn't feel the same way about me. I just didn't realize it was because you thought I was *gay*. Did you not feel that way about me because you thought I was gay, or..."

Christ, he really wanted an answer. I had to go back and search some pretty early memories of Nathan to figure out when it was I thought he was gay. And how I felt before that.

"Well, I obviously had a crush on you the second I saw you. I was ten, for God's sake." I laughed a little, but he didn't. "I don't know, Nathan, that's asking me to forget the last ten years and pretend I'm seeing you again for the first time. I can't do that." Suddenly, I felt tears stinging my eyes. I could see on his face that this was breaking his heart, and that's not what I came here to do. "I'm sorry," I whispered.

That's all I could say. There was too damn much to sort through if we really wanted to. But, I didn't. He was my best friend and I wanted to keep that relationship, if I could.

"Jesus, don't be sorry, Savannah," Nathan sighed as he pulled me into a hug. "I had years of chances to come clean with you about my feelings. I didn't. That's not your fault."

"Wow, we're a mess." I sniffed and chuckled.

He laughed, too, this time.

"I still love you, though, okay? I don't ever want to see you get hurt. Especially by Fitzgerald."

I tensed instantly and pulled away from Nathan's body. "What are you talking about?"

"Savannah..." He rolled his eyes and looked exasperated.

"Nathan," I arched my eyebrow, "I told you—I'm not in love with him."

"Yeah? And how long are you going to tell yourself that?"

I stood, holding out my arms. "What the hell is your problem all of a sudden? He's our professor. I see him three times a week for an hour. And, he's a pompous ass."

Nathan shook his head at me then spoke in a low, urgent tone. "Everyone's been talking about it, Savannah. Everyone has seen how you two interact." His eyes narrowed at me as he spoke.

I dropped my jaw. "Are you standing here, right now, insinuating that I'm having an affair with my professor?"

"Well, if you're not, I suggest you figure out what it is, exactly, that you want from him. Before not dealing with your feelings at all leads one of you to make a huge mistake."

Silence.

My cheeks betrayed me as they heated under Nathan's words. Slowly looking up at his face, I saw him wince a little. Maybe at what he said. Maybe at my reaction.

Either way, he took a slow step toward me and placed a hand on my shoulder.

Softly, he said, "I don't want you to get hurt, Savannah."

I stepped out of his touch. "You've mentioned that, Nathan. But you're the only one who's managed to hurt me lately. Despite everything we've already talked about, you claim to know my feelings better than I know them, and demand action from me."

"That's not what—"

"That's exactly what you're doing, Nathan, and it's not fair. Being my best friend doesn't mean you're director of my feelings. I...I need to go. Look," I took a deep breath as I paced toward my coat, "I don't want to put all kinds of stress on you before your recital in a couple of weeks. Just...we're fine, right?" I made myself sound convincing enough.

I knew how emotional Nathan could get, and his performance nerves were always all over the place. I cared about him enough in that moment to want him not to blow his final task in school.

"Yes. Savannah..." He dropped his arms and met me at the door, his eyes pleading.

I shook my head. "Don't say anything, Nathan. Please. We've both said enough. Let's just get through the end of the semester in one piece, okay?"

He nodded, swallowing hard as he looked to the floor.

Without another word, I zipped my coat and left Nathan's apartment. When I reached the front steps, I was grateful for the rain. Closing my eyes and tilting my face to the sky, I let the cold, grey water wash over me.

It was only a few blocks down Huntington Ave back to the Conservatory and my room. I set off through the rain, trying to clear my mind. Nathan. Gregory. It was all just…too much. And as much as I loved walking in the rain under normal circumstances, even *that* was becoming too much. The rain was coming down in sheets, and it was getting cold.

Ahead of me, turning onto the block and walking quickly, I saw a man in a black overcoat with a black umbrella and matching hair. From behind it almost looked like…it was.

I ran, my feet splashing up dirty rainwater, and ducked under the umbrella.

Gregory came to a shocked stop, and I realized that underneath the umbrella I could hear the rain pounding against the fabric.

"What are you doing?" He had to shout to be heard.

"Trying to get out of the rain!"

A gust of wind blew the rain at us, almost horizontal, and the umbrella nearly collapsed. Gregory looked around and then grabbed my upper arm in his right hand. "Come!" he shouted, then pulled me toward the next building an underneath an awning.

By the time we got under the awning, his umbrella was in shreds, the fabric completely torn from the wire spokes. He looked at it in frustration for a second, shaking it, as if giving it a stern look or a strong lecture might force it back into shape.

Finally he tossed it aside. I wrapped my arms across my chest, my teeth chattering. My coat had soaked through.

The rain was coming down harder now. Hard enough I could hear it rattle off the awning and the nearest cars, a roar of a sound. Behind us, the walls and windows were covered with signs reading *Boston Shawarma: Lamb, Kebab, Hummus, We Deliver!* To both sides and our front, a wall of rain, almost completely blocking the view of the street.

Right in front of me...his face. Rain still dripped from his hair, past his sapphire eyes. Eyes that were fixed on me. I couldn't hear my heartbeat over the pounding of the rain. But I could feel it, rushing in my ears. Because he brought his hands up, cupping my face. As he did I reflexively raised my hands, placing them flat on his chest, as if to hold him back.

"Why didn't you have an umbrella?" he asked.

I swallowed. I didn't know how to answer that. So I told the truth. "I don't like having to prepare for rain."

He shook his head, just slightly, and his mouth quirked up into a grin, one eyebrow raising. Then he threw his head back and laughed, a loud, hearty belly laugh. Without thinking, I shifted my hands to both sides of his face. And I leaned up and kissed him, hard, on the lips.

Gregory froze. For maybe a quarter second. Then his arms instantly wrapped around me, one hand slipping through my soaked hair and gripping the back of my head, and then our lips and mouths were open, working together, his tongue touching mine, and I let out a low whimper.

I heard a bell ring as the door to the Shawarma place opened toward us, and I pushed, hard, shoving back away from him.

Three girls...*students from the Conservatory*...stepped out of the door. One of them groaned, looking out into the rain. "We'll never make it without getting soaked," she said.

In between the girls and me, Gregory just stood there. Staring at me with those eyes that grabbed my heart and twisted it in knots.

I shook my head just slightly then backed out from under the awning and into the rain.

I turned and ran.

Chapter 10

SAVANNAH

I DON'T KNOW HOW the rumors started, but they made quick work of spreading. Somehow, someone heard my shouting match with Gregory the week after spring break. *God, I shouted at a teacher. What was that about?* Marcia came back to the room one day and joked that she was checking to see if I was still alive after going a few rounds with the insufferable cellist. From there, things only got more speculative when Nathan and I stopped talking. A few girls in class whispered to me things like, *Is it true? Are you dating a teacher?* All I could do was thank God no one had seen that kiss.

In spite of myself, my eyes wandered to Gregory Fitzgerald every four minutes or so throughout our final exam in his music theory class. I'd taken enough practice tests and studied what I knew he expected out of us, and planned to get through the exam with little to no argument from him. Analyzing the notes in front of me wasn't the challenge. It was, as Gregory drilled into us all semester, fairly straightforward on a face-value level. The challenge was ignoring the holes Nathan was staring into the back of my head. Him and the others.

I was horrified. Not only did I have more respect for myself than to date a professor, I certainly wanted no part in messing with his career—since that was all that tethered him to the land of the living.

Or was.

The way he'd kissed me back under that awning showed me something...more. There was life in those eyes. Sensation in those lips. Lust in his tongue.

He kissed me back.

Jesus, what now? I thought to myself as I scribbled answers inside a blue book.

Nothing. Semester over, problem solved. Pretend it never happened.

Chewing on my pen cap as I neared the end of the exam, with loads of time to spare, I glanced across the room at Nathan. As if sensing my eyes on him, he looked up from his paper and toward me. He'd texted me wanting to know if I was okay. I wasn't, and I hated that I couldn't talk to him about it because, for one thing, I'd lied to him. I'd known for weeks that what I'd been feeling for Gregory was nothing short of a crush but it was so, so much more. I hadn't told him about the kiss, either, because I was afraid. Or ashamed.

I really wished, in that moment, that I had my best friend but...this seemed like something I'd have to deal with on my own for a while. But, I wanted Nathan and I to really be okay. We'd been friends for too long to let miscommunication screw us up now. So, I smiled at him. As I did, I watched his shoulders relax as he smiled back. Nathan was graduating in two weeks, and I knew he'd been auditioning for a few symphonies, and, well, I was going to miss him.

I gathered my things and took another look at my paper, scrawling one last thing on it before heading to Gregory's desk, where he sat looking at pages of music I couldn't readily identify.

"Here you go, Mr. Fitzgerald." I couldn't even fake a smile as I shakily placed the paper in front of him. I didn't know if he had heard about the rumors involving the two of us. Probably not. If he had heard them, however, I found myself hoping he wasn't furious with me for kissing him in the first place.

Even though he'd kissed me back.

"Thank you, Miss Marshall," he muttered without looking up from his papers. That made my stomach turn. He wouldn't look me in the eyes. Couldn't, maybe. If he'd had any respect for me at all through the semester I'd made quick work of erasing it with a single kiss.

"You're welcome," I whispered, turning slowly from his desk, fighting tears all of a sudden.

"Savannah," he called softly. Of course, a few heads in the front row popped up, undoubtedly studying our interaction.

I cleared my throat and turned back toward him, where I found his piercing blue eyes scanning my face. "Yes?"

He squared his shoulders a bit and I watched him swallow before he said, "Good luck."

I nodded and left the classroom quickly, without saying thank you. I'd intended to wait for Nathan, but I was too big of a mess. I sprinted back to my dorm, tears streaming down my face.

Bursting through my door, I was relieved Marcia was still in her exam and I had the room to myself. I tossed my backpack on the floor and collapsed, facedown on my bed, sobbing into my pillow. The rumors didn't bother me. The school year was over and before anyone realized it, something else would happen to get people talking. I'd survived a class with the notorious Gregory Fitzgerald and was pretty sure I'd end up with a decent grade.

If he could even objectively grade my exam at this point.

I gripped my comforter as the tears came harder, at the realization of their purpose in the first place. I was going to miss him. I was going to miss Gregory. Not his broody, insufferable, uptight exterior, but what I knew was inside of that. His passion, his musicianship. It was the music. It was him. They were one and the same, even if he couldn't see it. I was going to miss the times he brought his cello to class and played examples for us about what he was lecturing about. Those moments where I felt like there was no one else in the room, because as soon as his bow slid across the strings I felt like it was just me, and him, and the music. God, the music.

His lips.

I'd only tasted his lips once, and the thought of never again curled me into the fetal position. I needed another way. Another way for this end, other than goodbye.

There was none. This was it.

Sitting up after several minutes, I forced myself to take a few deep breaths as I dried my tears. It was for the best that the year was over. I still had another year left at the Conservatory and was bound to run into him at one time or another. I needed to learn to behave in a professional manner if I was ever going to get into a symphony when I left here—if that's even what I wanted.

My phone rang, interrupting my spiraling train of thought. I smiled, seeing it was Madeline White. I couldn't wait until fall, when I could resume instruction with her.

"Hello?"

"Savannah, dear, how are you? You sound like you've been crying." She sounded genuinely concerned.

"Oh, you know," I tried to sound nonchalant, "just finished my music theory final." I laughed a little.

"That would do it to me, too." She echoed my laugh. "Anyway, I've been waiting for you to finish up the last of your finals so I could talk to you about something."

I sat up a little straighter as her tone brightened. "Yes?"

"As you know, I instruct at the Tanglewood Institute every summer."

"Mm-hmm." I nodded, and started pacing around my room, clearing all the Gregory clutter from my brain.

That's where I first met Madeline, when I was a freshman in high school. The Institute is open to students entering ninth grade through those entering their sophomore year of college. I'd attended every year I was eligible to, and, frankly, missed it greatly last summer.

"Well, this is completely unprecedented, and I had to make lots of noise and jump through several hoops to make this happen, but...I want you to shadow me there this summer, Savannah. I'd like you to work with me and instruct with me at the Institute."

"What?" My pulse raced as I tried to piece her words together in an order that made sense. "Is that...how did you?" Words fell rapidly from my brain and landed on the floor around me.

She laughed sweetly. "You're incredibly talented, Savannah. No one can deny that. I wouldn't normally share this information with any student of mine, but you're the best flutist at the Conservatory right now. And, frankly, the best we've seen in years. This will provide you an opportunity you simply wouldn't get anywhere else. I hope you'll consider—"

"Yes!" I squealed before she could finish her sentence.

"Oh fantastic! Stop by my office sometime today and I'll go over the details with you. I'm thrilled, Savannah, really. I think this will be a fabulous opportunity for you."

Happy tears washed over the old ones. "Thank you, Madeline. See you this afternoon."

I tossed my phone on the bed and stretched my arms over my head, grateful that my summer would be filled with nothing but music and sunshine.

Grateful for something to distract me from the love I felt for Gregory that I knew he wouldn't return.

GREGORY

AS MY THEORY class went through their final, I went through the music I'd given Robert to study this week. Somehow, despite my objections, I'd been drawn into guiding his curriculum, even if one of my former students was handling the lessons. For only two months of practice, he was coming along surprisingly well.

I heard Savannah sigh. The room was otherwise silent as the rest of the class was finishing their final exam. Some had already finished and left, and I knew Savannah wouldn't be far behind. Over the last several weeks, she'd shown incredible command over the material in both her assignments and exams.

Something had changed.

It had changed in me, too, the moment I felt her mouth on mine. The moment I licked rainwater off of her lips before she opened her mouth to me.

Savannah seemed to still be in rocky territory with Nathan, and she'd stopped coloring outside the lines in her assignments. While she'd been the one to initiate our kiss, I did exactly nothing to stop it. I tangled my hands through her rain-soaked waves and pulled her closer. I'd dreamt of feeling the silkiness of her hair against my fingers for far too long to let the opportunity get away. The sound she made as I pressed my mouth harder into hers nearly brought me to my knees.

I'd thought of kissing her too many times during the semester. None of them included being right before finals in front of a piss-poor excuse for a Greek restaurant. In spite of my intentions to help foster her abilities and career, I'd done some damage. That much was clear given her emotional response to me and those around her. She likely thought I was a pig, a professor abusing his authority by preying on young and dumb students.

She was neither of those things, and I hoped to God she didn't think those things of me.

Not that it mattered if she did.

Those few seconds were all we'd ever have.

Jesus. I closed my eyes for a moment and let myself feel her against me one more time. Her lips, cold and shivering but making me feel like I was on fire...

Stop.

I'd spent months discussing keeping lines between personal and professional. And now I'd harmed her ability to do just that. I'd watched her play at her flute ensemble concert, and I could pick her sound out of the group of six flutists in a second—her tone was breathtaking. But, her face looked empty and her vibrato was a little off. While that was only a small performance, if she continued to let her emotions spill into her music like that it could prove disastrous in the future.

Looking up, I found her smiling at Nathan for a moment before returning to her paper. Maybe things had smoothed out between them. I knew she cared about him. But the thought made my stomach clench all the same.

After a few minutes, Savannah stood, wrote one last thing at the bottom of her paper, and gracefully made her way to my desk.

"Here you go, Mr. Fitzgerald." Her exam shook slightly in her hand as she placed it on my desk.

Keeping my eyes trained on the sheet music in front of me, I mumbled, "Thank you, Miss Marshall," effectively excusing her from my desk.

"You're welcome," she responded. Her voice was soft and distant, causing me to look up. She was turning slowly away, her head lowered slightly. It made me want to reach out to her, inexplicably, and ask her what was wrong.

"Savannah," I called after her as quietly as possible, before I could stop myself. A couple of students in the front row looked up for a second, before I raised my eyebrow and narrowed my eyes at them.

They quickly found more interesting things to look at. Such as their exams.

As she raised her head and turned back to my desk, she cleared her throat slightly. "Yes?" she replied, her brown eyes still dark and slightly glassed over.

Realizing I hadn't thought through what I was going to say after calling her name, I straightened my shoulders and swallowed before saying, "Good luck."

Her eyebrows came together for a second as she nodded and hastily left the classroom. Glancing down at her exam, I found a note written on the bottom right hand corner. Mr. Fitzgerald, she wrote, I know we disagreed about the material, and I'm sorry for all the trouble I gave you. But, I loved it—the music.

All the trouble? Knowing that Savannah would contest nearly every other word I said in class this semester made coming to class something to look forward to, despite the fact that I'd dreaded taking on the class in the first place. Regardless of the fact that I found her opinions ridiculous much of the time, it was her passion that I admired. While I maintained my stance that she needed to be appropriately trained in order to reach her maximum potential, I found myself hoping she didn't lose her desire to break the rules.

It put life in her eyes. Life that drowned out the sound of a pounding rainstorm in the middle of a crowded city.

Shaking my head as I placed Savannah's exam on the bottom of the pile, my eyes scanned the class, where I found Nathan Connors staring at me with an indignant expression on his face. He shook his head, and I saw him clench his jaw slightly before he turned back to his exam.

That boy was a nuisance. It didn't really surprise me that he and Savannah were friends, or whatever they were. She, however, could get much further than he ever would, given his volatile behavior at school. I wouldn't put it past him to one day genuinely lose his temper in a professional environment.

An hour later, after the last of the students shuffled out of my classroom, I made my way back to my office. Exhausted at the prospect of having to sort through the exams and tally final grades, I stopped when I saw Madeline White's office door propped open.

"Come in," she chirped when I knocked.

Madeline was my age and had gone through the Conservatory with James and myself. Though, I admit, she looked much younger than both of us. Her olive skin and long black hair made her look like a student and garnered her much male student attention on campus, from what I heard through droll pre-classroom discussions. She took it all in stride, though. Which I suppose was easier to do given she only had two male students to instruct.

"Sorry to interrupt, Madeline, but I just wanted to stop in and see how you are feeling?"

She waved her hand toward the chair in front of her desk. "Nonsense, Gregory, you're never interrupting. Sit." I did, as she continued. "Thank you again for taking on that class for me. I hope they didn't give you too much trouble? You know how upperclassmen can be."

"I do," I sighed. "They were just fine, Madeline. Some more...difficult than others."

Madeline sat and crossed her arms. "How did Savannah Marshall do in the class?"

My pulse started to race at the mention of her name, and my mind reeled back to the conversation I'd had with James a few weeks ago about the rumors floating around about us. Certainly Madeline hadn't caught wind of them. She'd been off campus recovering from her surgery since December. If she'd heard the rumors, things were worse than I thought.

"Fine," I tried for a dismissive tone, examining Madeline's face. "She's definitely a student of yours, that's for sure. I've heard her play some throughout the semester and she's wildly talented. Her discipline in coursework, though..." I set my jaw and looked at Madeline, who seemed amused.

"Oh, come on, Gregory," she rolled her eyes, "just because a student doesn't agree with your ways doesn't mean they're undisciplined. I hope you didn't knock her grade because of it."

"I wouldn't do such a thing, Madeline. I take my job seriously." I forced myself to say the right thing. The thing professors say when they're not busy making out with a student.

"Of course you do. And, I know what you mean about Savannah. She's definitely a free spirit. Hey, you're teaching at the Institute again this summer, right?"

"Yes. I don't know why it took me so long to agree to do it, honestly. Last summer was wonderful." Last summer was the first time I'd taught at the Tanglewood Institute. Young musicians preparing for a professional career, from largely upstanding backgrounds. It was a thoroughly satisfying experience.

"Excellent. I'll be there, too. That's why I took this past semester completely off, so I could be in top form for Tanglewood. I'm glad Savannah did well in your class, she needed to complete it for this summer."

I shook my head, not understanding where Madeline was headed with her train of thought. Savannah was too old to attend the Institute.

Thankfully sensing my confusion, she offered more information. "I got the okay to have Savannah shadow me this summer at the Institute. She'll be with me instructing private lessons and in the classroom setting."

Leaning forward, trying to control the sudden bout of lightheadedness I was feeling, I looked Madeline in the eyes. "I'm sorry, what did you just say? Instructing with you? That's absurd, she's a student."

"Oh, Gregory," she waved her hand in front of me, "get over yourself. She won't get in your way." Suddenly, Madeline turned more serious than I was used to seeing as she rested her elbows on the desk. "You know as well as I do that she has the talent to instruct anyone who wants to play. I've seen her work with younger kids; she's kind but stern. Maybe you haven't heard her play as much as I have, so you'll have to take my word for it, but this girl is the real deal. I want to give her as many opportunities for success as I can, since, unfortunately, I'm not sure if playing professionally is what she wants to do upon graduation."

Controlling my physical reaction to this conversation was growing increasingly difficult. "I stand corrected. That's absurd. What gives you the impression she wouldn't want to play professionally?" I felt the anxiety rising through my voice but couldn't stop it. A player with her pure musical beauty simply had to pursue a professional career. "What sense would it even make for her to attend here if not to play professionally?"

Madeline lowered her eyes slightly, rubbing her forehead. "I don't know...I'm concerned it has something to do with her mother, but I can't be sure."

"What does her mother have to do with any of this?" I scoffed incredulously. Letting others affect my playing is not something I've ever stood for.

"It's not really my place to get into her family politics with you, Greg. But, I will say I'm hoping you won't throw too much of a fit when I ask the group of instructors if she can play with us in our ensemble this summer. She can keep up, that I'm sure of. I want to encourage her to keep playing, but it needs to be done carefully. If she feels pushed, she's likely to pull back."

I stood, beads of sweat starting to form on my forehead. Pacing to the back of my chair, I rested my hands on it and took a breath before addressing Madeline. "Fine," I managed, "you won't get any resistance from me about her playing with us. But, she better keep up, like you say she can."

"It's supposed to be fun, Gregory." Madeline rolled her eyes and stood, meeting me by the door.

"And, it can be fun, when people put in the work," I retorted.

She playfully slapped my shoulder. "Get the hell out of here," she chuckled, "before you have a panic attack. She might be a student, but she's more than mature enough to handle this."

"I hope you're right," I called over my shoulder as I walked measuredly down the hallway.

"Be nice to her this summer, Gregory. I think you stressed her out in class enough this semester."

I grumbled my response and headed for the exit. Once I reached the mild spring air, I ran my hands through my hair and took a deep breath. There was no way I could spend the entire summer around her. Not after what I did to her. To hurt her like that...and possibly confuse her, if what Madeline said held any truth.

My feet matched the speed of my thoughts as I raced back to my office. That Savannah Marshall could possibly be considering a future that did not involve a professional career was beyond the grasp of my comprehension. I wouldn't ever tell anyone this, but after she graduated next year, she could easily land a seat at the BSO, if there was an opening. God, that she was considering something other than a professional playing career was...IT was all my fault and I'd have to right it. Somehow.

Finally ascending the steps of the building, I sighed as I turned the key in the lock to my door— suddenly extremely invested in making sure that playing professionally was exactly what Savannah Marshall intended to do with her life.

Chapter 11

GREGORY

I WALKED INTO MY office and sat heavily in my seat. I needed to pack my things, as I wouldn't be back in here until classes started again in September. But I found myself oddly devoid of motivation. I didn't care for classroom teaching in the first place. My salary with the symphony was more than enough for my needs, or it was, until I mortgaged my home in order to pay for my cello. My entire check from the Conservatory went to those payments.

One thought I could not get out of my mind. *I'm not sure if playing professionally is what she wants to do upon graduation.*

What *else* did she have in mind? Was she considering teaching or nursing or working in a pizza parlor? What possible alternative was there for a musician so incredibly gifted? The thought kept winding through my mind, and the more I thought about it, the more agitated I became. It was essential that she continue her path. The truth was, it would be a tremendous loss to…to the world…if she didn't continue, practice more, become more…more of what she was. I was losing track of my thoughts, and I found myself pacing back and forth in my tiny office, thinking.

Why hadn't she come to me?

The question was patently ridiculous. Why *would* she come to me, of all people?

She saw me as a tormentor. Someone who made her foray through music theory a matter of aggravation and obligation. Someone who she disagreed with so much that she was simply unable to control herself in class.

And then there was that odd moment during spring break, when we'd touched hands in the coffee shop. And the kiss....a kiss we never talked about. Then the semester was over, and I knew she wondered about that kiss as much as I did. She probably hated me for hiding it, for driving that kiss into the darkness, for not discussing it. For leaving it there in the storm instead of bringing it out into the light where it belonged.

I closed my eyes. None of that mattered. Not in the face of the music.

Was she having doubts *because of the way I had treated her?* Three weeks ago she'd been in my office, screaming about her grade. But more specifically, she'd voiced a complaint that I'd been too harsh, that I'd somehow persecuted her because of who her mother was. Our odd, strained relationship might be the catalyst. Impulsively I promised myself that I would pay more attention. Understand her better. Because if I were the one who drove her from what she was so clearly fated to be, I would never forgive myself.

I was so absorbed in my thoughts, I barely noticed when there was a knock at my door, and I found myself face to face with Nathan Connors. I stopped in my tracks. What was he doing here? Did it have to do with her? I didn't speak for a moment, simply staring at him.

Nathan, unusually, didn't wilt in front of my gaze. His jaw was pressed forward, an insolent expression on his face.

"Is there something I can help you with, Mr. Connors?"

He pulled the door shut and turned to face me again. The boy was shaking. I couldn't tell if it was fear or anger. Until he spoke, and his nostrils flared.

"I came here to tell you...to stay away from Savannah."

"Indeed." I spoke in the drollest tone I could. "Aren't you a little late, Mr. Connors? Our class is over, and she's hardly likely to sign up for anything I'm teaching next year."

"I don't care about that," he said. "Just...leave her alone."

"Young man, you're not making the slightest bit of sense."

He leaned close, as if he were trying to intimidate me. Both of us were tall, and perhaps because of that he was accustomed to intimidating schoolboys, but with me, it wasn't working.

"Fitzgerald...I don't know what kind of game you're playing with her. But stop. You'll break her heart. She doesn't deserve that. She deserves better than you."

I snorted. "She despises me, Connors. Even if I was interested...and I am not...this would still be a pointless conversation. You are out of line."

"She's in love with you, you son of a bitch. And you toy with her like...like...she's just a kid."

"She *is* a kid, Connors. Get out of my office. And then we'll forget this conversation ever happened."

His face took became even more hostile. "What? Are you going to fail me if I don't? Are you threatening me?"

I narrowed my eyes. "You'll get exactly the mediocre grade you've earned. However, if you don't leave my office in the next five seconds, I'll call security and let *them* deal with you. And I suggest you sober up, or start thinking straight for a change."

For just a second...just the barest second...I actually thought he was going to hit me. His face went red, and his fists clenched as an angry crease formed down his forehead. Then he seemed to deflate, as if he'd been punctured. He stepped back and opened the door. Walked through. Then he looked back and said, "If you break her heart, I'll do whatever it takes to tear you down."

Then he walked away. I didn't even realize I was holding my breath until he was out of sight.

My mind was thoroughly muddled. For the first time in my career, I was questioning everything. My motives, my actions, my very emotions. The only thing I didn't question was the music.

What had she said to Nathan? What sort of discussion had they had? Did Nathan know that...we'd kissed?

I found myself urgently packing my few personal things in the office, then locked up and got out of there. Twenty minutes later I was home. My mind was still everywhere. Thinking about Savannah. Nathan. The strange, confusing year it has been. I needed to get inside; I needed to get to my cello and practice until the sweat rolled off me and my arms trembled. I needed to center myself, and that was the only thing in the world that could do it.

Unfortunately, as I walked up to the front door of my home, I discovered Karin sitting on the front step.

She was hunched over, her arms wrapped across her chest, staring off into space. Her eyes avoided me as I walked up to the house. I slowed my pace as I approached the house, distressed to find her there. I swallowed then drifted to a stop a few feet away from her.

"Karin," I said.

She looked up at me then looked back down. Idly, her left hand played with a lock of her hair, twisting and untwisting it. "Tell me what's happening, Gregory."

"I don't know what you mean."

Abruptly she moved, tensing up. "Don't be an idiot. You get in a fight with a student that half the school has been talking about, a *shouting match*. Students are spreading rumors that you're sleeping with her, and at the same time you cancel our dates with text messages. I haven't heard from you in two weeks."

I grimaced. It seemed the entire world was intent on shoving Savannah in my face today. "We were arguing over a grade. And the rumors are ridiculous. I'd never touch a student."

Except I had. She initiated the kiss. But I kissed back.

"Then why haven't you called me? Why cancel our dates?"

"I've been busy, Karin. It's been finals, in case you missed it."

She rolled her eyes. And I froze in place. Because her eyes were glassy with tears.

"I thought we were going someplace, Gregory. But I've seen the way you look at that girl. I brushed it off the time we went dancing because, well, she's stunning and everyone was looking at her. But the night of the opera...you have a sorry poker face."

I looked away, grinding my teeth, working my jaw. Apparently my feelings about Savannah were obvious to everyone on earth. And that could pose a major problem. Above all, it was infuriating.

"I am perfectly capable of being concerned about a student's education without being involved with them. I've told you this before. The last thing I need is...distractions."

She winced. "What are you saying? Am I a distraction?"

Hardly.

I rubbed my hand against my forehead. "Listen to me, please. I don't know what you think is going on, or why anyone at the Conservatory would wish to involve me in their grade-school rumors, but this...all of this...is unnecessary. I am what I am, Karin. I'm a musician first. My music will *always* come first."

She shook her head. "Get your shit together, Gregory. Until then, I don't want to hear from you."

She stood and looked at me, making an effort to contain herself, but I could see she was on the verge of crying. I stood there like an idiot, not having the faintest clue what to say or do. What exactly did she want with me? To disavow a relationship that barely existed? To throw myself at her feet, or chase her down? To give up my commitment to the music? We'd dated off and on for several months now. Did she expect me to make some proclamation of love?

I just stood there. Helpless. She looked at me, then shook her head and walked away. I stayed in place, watching. Thinking. Then I unlocked my front door and walked in.

The Montagnana was in its case in the corner. The case was fireproof, expensive, intended to make the instrument armored, untouchable, pristine. I stared at it, feeling an unfamiliar hostility. This was the center of my life. The center of my being. I'd long since promised myself that I would let nothing interfere with that. Nothing.

But the instrument in its armored case seemed to be mocking me now. For the first time since I was twelve years old, I didn't *want* to play.

And that's why I must. Now.

Taking my time, I unlocked the case, unsnapped the latches one by one, and opened it. I stared at the instrument. Four hundred years old, the wood burnished, sometimes it seemed to glow. I unbuttoned my shirt and threw it haphazardly on the couch. It was a little bit chilly in the house, but my t-shirt would be too much once I'd been playing for a while. Then I reached out and took the cello out of its case, respectfully, carefully.

I could see Savannah in my mind. The sway of her shoulders as she raised the flute to her lips. The swinging of her body as she danced, her hips moving in seductive circles. The red on her cheeks as she confronted me in class. I saw Nathan, his nostrils flaring, anger written on his face. I saw Karin, on my front step. *Am I a distraction?* With the force borne along by determination and rage, I swept them out of my mind.

I positioned myself on the practice stool. Flexed my muscles, and slowly rolled my head forward then in a loose circle, loosening the muscles in my neck. I put the bow to the strings. Not moving yet. I could feel the latent vibration in the bow, the music locked inside. I reminded myself that *this* was why I lived. Then I closed my eyes, and I summoned the music.

SAVANNAH

IT WAS THE Friday before graduation, and I was finishing packing my things in my dorm. Marcia had fled campus after her last final in order to start a summer internship program with the San Diego ballet. I stuck around so I could watch Nathan graduate on Sunday. We hadn't spoken much in the last week and a half because he had his recital—which was phenomenal—and auditions for things he still hadn't told me about. Superstitions and all.

Butterflies filled my stomach and, really, the entire space around me as I waited for Nathan to call me back. I'd called him to ask if we could talk before graduation. I hated the way things were between us. He was my best friend and I needed him, no matter where he was going to be in the fall while I finished out my senior year at the Conservatory.

"Knock, knock." I could hear Nathan's smile as he spoke, pushing my door all the way open.

"Nathan! I thought you were blowing me off, you didn't call me back!" I dropped the books I was packing and gave him a tight hug.

"I wouldn't blow you off, Savannah." He sighed as he squeezed me back.

"I'm just going to say it, Nathan. I'm sorry. I want things to be okay with us. You're my best friend." I was speaking so quickly I wasn't sure if he was able to understand me.

He didn't let go of our hug, and I was okay with that. "I'm sorry, too, Savannah. I'm going to miss you like crazy, you know that?"

I nodded, tears stinging my eyes. Pulling away, I playfully slapped his chest. "I'd say I'll miss you, too, but I don't even know where you're going to be. Did you audition anywhere, you cryptic freak?"

Nathan bit his lip; his face looking like it was going to explode with pride.

"Spill it, Nathan Connors, or I'll call your mother and ask her!" I was bouncing on the balls of my feet, buzzing with anticipation.

"Chicago!" He raised his arms in victory as I stared at him bug-eyed for a second.

"What?" I squealed. "Nathan!" I screamed as I threw my arms around his neck, jumping up and wrapping my legs around his waist without much thought.

This was big. The Chicago Symphony Orchestra was one of the United States "Big Five" orchestras, along with New York, Philadelphia, Cleveland and, of course, Boston.

After turning me around once, Nathan cleared his throat and carefully set me down. Okay, things weren't going to go all the way back to normal...he was awkward and stepped out of arms' reach. I took a breath, resisting the urge to kiss him, which is exactly what I would have done a couple of months ago. Settling instead for a smile, I wiped tears from my eyes.

"God, Nathan, I'm so fucking *proud* of you! When the hell did you sneak away to Chicago?" I asked, suddenly needing to sit.

"I had my final audition last weekend." He sat next to me, the smile still beaming off his face.

"So...when do you leave?"

"The position is open for the start of the season in the fall. I'll be staying with my brother this summer until I find a place."

"Wow," I whispered.

We sat in silence for a few minutes. I wasn't worried about missing him. Our friendship formed around seeing each other during summers only, since I was from Philadelphia and he was from Chicago. I was thrilled for him that he got a position at his hometown orchestra—it's what he's always wanted, and getting a spot with one of the big five the first time out was nearly unheard of. He's in love with the city and decided sitting in the audience at one of their performances that he wanted to make a life for himself playing the flute.

"Listen," he said, snapping us out of our respective introspections, "I've got to get to my final rehearsal. Want to grab a drink later?" His dimple appeared, and I knew we would be okay.

"You bet. I'll come to your place around nine, okay? I'll walk out with you. I have to go see Madeline."

Nathan walked me across campus to Madeline's office before heading to graduation rehearsal. Relieved that things with Nathan were settled, I was able to head into Madeline's office with excitement about the summer. I'm sure I would have been useless to Madeline if Nathan and I hadn't mended things before I headed to Tanglewood.

"Savannah Marshall, what am I going to do with you?" Madeline teased as I peered my head into her office with a playful look of innocence on my face. She'd asked me to stop into her office a couple of weeks ago, but...life.

"Sorry, Madeline." I smiled as I sat in the seat across from her desk. "I'm sure you've heard Nathan's good news?" I'd been smiling for the last half hour and my cheeks were starting to hurt.

She nodded. "I had no doubts he'd get in. It was keeping his auditions a secret that was the challenge for me. So, Savannah, I'm glad you came in to get your materials for the Institute, but, I must apologize," she took a careful breath before continuing, "I wasn't aware that your mother was retiring this season and would be coming back to the States. Are you sure you want to spend your summer in Lenox?"

"She won't be back till fall," I spit out, causing Madeline's eyebrow to arch. "Uh, my dad is going over there to see her last performances, then they're going to spend the summer travelling Europe together before coming back home. Kind of an emotional farewell for her, I guess." I shrugged.

"And you didn't want to go?"

"Madeline," I exhaled slowly, looking just past her, "I lived in Italy until I was twelve and got to travel a lot then. I've had to share my mother with Europe for the last decade, and, honestly, I have no desire to tag along for another summer."

Madeline's known me since I was fourteen; she's the only one I could be that honest with.

"Of course. Well, here's all the information you'll need," she deftly changed the subject, handing me a green folder. "I'll be running the flute workshop, as usual, and you'll be shadowing me the whole time. During the Young Artists Orchestra, we'll have lots of different things for you to do. The faculty also usually has private ensembles throughout the summer. Usually the woodwinds and strings play together, and we're hoping you'll join us."

Almost on command, my throat started to close. I was able to hold my own and excel in the company of my peers. But the instructors at the Institute, Madeline included, were at the absolute top of their game. What could they possibly want with me?

"No need to get all red-faced, Savannah," Madeline cut into my impending panic attack. "I've played with you for years, and I know not only will you learn from us, but you can keep up. You know that, too." Just as I started to breathe normally again, and take a sip from my water bottle, she interjected one last thought. "Don't worry. I've kindly asked Gregory Fitzgerald to treat you as a colleague and not a student, as would be his inclination."

Sputtering and coughing. That's how I responded.

"What? What are you talking about? Mr. Fitzgerald doesn't work for the Institute...does he?"

"Last year was his first year. Naturally, he excelled at it and produced some great things from his students."

Of course he instructs there now, I thought. *Shit.*

"You did well in the class, though. An 'A', judging by your transcript," she said, holding out a piece of paper.

"*What?*" I snatched the transcript from her and scanned down the page until my eyes fell on *Music Theory, G. Fitzgerald*. Where, as Madeline stated, was the letter 'A'.

"Savannah, you look pale. What the heck went on in that class?"

Realizing Madeline must have been deaf to the rumors that had floated for a few weeks around Gregory and me, I quickly got my shit together.

"I, uh, just argued with him constantly in class. It seemed to really piss him off." I shook my head at the 'A' that seemed to blink on the paper.

"Well, maybe something got through." She shrugged and patted my shoulder. "As you know, I have a summer home in Lenox," she continued, "and you're welcome to stay with me if you don't want to reside on campus."

"Oh, Madeline, that's so kind of you. Thank you so much." I gave her a quick hug before walking, slightly dazed, back to my dorm.

Yes, stay with Madeline. And far away from Gregory Fitzgerald.

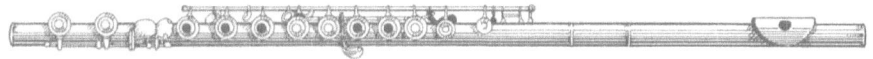

Chapter 12

GREGORY

B ACK HOME AFTER a long, but satisfying day, I set the keys on the table by the door and headed for my cello. *Home* being James's summer condo in Lenox, Massachusetts, near Tanglewood. Much of the BSO, and some of the Conservatory faculty, had second homes or timeshares here, given the frequency with which the symphony plays here.

The area was picturesque, exclusive, and, most importantly, quiet. I'd had the house to myself most of the summer, though James would be arriving shortly from Boston. He wasn't teaching at Tanglewood this year but had been recruited for a master class for the Young Artists Orchestra, a two-week program which looked very promising this year, and would be conducting our ensemble starting next week.

The summer had been smooth so far. Generally I dislike teaching—apart from private instruction—but I was coming to realize it had less to do with teaching itself than it had to do with the caliber and willingness of the students. As disturbing as it had been, with Savannah's constant challenges, I'd sorely missed teaching music theory when the school year came to an end. Teaching excited, brilliant students—that was a reward, and one I'd never expected. And the students who came to the Tanglewood summer program were exactly that: promising, intelligent, and hardworking. I was in my element here.

I'd found myself wondering if perhaps I should have taught Robert, the blind boy, back in the spring. The more I thought about how I'd passed the boy off to a former student, the less comfortable I felt.

Up until now, I'd managed to avoid Savannah most of the summer, with some exceptions. That was likely to change shortly. The faculty had formed a small ensemble, which would begin practice Tuesday evening. Madeline was part of the ensemble, as was her shadow, and there would be no avoiding her.

In truth...I didn't want to avoid her. I didn't want to, but I *had* to.

I hadn't been completely successful in keeping my distance. Three weeks before, the entire faculty and incoming students had met in a large auditorium for a welcome and introduction. I had been standing roughly halfway up the middle aisle, looking for a seat when I saw her near the orchestra pit, standing beside and just behind Madeline.

She had a smile on her face as they spoke with Joseph McIntosh, who would be directing the Young Artists Orchestra this year. McIntosh was an up and coming conductor who had taken over the Cleveland Orchestra only last year. Slightly shorter than me, with tousled hair and a youthful, always smiling expression, he spoke in an animated fashion, his hands waving all over the place. I froze, watching them, not able to help the fact that I hated her talking with him, even though it was none of my business.

But then her eyes wandered and locked on mine.

I froze in place, staring at her. Her eyes, her face, her hair. Her eyes widened a little, and she smiled. Just a little smile, at the corners of her mouth.

I kept my composure. I returned the smile, nodding to her, and then taking what felt like a thousand breaths to slowly turn away, I found my seat. The sight of her eyes, of that smile, stayed with me for hours.

That's not true. I could still see her. Every time I closed my eyes.

The taste of her lips...

The two-week workshops were intense, and we didn't get to spend much time with those in a different instrument from ours, so I saw a marked change in Savannah Marshall by the time the final performances rolled around. Madeline had told me she was a natural with the students, and she was right. Despite helping instruct students who were close to her in age—some only two years younger than her—I saw an effortless authority flow from her. The hot-tempered young woman who couldn't wait to challenge my every word morphed into a mature professional before my eyes. She laughed with her students before the performance and commanded their undivided attention as she led them through their piece. She made it look easy.

Madeline's inference at the end of the semester that Savannah might not be interested in pursuing a professional playing career, paired with her obvious natural ability instructing other musicians, concerned me. While I initially had reservations about Savannah playing with us in our kind of private ensemble in the next couple of weeks, those were now washed away. With any luck, playing with us would be encouraging to her. She'd be able to keep up; there was no question there. I'd listened to her audition recording several times over the last three years, blown away each time by the confident skill of that seventeen year-old. Doing anything else with her career but playing as long as she could simply wasn't an option. I intended on doing my part to make her see that.

Just as I sat down and pulled my cello from its case, a car pulled in the driveway. Sighing, I latched the case, figuring it was James, and he'd want to catch up. Regardless of what I was in the middle of doing. As he opened the door, I lifted an eyebrow at the number of grocery bags he was carrying. I had food here, and he was just in for the weekend.

"James." I nodded, walking over to him and taking a bag that was teetering from his grasp.

"Thanks, man," he replied as he set his bags on the table.

I gestured to the groceries. "What's...all this?"

"Dinner." He smiled and started unpacking steak, asparagus, and potatoes. "How was the workshop?"

"Fantastic, actually. There are some incredibly talented strings this year. More so than last year, I'd say. The students from last year got exponentially better, and the new ones are just..." I trailed off, watching him pour marinade over the steaks. "I appreciate you cooking dinner, but isn't that a lot of food for the two of us?"

"We're having guests tonight, Gregory. Madeline lives around the corner, and she and Savannah will be joining us."

I nodded, taking a deep breath as I ran my tongue across my lips. Savannah would be here for dinner.

"Madeline lives around the corner, you say?"

James was already skeptical of my feelings for Savannah, and I didn't need to add to that. Especially if we were all going to be in the same room shortly.

James nodded and spoke to me as if I were simple. "She does, you know that, Gregory. Her parents owned the house while we were in the Conservatory."

"Yes, of course. Of course." I knew that. I'd been to the house before, for goodness sake. What I'd meant was, *Savannah's been right around the corner this whole time?*

"Just try to be nice to Savannah, please, okay?" James set the knife down, giving me a pointed look.

"Why does everyone keep saying that?" Rolling my eyes, I took a knife from the butcher's block and began dicing the red potatoes.

"Who keeps saying that?"

"You. Madeline said it a few weeks ago in her office. I've never been mean to the girl, James. She was a student. One who found my authority up for discussion."

James laughed. "It wasn't your authority she found debatable, Gregory. It was your opinions."

"What's the difference?" I scoffed. "Plus, how would you know what she thought?" James seemed to know more about Savannah than I'd given him credit.

"Madeline told me. She said Savannah seemed nervous about being here this summer with you, worried she'd pissed you off all semester." He shrugged and took olive oil from a cabinet, handing it to me to drizzle over the potatoes.

"You spoke with Madeline about my interactions with Savannah?" My throat was stiff as I asked the question. As far as I knew, Madeline wasn't aware of the brief affair rumors that had run through campus, as she was off campus for the entire semester.

"Relax, she doesn't know about the rumors. At least, she's never mentioned them to me. But, yes, Savannah's come up. Madeline and I have been on a few dates, and we talk about work sometimes. Naturally, our most promising students enter the conversation and, Savannah is Madeline's."

Trying to regulate my sigh of relief I waved my hand. "Of course, of course. I didn't realize you and Madeline..."

He smiled. "Well...it's very new."

I nodded then said, my tone stiff, "And may I ask, why did you not mention dinner before now?"

James rested his hands on the counter and gave me a searching look. "Because it's obvious you are hung up on the girl. I thought it best to not leave you stewing in your own juices, and since the school year is over, perhaps the two of you can be around each other now without acting like idiots."

I squeezed my eyes shut for a second. "Your thought process is bizarre."

He chuckled. "Maybe. But isn't it true that if I'd warned you, you would have suddenly found something else to do this evening?"

I grunted. "Perhaps that would have been best."

SAVANNAH

As I FOLLOWED Madeline up the steps of the house, I found myself wondering for the fiftieth time if I should have gone out somewhere else. The past few weeks had been wonderful. I'd attended Tanglewood as a student during my summers in high school, but I'd never guessed that it was just as much an education for the instructors as it is for the students. And one thing I'd learned in the last few weeks was that I was a good teacher.

It was gratifying that I wasn't the only one who felt that way. Increasingly, Madeline had left me to my own devices as she became more confident in my abilities.

All the same, I was still a bit of a loner. Not really an instructor, though technically I was on the faculty for the summer. I was separated by age and by the fact that the rest of the faculty were professional musicians, most of them with tenured positions at the Boston Symphony Orchestra. More than one of them had given me the cold shoulder because of my youth and status as a not yet graduated student at the

Conservatory. At the same time, I was four years older than most of the students.

Madeline had brought up dinner casually a couple of days before. "I'm going to be having dinner Friday night with James Mahone. You know him? He's an oboe instructor at the Conservatory."

"He was on the panel for my audition," I had replied. "He seems like a nice guy, I've seen him around school."

So here we were. I was still a little lost in my thoughts as she knocked on the door, my eyes on the wooden porch, so when I looked up and saw Gregory Fitzgerald standing in the doorway, I sucked in a quick breath.

Gregory wore a tight black t-shirt and black pants. Typical. Slim, fit, with his muscular arms and shoulders, he was more than a little bit unnerving. He was obviously relaxed, padding around in his black socks with no shoes. *What is he doing here?* Stupid question, I guess. I knew James and Gregory were friends, or at least I'd seen them off campus drinking together. I'd managed to avoid Gregory so far this summer. Because really, what's the point of spending time with someone you're falling for, if they don't return the feeling? And I'd finally admitted to myself, just a little, that I was falling for Gregory. It was more than a passing kiss in a rainstorm. It was that I wanted to kiss him again. In the rain, in the sun, anywhere I could.

But I couldn't. He didn't want that.

I swallowed. Why did he have to be here? Why didn't Madeline warn me? Ugh, she wouldn't know to warn me, I guess, given she knew nothing of the rumors from the past semester. That was long gone, and we were both adults. She certainly didn't know about the kiss.

I actually wanted to run. My throat was dry, my hands trembling, as Gregory gave a tight half smile and said, "Madeline...S-Miss Marshall...please come in."

He stepped back away from the door, and I followed Madeline in. My muscles were tight as I walked past him, and I had no idea where to set my eyes. As he reached to close the door behind me, he brushed against my shoulder. I jerked back a little bit. His touch lit me up more than I was comfortable with, given the setting. I forced my eyes anywhere but on him because I needed to cool the heat circling around my neck.

"It's very good to see you again," he said in a low rumble.

My breath caught a little, and I whispered, "You too, Mr. Fitzgerald."

Madeline gave Gregory an annoyed smile. "I don't think the two of you need to stand on ceremony any more. After all, she's on the faculty this summer."

Gregory's eyes flashed at Madeline, then back to me. He nodded, and spoke in a low, tense voice, as his eyes locked on mine. Their bright crystal reflection made my heart race. "Of course. Savannah."

Pulling my shoulders back slightly to fake some confidence, I nodded. "Gregory. Nice to see you." Smiling because I'd made his eyes widen a little at my response, I shuffled by him and tucked a strand of hair behind my ear.

James met us in the living room. "Thank you both for coming." He gave Madeline a quick hug and a peck on the cheek, and echoed the greeting with me. I liked James a lot, and I was interested to find out more about how he and Madeline maintained their friendship with Gregory for so long without doing him any physical harm.

"Thank you for having us over. You have a lovely home. I brought this to have with dinner." I held out my hand, giving him the bottle of Cabernet Franc I brought.

James eyed the label. "Impressive. A vintage? From Villa Vignamaggio?" He looked at me, surprised.

I nodded, my cheeks heating slightly. "It's the best. Most of their vineyard produces Chianti, but, some of their land is reserved for this Cabernet Franc, and it's incredible." James held the bottle out to Gregory, who took it and studied it with the same reverence I'd seen him use while looking over sheet music. "Their vineyard is stunning in the summer," I added with a smile.

"You've been?" Gregory met my eyes, and I saw a flicker of life pass through his eyes. It was the same look I'd caught on his face when Nathan spun me around on the dance floor of that salsa club in Boston. Passion, maybe? Internally I caught myself about to roll my eyes, wondering if he was a wine snob, too. I decided, however, to play nice.

"Yes," I nodded, "my mom...I spent a lot of summers in Europe before entering the Institute." I shrugged and held out my hand. "Shall I open it?" Wrapping my hand around the neck of the bottle, my pinky grazed his thumb, making me pull my hand away quickly.

"I'll do it." Gregory turned on his heels and paced into the kitchen, where I heard the familiar *pop* of the cork a few seconds later.

"Please, come sit. I'll help Gregory with the wine, and I'll bring out the food." James gestured to the large black lacquered dining table.

"This is a great place," I whispered to Madeline as she sat next to me.

"It's been in James's family for years. We all used to come here on break when we were in the Conservatory together." She smiled and looked around, undoubtedly scanning memories from years spent inside these walls. Her smile brightened, her eyes creasing at the corners, as James walked into the room and handed her a wine glass.

He set mine in front of me, but his eyes lingered for a second on Madeline. There was certainly something lovely pass-

ing between the two of them, but given my recent indepen-
dent study on the origin of rumors, I decided to refrain from
speculation. Luckily, Gregory appeared with our dinner.

"Before we start," James began our meal by raising his
glass in the air, "I'd like to toast to good friends. Old and new,
and time spent doing what we love. Music. Savannah," James
looked at me, and Gregory followed, "I've heard nothing but
excellent things about your work here so far this summer. I
can't say that I'm surprised, given how talented you are. But,
it takes a special kind of musician to both play and instruct
with equal passion, as you've managed to do."

I started to blush. Not because of what James was saying,
but because Gregory was nodding along with him.

He thinks I'm talented? He thinks I'm talented.

That thought spread a smile wide across my face, but it
also made me berate myself a little. What did I care that a reclusive misanthrope musical prodigy thought I was talented.
What's wrong with me?

"Thank you, James. Really, it's been a great privilege to
work with everyone the last few weeks. I'm looking forward
to the orchestra work this week." I took a large sip of my
wine, anxious to turn the conversation away from me. "So,
how long have you three known each other?"

"Day one of classes at the Conservatory." Madeline
shrugged and lifted her glass to her lips. "Our professor for
that class was a bit of an ass—"

"Yes, and James chose to lock horns with him as much
as possible," Gregory interjected, shaking his head. His tone
was about as playful as I'd ever heard.

"I guess I can appreciate that." The words were out of my
mouth before I could stop them, and I silently cursed the
glass of wine that sat nearly empty beside my plate. Quickly,
I took a bite of asparagus.

James let out a full-throated laugh, and Madeline followed. My cheeks burned as I chewed, and I reached for my glass, swallowing the last bit of wine.

"Oh," my breath caught in my throat as I saw Gregory watching me carefully with an unreadable expression on his face, "I didn't mean you were an ass...I mean...me challenging..."

Mortified, I bit my lip and looked down.

This made Madeline and James laugh even harder. And, right then, I wanted to fall through the floor.

"It's quite all right Miss Marsh—Savannah." Gregory seemed to silence his own verbal stumble with a sip of his wine.

"Okay, you two." Madeline set her glass down and volleyed her gaze between Gregory and me. "Spring semester is over, and I think it's time both of you get over that foolish little rumor."

Well. That did it. Gregory choked a bit on his wine, and I turned to Madeline, my eyes widening as my face got even hotter.

"Madeline," I whispered. "You know about that?"

"Everyone knows, dear. It happens all the time, every semester. Different professor, different student, same story. Luckily this particular rumor was especially laughable and died down quickly."

Especially laughable? What exactly does that mean? I was a little irritated by that, and by the fact that I was irritated. Did she think I wasn't good enough for him? Seriously? I rubbed my eyes, ignoring my eye makeup and set my forehead in my hands for a second. When I pulled my head up, I was thankful to find Gregory's skin nearing a nice shade of crimson.

"Madeline," James cut in dryly, "could we talk about something else? I think...I think Gregory's head is about to explode."

At once, Madeline and James burst into laughter again, and I couldn't help myself. I folded my arms on the table, set my forehead on them, and began laughing along with them. What else was I supposed to do? It was all so ridiculous.

Ridiculous.

After a minute or so of the most uncomfortable laughter I've ever engaged in, Gregory cleared his throat. "Yes, we're lucky the rumor was so...ridiculous, or that could have caused a lot of problems for both Savannah and myself."

It was like he plucked the word right from my brain. Ridiculous. I found myself thinking that it wasn't *that* ridiculous of a rumor but stopped that train of thought. Quickly.

James slapped Gregory on the shoulder. "Lighten up, Greg. It's just us. We'll stop, though. Promise."

James and Madeline tried to suppress their giggles. James got up and retrieved another bottle of wine from the kitchen.

Greg. Hmm, I didn't like how that sounded, really. Gregory didn't seem to, either. His mouth pressed into a tight line as James said it. I guessed this was something James, and probably Madeline, did to tick him off. I was a bit relieved to know that it wasn't just me he seemed to be uptight around. He was this way with friends he'd known for over ten years. But, why?

Madeline placed her hand on my leg. "Sorry, Savannah, but you really need a thick skin for this business. Especially if you want to have a professional career." She leaned back in her chair, swirling what was left of her Cab Franc around in her glass. "When you're working incredibly long days with the same group of people you sometimes travel with...it becomes like a family. And, sometimes relationships develop," she paused, still looking down, and a ghost of a grin crossed her lips, "but, more often than not, lots of whispers and rumors start. It's just the nature of things. Add in a few hundred hormone-driven young adults and, bam, instant student-teacher rumors."

"That makes sense." I nodded, unable to look at Gregory. But, I had to—I needed to be a grown-up about this. "Gregory," I cleared my throat as all eyes fell on me.

"Yes?" His eyes were intense, and I almost lost my words.

"I just wanted to assure you that I had nothing to do with those rumors spreading—"

He waved his hand, as he always did when he found something exasperating. "Please, Savannah, the thought never crossed my mind."

"Okay, I just wanted to make sure, because...I know how stressful things can get for students academically, and the lengths some students would go to get a good grade. I would never—"

"Savannah," he cut me off sternly but with a softness in his eyes I'd never seen. "I never once thought that of you. You're an excellent student with a good head on your shoulders. Well, I suppose you're no longer a student..." He cleared his throat before continuing. "Despite your regular disregard for my authority in the classroom—"

"What?" I cut him off with a chuckle. Watching the corners of his mouth turn up in a grin, I caught on. "Oh, you're baiting me..." I looked down, heat filling my face as I bit my lip.

"I learned from the best." He laughed freely, patting James on the shoulder as he stood and began collecting our plates from the table.

I'd only heard him laugh once before. And that precipitated our kiss. I had to freeze and isolate that awareness. Because his laugh did things to my emotional makeup I couldn't even identify. So I pretended, and the rest of us joined him in apparently comfortable laughter.

Gregory re-entered the dining room, looking far more relaxed than I'd ever seen. He still had a slight crease between his eyebrows, though, and I began to wonder what he was holding in there. "Would you ladies like to stay for some coffee?"

Madeline and James shared a shocked look. I smiled, and without asking what Madeline wanted to do, I replied, "I'd like that."

GREGORY

"HOW HOSPITABLE OF you." James arched his eyebrow as he reached behind me to grab four coffee mugs.

"Sarcasm?" I shot back just as sarcastically.

"You nearly passed out when you found out who was coming to dinner, and after that whole rumor conversation I figured you'd want them out of here as soon as possible." He turned so his back was against the counter, crossing his arms across his chest.

Keeping my voice quiet, I answered. "I had no idea that Savannah thought I'd assume she'd had anything to do with those rumors. The thought never crossed my mind."

"Why do you care what she thought, Gregory? You don't care what anyone thinks," he challenged.

"That's not true." What was he talking about? Of course I cared. Well. I felt my eyebrow wrinkle a little, and I thought about it. Okay, so I usually didn't care. But...I was starting to care a great deal about what Savannah Marshall thought...of me.

I went on. "I didn't realize how much a rumor like this could affect a student. You and I know how foolish rumors are, but the students don't, apparently. You and Madeline were right, James. Savannah's talented and works hard. I'll help support that any way I can." My hands shook slightly as I poured the coffee, and I realized that my monologue wasn't making a lot of sense.

That's because my thoughts were muddled. After only two weeks of helping Madeline, it was clear Savannah was a natural teacher as well. That was troubling, given Madeline's hypothesis that Savannah might not be fully committed to a career in playing.

"Just be careful," he muttered as he took two mugs and shuffled into the living room.

Carrying the other two mugs into the living room, my breath involuntarily caught at the sight of Savannah on the oversized leather loveseat. She was sitting up straight, highlighting her years of orchestral training. Her poise was evident in the way her long, tanned legs were crossed at the ankles and her hands were resting in the lap of her green summer dress. The soft waves of her golden hair were hanging carelessly over her shoulders, as they always did. Her smile interrupted my staring.

"Thank you." Savannah smiled brighter as she took the mug, wrapping her long fingers around it and leaning back against the couch.

James and Madeline were sitting rather close on the opposite couch, so I took a seat next to Savannah. Sitting slowly, I thought I felt her eyes on me, but when I looked up she was simply staring into her coffee cup. She hadn't yet taken a sip.

"So, Savannah," James leaned forward, "I'm dying to know what it was like growing up with Vita Carulli. It must have been a fascinating experience."

Had he gone mad? Madeline seemed to think so too, given the crooked glance she shot in his direction. Savannah had brought up her mother's name in my presence exactly once, and in a tone that made it clear she felt overshadowed, uncomfortable. And the one time I met her mother, in her presence,

Savannah was reserved. Tense even. I didn't know what the reasons were, but it was clear that relationship was extremely strained.

"James, certainly we can find something else to discuss—" I tried to offer an exit from an already uncomfortable evening for Savannah, but she cut me off.

"Oh, no, it's fine." She spoke softly as she placed her mug on the side table.

Though she pulled off a practiced smile, her two-second blink before she started speaking suggested I should pay very close attention. Savannah ran a hand through her long hair and started talking.

"*Growing up* with Vita Carulli is...a loose term, James. The three of us lived in Italy together until I was twelve. Any growing up I did after that was with my father and his parents in Philadelphia."

Her voice and expression seemed wistful, but apparently James was tone deaf to it, because he kept talking.

"Wow, what did you like most about Italy?"

"Well, I have the most vivid memories from the Teatro dell'opera di Roma. My mother spent most of her time in Milan at the Teatro Alla Scala, but what's beautiful about the theater in Rome is, the shows aren't held in that theater in the summer."

Her smile turned genuine and her face lit up. "In the summer, they move the theater and dance performances to the ancient Baths of Caracalla..." her voice trailed off along with her eyes.

"That must have been beautiful," Madeline interjected.

I was stricken speechless by Savannah's seemingly perfect Italian accent as she spoke the names of the theaters, leaving me to wonder if she still spoke any, as I'm sure she had to know some when she was younger.

Savannah's hazel eyes grew wide as she looked to Madeline. "Oh, Madeline, you have no idea. There's absolutely nothing on earth like opera under the stars. The first year my mother was prima donna there, Malcolm Carroll was conducting, and it was...a powerhouse. Just...amazing."

Closing my eyes for a second, I put myself there. Under the stars in Rome, watching the opera with Savannah.

"Now you didn't start playing the flute until you were nine. How did you get the inspiration to do that? Your father is a French horn player, right?"

While James's questions were bordering on interrogation, I wanted to hear the answers as well. She'd told me before, in the coffee shop as she played with my hands. I seemed to have gone deaf the second her skin came in contact with mine because I had no recollection of what she'd said.

"Right," she nodded, her smile fading, "he's horn, and my mother..." Savannah continued on to the story she'd told me that day.

I found myself drawn to her hands. Remembering.

"Anyway," she continued, "I always thought the flutes and the strings sounded the most beautiful out of the entire orchestra."

"Strings, huh?" I interjected, growing slightly uncomfortable in my own silence. "What made you settle on the flute?"

A mischievous grin played on her lips. "The flute was prettier." She shrugged unapologetically.

"How honest of you, Ms. Marshall," I teased, chuckling a little.

"My mother was as supportive as she could be, and my dad..." Savannah sighed, leaning forward and running an index finger along the rim of her mug, staring again into her untouched coffee. "My dad was as supportive as he could be for knowing what kind of life I was preparing to lead."

I chose an entirely different career path than my parents, leading to decades of tense half-conversations over the phone and tight greetings on holidays. Apart from her mother, I knew Savannah's father was an accomplished musician, as well. To willingly step into a life mastered by one's parents, and to try to make it one's own? That took a certain constitution. Backbone. *She* wanted to do this, and not rest on her parents' laurels. At least, that's what she started out wanting. Her enthusiasm for instruction was growing more concerning. I'd caught her practicing after instruction was done for the day, and she was gaining ground in technique. She had to keep playing. Savannah straightened her shoulders, which pulled the fabric on her dress tighter across her chest. I checked my watch.

"Tired, Gregory?" Madeline set her now-empty mug on the coffee table, eyeing me teasingly.

I was tired. But, I wanted to listen to Savannah tell more of her story. Her history. Truth be told? I wanted to sit and listen to her voice until sunrise. It was as melodic as the notes that came from her flute.

"I know I am." Savannah yawned and stood. "Thank you both for dinner, it was lovely." Her eyes lingered on mine and I couldn't look away. I didn't want to.

James held out his hand for Madeline. "I'll walk you to your car."

"Thank you," Madeline whispered.

As they walked through the door, Savannah stepped forward and around the coffee table. As she slid past me I caught a whiff of her perfume. She still smelled like lilies. Clearing my throat, I caught up to her as she reached the door.

"Savannah, I enjoyed chatting with you this evening." My voice shook with an unsteadiness foreign to me.

Her tender smile calmed the buzzing through my body. "I did, too, Gregory. Thank you."

As she turned for the door again, I found myself not wanting her to leave. But I had no reason for her to stay. Maybe just a few more seconds. "Savannah, you didn't touch your coffee, was something wrong with it?"

She said she'd like some coffee, I'm sure of it. I'd asked if they wanted to stay for coffee, and she said, *I'd like that*. With her back to me, I watched the tops of her ears lift a bit as she smiled.

Looking back over her shoulder, she spoke quietly. "I don't drink coffee." Biting her lip, her eyelashes brushed the apples of her cheeks as she looked down and away and headed toward Madeline's car.

My heart raced as I watched them pull out of the driveway and down the street.

I don't drink coffee, either.

Chapter 13

S AVANNAH

I T HAD BEEN a few days since Madeline and I had dinner with James and Gregory, and here the four of us were, sitting in the faculty ensemble together near the end of the first week of orchestra camp. While most of the staff played together in the BSO or other ensembles, I felt like I didn't belong. At all. Sure, they were all nice and welcoming when I sat down. But, as James handed out a few sheets of music he wanted us all to play, my nerves started firing.

I can't blame it all on the music though. Gregory was only a few seats down from me, sitting behind his cello. I knew that was *the* one. I couldn't remember the maker, or how old it was, but I'd read in *Music Trades* that he'd taken out a mortgage on his family home on Beacon Hill to purchase it.

The man had more interaction with his cello than with any human. Realistically, I knew this to be more the rule than the exception with musicians and other performers. Most musicians are married to their craft. Except maybe my father, who walked away from his life in the orchestra pit to raise me as normally as possible. He had shared his wife with the opera for over twenty years. Now I often wondered how their relationship would look once they resumed life in the States.

As Gregory warmed up, the muscles in his shoulders and forearms flexed and relaxed with each note. It bothered me that his stomach-clenching eyes were closed, but it also gave me an excuse to study the rest of his face. I often had to remind myself how young he was. He was barely thirty-one, even though his attitude, manner of speech, and general outlook on life suggested he was much older.

"Don't be nervous, Savannah." Madeline playfully nudged me with her elbow. "I wouldn't have asked you to join us if I didn't think you could handle it. You're going to do just fine. This is supposed to be fun."

"Fun?" I chuckled. "*Fun* is playing on a city street corner or in the grass somewhere. Fun is not sitting in a room full of musicians you've admired your whole life, preparing to play with them. It's exciting…I'll get back to you on the *fun*." I arched my eyebrow and took a deep breath as James commanded our attention. I thumbed through our music as he spoke.

"First of all, I want to thank you all for a great first week with the students. I know it's not over yet, but I think we can all agree that the students get more talented each year. While that makes some parts of our job easier, the challenge lies in continuously pushing them to do better. We have a great staff on hand to accomplish just that." James nodded once to Gregory, who nodded back.

The cellists on campus were all thrilled to be working with Gregory, by the sounds of things, while all the other girls swooned every time he walked by. Watching him roll his tight shoulders back and stretch his neck side to side caused my mind to drift to what it would feel like to be pressed up against his muscles.

For three weeks I'd watched the high school students part as he walked down the hallway…whispering behind their hands, eyes wide. I wondered if I would have giggled along with them if I was a student.

Yes.

His quiet command, even when doing something as common as eating a sandwich, left me staring. The way his jaw worked, how his eyes scanned the room as he took a drink... every little thing about him pulled me in.

Viewing him as a colleague over the last few weeks, and the casual environment of James's house for dinner, I was intrigued to see another side of him. While he was still reserved, it no longer looked pretentious. He looked focused, passionate, and intense. I found myself anxious to know what was going through his head most of the time.

I'd caught the tail end of some of his private sessions, as I was walking through the halls. While he was stern with his students, he taught them to let the instrument tell the song's story. Such a beautiful statement that he never once shared in class. I wondered why. He was certainly expressive whenever he played; it was his rigid ideas of what music could be that I found...frustrating. Why not bend the rules and create something new when he had such command over everything else?

"This year," James continued, "we want to have more fun and play around with duets and smaller groups apart from larger pieces. It's not often some of us get to play together one on one..." He continued his introduction as I turned more pages of sheet music.

The pieces were fairly standard, easy if you'd been playing for twenty years, I suppose. I liked that. Madeline might have been right, maybe they really did view this as fun. Playing pieces everyone knew well gave the opportunity to make them sound out of this world. And, maybe have a little fun with them? Glancing quickly at Gregory, I guessed there wouldn't be much rule bending here. His eyes met mine and he gave a slight nod and a half-smile.

Holy shit, a smile.

Moving my eyes back to the music, I gasped when I turned to the last page.

"What's wrong?" Madeline leaned in to see what I was looking at.

I whispered, as James was still rambling about something. Man, he was long winded. "This is the third movement of Assobio a Jato. I *know* this."

"What? Why don't I know that you know this?" Madeline twisted her lips accusingly. She knew better than to think I'd stick solely with the music she assigned.

"It's nothing. I was thinking about playing this at my senior recital and asking Marcia to accompany me."

Madeline's eyebrows shot sky-high. "Oh, you were just thinking of adding this to your recital program and are just mentioning it now?" Her playful tone caused me to roll my eyes.

"Just...shh," I teased, sitting back in my chair.

"Okay," James seemed to be finally wrapping up, "why don't we let Gregory pick the first duet piece. We have lots of string opportunities since we have lots of strings hanging around this year." James laughed a little as he headed to his seat, where his violin sat in wait.

"Let's try the Assobio a Jato." Gregory stood and moved to the seat in front of the ensemble.

What? This piece was not up Gregory's alley—at all. Was he trying to branch out? For someone who seemed to be musically stuck in the nineteenth century, this was odd.

"Have fun, Madeline," I teased, grinning from ear-to-ear. Madeline and I were the only flutes in the ensemble. Since she and Gregory had known each other for a lot of years, I figured she'd played with him at least once or twice. But, Madeline is a lot like me—free in her interpretation of sound. I was anxious to see how she would play with him in this piece.

"Uh-uh." Her grin mirrored mine and made me nervous. "You want to practice this piece for your senior recital without telling me? Get up there and prove it."

My pulse raced. She couldn't be serious. "No way. Stop. Just...get up there."

"Madeline?" James raised an eyebrow in our direction from his seat.

"Actually, Savannah should do this one. She's been practicing this for her senior recital...evidently."

Gregory's eyes shot to mine and my stomach plummeted through the floor. This wasn't happening.

"Really? Fantastic." Damn James and his cheerful attitude.

"I, uh," I cleared my throat, shaking my head, "it's...I shouldn't..."

Gregory's eyebrows pulled in, and I watched him take a careful breath. "Nonsense, Savannah. Come on up."

Not wanting to make a further bumbling spectacle of myself, I took my own measured breath, stood somewhat shakily, and made my way to the other seat.

"Do you mind if I stand? It sounds better when I stand," I whispered.

"By all means." He gestured awkwardly with his hand.

I couldn't believe I was about to do this. I wasn't nervous about the notes—I'd mastered those months ago. I wasn't concerned with the other members watching me play—I'd played solos for most of them at one time or another during my years as a student here.

It was him.

Any time he played, either in the classroom or with the BSO, I was rendered speechless. He commanded my full physical attention with each note he drew from his strings. When he played, it was like it was the only time I was granted access inside his head. It was fascinating, and frightening, and heartbreaking. So much so that I often held my breath as he played, paralyzed by the sheer beauty of the music swallowing every negative assumption I had of him. Now, I was expected to play with him. God, I was about to play with Gregory Fitzgerald.

Shake it off. You've played in front of him before.

Once I adjusted my stand, I looked down at him and gave a nervous smile. His eyes smiled back, and he nodded once before starting the piece. He had twelve notes before I had to enter, and I used all of them watching the way his body moved behind the cello.

GREGORY

As always, Savannah's posture was perfect, back straight, her feet spread shoulder width apart. For perhaps a fraction of a second she met my eyes, and I jerked my eyes away, down to the level of her hips. Then I set the bow to the strings, mentally preparing myself for the first notes. I knew this piece well, though it was an unusual one for me.

Unusual because two months before, I'd walked by the practice rooms late in the evening at the Conservatory. I'd heard her playing before I saw the door to one of the practice rooms cracked, just enough to let the music out. She'd been practicing it.

I recognized the notes, of course, but it wasn't one I'd played before. A flute-cello duet. Later that evening I'd gone home and practiced until the music became part of me.

Now, she adjusted her music stand then looked at me with a quick smile, quickly gone. I nodded, encouraging her. Despite myself, I found myself take in a sharp breath as she raised the flute to her lips.

Six notes, repeated twice, from the cello. Two measures, rising arpeggios, slightly dissonant, and as I played them she took a breath, her back straightening, arms riding slightly in the air, and then she began to play the melody as I continued the bass rhythm underneath. I'd played this part through a hundred times by now and knew it as intimately as any music I'd ever played. So, while I did not divert attention from my own playing...I watched her, making slight adjustments to match her volume and pitch—which was impeccable—as she began to play the fanciful, almost playful melody.

To my surprise, I found that the longer we played together, the less I had to think about it. It became effortless. I knew this music by heart, and it seemed she did too, and her eyes moved as she played, focusing on me, then away, then back. They were liquid, huge, and as her body swayed slightly forward during a particularly difficult run, I caught my breath because it was as if she was speaking to me in a private language only we knew. The room had somehow narrowed, only the two of us, and the music between us.

I don't think I'd realized before *just how beautiful* Savannah Marshall was. It's not that I'd never noticed her...I'd observed her dirty blonde hair which she usually left free and wild, her large brown eyes, the dimples that sometimes appeared on her cheeks when she smiled. Her free and loud laugh when she found something amusing. The curve of her hips, which swayed as she walked, the swell of her breasts. I'd seen all of these things. And felt a tiny scar on her bottom lip as my tongue swept slowly across it.

I'd also seen her mind: quick witted, incredibly intelligent, opinionated, talented, *brilliant*. Her talent, her intellect, surpassed that of the vast majority of students or adults I'd known, and it was breathtakingly attractive.

And then, there was the music. The beautiful sound of her flute playing drifting down the hall of the practice rooms was commonplace in the quiet moments of my mind. Even three years ago during her audition she'd shown poise, talent and practiced skill that surpassed virtually all of her peers.

But here? Sitting across from her in the semicircle of our peers on the faculty, our eyes occasionally met, softening, bridging the distance of what had been a tempestuous relationship. Here, the tendrils of music emanated from us both for the first time, winding together like a braid, the threads tightening together, faster, more in sync, beautifully wound up into something much bigger than the separate cello and flute parts that each of us played alone.

As we reached the crescendo I looked in her eyes and found her looking right into mine. I sucked in a quick breath, trying to keep it quiet while my head felt light, my hands now playing the notes on the cello on instinct. Her face was flushed, eyes wide and slightly watering, and I almost felt as if we had somehow moved closer together in that room. Our bodies were the same distance apart as they were when we'd started, but something had changed between us. She hadn't simply just become my musical peer. There was something more humming in the vibrato between our bodies.

I almost stumbled when she shifted the melody, changing the rhythm and dynamics several times on the fly. My brows pulled together and I adjusted the baseline, watching her eyes closely. She met my eyes...then had the nerve to wink at me. Against my will, I found myself grinning as I adjusted to her change. We continued from there, playing the song, but with playful adjustments that suited the light mood we'd created.

As I drew out the final measure, the final note from my cello, I was momentarily at a loss. She took a deep breath, lowering her flute to her side. I looked at her red tinted cheeks, her full, passionate eyes, and I surrendered to it.

The music.

Her lips.

I wanted her.

SAVANNAH

MY CELL PHONE rang as I got ready for our second to last day with students. I nearly jumped out of my skin in excitement as I saw Nathan's name pop up on my screen.

"Hey you!" I shrieked into the phone.

"Hey, doll. That's quite a greeting. Summer's going well, I take it?"

I could tell he was wearing his best dimpled smile.

"It's been amazing, Nathan. So much more than I expected. The workshops were intense, but the students were great. I've missed you, though."

He sighed, long and heavy. "I know. I've missed you, too. It's just been so—"

"I get it. I *really* get it. No need to explain."

Nathan and I had spent most of the summer texting here and there, but hadn't had much time to talk on the phone. I was busy with the Institute, and he was settling into his new Chicago apartment and starting rehearsal with the symphony. He was practicing extremely long hours and, for Nathan, I was impressed. He knew as well as I did how rare it was for someone right out of school to get a seat with one of the Big Five, and he did. He was determined to keep it and developed an incredible work ethic seemingly overnight.

That meant less time to talk, though. Or to have much of a life at all. I knew he was practicing extra hard to make an impression and really "earn his keep," but it still had me wondering if the professional performance life was for me. At least at a major symphony like that. I hadn't talked about it with anyone—my thoughts about doing something other than playing for a symphony once I graduated—because no one asked. As I excelled further and further in my skill at the flute, it seemed to be assumed by everyone—myself included—that this would be my life. Playing. Going as far as possible and staying there until I couldn't do it anymore. Following in my mother's footsteps. And my father's, at least until he chose me over the orchestra pit.

I didn't know if I wanted to have an either/or life. Was that my only choice? Looking around at all the people I admired most, it seemed that was surely the case. My parents did the best they could with a compromise situation, but that resulted in some combination of us feeling lonely at one time or another. My mother asked me to Italy whenever she had the chance, and it got harder to go the older I got. And, while James and Madeline seemed to be engaging in some heavy-duty flirting—though I was too shy to ask her about it—they worked in the same place and played for the same orchestra. That could be easy for them. Not many people are lucky enough to find someone at work. Then, there was Gregory. Married to his craft. His only friends were Madeline and James, that I knew of. I hadn't seen much of that woman from the campus offices—Karin, I think her name was—since the night I saw them out dancing. I often teased him internally for being broody and dramatic, but I had no idea if he was lonely.

"Savannah?" Nathan interrupted my internal ramble.

"Yeah?"

"I said, are you okay? Your voice seems...off."

"I don't know if I want to do this, Nathan." My heartbeat nearly tripled, as I was about to admit what had been swirling in my brain for over a year.

"Do what? What are you talking about?"

I took a huge breath, nearly sighing my answer. "I don't know if I want to play professionally, Nathan. I don't...I don't think it's for me."

"Savannah..." His voice was agitated, anxious as he spoke my name, but he clipped off the rest of the sentence and let out a frustrated breath. "Is this about your—"

"Yes," I cut him off, "it is. It's about my mom. It's about her and the fact that she and my dad had to live an ocean apart because she couldn't have the kind of life with the opera here that she could over there. It's about the last few weeks here at the Institute. I've loved teaching, Nathan. I've loved nurturing young talent; preparing them for a life of their choosing. Should they have a choice..." My throat closed as I considered the implications of what I was saying.

Nathan was quiet for a few seconds and then started speaking in an uncharacteristically even tone. "You have a choice, Savannah."

"Do I? At the end of last week I played that Assobio piece with Gregory—"

"It's Gregory now?" Nathan sounded annoyed.

"They've all insisted I call them by their first names, since I'm technically a colleague. Anyway, we played that piece together during the instructor ensemble time, and..."

"And what, Savannah?"

My words came out as a whisper. "It was the single most moving experience while playing that I've ever had in my entire life. It swallowed me. We've never played together, Nathan and it was...*perfect*. We didn't stop or stall or trip up. Not once."

"I'm...confused, Savannah. What does that have to do with you not wanting to be a performing musician?"

"In just a second, I got it, Nathan. I was consumed by the song, the notes, the scene. It was like a drug that was instantly addicting. I've always loved performing and playing, Nathan, you know that. But, in that moment, playing with a world-class musician and playing a song I've spent months working on...I wanted that and absolutely nothing else. And, it scared me."

"Look, Savannah," Nathan sighed again, and I could picture him raking his long fingers through his disorganized curls, "I know that you've struggled off and on with performing as a career. You've never said it, but we've talked enough about your family life for me to...get it. But, I don't think what happened with *Gregory* scared you about playing professionally."

"What was it then?"

Nathan's tone turned dark, and I could tell he was speaking through clenched teeth, though he didn't sound angry. He repeated the same words from our earlier argument. His words that made no sense, but made too much sense. "You're in love with him, Savannah."

I thought back to standing next to Gregory as we played, and one by one the faculty disappeared from my view until all I saw was him and the notes. And all I heard was the beating of my heart.

"I know," I whispered, covering my mouth to silence the clamor of my tears.

I knew.

I was in love with him.

And it was a horrible mistake.

Chapter 14

SAVANNAH

*T*AKE A DEEP *breath, Savannah. It's just a bar.*

Smoothing down the front of my favorite red dress, I knew damn well it wasn't *just* a bar. I'd made it through the second week of orchestra camp at the Tanglewood Institute, and the staff was gathering at Magnolia's for end of the summer drinks and dancing. He was going to be there.

Overwhelmed by the time we played together during the instructors' ensemble, and my admission to Nathan on the phone several days later, I'd done my best to avoid Gregory Fitzgerald.

I loved him.

Not only had I kissed him, but I was falling in love with him, and I didn't know what to do about it.

If anything.

I hadn't spoken to Nathan since that phone call. He seemed tense over the fact that I admitted my feelings for Gregory. He said while he saw I *was* in love with him, he didn't understand why. We never spoke to each other outside of the classroom, he said. And, when we did speak, he was certain to remind me, our interactions were less than cordial. No hearts. No flowers.

I never did tell him about the kiss.

There wasn't anything tangible about Gregory Fitzgerald that screamed for me to be in love with him. It was all beneath the surface. I felt a pull toward him since the first time he played for us on our first day of music theory. My first perceptions of him—since the day he offhandedly dismissed me from the stage at my audition—was all wrong. At least, I hoped it was wrong.

The passion and intensity behind our kiss shattered that first impression.

I'd told Madeline I needed to walk to the bar alone to gather my thoughts. And steel my nerves. It was absurd, really. I wasn't his student anymore, and I'll be damned if he didn't feel something when we played that piece together, too. I know he felt something. I intended to figure out exactly what that was.

I was here. Magnolia's.

One more deep breath.

Clearing my throat and rolling my shoulders back, I opened the door and was greeted by nerve-calming dance music. Heavy beats graciously drowned out the sound of my heart.

"Savannah, over here!" Madeline flagged me down the second I walked in. She and James were sitting next to each other, but turned in so their knees were touching.

A second later, I spotted Gregory sitting on the other side of James. Always in black. It looked different this time, though. I knew how his arms looked as they drew music from his cello. How his muscles flexed. He had a suit coat on over what I was certain was a t-shirt, and I rolled my eyes as I smiled and walked toward the trio.

"You okay, sweetie? You seemed stressed earlier." Madeline playfully tugged the skirt of my dress and I noticed Gregory's eyes flicker to my legs.

"I'm fine. I just needed some fresh air, so I walked."

He was still looking at my legs. I softly bit a grin away from my lips.

James leaned his back against the bar. "Well, Savannah, I must say, you've thoroughly impressed not only the staff here this summer, but the parents and students, too."

"Thank you, James. I had a great time."

Gregory broke his standard pensive silence. And his study of my calves. "Can I get you something to drink, Savannah?"

I let out a surprised giggle, and James and Madeline looked askance at both of us. His face twisted up a bit as we all stared at him, and I suppressed the startled giggle.

"What?" He held out his hands. "She's been here for two minutes and no one's offered her a drink. I figured one of us should be polite."

Something behind his eyes looked less than polite and innocent. Rather than make me nervous, confidence took over.

I arched an eyebrow as I answered. "Tequila."

"Tequila?" He questioned with a sour look on his face.

"Yes. A shot. Please." I grinned and watched his eyes land on my mouth. It made my heart tick up a few beats.

"Make it four!" James playfully slapped the bar and raised his eyebrows as Madeline giggled.

"Four?" Gregory questioned.

"One for all of us, Gregory. Come on." Madeline batted her eyelashes mockingly. I loved watching the three of them in action, as if no time had passed from their days as students at the Conservatory.

The bartender leaned into Gregory, who held up three fingers while making a displeased face.

"Spoil sport," Madeline snorted as three shot glasses were set on the bar in front of us.

"Drink that bathwater, if you must. I'll stick to my gin, thank you."

Despite myself, I let out a loud laugh.

"Something funny?" Gregory lifted an eyebrow at me.

"You're just…" I trailed off as the tequila was poured and I clinked glasses with Madeline and James as Gregory rolled his eyes. As the tequila warmed my throat, my resolve followed suit.

"You were saying, Savannah?" Gregory challenged as Madeline and James ordered another shot for themselves. "I'm just?"

"Dance with me." I ignored the pointed stares from James and Madeline.

"Dance with you?"

I'd think he was blowing me off had I not caught him swallow hard.

"Yes," I said with all the confidence I could muster. "Dance with me. Hear the music? See the people? Take off that God-awful, stuffy coat and dance with me." I held out my hand, praying that it wasn't shaking as noticeably as my nerves were.

Jesus, I just asked my professor to dance with me. I had no plan beyond that. That was all I'd managed to come up with on my walk to the bar—that I wanted him to dance with me. People usually loosen up while they dance, and I was hoping he'd be no exception. Though, standing there with my hand suspended in air while he stared skeptically at me, I had my doubts. Maybe our kiss had ruined any chance I might have. In a second his coat was on the back of his chair and his hand was in mine. His eyes challenging.

Maybe not.

"Let's go." He shrugged as his voice turned husky.

Just then, a new song started. It was fast, which was all my nerves and my pulse could handle, anyway. His hands were firm, tight, just like I remembered. My knees were a little weak, and I regretted not taking one more shot of tequila before heading onto the dance floor.

Suck it up, Savannah. This is what you wanted. Just. Dance.

I spun around with a smile on my face and found Gregory assessing my legs.

"That is a lovely dress." His eyes volleyed around the space between our bodies, struggling to find a place to settle.

"Thank you." I knew he liked it. He looked at me the same way when he saw me in this dress in that club in Boston.

Though we'd been on the dance floor for five seconds, he'd made no move to take the lead. He seemed stuck. Thankfully, a waitress weaved through the crowd with a tray full of shots.

"Thank *God*," I sighed as I took one, placed some cash on the waitress's tray, and poured it quickly down my throat. "Want one?"

He shook his head. "What was that?"

I looked up at the ceiling, giving myself a second to taste it. "Rum? Yes. Rum." I nodded, licking my lips.

He opened his mouth to say something, but I silenced him by grabbing his hands and anchoring them on my hips. Before I could assess how much I loved the way his hands felt on my body, I gripped his shoulders. His lips parted slightly as I refused to move my eyes from his gaze.

"I know you can dance, Gregory. I saw you that night in Boston..." I felt his fingers press into my hips for a second as he seemed to consider whether he'd lighten up or not.

"I know you can dance, too, Savannah." His face didn't change as I realized we were both standing static on the dance floor.

I closed my eyes, and a breath later, started moving my hips in slow circles. I left my eyes closed for another second, letting the music pour through me and out my hips and feet as I moved, faster now. Tossing my hair over one shoulder, I opened my eyes to find Gregory's face more relaxed, but his eyes were still incredibly focused on my face. I wanted to look away, to take a break from their intensity, but I couldn't.

As the song headed toward the chorus, I realized Gregory was keeping a measured distance from me. Our bodies were too far apart to be dancing to a song like this. Too far apart to be dancing at all. As the rhythm picked up, I moved in a step closer, sliding my hands from his shoulders to the back of his neck.

He sucked in a breath I know I wasn't meant to hear. A breath that made me want to run my fingers through the back of his hair. I knew if I lifted my chin just a fraction of an inch, I'd be well within kissing distance of his lips. Goosebumps sprouted down my back, and my lips felt like they were pulsing just at the thought of his mouth on mine. I wanted to kiss him. I wanted him to kiss me. He wanted it too. Any insecurities I had about kissing him vanished as I watched his pupils dilate as he licked his lips. This summer had changed things for me, and judging by the way his eyes were moving across my collarbone, they'd changed things for him, too.

No.

Not here.

My head was clouded with the music, the nerves buzzing through my brain, and how his hands felt as they tightly held my hips.

"You can really dance." I bit my lip to prevent myself from kissing him right there on the dance floor. I chuckled, realizing that he was now leading us in the dance. Only Gregory Fitzgerald could change who was leading without the other person noticing.

He simply grinned, half his mouth turning up in a way that would make the Cheshire cat jealous. Seeming to relax into the music, and our dance, he lifted his arm and spun me out away from his body, his ice-blue eyes watching me the entire time.

GREGORY

MY HEART RACED as she spun in a circle at the end of my arm, the bottom of her dress flaring out, my eyes once again falling to her calves, her knees, the swell of her breasts. Then I pulled her back, and her body came back into contact with mine, leaning back against my arm just as the song came to an end.

Savannah's cheeks were flushed red, and for just a second our eyes met again, as they had over our instruments just a few short days before. I steadied her back to her feet, careful to not touch her anywhere inappropriate in front of all of these people.

But I ached to touch her. I was out of control, my body aching with unchecked lust. The lights lowered as the next song began, a slow song, a ballad. Instinctively I started to let go, my hands loosening.

Why not?

The thought was…unnecessary, wrong. But without transition my hands slipped from her arms down to her waist. I pulled her to me as her hands rose to my shoulders. The touch of her skin, shifting just beneath that insubstantial dress, was intoxicating.

"You dance remarkably well." As I spoke I tried to keep my breathing under control. I tried to keep my thoughts and emotions under control. *She was a student.* No matter that she'd spent the summer on the faculty at Tanglewood, in a matter of two weeks we would be back at the Conservatory, back to our normal roles.

Struggling to get my thoughts under control, I said, "Where did you take lessons?"

She raised one eyebrow, as she leaned back just slightly to look in my eyes. "Lessons? You don't need lessons to dance, Gregory, you just move with the music."

With her in my arms, my hands just touching her waist, I wasn't even conscious of any music playing. I took a breath as we moved slightly closer to each other. Too close, really. Her dress was a light fabric, smooth and barely there. The muscles at the base of her back seemed to tense where my hands rested. "Chaotic as always, Miss Marshall."

She grinned. "We're back to *Miss Marshall* now?"

"Savannah. I was commenting on your resistance to structure."

She shook her head slightly. "What's your deal, Gregory? I don't get it."

I turned us in a gentle circle and said, "My *deal*? Please explain, I don't understand."

Her eyebrows worked. I'd seen them before, moving independently of each other sometimes, as if they had minds of their own. I was certain it was completely unconscious. Fascinating, and somehow insanely attractive.

"You're always so...structured. But broody. Dark. Sometimes I think there's something inside of you just ready to explode."

I swallowed. "I assure you, Savannah, I am what you see. A musician."

My fingertips touched at the small of her back as we moved closer to each other. An intense urge to run my hands over the refined curve of her backside flashed through me. The thought made me suck in a quick breath.

"I don't think so, Gregory. I think there's a lot more inside than you show."

I wanted to tell her more. I wanted to tell her how it felt the first time I heard the cello. The first time my hands brought a note, alive and amazing, from that instrument. Sometimes I felt there was nothing more important than music...that when the writing and words and pretensions people used as barriers were all stripped away, in the end it was only music that could truly be shared as a universal language.

I didn't know how to say any of that. And, no one had ever asked me to. But looking in her eyes, swimming in those eyes, I thought she understood. For the first time in my life I felt a gaping empty wound in myself, a wound I'd stuffed with nothing more than melody for all those years and suddenly that *wasn't enough*.

"Perhaps," I replied. "But all music has depths that don't show on the surface."

She gave me a quirky grin at that, and against my better judgment, I pulled her a little bit closer. Our bodies touched down their entire length, and my breath was coming in short, fractured moments. In my arms she felt right...real, and our faces were almost touching. We swayed slightly with the music, and her full, shiny lips grinned a little wider as our eyes met. Against my will, I found my own mouth curving up into a smile.

That made her eyes widen. "I don't think I've ever seen you smile. Does that hurt?"

Good god. I felt myself laugh a little. "You are one smart-mouthed young woman."

That made her smile even wider. "You are an ill-tempered old man, which makes no sense considering how young you are. I don't get it. Most musicians would kill for what you have."

I stumbled over her statement. What I had? Did she mean *her* in my arms right now? It was true. But then I realized she was talking about something else entirely when she continued.

"You're probably the most talented cellist the BSO has fielded in years, and it's not enough?"

I was oddly disappointed. Because the experience of having her in my arms, dancing, was...unique. Fascinating. It had a music all its own. But I kept my thoughts to myself and kept the conversation away from that.

"I always strive to improve."

"To what end?"

"Mastery."

She smiled and shook her head. "You amaze and appall me at the same time."

I found myself grinning. "In that, Savannah, the feeling is completely mutual."

Her eyes widened. They were dark eyes, but beautiful. Her voice breathy as she spoke the next words. "I amaze you?"

"You do. You're...erratic. Dynamic. Incredibly talented. Brilliant. There were days in my class where I wanted to shake you."

She raised her eyebrows. "Shake me?"

"In...frustration. In..."

I found myself floundering. I'm only articulate with bow and cello in hand. What I wanted to say was...that I wanted to touch her. That I wanted to hold her, just like this. That I wanted to look in her eyes and see admiration. Affection.

"Savannah..." my voice trailed off. Our lips were so close, I would only have to move a fraction, a few bare centimeters, and they would have touched.

"Gregory?" When she replied, her voice sounded small, shaky. Confused. She sounded almost as confused as I felt.

What I really wanted to do at that moment was lean in. Closer. Her eyes seemed huge as I took a deep breath and considered my options.

And that's when I realized the song had ended, and a new one started. A loud, raucous pop song, and dancers were moving onto the floor around us. The change broke the mood, suddenly, and she stepped back, away from me.

She had a wounded look in her eyes as she said, "I have to go to the ladies' room. Um...I'll be...I'll be back." She backed away from me, quickly, stumbling a little, then turned and walked quickly away.

I stood in the middle of the dance floor, my breath slowing, feeling bereft, and an unfamiliar ache in my chest.

That's when I heard an all *too* familiar voice. "Gregory!"

I turned around and felt my face slip into a mask. *Karin* stood on the edge of the dance floor. Where had she come from? What was she doing here? Mechanically, my limbs almost numb, I moved toward her.

"Karin, what are you doing here?"

She gave me a piercing look. "I came to see you. This is the last night for the Institute, right? You told me weeks ago all the instructors blew off some steam tonight."

I swallowed. Indeed, I had told her that. I'd mentioned it in passing quite a long time ago, but I hadn't exactly intended it as an invitation. Nor had we really spoken since she'd given me her...not exactly an ultimatum...back in the spring.

"Anyway," she said, "I came here hoping to find you, but it seems you've found Savannah Marshall."

I shook my head slightly. Nothing was going on with Savannah. If I repeated that enough times, the reason *why* might resurface in my conscience. I swallowed.

"Just dancing," I said. The words seemed to stick in my throat. Because they were a lie. That was much more than merely dancing. I could still feel Savannah's body against mine.

"Can we talk then?" Karin asked.

I didn't know what to say. I didn't really want to talk. Not to her. Not now.

As I looked over my shoulder to the restrooms, I saw Savannah move past the bar. She was in a hurry for the front door, it seemed. Her back was rigid, her steps furious.

"Karin," I said. "Perhaps later..."

Then I stopped talking. I stopped breathing. I stopped thinking, because the pain was too much. At the door, Savannah looked over her shoulder. Her eyes fell on me, and on Karin, at the edge of the dance floor. Her face held an indescribable expression, an expression that I'd do anything to capture in a song, but also an expression I'd do anything to erase. The bleak turmoil in her eyes speared my chest like a blade.

Her eyes swept away from me.

Then, she was gone.

Chapter 15

G REGORY

MY EYELIDS WERE heavy and felt as though they were lined with sandpaper. The tension I felt seared through my chest and shoulders. I'd been up for hours. Not voluntarily. Once I'd finally seen a disappointed Karin off, I'd returned to the house only to lie awake, staring at the ceiling. Each time I closed my eyes, I saw a hurt and distressed Savannah hurrying for the door of the bar.

I'd almost kissed her. Almost. We'd been so close to each other, and instead of an intrusion, she'd felt…at home there.

I wanted her, and she ran.

I finally drifted off to a restless, unsatisfying sleep at midnight, but then my eyes snapped open again, and fell on the clock, only to see that it was merely 2:30 a.m. I rolled over, unable to clear my mind of thoughts of her. Of her lips, of her eyes, my hands on her hips. The music pounding into our bodies as we danced.

I tried to go back to sleep. But I failed. Which is why I found myself standing in front of Madeline's house at 3 o'clock in the morning. My head felt cloudy, my thoughts making little sense.

I knew Savannah was here alone. Madeline and James had returned to his room together, which gave me even more reason to leave the house. They'd have been embarrassed if they'd known I was awake.

I stood there at the door for possibly five—or a thousand—minutes, my hand hovering over the doorbell.

Before I could press it, the door opened.

Savannah stood in the doorway, Her eyes were blurry, red rimmed. I couldn't tell if I'd woken her or she'd been tossing and turning as I had. She wore a long white t-shirt that fell to her knees, and her blonde hair was tousled. It was all I could do to prevent myself from reaching out and touching it.

She blinked at me three or four times. Waiting, perhaps, for me to say something.

"Savannah..."

Without a word, she grabbed my hands and pulled me into the house.

She shook her head. "What are you doing here?"

"I'm here to see you."

Her eyes darted to the floor, her long eyelashes sweeping down. She swallowed, then her face set in a grim expression and she looked back up at me. "Why?"

Unexpectedly, I found myself shaking. "I had to see you."

She slightly shook her head, an infinitesimal movement. "You're a professor, Gregory."

"Does that matter? I'm not *your* professor."

She looked away from me. "It should."

I took a deep breath. "I know it should. But it doesn't. Not to me."

"What do you want from me?" She looked right through me as she said the words. The resignation in her tone chilled my core.

My heart was pounding. What did I want from her? How could I answer that? How could I explain to her what I wanted, when I had no idea myself? I wanted to make love to her. I wanted to make music with her. I thought about that moment when she raised her flute and I touched bow to string for the first time, and we looked at each other across those bare feet of space, and wove our song together. I wanted that again. I'd never experienced that with anyone else. Right there in front of our colleagues, I felt as if I'd performed the most intimate of acts. How could I say that? How could I tell her that I desperately wanted to touch her. That I wanted to kiss those lips. That for the first time in my life I wanted to experience a deep emotional connection with a woman, a connection that transcended everything.

My mind frantically sought an acceptable and normal response to her question. Without a conscious decision, I spoke. "You're doing the Assobio a Jato for your senior recital, yes? I'll practice it with you...perform it with you."

Her face looked confused...then disappointed. Her shoulders dropped a fraction as she exhaled, and then she said, "You showed up here at three in the morning for that?"

I closed my eyes. The tension in my body and throat was worse than any recital or performance, worse than any audition I'd ever performed. It was almost painful to speak. My voice came out strangled, too fast, too much force, too much *everything*. "I want much more than that, Savannah. But as you said..." I trailed off, not wanting to remind her of her protests.

Her eyes watered a little and she blinked, moving inches from my body in one graceful motion. "This isn't...it isn't right. For either one of us."

"I don't care." The words came out in a rush of breath.

I closed the remaining distance between us. She pressed her palm against my chest, as if to stop me. She leaned her head back, and my eyes fell to her lips. She took a deep breath. The very same spot where her hand had rested when we stood in the rain. Where we kissed.

"I care," she whispered. "I can't do this." But her hand, which was poised to push me away, curled up, bunching my shirt up into her fist, and she pulled herself toward me.

"I can't either," I said. "We'll be back at the Conservatory in two weeks. It's too dangerous. You're too dangerous."

Her face paled, and her tone sharpened, but she never released my shirt. "What the hell is that supposed to mean?"

I closed my eyes. My whole body was tense, the muscles in my shoulders ready for a rehearsal, or a performance...or a war. I opened my eyes and looked in hers. Her brown eyes. So young. So confused. Intense.

Before I could stop myself or think or do anything that made any sense at all, I spoke.

"Savannah..."

Then I stopped talking. She was so close to me, her slender fist bunched up in my shirt, her eyes huge, her lips so close I couldn't stop myself from touching them, and I was compelled to know what those lips felt like again.

"Gregory, I..."

Her words were cut off when my lips touched hers, and I felt a wave of euphoria wash over me. This was no slow, gentle kiss. Our mouths opened immediately, and she gripped the back of my neck, pushing us together closer, a low moan like a growl rising from her throat as she pressed her body against mine, hard.

SAVANNAH

I gave him as many chances as I could to turn and leave. To come to his senses. I wouldn't ask anymore, not with the way his tongue danced greedily inside my mouth. Or the feel of his goatee against my skin. Rough. It fired sensations through my body faster than I could keep up with.

I managed to pry myself away from the kiss. "This way."

I led him up the stairs and stumbled on the next to the last. Gregory caught me, and we quickly moved to the guest room that had been my home for the past several weeks, and closed the door.

My shirt was on the floor and my hands were working on his shirt before the latch clicked into place. Gregory raised his arms overhead, the muscles in his arms bunching as he grabbed the back of his shirt and pulled it over his head and the rest of the way off. I pressed my almost-bare chest into his, letting out a small moan at the feeling of his hard muscles against my breasts. His hands moved from my lower back to the clasp of my bra, where he fumbled for a moment before successfully freeing it. And me.

"Jesus." His lips stayed parted as I backed away to slide the black lace barrier off my shoulders.

In here, there was no sign of the passionless music theory professor. This was the man who closed his eyes and swayed as he coaxed adoration from his cello, the man whose eyes froze me in place every time he looked at me, the man who returned my kiss in the rain and made my heart crave completeness I didn't even know I was missing. He was quite still, but the hard lines around his eyes and mouth morphed from tension to reverence as I set my hands on his hips and stepped back into his hold.

His head bowed just a bit, as though he wanted to kiss me. Before he reached my lips, I tilted my head to the side and kissed his chest, moving my lips slowly across his scorching bare skin until my tongue centered on his nipple. Gregory sucked in a loud, fast breath through his teeth as my tongue worked him over. Teasing. Testing.

"Come here." His growl made me weak, and I looked up to find his eyes alive with purpose. He grabbed my face and kissed me again, hard, and I was suddenly aware that I was the only one completely naked. I had no recollection as to when I'd discarded my panties, but now wasn't the time to wonder about their whereabouts.

As our mouths and tongues hungrily explored each other, I deftly undid his belt with one hand as my other tugged at his hair. Each time I tugged, he gripped my hips harder. The blurred lines between pain and pleasure swirled around me, and all I knew was I wanted more of him. Now. As his pants fell to his ankles, Gregory kicked off his shoes and stepped out and away from his wrinkled khakis. He stood before me in nothing but his grey boxer briefs and I gaped at his form.

Immaculate.

His arms, shoulders and the tight, bunched muscles of his torso were toned from thousands of hours at the cello, more than I'd ever realized until now. They begged to be touched.

"Don't move," I whispered against his lips. Kissing him once, nibbling on his swollen bottom lip as I pulled away, I moved my hands to the waistband of his last article of closing.

I squatted slowly as I pulled them down, kneeling in front of him as they settled around his ankles. I led the tips of my fingers slowly up the sides of his legs, feeling goosebumps pop up as soon as I made contact. He was so ready for me, the ache between my legs made me moan as I knelt before him. I let one hand reach his hip as I slowly circled the other around him. His hips twitched as my mouth inched closer.

"Savannah." He said my name inside of a ragged breath, stopping me less than an inch away from him.

I arched my eyebrow as I looked up at him, grinning mockingly. "I said...don't move."

As slowly as I could handle, I wrapped my lips around him, and let my tongue gently follow. Gregory felt for the hand I'd left on his hip and gripped it tightly as I took more of him in. As much as his size would allow before I couldn't take anymore. He groaned in ecstasy, a deep, carnal sound that made me echo with my own delighted sound.

I couldn't take it anymore.

I pulled away, kissing from his hips up to his mouth, where he earnestly welcomed me in. I took one, two steps forward and as the backs of his legs bumped up against my mattress, he sat, his hands on my hips as my fingernails dug into his shoulders.

"Lie back," I commanded, not breaking his fiery gaze.

"Are you...do you..."

I nodded. "Pill." As he scooted up the bed, I climbed over his body, straddling his narrow hips.

"God..." As reticent as he was in the classroom, he seemed more at a loss for words as I leaned over him and bit his collarbone. That elicited another incoherent noise from the depths of his want.

I pulled back a little, raising myself up enough to slide onto him. I went slowly, tossing my head back and wincing before sighing in blissful relief as he filled every part of me. Once I settled all the way onto him I paused for a moment and looked at him. I was almost startled to find him staring right back at me, eyes calm as his chest rose and fell erratically.

I rocked forward and back, slowly at first, as we adjusted to each other. Our eyes never once strayed, as my movements got faster...harder. Soon, the intensity of his hands guiding my hips up and down became so much that I had to close my eyes, crying out with each hard thrust downward.

Leaning forward slightly, I clenched the sheets as I kissed him. This new angle of our bodies caused me to shake in anticipation of the orgasm it would bring. I worked faster, digging my knees into the bed as I pushed on him harder, making him go deeper inside me than anyone had been before.

Warmth circled my insides and I knew it was only a matter of seconds.

Pressure building inside of me, I pressed my forehead into his shoulder and screamed his name as my knees went weak and the orgasm took over. Every muscle from my waist down seized around him, releasing and tightening four, five, six times as he continued to relentlessly push against me.

"God...Savannah!"

"Don't stop!" I cried out, despite having nothing left to give.

"Roll over." Abruptly serious through unsteady breaths, Gregory moved his hands from my hips to my shoulders.

I still felt the heat from his hands on my hips as I carefully slid off him. My insides remained on fire as I settled onto my back, anticipating his next move. The only warning I had was a flicker of desperate mischief in his eyes before he plunged into me.

"Shit!" I gripped the backs of his legs, bracing myself.

"Look at me," he ordered as sweat trickled down his neck and chest.

My eyes were closed tight, bracing my body for the on-slaught of his. It felt so good I didn't want to stop. I didn't want to break this moment.

"Look at me," he demanded once more, a demanding rumble coming from his throat.

He started working faster, his movements becoming more syncopated. As instructed, I opened my eyes. His eyes met me expectantly, waiting for me to obey him. When I did, he threw his head back and let out an animal howl, pulsing hard as he warmed me. Filled me.

Our slick skin glided across each other as he lay down on top of me. I felt his pulse against my breast and my inner thigh as we both lay in a ragged heap across my bed. I was dizzy as his mouth found my nipple and his tongue turned in lazy circles around it.

Once I regained most of my senses, I dragged my hands through his damp hair, lifting his face from my chest. It was there again. The calm. Like a quiet lake lapping onto a lonely shore, Gregory's eyes caused me to catch my breath.

"What?" he asked, kissing the side of my breast before resting his chin there. A contented smile worked its way tentatively across his lips.

It had been happening before that moment. Feelings set in motion before I'd taken my first exam in his class, and certainly well before our first kiss. But there, with Gregory lying on top of me as he smoothed my hair away from my face, I knew.

I loved him and there was no turning back.

Ever.

No matter what.

I T WAS A few minutes past 4:00 a.m. when we'd fallen asleep, legs wrapped around each other and my head on his chest. Daylight didn't wait for us to be ready; it came on schedule and poured harsh light into my bedroom. I shifted, rubbing my cheek against his chest as I savored the sensation of his skin against mine.

"I love you, Savannah." Gregory caressed my shoulder blade as he spoke.

"I love you, too." I smiled and looked up, resting my chin on his chest.

His thumb kept moving across my skin, but his mouth was frozen in a firm line. His eyes were a mess. Tired, bloodshot, but strikingly vulnerable. He'd meant what he'd just said. I felt it in his voice, but he wasn't looking at me.

I sat up a little, moving my head into his line of vision. "Hey..."

He sat up against the headboard, the sheet falling away from his chest, and ran a hand through his rumpled hair. "I'm sorry, Savannah."

"What are you sorry for?" I reflexively clenched my fists, sitting up and facing him, not liking the sudden dread settling over my chest. Even though Madeline wasn't home, I spoke in a near-whisper. "You just told me you love me."

He clenched his jaw, as if what he was about to say hurt. "I am in love with you, but there's nothing I can do about it, and I'm sorry for that."

I'd never been punched in the stomach before, but if it felt anything like what hearing that felt like, I was all set. I started to pull my hand away, but inexplicably, he laced his fingers through mine. He pressed my hand tighter into his chest.

"What do you mean there's nothing you can do about it? Why would you tell me—" I peeled my eyes away from his and sought for anywhere else to look. Anywhere except complete heartbreak that took over my life inside two seconds.

He tilted his head until I was forced to look into those blue eyes again. "I needed to be honest with you, Savannah."

"Why?"

"I...It...it's the right thing to do. To be honest." His eyebrows pulled together again, as if what he was telling me was an absolute truth—even when it meant shattering someone's heart.

"How long?" I finally managed to disentangle my hand from his and crossed my arms over my chest as I wrapped the sheet around me.

"How long what?"

"Have you been in love with me, Gregory? And, why do you get to be the one to decide we can't do anything about it?" Actively fighting tears, I took a deep breath and exhaled, puffing out my cheeks.

He responded in a stiff fashion better suited for the classroom than the bedroom. A tone that sat me up straight. "Which do you want me to answer first?"

I swung my legs over the side of the bed and stood, searching the floor for my panties.

"Savannah...fine. I can't do anything about it because you're a student—"

"I'm not *your* student," I shot back.

Finally locating my panties, I slid them on under the sheet and reached for my bra, which was sprawled across the desk.

"You know that doesn't matter. I'm a member of the faculty and you're a member of the student body."

I let the sheet fall as I fastened my bra and began collecting his clothes from the floor.

"Savannah, what are you doing?" Gregory moved to the edge of the bed, watching me cautiously.

In response to his question, I picked up one of his shoes and threw it across the room. He dodged it, raising one arm to shield his head.

"You can't *do anything* about it?" The shoe was followed by his pants, which smacked him in the face. My next words came out in a high-pitched scream. "What the *fuck* do you call what we just did?"

He didn't respond, nor did he start getting dressed. Which prompted me to throw the other shoe.

"Get dressed if you can't do anything about it!" I placed my hands on my hips as I tried to slow my breathing, staring at him as I clenched my teeth. I would *not* cry. Not now.

His eyes didn't move from mine as he slowly reached for his underwear and began to pull them up. His eyes were nervous, as if he were saying in his head *she's more scared of you than you are of her.* Then he spoke in a calm, condescending voice, like you might use with a child. "Savannah, I don't understand why you're so angry."

That did it.

I reached for the nearest object, which happened to be my composition notebook on the desk, and sent it toward his head. His hands couldn't move up in time so he overcompensated with an exaggerated duck, knocking him off balance and planting him on his ass.

There.

"*Stop!*" he yelled. "Stop throwing shit at me for a second and listen to me."

Not trusting myself, I crossed my arms in front of me and took a step back as he righted himself on his feet, dressing the rest of the way. He pulled his shirt over his head and walked toward me, tentatively bringing his hands to my shoulders.

"*Don't* touch me." I didn't attempt to move out of his hold, though. He just needed to know that I didn't *want* to want him to touch me.

But I did. Still.

"Savannah." He took a deep breath and, instinctively, as if we were starting our piece together, I took one in time with him. "You asked what I'd call last night. Fucking amazing. That's what last night was." His voice shook as his hands worked over my shoulders in a conciliatory manner I didn't care for.

"Don't you dare tell me you just got swept up in the moment, Gregory. What you did in that bed was more than getting *carried away.*" My goddamn chin quivered then, but I bit the inside of my lip to make it stop. It didn't work.

Gregory shook his head. "I didn't get carried away this morning Savannah. I got carried away by you long before last night. That alone doesn't mean this can go on..."

"Then why did you stay when we were finished?" I whispered, looking down.

"Look at me."

It was in a different tone than a couple of hours earlier but caused the same internal reaction in my gut. I lifted my eyes.

"I stayed because I love you, and cutting the past few hours even minutes shorter would have been excruciating."

"You don't tell someone you're in love with them and take it away all in the same breath, Gregory. That's not fair."

"I haven't taken anything away, Savannah. I do love you."

"Stop saying it!" I stepped out of his grasp and ran a hand through my hair as I walked out of the bedroom and headed down the stairs, trying to distance myself from the oncoming tears.

I heard him sigh with a little growl at the tail end of it as he followed me down the stairs. That better not have been directed toward me. He was the one ruining everything.

"I need you to leave." I *hated* that my voice shook as I spoke the words. I reached for the doorknob, but his hand stopped me, fingers wrapping tightly around my wrist.

"Don't do this, Savannah," he pleaded, tilting his head to the side the way he had before he kissed me last night.

"You don't do *this* then, Gregory. Don't tell me we have to leave what happened between us upstairs."

I knew if I didn't blink then the tears couldn't fall, and he couldn't watch my heart breaking all the way down my cheeks. But, we all have to blink sometime.

Gregory grabbed me and pulled me in, holding my head against his chest. "You know we have to, Savannah. At least for now."

I nodded. He was right. There was no way we could continue while I was still in school. I scrambled around inside my brain, searching for a way.

"You...you'll still work on the piece with me, though. Right?" I was committing emotional suicide inside my request, but there was no other way for us to be...an *us*.

"Are you sure?" He held me at arms' length and seemed to be studying my face.

I nodded my head, rapidly, unsure of my words. I chewed on them for a moment, and then I said, "Just...one thing. You never...asked me how long."

"How long what?" He gently shook his head in apparent confusion.

"You didn't ask me how long I've been in love with you."

I reached for the doorknob again, allowing us onto the porch and into the thick late-August air.

He swallowed hard and looked past my shoulder for a split second before meeting my eyes again. "How long have you... been in love with me?" It was like he was afraid of my answer, the way he had to pull his own words out of this mouth.

Leaning forward, I took both his hands in mine, looking up just slightly, and waited for his eyes to fall on me. When they did, I took a resolute breath. "I think always." With a puzzled look on his face, he looked like he was going to respond, but I cut him off. "Let me finish. I remember staring at you during my audition. I knew who you were and I knew how tough you were. I wanted to get in, more than anything, but I also wanted to impress *you*. Then I didn't see you again until class last semester. I still had this desire to make you notice me, to make you notice my music. Then, you hated me."

"No, I never hated you, Savannah. I was just—"

"Falling in love with me," I whispered.

He just nodded.

"So, what now?"

He sighed. And my stomach sank as he reached up and moved a piece of hair out of my face and tucked it behind my ear. "Now? Now we practice together. We spend the year preparing you for your senior recital. I can help you work with Madeline to select pieces to audition with, if you'd like. But, we respect each other. I respect your position as a student, and you respect mine as a professor. We move forward cautiously and responsibly. No surprises. You're a student." He seemed to be reminding himself of that measly little fact any chance he got.

Grasping at straws, trying to fight my way back through the wall he was slowly rebuilding, I blurted out, "Not for another two weeks."

"What?"

"Until classes start again. Not until we start practicing together. I'm not a student for another two weeks." My tone may have sounded slightly panicked.

"Savannah, I don't see what that has—"

Before I could think further than the next ten seconds, I shook my hands from his and placed them on either side of his face, pulling his lips to mine. His lips were tight as he inhaled sharply through his nose. I wasn't letting go. Not until he kissed me back. He exhaled slowly, his shoulders sinking as he ran his hands up my sides and wrapped them behind my neck. As his fingers knotted gently through the back of my hair, his mouth opened slightly. Just barely. It was enough for me to deepen the kiss, so I did. A soft and low moan, barely audible, vibrated from Gregory's throat as he pulled me in even tighter, his soft tongue gently caressing mine.

In two weeks we would have to pretend. To ignore how we felt. I wanted to perform with him, without question. But, during those few seconds kissing him, I had the fleeting desire to walk away from everything and run off with him. With that thought I hastily pulled away from our kiss, resting my forehead on his, both of us breathing heavily. Before either one of us could say anything, before we could even open our eyes, the shutting of a car door kicked us back to reality.

Madeline. Shit.

Gregory dropped his hands to his hips and looked down, closing his eyes tightly as if trying to wake himself up. Unfortunately, this was no dream. Madeline was walking toward us quite calmly. Rather than cross my arms in front of my chest as if I'd done something wrong, I stood a little straighter and gave her a smile.

"Good morning, Madeline." My voice was embarrassingly squeaky.

"Morning, Savannah. Gregory." Her tone was darkly playful.

Gregory slowly turned around. "Madeline," he said through clenched teeth, as if he were trying to prevent himself from throwing up.

Madeline looked between the two of us a few times. Smacking her lips and arching her eyebrow, she finally spoke. "I trust that now that the two of you have gotten that out of your system, there won't be any problems this semester?" It was less of a question, and, really, more a statement. A requirement. She didn't wait for our answer before turning on her heels and walking inside, closing the door I'd left open behind her.

Shit. I blew it. I thought for sure Gregory would be incensed that I could have just caused a *major* problem for the both of us. We were lucky, all things considered, that it was Madeline who happened upon us. And that it had been out here on the porch and *not* the second floor of her house. I felt my cheeks heat as I nervously looked at him.

"I'm sorry, Gregory," I cleared my throat, trying to regain some semblance of composure, "I didn't mean to—"

Gregory's index finger lifted my chin. "Don't be." His thumb gently stroked my cheek, as his eyes danced back and forth across from mine. His tone was gentle, soothing. Reassuring. "It can't happen again, though, Savannah. Understood?"

I bit my lip and nodded. "Understood."

The next five seconds held us in space, looking into each other's eyes at the truths we were going to have to ignore in order to come out of the next year in one piece. With our careers intact. Finally, Gregory let his hand drop from my face, and without another word, he put his hands in his pockets and turned away from me, walking gracefully down the stairs and toward his car.

I watched until he was out of sight. Just standing on the porch in my t-shirt, with the memory of his touch burned into my body.

Chapter 16

GREGORY

I T CAN'T HAPPEN *again.*

Walking down the narrow hall to the practice rooms, I mentally repeated my command to Savannah from the front porch of Madeline's house two short weeks ago. She had nodded her understanding through flushed cheeks and those wide brown eyes of hers before responding. I had to repeat it, because I was about to see her for the first time since that morning.

We'd managed to arrange our practice session with a minimum amount of awkwardness. Granted, the exchange was through email, but her language suggested she was ready to forge ahead with the Assobio a Jato piece in preparation for her recital without hesitation. I planned to suggest pieces for her to audition for orchestras. I'd been through and to enough auditions to know what would easily get her a spot.

She *would* be auditioning for major companies. I would see to it with everything I had. If Nathan Connors could land Chicago—the thought caused me to roll my eyes as I rounded the corner—Savannah could have her pick of orchestras. I'd heard her play; she could have her pick of any orchestra in the world.

I saw the door to the last room on the right was open, and I knew Savannah would be in there. She often left the door open while practicing. Not all the way, but enough that I could hear a bit of her sessions if I happened to pass by, the way one might catch the scent of the tulips as they walked through the Common in the middle of spring.

The sound coming through the space in the door wasn't her flute, though it was equally as beautiful. It was her voice. She was on her phone. Despite the carefree resonance of her laugh, I felt rising irritation that she wasn't warming up in preparation for our session.

At the sight of her, I had to immediately push away thoughts. Her bare skin, and how it felt under my fingertips. Her hair, damp with sweat, splayed out on the pillow as she arched her head back. The soft heat of her lips as they pressed into mine, breaking every code of conduct I'd established for myself. I had to force my mind away from all of that. This was about the music. This was about our lesson. I reminded myself that her discipline to the craft needed some serious attention.

Savannah sucked in a quick, startled breath as I unceremoniously marched through the door, set down my cello case, and pointedly closed the door behind me.

She smiled when she saw me, and I almost regretted my gruff entrance. "Hey, uh, he's here. I have to go. Good luck tonight, we'll talk more later. Love you."

She shut her phone and leaned over to set it in her bag. Her yellow tank top clung to her body in a way that recalled how she looked without it. Flawless. Sun-kissed skin from her head down her breathtakingly long legs.

Love you? Who is she talking to? Who makes her face light up like that?

"Turn it off first." I used the same tone with her that I used with all of my first-time students. I knew she wasn't a student of *mine*, but she was a student I was working with, and I intended to hold her to the same expectations. Regardless of how her skin felt beneath my lips.

It can't happen again. Ever.

Her eyes shot to mine as her smile faded. "Sorry." With blushing cheeks, she turned off her phone before tucking it into her bag. I was the one who was sorry, in that instant.

I hated seeing that smile leave her face.

But we'd been wrong. And I had to be the one to set the expectations and tone of our relationship. It killed me to hurt her. But I couldn't give her any illusions at all. Our relationship *would* be professional.

"I expect that when we practice together, Savannah, you're ready to go at the start of our time. I know I suggested we collaborate on this piece for your recital, but neither of us have an excess of time. I've been playing all morning, so I'm warmed up. I expect you to be warmed up, as well." While this was my normal spiel, and it usually produced the same sheepish response from students, it lit a familiar fire in Savannah's eyes.

"I've been ready." She gestured to her flute, set on its stand, that I'd failed to notice upon entering the room. "And I'm warmed up. Anything else, Gregory, or shall we tune and get on with it?"

She arched her eyebrow to accentuate her challenging tone.

That kind of attitude should have infuriated me—a student speaking to me in such a self-righteous tone. But, Savannah was no longer just a student. Not after that night. What she *was*, though, I had no clear idea.

I thought maybe we should reiterate the boundaries conversation we had after pulling away from our kiss on Madeline's porch. A kiss, thankfully, gone unmentioned to me by Madeline *or* James. It wasn't really a boundaries conversation, though; it was more a declaration that it could simply *never* happen again. Not while she was still a student.

"Who was that on the phone?" I asked, despite myself, as I took my cello out of its case.

She sighed and glanced at me out of the corner of her eye. "Nathan."

I cleared my throat. "Connors? I thought he wasn't your boyfriend." I couldn't stop the words from coming out of my mouth.

"He's not." She grinned and shook her head just slightly.

"But you said *love you* when you hung up."

"Because I love him, Gregory. He's my friend." She shrugged, brought her flute to her lips, and ran through a scale, seeming to study my reaction the entire time. "What?" she asked when she finished.

"You two were awfully...close in my class last semester. And all around town, if I remember correctly."

"I told you he's not my boyfriend." She chuckled and shifted the music on her stand once more. "Are you ready? The first twelve notes are all you."

But she loved him? This woman made no sense.

"Does he tell you he loves you, too?"

She swallowed hard. "Yes. We've been friends since we were, like, ten, Gregory. We grew up together. He...can we play, please?" Bemused, she shook her head again.

"Certainly, let's tune. C?" She nodded and I just set my bow across the strings, when she stopped me.

"And, what do you care if he's my boyfriend anyway? What was it you said? Your instructions...*it can't happen again.*" She said the words in a stentorian tone, mocking me.

I'd foolishly hoped we could make it through one practice without discussing the night we'd spent together.

"Sav—"

"Don't." She put up her hand and straightened her posture. "Let's just play, okay? You start."

I set my bow across the strings once again and took a measured breath. She took one too, in time with mine. I couldn't possibly start without discussing this with her further. This was the precise reason I never mixed life with music. Things got messy. I didn't want to turn down the opportunity to play with her, though, so I had to figure it out. Fast.

My breath turned into a heavy sigh as I leaned my cello against its stand and set the bow down. Savannah rolled her eyes and put her flute on its upright stand, clasping her hands on her lap.

"Is there a problem?"

My proximity to her was maddening.

The last time I was this close to her we were in bed...I couldn't stand to be this close to her without touching her, and that was going to be a massive problem if we were to continue working together. I didn't want it to be...I just wanted to touch her. Just one more time.

So I did.

I reached across the restless space between our bodies and gently set my hand on her thigh. The muscles up and down her thigh tensed in response.

"W-what are you doing?" Her voice staggered a bit as her eyes fell to my hand and made their way up my arm before resting on mine. Her brown eyes were nearly black as her large pupils took me in, and her chest was moving faster as her breathing became softly more erratic.

My mind froze. I had no clue what I was doing. I had no rational explanation for why I was sitting in a practice room at the Conservatory with a student, helping her prepare for her senior recital on an instrument I knew little about. Or why my hand was on her thigh.

My lips barely opened. "I don't know."

She swallowed hard, never blinking or flicking her gaze elsewhere. "Don't stop."

I leaned forward, watching the hue of her cheeks turn from sun-kissed pink to breathless red as I got closer. Never once did she look away from me. She shifted in her seat, turning her knees toward me. My hand trembled as I slid it from her thigh, over the curve of her hip and up her side until it came to rest at the base of her neck where I cradled her chin in my hand. Her eyebrows pulled in a little and she leaned her head into my hand, sucking in a long, deep breath. Her lips looked fuller, begging to be kissed.

I considered pulling back, stopping this right then and there, but all the reasons I shouldn't have been doing what I was doing vanished as her tongue tentatively slid across her lips, then disappeared back into her beautiful mouth. I brought my other hand to the opposite side of her face and pulled her face to mine. The tips of our noses touched as our mouths stood in a standoff, millimeters from each other.

Exactly enough distance to make a fatal error.

Nothing about her mouth was wrong, though. Nothing about the smell of lilies coming from somewhere between her neck and her hair was immoral. Nothing about my absolute desire for her was deniable.

In the span of the blink of an eye, our lips were pressed together as if by a force outside either one of us. Her hands clenched the sides of my torso as a high-pitched sigh found its way from her throat into my mouth. Needing to feel her hair between my fingers, I slid one of my hands around the back of her neck and through her long, wild, impossibly soft hair. I was lost to her in that moment, and I never wanted to find my way out of that hole.

SAVANNAH

T HE FIRST THING I noticed the morning after Gregory kissed me in the practice room was that my lips were swollen, and my muscles tense and aroused. But it wasn't the physical impact...it was the emotional. Everything had changed. Again. We'd broken all the rules...then set new ones, and then broke those. That afternoon we kissed...then practiced... then kissed more. The feel of his lips against mine was unexpectedly intense, fraught with tension, and thinking about it the next morning made me moan a little.

I'd gotten back to my room that night after practice, and Marcia immediately saw something was going on. So, in slow, hesitant sentences, every moment thinking I was going to be judged by her, I told Marcia the story.

Instead of the condemnation I expected, I got a hug. And then a near whispered, urgent request for details. We sat on her bed, talking and laughing, and for the first time since all of this started with Gregory, I didn't feel like I needed to hide. After all, no matter how close we were, Nathan would never understand or support my love for Gregory. He would never approve. Honestly, I didn't know if I even approved. Of myself. The more we kissed, however, and the more we said we loved each other, the less I cared.

The next day I arrived to practice early. He was already there, and the door was slightly open, so I heard him playing as I walked down the length of the practice hall, my heart thumping with each step. I stopped outside the room to watch and listen. He was playing Max Bruch's *Kol Nidrei*, a haunting and melodic composition.

His back was to the door. I stood watching, my eyes taking in the muscles of his shoulders and the slight sway of his head as he played. For a man who kept his emotions under such tight constraints, the passion in his music was heart stopping. I stood, watching, arrested, until he finished. As I watched him play, I realized I was incredibly unsure of myself. Unsure of what our strange make out session in the practice room meant.

Nothing about our situation had changed. I was still a student. He was still a professor. Moreover, he was still an arrogant, obsessed man who claimed that personal relationships had no place in his life. No amount of kissing could cure that.

My insecurity washed away in an instant when he turned around, his blue eyes meeting mine. I felt his gaze all the way down my spine, and his eyes barely left me throughout the practice session.

When we were finished, he set his cello in its stand and approached me. He lifted his left hand, tenderly cupping my chin.

"Savannah..."

I swallowed.

"We can't do this," I whispered. "Not here."

"Monday. Practice at my house. Six o'clock."

I nodded. Monday. His thumb slowly ran along my jaw, and I closed my eyes, leaning my head back slightly, my breath sucking in slowly.

The moment ended too quickly. His eyes darted to the narrow window in the practice room door. We'd taken a terrible risk the previous day. The kind of risk that could end his teaching career and destroy my reputation.

I couldn't help but ask myself if the risk...the thrill of that risk...had enhanced the moment.

Then he was gone, packing up his cello and leaving in record time, leaving me confused and lonely and unsure.

The following Monday, I tentatively walked up Pinckney Street in Beacon Hill, my flute case in my right hand. It was a beautiful day, the sky clear, everything crisp. I could barely feel the slightest chill in the air, not autumn yet for some time, but the beginning breath of fall just touching me. It calmed my nerves, reminding me that he had invited me here. He'd said, "I love you."

Of course, in the back of my head, his full sentence continued to play out in my mind, because the words he'd said weren't simply, "I love you." They were *I am in love with you, but there's nothing I can do about it, and I'm sorry for that.*

Who says that?

Gregory fucking Fitzgerald says that. Leaving me wondering what he was looking for, what did he want? Was he just playing with me? Was he looking for some excitement? Was he planning to have his fun then toss me aside, did he even know what the hell he was doing? Did he even know what love was? Because you don't tag any stipulations onto the end of *I love you*. You just don't.

My thoughts and emotions were completely tied up in knots by the time I knocked on the door of his townhouse on Beacon Hill. Through the door, I could faintly hear his cello...he was practicing the *Kol Nidrei* again and didn't stop. I knocked again a second time, but he obviously didn't hear me, because he didn't stop playing. I shifted on my feet, my emotions shifting from irritation that he wasn't answering the door to...what?

I couldn't put my finger on it, until I saw a woman walking down the street toward me, walking her dog, which was roughly the size and appearance of a Shetland pony. I felt my eyes dart away from her, and I knocked again, harder. I swallowed as I avoided the woman's eyes, trying to mute the confusion of my thoughts and feelings. Part of me was incredibly excited to be here, because I knew that while we'd practice, we'd likely be doing far more than that. But part of me was uncomfortable that I hadn't demanded clarity from him, that I hadn't insisted we explore exactly what those words meant when he said, *I am in love with you, but there's nothing I can do about it, and I'm sorry for that.* Because I kept asking myself what my friends would think, what my parents would think.

I shook my head as I finally raised a fist and slammed it into the door. I was almost ready to walk away. I felt like a stereotype, the young student with a crush on a professor, and it made me confused and ashamed and angry.

After all that knocking, I was startled when he finally stopped playing and I heard the bolts slide back. He opened the door and stood there for a second, his eyes glassy, his breathing heavy. He wore black jeans and a plain white t-shirt, and the faintest sheen of sweat made his forehead and neck reflect the sunlight.

For the barest fraction of a second he stared right through me, as if he didn't recognize me. Then his eyes darted to the woman across the street, then back to me. "You're late for your lesson," he said, loud enough for the woman to hear, then turned his back on me.

I wanted to hit him.

Instead, I followed him inside the house, closing the door behind me. All of my instincts were screaming at me to turn around and leave. He'd been hideously rude to me, and there was no reason for it. None at all. When his eyes darted to that woman and he'd spoken to me in the tone he had, he'd made it very clear. He was ashamed of me.

He turned back toward me when he neared his cello. It was a beautiful instrument, not the workmanlike one he normally carried at the Conservatory. This instrument was remarkable, and as he turned toward me, one of his hands moved over the curve of the instrument in a caress, the way a man touched a woman.

I wanted to be touched that way.

Wordless, I unsnapped the case for my flute and began assembling it, trying to still my confused thoughts.

"Shall we begin where we left off Friday?" he asked, softly.

I wanted to snort. Where *did* we leave off Friday? With his hand cupping my chin. With my entire body trembling in anticipation. With my emotions in tatters.

It was better to take the question literally. "Yes."

And so we began to play. And no matter the chaos in my head, the music was anything but muddled or unclear. For the next ninety minutes we played without pause, and with barely a word spoken between us. It was intense, emotional, and brutal. As the melody passed back and forth between us, sometimes alternating, sometimes in unison, our eyes repeatedly met, and each time I felt raw, as if he were stroking the bow across my soul instead of the strings of his cello.

For that hour and a half, I felt as connected to Gregory as I'd felt when we were making love. In truth, I felt as connected to him as I'd ever felt with *anyone*. What we created between the two of us was so much bigger than what either of us did alone. I literally felt the walls of my ego and isolation fall away, leaving me open, raw...and vulnerable. I felt ecstatic. Beautiful. In love.

Finally, he signaled enough. And as I placed my flute on its stand, he leaned his cello into his and abruptly walked out of the room. I flinched, my emotions suddenly going into a tailspin.

Not a word? Not a sign that he'd felt anything?

Tentatively, I followed him into the kitchen. He stood facing the center island, his arms trembling from the continuous exertion of our practice, his back to me.

I swallowed. I was afraid. I was afraid of what he might say right then. What was going through his mind? And so, slowly, I reached out and put my hand on his back, my fingers splayed out, feeling the tension in his shoulder and back muscles.

He abruptly turned toward me. "I don't know what I was thinking," he muttered.

"What?" I said. Stupidly.

"Savannah...you're a student. Can you imagine what it would do...my career...the Conservatory..."

I stared at him. Unable to move. Unable to think. He invited me over here to say *that*? "I see. Well..." I cleared my throat and took a deep breath. "I'll, uh, just be on my way then. I'll see you later this week, right? Wednesday? Let's go back to the practice rooms, though, if you don't mind."

I hurried over to where my flute stood on its stand.

I quickly disassembled it and put it in its case without drying out the inside first. I would do it later. Right now, I needed to get the hell out of Gregory Fitzgerald's house without bursting into tears.

"Savannah, where are you going? We haven't finished." I couldn't decipher if his tone had changed to one of arrogance again, or if it had remained the same this whole time and I'd become deaf to it. Either way, it infuriated me.

"We *are* finished. I'll see you Wednesday." Brushing past him and racing to the door and down the stairs, I mumbled, "I can't believe I was so stupid..."

I grinned just slightly, imagining how up in arms he must feel to have a pissed off woman fleeing his apartment, on the brink of causing a scene. Gregory doesn't *do* scenes. The grin didn't last long though, as the weight of what I was actually feeling pressed down on my shoulders.

"Savannah, *wait*." It wasn't a yell, but his tone was commanding, sending chills down my spine.

I didn't stop. He didn't *get* to give me commands. I couldn't turn around and face him. Not like this. He'd just made it very clear that what we were doing was an inconvenience. Some sort of a fling. Nothing that matched what I felt for him. He'd told me in Lenox that he was in love with me. And I believed him. Shit. I believed him, when all he wanted was to fool around with me behind closed doors. How did I fall into the pathetic professor/student stereotype? *God.*

Shit.

After a few minutes, and rounding my second corner, his footsteps were no longer following me. Looking over my shoulder I found nothing but an empty sidewalk. I'd taken the back way around his block and was now at the end of Mt. Vernon St., taking a left onto West Cedar, the school in my sights.

I would ask Marcia to just do the piece with me for my recital. She'd love it. She was a little disappointed when I told her Gregory had offered to play with me, but as a musician she understood that he'd be able to pull my best out of me. Except for now. All he was able to pull out of me today was tears and the feeling of being cheap. Used. Part of some lonely musician's premature mid-life crisis.

"Savannah! Stop!"

I did. Because it took me by surprise to see Gregory Fitzgerald running toward me. Running. I'd never seen him run, because he's too important for things like rushing around. The world waits for him. Or, so he thinks.

As soon as it registered it was him, I walked faster. Not quite running, because I didn't want to cause a scene. He caught up to me as I was about to turn left and make a break for the school. Wrapping his long fingers firmly around my upper arm, he spun me around. The force of the physics jam-up of our differing directions of movement caused us to slam into each other. His other hand grabbed my other shoulder and we stood there, unmoving, apart from our ragged breathing.

"What do you want?" I looked right into his eyes, not wanting to allow him respite from the hurt I knew would be washing through them.

People passed by on either side of us, hurrying to their appointments, classes, work, wherever. They had no idea I was staring into the eyes of the person I'd fallen unwillingly in love with. The person who held my heart in their hands. The person who'd just broken it by dismissing me so easily. So coldly.

"I'm sorry. That came out wrong back at my place. I didn't...I didn't want you to leave, Savannah. I just...this is new territory for me."

"For *you?* Ah, yes, so you assume I've been down this road before. That screwing professors is just *something I do*." I pulled back, wanting to sink through the sidewalk.

"Damn it, Savannah," he huffed through clenched teeth, "that's *not* what I meant." His jaw beat against his cheek like a bass drum as he considered his next words. Carefully, and so only I could hear him, he said, "I'm madly in love with you, Savannah. Madly. I can't remember when it started, or how we ended up *here*, but I love you. It makes no sense, it's incredibly risky, and, for the life of me, I just don't care. I froze up back at my place, and I'm sorry. I've just never felt like this before. About anyone."

I relaxed a little, exhaling as I rested my forehead on his chin. Tilting my head back up, I saw his eyes were soft as he looked over my face expectantly.

"I love you, too, Gregory. And I don't care, either."

And right there, in broad daylight, on the corner of West Cedar and Acorn St., Gregory Fitzgerald pulled me into a deep, knee-weakening kiss.

And the world disappeared.

Chapter 17

SAVANNAH

AN HOUR LATER I returned to my dorm room. Breathless, and with weak legs, I'd walked around the block once to calm down after Gregory gave me a slow grin and turned to walk back to his place. He loved me. He said it. Again. I believed him because I had no reason not to. I loved him, too, and we were both keenly aware of the catastrophic risk we were taking. Turns out the Tin Man had a heart after all, and right there on the sidewalk he gave it to me. Risks and all.

"Well...you're glowing," Marcia deadpanned as I closed the door to our dorm and leaned my back against it.

"Mm-hmm." I nodded, biting my lip as I fought off a foolish grin.

"I take it things went, uh, well at his place?" The way she arched her eyebrow caused me to blush even deeper.

I shook my head and made my way to sit next to her on her bed. "Not like that, Marcia. Jesus. We *do* practice, you know..."

"Uh-huh, in between heavy make out sessions?"

My smile faded as I looked to the floor.

"Hey," she nudged me, "I'm just playing around. Not judging. I think it's great...as long as you're being careful."

We *had* been careful, apart from that kiss on the busy Boston sidewalk an hour before. And Boston was a big city. No one has time to look around. For once, I was grateful for that.

"We are being careful, Marcia. No one sees—"

"I don't mean just that, Savannah. I mean with your heart. I know he's said he's in love with you. And, *believe me*, if there was anyone on this planet that I would choose to thaw that frozen excuse for a soul of his it would be you, but just...be careful, okay? I don't want you to get hurt."

I gave her a quick hug. "Thanks, Marcia." I slid off her bed and bounced over to mine, picking up my phone.

"You should staple that thing to your forehead. It was ringing off the hook before you came back."

As I scrolled through the missed calls, my smile faded, and I'm sure my glow dimmed to a panicked pallor. I had nine missed calls—all from Madeline's office.

"What?" Marcia asked, her eyebrows moving together.

I shook my head in confusion as I dialed Madeline's number.

"Madeline White." She answered on the first ring, sounding less than calm.

"Madeline, it's Sav—"

"Savannah, where the hell are you?" Her clipped, anxious tone set my heart racing.

"I'm...in my dorm..."

"Have you been there all afternoon?"

Swallowing hard, I shook my head as I answered, "No, why?"

"Come to my office. Now." With that, she hung up. Madeline never used a tone like that.

Marcia never moved her eyes from the scene. "What's going on?"

I cleared my throat. "That was, uh, Madeline." Slowly, I stood and dropped my phone into my backpack and slid the straps over my shoulders.

"Everything okay?"

"Yeah," I lied. "She just needs to see me right away. See you later."

There's no way...

I whispered that to myself over and over on my short walk to Madeline's office. There was a way, however, and it was written all over her face as soon as I closed her office door behind me. She was standing cross-armed in front of her desk, leaning against it, not blinking. She didn't look angry. Worse. She looked disappointed.

"I thought it was just the one kiss." She cut right to the chase and I had no defenses. No excuses.

"I..."

"Damn it, Savannah, right on the street?" she yelled.

"Who—"

"Janna Wilson. And, probably her entire class since you chose the end of a period to make out with a professor in front of the school. What were you thinking? What was *he* thinking? Do you know what this could do to his career?" Madeline ran a hand through her hair, and I sat in the chair across from her, resting my forehead on my hands.

"Shit," I whispered.

Janna Wilson was a sophomore flute player. I guess I should have been thankful she called our instructor, rather than absolutely anyone else. But gratefulness was hard to pick up off the floor, what with my dignity scattered all around it and all.

"It was just a kiss, Madeline, I swear. We're not sleeping together. At least, not since school started again. We've just been working on the Assobio piece." I said it as if, somehow, this would erase the gross breach in ethics we'd committed. More than once, whether anyone was watching or not.

In the several second silence that followed, my mind raced through all of the best and worst case scenarios. Best case? Only Janna, and now, Madeline knew. Worst case...worst case was that Gregory would find out people saw us. He would completely lose it. Madeline gently placed her hand on my shoulder.

"I didn't realize...you slept with him, Savannah?" She shook her head then spoke in a firm, clear voice. "This has to stop. Whatever the hell it is, it has to stop. Find another cellist to help you prepare your recital piece. Do not, under any circumstances take any classes of his next semester, and cut off contact with him altogether. That's all you can do at this point to prevent a mess."

"For him," I murmured.

"What?" When I looked up, I found Madeline looking confused.

"A mess for him, you mean. There's never a mess for a student in a situation like this. You just said it. Do I know what this could do to his career? Of course I know. You and Gregory operate in a completely different world than I do. I get it, Madeline. He's an elite musician. He's with the *Boston Symphony* and the *Conservatory* and there can't be any *scandal*." I repeated the emphasis, finding myself increasingly sarcastic with every word.

I stood, watching Madeline's mouth open and close a few times as she struggled to form a response.

Madeline spoke slowly. "I don't want you to get hurt. I've known Gregory a long time, and—"

"Exactly," I cut her off. "You've known him a long time, and he's one of your best friends. This isn't about me getting hurt, Madeline. It's about making sure your friend doesn't lose his job over some mistake with a student."

I knew Madeline cared about me. She'd been in my life for several years, often acting as a mother figure when mine couldn't be bothered to be around. And really, that's what I needed right now. I was no kid, and I hadn't needed a mother in a long time. But, sometimes a little understanding—a little care—makes all the difference in the world. What I needed was for her to understand that this could break my heart.

Instead, she was closing ranks.

In that moment, I'd never felt so isolated. I wasn't part of their world. No matter how welcoming they tried to be, or how encouraging they'd been, I wasn't one of them yet. One of the elite. Taking a quick glance around Madeline's office, I knew I never wanted to be. Not if it made others feel the way I was feeling.

"Savannah…" Madeline's shoulders sank in apparent defeat as I crossed back toward the door.

"Does he know yet? Gregory. Have you talked to him? Does he know that Janna saw?" Clenching my teeth, I gripped the door handle.

Madeline shot her eyes to the floor, without answering.

"Oh, of course," I scoffed. "James. Well…thanks." I clicked my tongue against my teeth once before taking a deep breath and leaving Madeline's office without further discussion.

Once out on the street, I retraced my steps on my way back to Gregory's home. I tried to breathe through the anger I felt simmering over Madeline's allegiance to the faculty over what I'd perceived over the last several years to be her care for me. She had no choice. If it came down to it, she'd have to side with Gregory.

If there were to be sides.

If this ever got out of hand.

It's going to be fine, I told myself. After all, *he* told me he loved me and *he* was the one who desperately kissed me on that sidewalk. We were adults in love. *We can work through this hiccup*, I thought.

I thought.

GREGORY

"AND A STUDENT that you've already dodged rumors about already, at that. Damn it, Gregory, what the hell?" James held his arms out, his face red with anger as we stood on the stairs in front of my house.

He'd met me on the stairs as I returned from chasing Savannah down.

Fuck.

Now James was making me answer for it.

"For God's sake, James, would you calm down? You're making a scene."

"I think you made enough of a scene for both of us, Greg." He clenched his jaw, and I started to panic just slightly. I'd never seen James so erratic before.

Looking side to side, I lowered my voice to an almost-whisper. "Back up a little for me. Who saw what, exactly?"

"A student of Madeline's who called her right away..."

As James gave the details about this girl who reported what she thought she saw to Madeline, my mind shifted to Savannah, and the desperation I felt as she fled my house.

Desperation causes people to make mistakes. To fail. There was no room in my life for failure.

"Okay, okay," I cut him off, waving my hand impatiently. "What do I do to fix this?"

"You cut off all contact with Savannah Marshall. Starting right this second."

The idea was preposterous. I was helping her with one of her recital pieces. We'd become close on a musicianship level, learning from each other as we practiced our piece together. All of that was secondary, evidenced by the fear rising through my chest. I loved her. I couldn't simply cut her off.

"That's irrational, James. I'm helping her with one of her recital pieces."

"She can find another cellist, James. I know you'd like to think you're the only one, but you're not," James scoffed.

"Won't that just work to confirm whatever rumors are floating about?" My pulse raced at the thought of never seeing Savannah again.

"It won't confirm them any more than making out with her in front of the school, Gregory. You've worked too hard for too long to let something like a fling with a student ruin everything for you. You could lose your job at the university and cause scandal for the orchestra. Not something either place, or you, need right now."

I had no other cards to play. No tricks left up my sleeve. Except one.

"I love her."

"Ha!" James let out a full-throated laugh. "Come on, Greg. You don't have to lie to me. You don't love anything but music, and you don't love anyone but yourself. You're a good guy, but we both know that relationships have never been a priority for you. Now is not the time to make them one. Especially not one with a student, Greg. You need to cut the shit. You're not in love with her. You're excited by her. Who wouldn't be? She's gorgeous. They're all gorgeous, Greg, and they're all talented. That's where it ends. *This* is where it ends. You need to stop seeing Savannah, starting immediately."

"I'm a goddamn adult, James. I've been in control of my own life for as long as I can remember, and I don't intend to have you standing on my stairs changing that now." Panic struck like lightning through my body at the thought of having to *end* things with Savannah. Whatever it was...it couldn't end.

James stepped up one stair so we were level. He spoke low and slow into my ear. "You'll lose everything, Gregory. Your position at the conservatory, for sure. While you'll stay in the orchestra, your reputation certainly won't. Think about it. Is she really worth all of that?"

She is.

"It's not as simple as that, James."

"Yes, it is, Gregory—"

"I love her!" My yell scattered a group of pigeons from the sidewalk in front of us.

"If you love her," James spoke carefully, "then release her from this. Think of how she'll be seen. Her senior year, as she's auditioning for symphonies, and she's fooling around with the principal cellist for the BSO? Come on, Greg, you don't want that stamp on her head as she starts off, do you?"

I set my hands on my hips and looked down. "Damn it..."

"You'll both be better off in the long run if you cut this off at the pass. But, you're already established in the community and she's not—"

" *I get it, James,*" I snapped. After a few seconds, I cleared my throat and nodded. "Okay. I'll end things with her. Today."

I had no choice. He was right.

"Just like that, huh?" Out of nowhere, Savannah's voice forced the full weight of what I'd just said onto my shoulders.

Shifting my gaze to the sidewalk, I found Savannah standing wide-eyed with her arms hanging loosely at her sides. Staring at me. Staring at the space between us that was filled with the words I'd just spoken designed to protect both of us from what everyone *else* would view as simply an affair.

"James," I asked, never breaking Savannah's stare, "can you give us a moment?"

"Uh..." James looked back and forth between me and Savannah, mouth hanging open.

Savannah addressed him, looking at me the entire time. "That won't be necessary, James." Her face was like stone; the only evidence of life coming from her was in the trembling of her voice.

"Savannah." I jogged down the stairs to meet her.

She took a deliberate step back and held up her hand. "Stay away from me."

At that she turned slowly away and marched with a stone-like cadence down the sidewalk, away from me.

I stood there, waiting for her to come back. Waiting for her to change her mind.

She never did.

Part Two

Five Years

Later

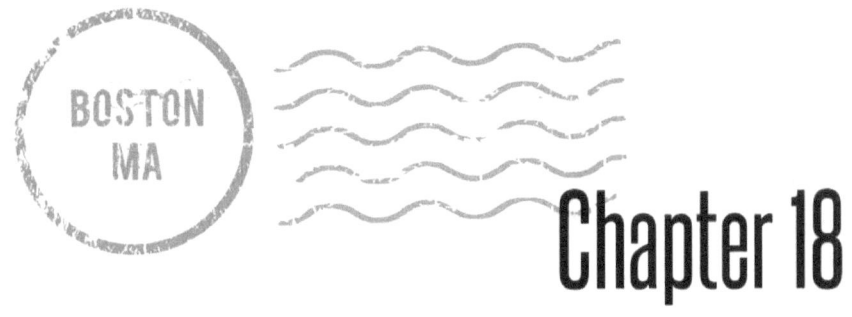

Chapter 18

SAVANNAH

THE SOFT STRAINS of Antonio Vivaldi played in the background. Men and women spilled out onto the lawn in their gowns and tuxedos, as the wait staff hurried here and there delivering champagne and caviar. I held a glass of Riesling in my left hand as my eyes scanned the crowd.

I wasn't seeking out anyone in particular. It was actually just the opposite. Until that morning in the cathedral, it had been more than five years since I'd seen Gregory Fitzgerald. Five years I'd spent mostly in Europe, living a life marked by travel and performances instead of a home and stability. A life much like my mother had, a life that sometimes felt amazing and sometimes felt desolate.

A few days ago, I'd left Moscow. The season was over for the Bolshoi Ballet, where I was first chair, and I was unsure of my plans to return. I thought maybe I could finish my final year of college and find a job teaching music somewhere, maybe in a high school near Philadelphia.

But who was I kidding? The lure of my musical career pulled me back every time I tried to walk away.

So here I was in Boston attending the wedding of my mentor Madeline, and James, Gregory's best friend. It was a beautiful ceremony, in Boston's largest Catholic cathedral, and *of course* Gregory was there, standing at the front of the wedding party as best man to his long time colleague and friend. At one point Gregory's eyes swept the congregation, and against my will I shrunk down in my seat a little, ducking my head behind a large man who sat in the pew in front of me. I didn't think he saw me. I didn't particularly want him to.

I shook my head, scoffing a little at myself. After all, while Gregory hurt me, badly, it had been more than five years. Five years was plenty of time to get over the rejection I felt as he effortlessly dismissed his feelings for me on the stone steps of his townhouse on Beacon Hill.

Five years was plenty of time to get over what was nothing more than infatuation in the first place. After all, Gregory was a selfish ass. The issue wasn't that he hadn't loved me. The issue was that he hadn't loved me enough to fight for me. Or to even really admit his feelings for me to James, who pushed him to cut off contact with me.

"Excuse me...you're Savannah Marshall, right?"

I blinked in surprise. I'd been lost in my thoughts as I stood there thinking of Gregory and hadn't noticed the woman approach. Cynthia Dillinger. Clarinet, and in my year at the conservatory. We hadn't been close, but it was nice to see a familiar face.

"Yes...Cynthia, right?"

Cynthia smiled. A fake smile, plastered on just like her makeup. "Oh, you remember me! I'm so pleased."

"Of course I remember you." I sipped my wine and returned the smile.

She turned her head away from me, scanning the crowd, then glanced back at me, and her tone of voice wasn't precisely unfriendly, but it wasn't all that warm either. "I wasn't so sure you would, I was never part of the *conservatory elect.*"

I raised an eyebrow. "I don't know what you mean."

She looked at me skeptically. "Of course you do. You...Nathan...Yon Park...the professors fluttered around you and your *talent*. The rest of us were rabble in comparison."

I could have tried to deny what she was saying, but there was nothing I could offer. I'd seen it happen in the years that led to me entering the conservatory, and it was no different when I was there. While I didn't notice the extra attention while I was a student, the second I stepped away I could see that I was being groomed for one of the Big Five, and no one bothered to ask if that was what I'd wanted.

Uncomfortable with the direction of the conversation, I shifted the subject. "What ever happened to Yon?"

"London Symphony." Her eye roll highlighted five years of resentment over her perceived place on the conservatory totem pole.

"Oh...I see. I've lost touch with a lot of people."

She gave me a speculative look and said, "I heard you went off to Europe right after you quit school."

I nodded. "I took about a year studying folk music in Eastern Europe, and I've mostly been touring since." I was understating it. I hadn't gone and studied folk music in Eastern Europe. I'd wandered, mostly by bus and train, from town to town. Meeting local musicians and learning their music. Busking in subway stations in Prague. I'd learned more about music in just a few months wandering around than I did in ten years of formal classes and lessons. I learned more about myself, too.

I hadn't left because of the sex, the kissing, or because of Gregory's stark rejection. Not even because of my mother, or my confusion about my goals in life. None of those things, or maybe all of them. It took several months of me trying to tease out my motivations for leaving the place I'd dreamed about since I was a girl, to realize that sometimes life just takes you in a certain direction whether you're on board or not. Motivations or not.

Cynthia smirked a little and said, "I will say, it made our senior year super interesting. There were rumors that you and Fitzgerald snuck off together."

"I can't imagine why," I said, running my hand over my navy eyelet dress.

"He disappeared the same day you did. Although he turned up with the BSO a week later."

I tilted my head and said, "What, did he take leave or something? What do you mean *disappeared?*"

She gave me a stare. "He stopped teaching. Surely you knew that."

I took a sharp breath, surprised. But maybe not. He hated teaching anyway. Though I wondered how he managed to pay for that giant monument to his ego...the one-of-a-kind cello he toted around as if it held the secrets to his soul.

It probably did.

"Savannah!"

The shout startled me, and immediately I felt a smile spread across my face.

Nathan!

"Excuse me," I said, and walked away from Cynthia without another word.

A moment later I was laughing as Nathan wrapped me into a warm hug. We squeezed each other tightly, and unexpectedly I began to choke up, tears flooding my eyes. I hadn't seen Nathan in years. We'd talked on the phone, emailed, and chatted online, of course. But I missed looking into his eyes and watching his dimples. I missed being hugged.

"Christ," he whispered. "I missed you so much."

I leaned back and looked up into his eyes. "Where were you earlier? I looked for you at the ceremony."

He shook his head. "Flight got delayed."

"We're going out for drinks this weekend. I need to spend some time with you."

He slipped his hands down to my shoulders. "How long are you in town?"

I shrugged. "I'm off for the summer. No firm plans."

He blinked then said, "We need to talk then. I've got a short term suggestion anyway."

Over his shoulder, I saw Madeline chatting with a small group of women. "Okay, let's talk later. We need to catch up, anyway, but let's go say hi to Madeline."

He nodded and fell into step beside me as I approached Madeline's group.

"She looks so happy," Nathan whispered as we neared Madeline. "Do you know how long she and James have been together?"

I chuckled a little. "I do. They started dating the summer I worked at Tanglewood with Madeline."

That dimple appeared as Nathan laughed, too. "That must have been interesting."

"That whole summer..." I trailed off, shaking my head at what I once thought was the best summer of my life. After all, a man I highly respected and found incredibly attractive told me he was falling in love with me.

It wasn't so great, after all.

"You okay? Is he here?" Nathan's eyes surfed the crowd briefly.

"He is," I nodded, "but I've been able to avoid him so far."

Despite the rocky road our friendship endured during Nathan's last year at the conservatory, I hadn't thought twice about showing up at his Chicago apartment unannounced a day after I quit school. I drove all night from Boston to Chicago, showing up at his apartment at around 3:30 a.m. Though I could see "I told you so" wired through his tense jaw as my chin quivered through the details of Gregory, he never said it.

Not once. He just handed me a pillow and a blanket and told me to get some sleep. Said I looked like crap. I left for Europe a week later.

"Madeline." I gently placed my hand on her lace-covered shoulder as Nathan and I stood behind her. Her long ginger hair was held in place at the base of her neck with a startlingly beautiful crystal clip. The skirt of her off-white gown rustled as she turned around.

"Savannah! Nathan!" Madeline hugged us at the same time and kissed our cheeks. "I'm thrilled to see the two of you. I wasn't sure you'd be able to make it," she said, looking at me through green eyes glittered with happiness.

"I wouldn't miss it, Madeline. I'm back for the summer." Even if I didn't know what my plans were from here, I could play the part.

Madeline nodded with a slight smile on her lips. Her eyes were warm as she took in my words. Reassuring, somehow. I would be just fine.

She turned to Nathan, asking him about how things were with the symphony. They discussed the unsteady finances of American orchestras as I tuned them out, feeling like a stranger to the conversation, and fixed my eyes on a familiar woman just across the group. It took a moment to recognize her, because her hair was now dyed almost black, and when I'd known her it was the color of honey.

Oh. Karin Briggs.

It was the woman from the conservatory's administrative office that Gregory casually dated during the semester I was his student. Her hair was cut into a reverse bob that fell just beneath her chin. She looked stunning in her floor-length chocolate colored gown.

When she caught me studying her I gave a polite smile, but she didn't return it. She seemed to pale a little, if anything, and I looked over my shoulder to see why, but found nothing there. Meeting her eyes again, she grinned a sort of half grin that did little to make one feel warm. Confused, I sipped the rest of my wine, set it on the tray of a passing waiter, and retrieved another one.

It was already shaping up to be a long night before I looked past Karin and saw Gregory Fitzgerald approaching from behind her. I'd seen him already at the church, but his proximity at the moment was disconcerting. My pulse raced as I realized it would do no good to try to hide. He would see me in a few seconds and that would be that.

His jet-black hair had just barely visible flecks of grey scattered throughout it. His tightly shaven goatee displayed a little more grey, but not much. He was devastatingly handsome in his tux—the only man I'd ever seen that looked comfortable in one.

Gregory handed Karin a drink and she turned slightly sideways as she sipped her drink and placed her hand awkwardly on his arm. I opened my mouth, contemplating saying *hello* before he realized I'd been watching him this whole time, but shut it as the movement of Karin's hand arrested my attention. It was her left hand. Adorned with an exquisite diamond solitaire, easily a carat given it looked large from several feet away, and a platinum band saddled up behind it on her slender finger.

I'd long since gotten over Gregory. I'd moved on. But all the same, I shut my mouth, clenching my teeth as my eyes moved over to his hand, which showcased a matching, though wider, platinum band.

Gregory and Karin. Married.

GREGORY

I THREADED MY WAY back through the wedding guests with our drinks in hand. I'd been unreasonably irritated all day, so I'd welcomed even a few minutes of space to go stand in line at the open bar and get drinks.

Halfway back I was stopped in place by Lillian James from the Pops, who wanted to ask me a question which was both work related and trivial. I answered her question, at the same time brushing her off a little. We were at a wedding...it was hardly the time.

After I turned away from her, I continued making my way through the crowd. This was a huge wedding, far larger than mine and Karin's had been. I'd insisted on a smaller, more private ceremony, though I think she'd have preferred the same sort of huge, lavish party as Madeline and James. This wasn't my style, an event that required a huge hall to house four hundred or more guests. Bluntly, I was feeling claustrophobic as I finally made it through the crowd and slid into place beside my wife.

"Here you are," I said, passing her the glass of wine.

She took the drink, then pressed her left hand into my arm, a touch that felt oddly awkward and uncomfortable. I took a too long sip of my gin and tonic and looked up, right into the eyes of Savannah Marshall.

I froze in place, involuntarily falling into Savannah's huge brown eyes as she took me in. She was standing right there in front of me, while Karin's grip on my upper arm squeezed a little bit tighter.

Savannah's lips parted when I met her eyes. Her hair was piled high on her head, leaving her graceful, beautiful neck bare. She wore a deep blue sleeveless dress, which accentuated every curve of her body, eyelets giving a tantalizing and constantly shifting guess at what might lie underneath.

She was...what? Twenty-six now? Twenty-seven, maybe, but I didn't know when her birthday was. She no longer had the too-young, intentionally challenging look of a teenager trying to prove her independence. Now she looked like a confident, professional woman. A bit of color touched her cheeks as her eyes met mine, and I swallowed as her tongue brushed against her lips. Running just over that tiny scar.

I couldn't see it from this distance, but I could still feel it.

Silence fell over the little group, and I don't know if that was because they saw the sudden tension or if I just didn't hear them anymore.

"Gregory," she said. I was instantly steeping in her rich voice.

I swallowed. "Savannah."

Karin's grip on my arm tightened. Which was odd, all things considered. Savannah and I had a frenzied love affair years ago. But that was long over.

"It's a pleasure to see you again," I said, trying to maintain an even tone.

Savannah huffed softly through her nose as her raspberry colored lips twitched into a quirky grin. "Yeah, you, too. Congratulations." She raised her glass just slightly as she nodded toward Karin and me. Her forced smile failed to light up her gorgeous eyes.

Karin's grip on my arm loosened just slightly. "Thank you," she answered Savannah as my mouth inexplicably ran dry.

"Yes," I cleared my throat and raised my glass back, "thank you."

As Madeline turned back around, she raised her eyebrow in my direction but turned away quickly again as more people approached her with congratulations. Nathan Connors appeared out of nowhere behind Madeline. Maybe he was standing there the whole time. It was hard for me to focus on anything besides the sinful curve of Savannah's breasts in that dress.

"Ready to find our table? They're about to serve dinner." She kept her eyes trained on me as he spoke. Finally his eyes followed. Then darkened.

"Yeah," she said, finally breaking her gaze from me, "let's go." She turned away from me and walked side-by-side with Nathan to their table. They didn't hold hands, and he didn't put his hand on the small of her back.

Foolish boy.

"Gregory?" Karin's irritated voice cut through my thoughts.

"Yes." I couldn't enunciate properly as I tried to find Savannah in the periphery of my vision. Of my past.

"I *said*, shall we sit for dinner?" She spoke through her teeth as her eyes unabashedly glared at the empty space created by Savannah's exit.

"Yes. Let's." I took Karin's hand and led her to our table.

"Your hand is sweating," she said, her voice sounding distant.

I shrugged. "It's hot in here."

Karin rolled her eyes as I pulled her chair out for her. Needing to change the course of our evening and fast, I leaned over her as she sat and pressed my lips softly against her cheek.

"You look absolutely stunning tonight, darling," I whispered into her ear.

The corners of her eyes creased as a large smile took residence in her face. "Thank you, Gregory."

Dinner went smoothly and the cake was served with mediocre coffee. I didn't finish chewing my second bite before Sadie Daniels, oboe, turned to Karin and said, "So, when are you two going to start *your* family?" As she rubbed her growing belly, I swallowed a mouthful of the bitter coffee to cover up nearly choking.

Not this conversation. Not here.

"Soon," Karin answered confidently as her hand glided over to my thigh underneath the crisp champagne colored linen tablecloth.

"Don't look so excited, Gregory," Sadie teased. Tasteless.

"Well," I was honest, "we haven't discussed it much, really. What with our work schedules and traveling this summer—"

"Traveling?" Karin dropped her hand and pulled her head back a bit.

"Yes, for the Big Five Tour," I said matter-of-factly. Because it was fact.

American orchestras had been losing money at an alarming rate since 2000. Each year, it seemed, there was another long-standing orchestra ending their year in the red for the first time in decades, or, ever. The Big Five decided to take initiative on the matter by forming an orchestra made up of members from each orchestra, and touring the United States. While the goal was to raise awareness of and increase excitement for classical music, the underlying goal was to gain new donors to keep this cornerstone of American arts above water.

"I thought we decided you were going to abstain from that tour." Karin worked to keep her voice even. "James and Madeline aren't participating."

I took a deep breath and tried to diffuse a potential scene. "James and Madeline have just gotten married, Karin. They'll be on their honeymoon when the tour starts in two weeks."

I agreed to participate in the tour before checking with Karin first. The idea of checking with another person for professional decisions still seemed foreign to me, even after three years of marriage. And then Karin declared during the winter that while the BSO was on break for the season in the summer, we would start trying to have a baby.

A baby.

Something she wanted without a doubt, and something we hadn't discussed much before getting married. Any time

I tried to have a rational discussion with her about it, she became defensive and overly emotional. Those discussions were short.

The discussion about my joining the tour during what was deemed by Karin to be a very important summer in our marriage, however, was anything but short. We'd just discussed it this morning, too. I told her this was beyond being important for *my* career, that it was important for music as a whole. Not something I expected her to fully understand, not being a musician herself. But something I thought she could accept. Staring at her in the middle of our friends' wedding, with all of our tablemates' eyes on us, however, it was apparent she did not, in fact, understand.

As the band cued up and the dancing started, I saw the blue eyelet dress twirling on the far end of the dance floor and I had to get out of there.

"Excuse me." I set my napkin on my chair, adjusted my bowtie, and headed for the bar. Karin wasn't far behind me.

"You can't run away from this discussion, Gregory," she snapped as I waited for the bartender to mix my drink.

"And you can't run away from my decision, Karin. This tour is important."

"To you!" Her voice was louder than I cared for.

"To music," I shot back through gritted teeth. "If you don't understand that..."

"What? If I don't understand you placing the tour...this *life* over *our* life? Over starting a family?" Her blue eyes filled with tears.

I leaned in close, not wanting to invite an audience. "Karin, we never discussed having children. I'm open to the discussion, but not open to being forced into fatherhood."

Her eyes cast to the floor for several seconds. When they looked up they were void of tears. Of any emotion at all. "I'm going home. I trust you can find your way there when you're finished up here?" She looked past my shoulder waiting for an answer.

I nodded. "Yes." At my response her eyes shot to mine as if she were shocked by my reply.

"Wow," she sighed, "you have no fight left in you for anything but music, do you?" She picked up her purse and made her way toward the exit.

"Sir?" the bartender called out, handing me my drink.

"Thanks," I mumbled, shoving a twenty into his tip jar before searching for a way outside that wasn't the way Karin went. I needed fresh air.

Leaning against a rail and taking a long sip of my gin, I thought about this summer. I was going. There wasn't much else to think about. Some colleagues I'd worked with during my days as a student at the conservatory who'd gone on to other orchestras would be participating, and it would be good to catch up. Before I could give it much more thought, Savannah's melodic laughter burst through the French doors opposite where I was standing. She and Nathan were fanning themselves and looking up at the starlit sky. This afforded me an extra second to take in the way her neck glistened under the moonlight before they saw me.

"Oh!" Savannah seemed startled as her smile faltered on her lips. "Sorry." She looked around the open space.

"No need to apologize. I'm just getting some air."

I didn't like the way Nathan Connors was eyeing me. It likely had to do with whatever Savannah told him about the last time we saw each other face-to-face, as I recklessly dismissed our relationship on the steps of my townhouse. I wondered if Savannah had received any of the emails I sent her in those first few weeks. She didn't reply to any of them. Once Madeline told me Savannah had left for Europe, I stopped emailing. Putting an ocean between us was signal enough. She wanted nothing to do with me.

"Can you give us a minute?" Savannah turned toward Nathan, who looked shocked at her request.

Not as shocked as I felt.

"Savannah..." Nathan cocked his head to the side as he took a frustrated breath.

"Nathan..." she retorted mockingly, mimicking his head tilt.

"You're impossible." He shook his head, gave her a playful smile, and headed inside without another word.

The click of the French doors shutting behind him lingered in the space between us, as she slowly turned around to face me. Her eyes were dark, longing, as she walked slowly toward me. My heart echoed the sound of her heels clicking against the paved patio as she walked toward me. Uneven steps. Uneven beats.

"I'm sorry I rushed off at the beginning of dinner," she started.

I waved my hand. "No worries." She laughed. Oh, her laugh. "What?" I asked.

"That thing you do with your hand. You do that when you're annoyed. You did that at my audition...and any time I came to your office."

"Any time you came into my office, Savannah, you were ready to argue points that didn't need arguing." I chuckled, sipping more of my drink, until the ice clinked against my teeth.

"Fair enough." She nodded. "How have you been? You and Karin, huh?" Her eyes were honest, endearing. With just a hint of the fire that sucked me in the first time I ever saw her.

"Yeah..."

"Everything okay?" She crossed her arms and took a step closer. Just close enough for me to smell the lilies.

"I'm sorry, Savannah," I blurted out as I set my glass down behind me and shoved my hands into my pockets.

She swallowed hard, her cheeks turning pink. "Gregory, you don't have to—"

"No," I stopped her, "I do. It was incredibly cruel of me to treat you the way I did that day. I thought at the time I was doing what was best for you, and for me...but you deserved better from me."

"Look," she cleared her throat and looked down for a moment before capturing me with her glistening gaze, "I didn't ask to speak with you so you could apologize. I wanted to tell you that I'm fine. Everything is fine and the past is in the past, okay?" She started to turn for the door.

"Savannah, wait." I reached out, taking hold of her hand.

She stopped and faced me again. Her lip was trembling slightly, and her eyes looked conflicted. She laced her fingers between mine. "What?"

"I..." I gently tugged her hand so she would take one more step toward me. My head was spinning, and I couldn't tell if it was from the gin or the feel of her hand in mine.

Our toes were touching and I stared into her eyes before my gaze fell to her cheeks, then her lips. The pull I felt to the woman standing before me was undeniable. Startling. It felt like we were standing on Madeline's porch five years ago. My lips parted as I fought to say something to get out of this. To get out of holding hands with Savannah at our friends' wedding.

Savannah bit her lip and gave a long sigh, leaning in so her mouth almost touched my ear. "You should go home to your wife, Gregory," she whispered before freeing her hand from mine and walking back inside without a backward glance.

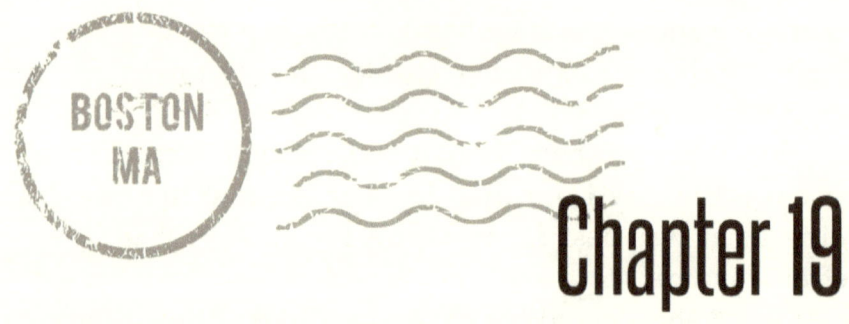

Chapter 19

GREGORY

WALKING HOME FROM checking in on James and Madeline's house, as they were off on their honeymoon, I found myself enjoying the silence. Peaceful silence. The kind of silence that allows you to hear the leaves hum the wind's song. Not the kind of dreadful emptiness that I knew awaited me at home.

Karin had never been one for the silent treatment. We actually hadn't fought much at all, until the night I came back from the wedding. She wanted to reopen the baby discussion, I told her that one a.m. simply wasn't the time, and I went to sleep. For three days I found myself watching the calendar, begging for the summer tour to start so I could escape the constant scrutiny.

Tossing my keys on the door upon entering my home, I saw Karin curled up on the couch in the formal living room, dabbing her eyes with a tissue. She seemed startled by my entrance and turned toward the south-facing window. Away from me. My chest felt heavy, seeing her in such a state. The silent anger I could handle. Hearing the sniffles of falling tears fill the space around her, however, I couldn't. She was beyond mad, now. She was hurting.

"Karin." I exhaled slowly and made my way to the couch, sitting gently next to her. She hadn't changed out of her pajamas yet, and her hair was snarled about her head.

"Leave me alone, Gregory. Please." Her voice shook as she rested her head on her knees.

Ignoring her, I placed my hand softly on her back.

"I *said* leave me alone," she repeated with no hesitation.

Removing my hand from her back, I clasped them in front of me, leaning forward so my elbows were resting on my knees. "I won't leave you alone, Karin. You're my wife and you're upset. I want to talk about whatever it is that's upsetting you enough to drape this place in silence for the last three days."

Karin chuckled softly, sardonically. "Three days of silence is too much for you, yet I'm supposed to smile and live with a ghost for the last five years?"

"I beg your pardon?"

"I could live with the idea of Savannah Marshall, Gregory. Her existence in the world, your history with her—"

"I have no history with Savannah, Karin," I lied.

"You still can't admit it! The top student at the conservatory leaves at the beginning of her senior year, and you resign within a week of that. Don't you *dare* tell me there's no history with you two, Gregory. Especially not after half of Glen Wild's fundamentals class saw you two making out on the street." With a petulant scoff, Karin leaned back and crossed her arms over her chest.

Taking a deep breath to keep my patience in check, I slowly faced Karin. "We've discussed my reasons for resigning from the conservatory. Those are also five years old. What I don't understand is what you mean by her *ghost*."

Wordlessly, Karin stood and walked over to the baby grand piano by the window, gliding her fingers over the glossy black wood before talking at the window.

"I'd heard the rumors, just like everyone else. But I thought they were simply rumors. You're a good man, Gregory, with strong ethics. I knew you'd never endanger your career by sleeping with a student. When you brushed me off in Lenox that summer, I thought that I was done with you. That you weren't interested in *anyone*, let alone me. You hadn't had a girlfriend since being in the conservatory yourself." Karin shrugged and turned toward me, leaning against the piano. "Then you kissed her. In the middle of Boston for all to see."

I swallowed hard, nodding. There was little I could do to refute that, especially given I never told her I'd slept with Savannah.

"Though you and I hadn't been on a date in several months by that point, it hurt me. The thought of you kissing Savannah—or anyone really. I'd cared a lot about you early on, and you just weren't interested in me."

Not knowing where she was going with this, I felt the need to stand and meet her at the Steinway that was hosting this discussion. "Karin, I love you..." I trailed off, taking her hands in mine.

"Then why haven't I ever had the Gregory Savannah Marshall got to have? The one who will go dancing without hours of persuasion? The one who will grab me on a busy street corner and kiss me like no one is watching?" My lips parted to retort, but she continued. "I get the ghost of you. Why that girl got that part of you no one had ever seen before, I'll never know..."

"Then why did you marry me?" I spit out distastefully.

"Because I love you!" Fresh tears spilled down her drained cheeks. "You're intelligent, passionate, talented...when we started dating again you said all the right things, did all the right things, and made me believe you'd changed. That you'd moved on from whatever it was that happened between you and Savannah." She shook her hands out of my hold and placed them on her hips, looking down.

I worked hard over the months after Savannah disappeared to regain my footing. To remind myself why I never got involved with anyone. It was too distracting to my career. Karin was safe, though. She understood my commitment to my craft and never questioned the long hours. She was patient and loving and didn't get in the way of my goals.

"What makes you think I haven't changed?" I asked, incredulously.

"The look on your face when you saw her at the wedding. You looked like you'd seen a ghost, and I realized I'd been living with one."

Frustrated at her accusations, I ran a hand through my hair and turned away, pacing to the other side of the living room. "Yes, it was surprising. I haven't seen or spoken to Savannah in five years, you know that. But for you to stand there and assert that the way I looked at her somehow disregards *our* entire relationship is foolish, Karin. I love you."

Karin's face changed. Calm, as she walked toward me, she looked up at me with wide eyes. "Then let's start a family, Gregory. Let's have a baby."

"Damn it, Karin!" I spoke through tightly clenched teeth.

She took a step back and furrowed her brow. "What?"

"You will *not* use this situation to emotionally blackmail me into having a baby with you." I turned quickly on my heels and headed for the kitchen to get a drink. And space.

Karin shouted after me as she followed. "Are you kidding me, Gregory? You think I'm *blackmailing* you?"

Slamming the refrigerator door shut after retrieving a bottle of water, I shouted, "Explain yourself, then. Explain how that senseless story about some student I kissed five years ago led to you asking me to concede to having children!"

Karin jumped. "*Concede?*" she shouted back. "That's what people do when they get married, Gregory. They get married and start a goddamn family!"

"No!" I slammed my fist on the granite island. "That's what people who want to have children do, Karin. People who discussed it while they dated, while they were engaged. We never discussed it! We discussed travelling and buying a second home somewhere..."

"You discussed it."

"What?" I asked, finally taking a sip of my water.

"*You* discussed those things, Gregory. You discussed travelling the world, hoping to maybe play with a symphony overseas for a time. *You* discussed buying a second home in the Berkshires. You never asked me what I thought of all of that. Or what I wanted. You put more thought into whether or not you were going to pick up lessons with that blind boy again than you did into fixing our marriage."

I shook my head violently. She *knew* I'd never felt equipped to teach Robert. "First of all, *that blind boy* has a name, and he's an accomplished musician and needs someone advanced to continue his lessons. Second. You agreed with what I was saying, Karin. You never spoke out against any of it. And, knowing what I wanted, you married me anyway, without ever mentioning your desire for children. What did you expect from me?"

Karin rolled her eyes. "I expected more. I expected a relationship." Contempt curled around her words as she looked through me.

"I don't have time for this, I have to practice." I sighed and left the kitchen, heading for my practice room.

"Excuse me? You're still considering going on this tour?" she shrieked.

I stopped abruptly and turned just as fast. "No," I spit out, "I'm not *considering* going. I am going. Practice starts in a few days and we're leaving at the end of next week and will be gone through June and July."

"You're a selfish bastard, you know that?" Her disdain for me was palpable.

Pinching the bridge of my nose, I sighed. "Perhaps you should stay at James and Madeline's house for a few days."

She gasped. "What did you just say?"

"We're not going to resolve this today, and I refuse to walk in this house every day feeling uncomfortable and looked down upon. James and Madeline will be out of town for the next two weeks. They're returning home a few days after I leave for the tour."

"I'm not leaving."

"This is my house, Karin."

"Oh fuck *off*, Gregory. This is *our* house. We're *married*." Karin never swore, and the conviction in her words irritated me.

"*Fine*. I'll go." Reaching into my practice room, I pulled out my cello case and walked to the front door.

"Just you and your cello, huh? Surprise, surprise." Karin didn't follow me down the hall. She leaned against the wall and watched me go.

Without engaging with her any further, I slammed the door behind me and made my way for James and Madeline's.

As soon as I settled into their living room, I set my iPod in the dock on their shelf and pressed play. Within seconds, I was playing Assobio a Jato along with the sounds of Savannah playing her flute during her brief senior year. We'd each recorded the other playing so we could practice in our spare time. Sometime after she left I moved my CD recording to my iPod, and this was the first time I pressed play.

Closing my eyes as I moved through each measure of the song, I watched Savannah's eyebrows pull together, strands of her golden hair falling into her face as she kept up with whatever tempo I set. I wanted to play harder and faster than this recording, but I stayed with Savannah, allowing her even tempo to wash over me, to calm the bitterness I felt toward Karin. *How dare Karin try to use her insecurities to guilt me into having children with her.*

Sweat formed across my brow and slid coolly down the side of my face as I was brought back into the practice rooms at the conservatory, where Savannah and I had stolen many kisses. Too many. Shaking my head slightly, I returned my thoughts to Karin. Perhaps I was unnecessarily cruel in suggesting she leave the house for a few days. I was the one with the issue. I was the one struggling with the idea of forming a family. Whether or not Karin could admit it now, this tour would give both of us time to cool off and reassess our goals. I was confident that by the time I returned in August, we would be able to start fresh, with clear expectations on moving forward.

As I neared the end of Assobio, the memory of Savanna's smile every time we successfully finished the piece left me breathless, and angry. I set down my cello and walked to the iHome, roughly tore my iPod out of it, and threw it against the wall with a growl.

Walking over to where it lay on the ground, I knelt down and picked it up. Thumbing back to Savannah's recording, I deleted it as quickly as I could.

SAVANNAH

"Are you sure about this, guys? I feel a little weird about it." Sitting across from Nathan and Marcia at a tiny coffee shop in Andover, I struggled over the decision to join the Big Five tour for the summer.

"What the hell is holding you back?" Marcia chuckled. "You're just home from Moscow and have zero plans for the summer. At least this will give you something to focus on. And keep you playing."

"Can't you come, too?" I looked to her pleadingly.

"I'd love to, you know that. I would have auditioned for it if I hadn't already committed to so many private lessons this summer. They start right when school ends." Marcia was a middle school band director in Andover and seemed to absolutely love her job.

Nathan feigned hurt. "What? I'm not enough?"

I laughed. "No, I'm thrilled you're going. But...that's the thing. Like Marcia just said, *she* would have to audition. Madeline said I could just...*take* her spot."

I shook my head thinking about the brief conversation I had with Madeline the day after her wedding. She told me the organizers of the tour would be more than happy to have me in her spot, especially since I played for the Bolshoi Ballet, and they knew I had maintained my training.

"Come on," Nathan cocked his head to the side the way he always did when he was being sweet, "don't you think the organizers— the ones from Boston anyway—are thrilled to get their hands on you again?"

"What does that mean?" I asked, biting the inside of my cheek.

Marcia smiled. "Savannah."

"Marcia," I shot back playfully.

"They love you," she continued warmly. "Not just because you're amazingly gifted, though that's a huge part of it. When you left it was like the star quarterback walking away from a zillion-dollar NFL deal, or something. You could have had any symphony you wanted, and they were all just waiting for you to decide."

I sighed, recalling the many emails and letters I'd received over the last five years asking me to come practice with, or audition for, orchestras from Boston to San Francisco. I ignored some, politely declined the others. That wasn't what I wanted then.

"We're not saying they're going to spend the summer scouting you, Savannah," Nathan entered. "But if you take yourself seriously on this tour, you could very well have your pick all over again…if that's what you want."

"All right, all right, I'll do it." I smiled, butterflies forming in my stomach over performing with the most elite musicians in America.

"Yes!" Nathan high-fived me. It would be great to spend the summer catching up with him, as well. "It's basically just going to be the youngest members of the symphonies anyway, since we're the ones who are going to lead them in a few short years. So, we'll be in good company. *And* you'll finally be able to meet Christine."

Christine was Nathan's girlfriend of the last six months. She was in the Chicago symphony with him. She graduated from Eastman the same year Nathan graduated from NEC and was one of two harp players with the Chicago Symphony. Nathan seemed fully smitten.

I smiled. "That'd be great. Well," I sighed, "I suppose I should call the number Madeline left me and get organized. Nate, you're not staying in the hotel for the next two weeks are you? We should just stay at Madeline's. She said to call her if we wanted to, and she'd cancel her house sitter."

Marcia played with her napkin as she spoke. "You're not going to stay with—"

"No," I cut her off. She and Nathan shared a sideways glance. "I don't want to talk about that right now, okay?"

"Okay," she shrugged, "let's talk about what we want to get at the liquor store this afternoon. You two aren't staying at Madeline's *or* in a hotel. You guys can stay with me. I own a house, remember? I'm all grown up and stuff."

We all laughed. For the first time in several years, aside from my experience with Bolshoi, I was feeling excitement over my prospects come the end of the summer.

Several hours later, I was sitting at a table outside the Hyatt Boston Harbor, overlooking the water. A refreshing breeze blew through my hair as I sipped a Chilean Sauvignon Blanc, watching tiny boats go back and forth across the harbor. From this distance, the city looked beautiful. Peaceful and inviting, taking in the view of Boston from this distance reminded me why I'd chosen NEC over Juilliard, despite the enticing scholarship package they'd offered. Even Nathan left his beloved Chicago to attend here. The proper blend of American history and contemporary excitement, I'd once hoped to call Boston home. Despite my best efforts, it was impossible for me to separate Boston from Gregory Fitzgerald. I was gazing at the place my heart was broken.

"Savannah, darling, we could have met somewhere *in* the city." My mother rushed to her seat, fifteen minutes late for our date, calling her drink order to a passing waitress.

Dressed in a sleeveless black dress that had a pencil skirt, which accentuated her thin frame, she wore bright red pumps and a matching patent belt round her tiny waist. I'd say it was a bit much for afternoon drinks, but she'd passed her expectations of style onto me, and I'd begun to follow them over the last several years—especially during my time in Moscow. I played with the bottom of my grey skirt as I addressed her.

"You know I love the view here, Mother." I sighed, drinking more of my wine.

"How was James and Madeline's wedding?"

"Lovely," I replied with a smile.

"Gregory Fitzgerald...was he there?"

"I'm not sure why you have to look at me that way," I commented on her accusing gaze. "But, yes, he was. He was the Best Man."

It was interesting that five years later, meeting in Boston brought Gregory to my mother's mind as well. She had been less than pleased to find out about what happened between Gregory and me, though she only knew about the kiss. When I fled Boston and went to Nathan's, she pulled it out of me on the phone one night. Incensed, she threatened to call the school and have him fired before I barely convinced her that he wasn't the reason I was leaving. I'm not sure if she bought it, because I couldn't tease out all of the reasons I was leaving myself, but she bought it enough to back down on her threats.

"Hmm," she paused briefly to plaster on her stage smile while accepting her Manhattan from the waitress, "did you speak with him?"

"Mother," I sighed, "it was five years ago. Move on. I have."

"You don't sound so convinced—"

"For God's sake, *Mother*, drop it!" My voice came out a bit louder than I, or my mother cared for, and the people at the next table looked up. Embarrassed, I picked up my wine glass and took a large gulp, shifting my gaze to the tiny white caps bobbing through the water.

"So, you've decided to join that Big Five tour, I hear?" my mother inquired after an acceptable length of silence.

My jaw failed me and dropped just enough for her to arch her eyebrow. "How did you..." I trailed off, not really need-

ing an answer. Her connections in the American music indus-
try ran so deep, it was hardly surprising that she found out
about a decision I'd made only hours before. "Never mind."

"And am I to assume that since we're having this conversation here, and not in Moscow, you've chosen to leave Bolshoi?"

I nodded without trying to disguise my exaggerated exhale. "We're on break for the summer, Mother. I'm not sure
what my plans are."

She clicked her tongue against her teeth and shook her
head, looking across the harbor with a sour look on her face.
"You simply can't settle down, can you?"

"Interesting choice of words, coming from you." I carefully
set my glass down and braced for her counterattack.

"Young lady, I'd watch my tone, if I were you."

"Well, we've established I'm *not* you, haven't we?" It had
been a year since I'd seen my mother, and I was rapidly regretting asking her for drinks. It was too long and cold of a swim
to make a break for it now, though.

My mother stood gracefully and tucked her clutch under
her arm. "I don't have to take this attitude from you, Savannah. I'll be on my way." After an elegant half turn and a single
step, I stopped her.

"Wow, this is getting easier for you." My pulse raced as I
prepared for what I would say next. "Being *on your way.* Is that
the same term you used on Dad when you left him last year?
That you'd be *on your way?*"

She turned around slowly and stared at me as ruffled as
I'd ever seen her. Her blue eyes darkened, and her mouth
swung open. I'd rendered Vita Carulli speechless. I'd never
addressed her leaving. Not with her, anyway. Not only had I
not seen her in a year, I hadn't spoken with her either. While
I received phone calls from both of them on the day she left, I
happened to answer my father's call first and got the raw ver-
sion of events. She wanted more, he said.

More than my father giving up his own career to raise me while she traveled the world doing what she loved.

More than having the entire opera world love her.

More than doing exactly what she wanted, when she wanted.

More than having my father wait lovingly for her for two decades and welcome her home with open arms to resume their life *together.*

She packed her things and moved to Boston. Fucking *Boston.* The city *I* loved.

Taking a page from her score, I slid my bag over my shoulder and stood to leave.

When I reached the place she was standing, shocked and unmoving at my words, I leaned in so only she could hear me. "*I'll* be on my way. *Mother.*"

Walking through the lobby of the hotel and out to the parking lot, I never turned around to see how long she stood there. In that moment, I didn't care if she stood there forever.

Alone.

Chapter 20

SAVANNAH

"**N**ERVOUS?" NATHAN LEANED in and whispered to me after we finished tuning.

I shook my head "no" as the comforting buzz of excitement coursed through my body. One benefit of being in the flute section is being seated near the front of the orchestra. While I wasn't nervous, because I wouldn't have to visually take in the entire orchestra to keep my eyes on the conductor, I reveled in feeling the power of the whole orchestra behind me.

Nathan and I arrived a little earlier than necessary. I knew no one was going to particularly care that I was there, if they even noticed. I wanted to be sure to make a good impression on the conductors we'd be working with, in the event that I wanted to audition for any of the orchestras represented in this room. Despite Nathan's insistence that I take the seat ahead of him, I demanded to sit last chair based on principle. Everyone else in the flute section was a member of one of the Big Five. I was an outsider.

I elbowed Nathan and whispered, "Hey, there's Tim Flannigan!" My cheeks heated as I pointed out the principal flute for Chicago. Not only was he currently my favorite flutist, he was shockingly easy on the eyes.

"Blush much?" Nathan teased, rolling his eyes. Of course Nathan knew Tim; they worked together.

Tim was tall, just like Nathan, but much more filled out. His broad back and narrow waist had him looking like a percussionist for a marching band.

I'd followed his career since I was old enough to care about such things, and his rise to the first chair with the Chicago Symphony was remarkable. The son of Irish immigrants, he'd come to this country when he was ten, though he started playing the flute a year prior. His parents couldn't afford to send him to a conservatory, so he studied music at his local college. Practicing every spare hour he could, he auditioned half a dozen times before getting in. Since his acceptance, he traveled the world doing solo performances before sold out crowds during the symphony's off-season.

He was only ten or twelve years older than me, but his skill made him sound like he'd been playing for a hundred years. His hair was completely salt and pepper, which did wonderful things for his green eyes. As he sat, he turned toward Nathan and me, extending his hand, which Nathan accepted.

"Tim, I'd like to introduce you to my friend—"

"Savannah Marshall." Tim leaned past Nathan and gently took my hand in his.

"Yes..." I trailed off, shaking my head in confusion.

Tim chuckled softly as he let go of my hand and ran his over his tightly cropped hair. "I'm a friend of Madeline White. She told me you'd be joining us this summer. She's talked a lot about you over the years, and I'm glad to finally meet you. That piece you played in your junior year flute ensemble was stunning. Well done, really."

"Were you there?" I asked, tucking a strand of hair behind my ear.

"No. Madeline sent me the video. She was showcasing the two of you." Tim pointed his finger between Nathan and me. "She was giving all of us a heads up on who to look out for over the next few years."

"Oh...wow." I exhaled softly as someone tapped Tim on the shoulder, calling his attention away from us.

"You okay?" Nathan asked, trying to follow my stare at the floor.

"I feel like I may have let Madeline down a bit."

Nathan rolled his eyes. "You just spent a year playing for Bolshoi. You're far from a disappointment."

I smiled and leaned my shoulder into his before going through our music selection. Apart from playing "The Stars and Stripes Forever" at the end of each performance, we would be rotating through a breathtakingly beautiful selection of music. On the order for today's rehearsal was Beethoven's Leonore Overture No. 73, "Theme from Schindler's List", which I could rarely play without tearing up, and Mendelssohn's Symphony No. 4 in A Major. There were more. Scores and scores of music that spanned centuries. Generations had lived and died under this music, and I was getting chills at the prospect of making the music come alive with all of the master musicians around me.

"Here come the bees," Nathan mumbled, tilting his chin toward the front of the stage, where a majority of the strings swarmed to their seats.

I laughed, thinking about my summers as a student at Tanglewood with Nathan, when he first pointed out to me that the strings huddled together and always took their seats together, looking and sounding like bees as they settled into their seats and began tuning.

"Oh, excellent," I whispered, "Zoey's here!" I caught the eye of one of our conservatory friends who'd gone on to Cleveland, and waved. She smiled and waved back.

My smile quickly vanished as the cellos made their way on stage. It didn't occur to me that Gregory Fitzgerald would want to participate in something like this, given his two best friends weren't participating, and loads of travel crammed into an eight-week, twenty-city tour didn't seem to be his cup of Earl Grey.

"*Nathan,*" I snipped.

"Yeah, doll—oh, for Christ's sake," he grumbled as he looked to where I was pointing.

"Did you know?"

"*Yeah,*" he spit out sarcastically, "I thought it would be a fucking blast to sucker you into spending two months with him on the road. I'm sorry, Savannah." Nathan leaned back in his chair, running a hand through his loose curls.

I shook my head, mocking Gregory's signature dismissive wave. "Don't be sorry. It's way old news. A heads up would have been spectacular, but, whatever...let's look over this piece."

Nathan and I got out our pencils, marking sections that we would each have to pay extra attention to in order to not make total fools out of ourselves. Every few seconds, my eyes would flicker to Gregory, and I found myself wondering what had him in a seemingly extra sour mood.

His eyes seemed ashen, bags under them that weren't there a couple of weeks ago at James and Madeline's wedding. His usually well-groomed goatee looked about a day or two past its scheduled maintenance, and he seemed to speak in clipped sentences to his section mates. Despite his usually gruff attitude toward the rest of the world, from what I'd seen, Gregory was always pleasant with his fellow cellists.

My stomach flipped as I waited for him to relax the muscles between his eyebrows. He didn't. Something was wrong, and wrong enough for him to let it show all over his face and body. I'm not sure what concerned me more, that something was definitely unsettled in his meticulously polished life, or that I cared.

And I wanted to make him feel better.

GREGORY

I DON'T UNDERSTAND WHY *you won't agree to have children with her.*

The voice of my mother grated in my ears every time I thought about it. After days of a cold standoff between Karin and me, I'd received an unexpected phone call. My mother, who barely left her home these days due to a host of ailments, most of them imaginary, wanted to meet for lunch. And *catch up.* That was her code for interfering in my life. I could have rehearsed her lines for her in advance; they were so predictable.

That lunch resulted in a shouting match later between Karin and me. How dare she involve my family in this discussion? The last two days our attempt at a silent argument over whether or not to have children had erupted into open warfare, and I'd left this morning in a rage.

All the same arguments kept running through my head as I carried my cello into the rehearsal hall. I'd told her more than once, many times really, that I had no desire for children. Did she think that was going to change after we got married? Did she think she could change it for me? *Did she want to change who I was?*

I didn't speak to the other cellists as I opened my case and very carefully leaned my instrument into its stand. I frowned as I saw a tiny mark near one of the f-holes. Very carefully, I wiped it with a polishing cloth then breathed a sigh of relief. Whatever had caused the mark, it wasn't permanent.

Finally I looked up at my section.

They were all prominent, first rate musicians. Colleagues. Looking at them, I was disoriented for a second. For my entire career, I'd been the youngest cellist. But of course, years had passed. Years in which I was one of the preeminent cellists in America, but also years in which I was aging. Most of the men and women in my section were much younger. I looked at them, and without a word signaled them to gather and began to issue instructions.

Normally I'm considerably more deft with people, but after the last several days of fights, of continual emotional battles with Karin, I had nothing left. For anyone. I kept my instructions terse, cold and functional. Then I turned my back on them and began to set up and tune my instrument. The tuning on the Montagnana is always delicate, in particular the G string, which tended to slip and loosen occasionally, sometimes even while in the middle of a performance. I always kept a close ear on it, a constant ongoing background tension, which kept me poised, alert, and responsive. In some ways, that constant tension was far better than having the pegs adjusted so they didn't slip.

But nothing today was going smoothly. From the moment I woke up and she started harping at me about the nonexistent *baby* before I'd had my first cup of tea, to the tearful scene at the front door...*nothing* had gone smoothly. And so, of course, this would be the one day the G string *refused* to tune properly. I sat there, in front of six younger cellists from other orchestras, looking like a rank amateur, as the frown on my face grew deeper and deeper. Finally, I got it right.

I closed my eyes. I leaned back in my seat, my right hand slowly caressing the curve of the body of the instrument. I opened my eyes.

And staring back at me, just ahead and to the right, was Savannah Marshall, her eyes wide and alarmed. She was sitting next to Nathan, of course. When she saw me looking at her, her eyes darted away. She leaned close to Nathan and whispered something. And I felt a sudden, reckless urge to stand up, walk to her and grab her arm. To say...*something*. I had no idea what.

Of course Savannah was here. Why hadn't I thought of it? The rumors had gotten back to me quickly. She'd left the Bolshoi, with virtually no notice. Were she a lesser musician, merely outstanding and top-ranked, she'd have never worked again after disappearing *twice*, once from the conservatory and now from the Bolshoi. As it was, however...she'd become one of the premier musicians in the world, and everyone knew it.

She was certainly as good as anyone else in this group.

Now she met my eyes with an almost dismissive look. Was she annoyed? Irritated to find me here? Was she angry? Did she even feel anything at all about me? And why the hell did it matter? I had a wife at home, after all. A wife I'd chosen to marry three years ago. A wife I'd married in spite of Savannah. A wife I'd married because...because she wouldn't complicate things. Because it made her happy and she wouldn't interfere with my life.

But now?

Now she wanted *children*.

The thought of Karin swept through my head like a migraine, and consequently, I was the first to look away from my unofficial little staring contest with Savannah. And I decided then and there I wouldn't look again. I wouldn't meet her eyes. I wouldn't talk with her before or after rehearsal, I wouldn't seek her out, I wouldn't discuss her, or, worst of all, *think* about her.

So I sat up straight in my seat. I looked at the conductor. I took a deep breath. And I tried to ignore that in my peripheral vision just to my right, she sat in the second chair in the flute section. I tried to ignore the fact that for the next eight weeks, this little traveling road show would be performing on stages large and small all over the United States.

And she would be a row away from me the entire time.

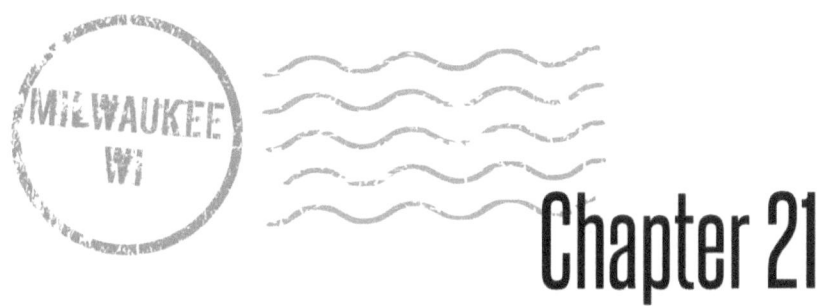

Chapter 21

SAVANNAH

TIM FLANNIGAN THREW his head back and let out a full-throated laugh and Nathan grinned. I smiled in response. I'd been telling the two of them yet another story of Sasha Nikulina, the Bolshoi's Prima Ballerina and a slightly crazy, waifish woman who had attacked her boyfriend with knitting needles midway through last season.

"You may think it's funny," I said, "but Boris didn't. He was in the hospital for two weeks. Knitting needles are serious weapons."

I tried to keep a straight face. I really did. But their laughter got to me. First one corner of my mouth quirked up, then the other, and then I was laughing along with Tim.

"All right. What happened to the young ballerina?" Tim asked.

I shrugged. "The police escorted her to the performance, waited, and then picked her up afterward to take her back to jail. Every night for the rest of the season."

"No way," Nathan said, staring at me incredulously.

I nodded. "Russians are serious about their ballet." What I didn't say was that Sasha's story wasn't even the weirdest. The politics and backstabbing at the Bolshoi was legendary, and even if I went back in the fall, I had the feeling I wouldn't stay much longer.

Tim gave me a quirky grin and said, "And that, my friends, is why I've never dated a ballerina."

Nathan laughed, but I just raised an eyebrow and said, in as droll a voice as I could manage, "You're assuming one would have you?"

He winked at me in response, and I felt a small thrill. But seconds later, Nathan's grin disappeared and he sat up, a clouded expression on his face. Tim raised an eyebrow.

I twisted around in my seat. Of course, that explained the sudden transition from laughter to sobriety. Mr. Personal Rain Cloud himself had walked into the room, trailing Joseph McIntosh, our conductor. For a change, Gregory wore light grey pants instead of black. How original, he seemed to be branching out. I had to force myself to not roll my eyes.

Tim stood up just as Joseph and Gregory reached him.

"Hey guys," Tim said.

Joseph spoke for the dour pair. "Tim, listen, we've got an interesting opportunity...and a strange one. The Tonight Show is looking to do a segment on the tour."

I raised an eyebrow. That *was* a surprise.

The tour was intended to raise interest across the country in symphony music. In simpler terms, it was an attempt to pull the collective asses of classical musicians out of the fire. In the wake of economic recession and war, symphonies were seeing subscription drops all over the country. Some had closed; others were laying off musicians and shortening their seasons, not to mention cutting pensions for those who'd been members longer than I'd been alive. This tour was an attempt to generate real interest in our music and included a lot of unusual venues: town centers in cities with no symphony, television shows, and malls.

"What can I do to help?" Tim asked.

"We need a duet. I went over a number of possible pieces with the producers and they want Assobio a Jato. Gregory knows it well, but we need a partner for him. Savannah, I understand you've played it with Gregory before?"

I took a deep breath. Joseph didn't see it, but I did: Gregory scowled, fiercely. *Asshole.* Of course he wouldn't want me involved in this.

"Maybe Tim?" I said, my voice trailing off.

Tim shook his head. "Difficult piece, and I've never played it. How much time do we have to prepare?"

"None," Joseph said. "You'll be playing live, tonight."

Tim shook his head. "Not possible. Savannah, I think it's going to have to be you if you know it. Is that okay?"

I spoke up again. "Perhaps a different piece…"

Joseph said, "No, this is the one they wanted. I need you to pull this one through, Savannah. It's important for the tour."

I could do this. Gregory might be a reclusive ass, but it was only a few hours anyway. I met Joseph's eyes. "I'd be happy to."

Gregory began to sputter, so I smiled at him, and in the sweetest tone of voice I could summon, I said, "Although if it's too difficult for you to do this one on such short notice, Gregory, I'm sure one of the other cellists could substitute."

I could feel the tension from him, so intense that his face just beside his right eye started to twitch.

My anger withdrew, leaving me deflated. He'd been visibly tense, angry, frustrated about something since the tour started. I'd carefully avoided him outside of practice and performances, so I had no idea what was wrong, but suddenly I didn't want to irritate him any more. I wanted to soothe whatever was bothering him.

It seemed I was too late. Red-faced, he said to me in a cold tone, "I'm certain we'll get through this somehow, Miss Marshall."

Joseph looked back and forth between us, concern on his face. He didn't verbalize the tension. Neither did Nathan, who rose to his feet.

Joseph shrugged. "Pack your bags then. We'll have a car brought around to take you to the airport."

Forty minutes later I was back in the lobby of the hotel. An uncomfortable looking Gregory stood at the door of the lobby. As I approached the door, Lyn, one of the production assistants, approached us both.

"Gregory? Savannah? Okay...you're on United Airlines, arriving in Los Angeles at three p.m. A car from the network will pick you up and get you to the hotel, and then pick you up again at seven p.m. to take you to the studio. Your flight tomorrow morning is to Lincoln, Nebraska; you'll meet us there. Those tickets are in the package as well."

I thanked Lyn as she pressed the folder with the airline tickets into my hand.

She handed another folder to Gregory. "You have an extra seat for your cello, of course," she said.

He mumbled his thanks to her in a barely civilized tone, and I whispered, "We'd better go before you accidentally say something polite."

Then I turned and walked outside to the waiting black Lincoln Town Car, praying that it was our car. Otherwise I'd be left standing there; dramatically making an idiot of myself after my not-so-grand exit.

It was the right car. A few moments later, his cello safely positioned in the trunk, Gregory got in the back seat beside me and slammed the door.

I pointedly looked out the window. The driver got in the front seat and the car pulled out in near silence. Buildings and traffic whisked by us as we pulled out onto the highway.

I snuck a glance.

Gregory was staring out the window, his elbow on the edge, and his chin resting on a clenched fist. At that moment, he bore more expression on his face than I'd ever seen. And it wasn't nice. His eyes wore a look of pain as he stared out the window. Desperation. Loneliness.

I stared at him in shock, one question repeatedly running through my mind.

What happened to him?

GREGORY

ITTING IN THE makeup chair next to Savannah, I was annoyed. The flight was quiet, with only a soft "excuse me" from her lips when she slid past me to use the restroom. We'd spent the past couple of weeks skillfully avoiding each other. Well, I was avoiding her, and it sure seemed she was avoiding me. She would look down whenever I scanned the orchestra, or would turn her back to me as I approached someone standing next to her. I couldn't worry about that right now, though, as I was still being punished by bi-hourly texts from Karin. I assured her this time apart would give us both a chance to breathe and assess our goals. Hers hadn't, and I knew wouldn't, change.

She wants a baby.

"What are you doing?" Savannah snapped to one of the stylists in front of her, pulling me from my silent battle with someone who wasn't here.

Looking at her in the mirror, I saw the stylist messing with the neckline of Savannah's dress. It was a gorgeous knee-length green dress that highlighted her bronzed skin. Similar in color to the gown she wore to her mother's performance five years ago, it tied around her neck. While I knew the night I met her mother that I'd never forget how Savannah looked in that dress, I cursed myself for the thought anyway.

Focusing on trying to figure out what Savannah was upset about, I followed the stylist's hands and saw them pulling the neckline down, exposing more cleavage than I'd ever seen from Savannah. Even more than that red dress she wore dancing. Twice.

"Honey," the young stylist sassed, annoyed, "the point of this tour of yours is to increase interest in classical music, is it not? To make centuries-old music accessible to people like us?"

"If I walk out there like this," Savannah slapped her hand away, "it will suggest there's far more about me that's accessible than my music."

She slid off the chair and walked skillfully in ridiculously high heels over to the full-length mirror, where she repositioned her dress and wiped the excessive color from her lips.

"Why did you do that?" the stylist shrieked.

With an eye roll, Savannah replied, "I'm not going to get this crap all over my ten thousand dollar flute. Thanks, though."

I was mid-way through a chuckle, impressed by her grace amidst surely feeling frustrated, when I felt someone's hands on my head.

"Damn it!" I ducked out of their reach. I lack grace when frustrated. *"What?"*

With a long sigh, a second stylist groaned, "We're stylists, I'm *styling your hair.*"

"It looks cute, Gregory," Savannah teased from across the room.

"Oooooh," a producer exaggerated, walking into the room with an oversized headset on her undersized head. "So, it's true then. The whole student-teacher thing from a few years back?"

That was the last straw.

Between things at home with Karin, the cold shoulder I'd been giving Savannah, which was growing physically painful for me to maintain as the days wore on, I tore the brush from Dwayne's hand and chucked it across the room, where it, thankfully, only hit the wall before hitting the ground with a clunk. In the brief second before I put my head in my hands, I caught Savannah's eyes studying me in the mirror, wide-eyed but calm.

She cleared her throat and addressed the people in the room. "Can we have a few minutes, please? I'm aware we're on in seven minutes. I can see the clock." She spoke quickly and with authority.

The pair of stylists and the pissed off producer obliged and left in a hurry, mumbling something about self entitlement as Savannah shut and locked the door behind them. As the sound of her heels against the tile got closer, I had to say something.

"Sorry about that…" I trailed off, having little else to offer.

Savannah swallowed hard as she turned my chair toward her. I was eye level with her chest, but it wasn't her breasts that interested me in that moment. It was her eyes. Laced with concern and vulnerability, the sliver of vulnerability her eyes always carried. She shook her head and picked up a comb, not saying a word.

"I can do it—" I started, leaning forward in my chair.

"Just sit," she whispered.

Gently lifting my chin with a nudge from her index finger, I could tell she was biting the inside of her cheek as she brought the comb to my hair, attempting to fix whatever it was Dwayne had done. After a few passes, she set the brush down and ran her fingers slowly down the sides of my head. Her touch ignited me, and I had to carefully measure my breathing to keep from giving myself away as thoughts of everything going wrong at home slipped away.

She slowly moved her fingers to the back of my head, leaning over me slightly, so her breasts were mere inches from my face. I closed my eyes, breathing in the fresh scent of lilies that seemed to come from every part of her body. Goosebumps sprang across my neck as her fingers grazed the skin just below my hairline. I prayed she couldn't feel them.

"There," she said after several seconds, taking a step back.

Looking in the mirror I saw that my hair was nearly exactly how it always was. Every day.

Widening my eyes, I looked between myself in the mirror, and her. "How did you--?"

With a soft chuckle, she met my eyes in the mirror. "And you thought I never paid attention in class. Come on, we have three minutes before we're on." She squeezed my shoulder once before exiting the room, leaving me in conflicted silence.

"Shit," I sighed as I exited the room, following the scent of lilies down the hallway.

Her eyes closed and her lips pursed correctly as I reached the second measure of the intro. Savannah took a quick breath, her shoulders falling back, her breasts just slightly rising as she inhaled, and then she was playing. It was like it was five years ago.

Her eyes met mine as we played. Boring into me. As if she were asking years' worth of questions. Why was I so angry? Why had I given up so easily five years ago? Why? Why didn't I fight for her?

I could feel the tension in the audience as she played the runs, rapid arpeggios scaling upwards. Aggressive, angry. This was a lighthearted piece. Or it was intended as such. With intense energy, with a shift in tone here and a difference in breath there, she had transformed it, to an emotional, oppressive piece of music.

I followed her lead, making the necessary changes to not only keep up, but to complement what she was doing. Probably no one in the audience knew what was happening, probably few even in the televised audience, for that matter. Those few who knew this music well would likely assume we'd simply modified it, played a slightly different arrangement.

Not one of them would believe that we were improvising, that right there on that stage she was telling a story of hurt and anger and betrayal. That she was telling me just how *much* I'd hurt her.

Hearing her pain through the notes broke my heart.

And I could hear it. I could see it in the shifts of her posture, and in her eyes as they drifted toward me. I responded the only way I knew how, by adjusting my own music—attempting to play my apology, my longing, my love. My failure.

Finally, we brought the music to a close, and as the audience stood, applauding, cheering, she peered up at me as she continued to breathe in and out, her eyes glassy with threatening tears.

After taking a bow, being whisked off stage, and packing up our instruments, we got in the town car and made our way back to the hotel.

"You played beautifully tonight, Savannah," I started, five minutes into our drive.

"Thank you." She smiled and bit her lip in a way that made me want to lean across the car and kiss it. "Thanks for playing along, so to speak." She laughed and looked out the window.

"Of course." I shrugged, not knowing what else to say about her acknowledgement that she'd meant to take the piece in the direction she did.

She stared out the window for a few more minutes. Lights from each passing car showed me her distant eyes for the briefest of seconds, before returning my view to that of her silent silhouette. A second later she tossed her hair over her shoulder and turned so she was facing me.

"Gregory..." Savannah looked down for a moment, taking a deep breath before finding my eyes again.

"Yes?" My heart raced, my chest rising and falling more rapidly with each second that passed. Each second of her silence increased my anxiety over what she was about to say.

As she opened her mouth to speak, her phone rang loudly, causing her to jump.

"Shit," she mumbled, glancing at the screen. I saw that it said *Nathan*.

"Go ahead." I rolled my eyes and looked out the window.

"Hey Nathan, were you watch—" Savannah clipped her sentence, starting again in a much more aggravated tone. "What? What the hell are you talking about?"

Looking over at her, I watched her run a hand through her hair, leaving it perched on the back of her neck as she pressed the side of her head into the window.

"Not this shit again, Nathan. Seriously. Yes...I remember. Don't talk to me like I'm an idiot. It was nothing." Savannah's cheeks reddened in an instant as she looked at me out of the corner of her eye. "Get a grip. Even if there was, it's not a shred of your business. I'll see you tomorrow. Bye." In a huff, she ended the call and shoved her phone into her purse.

"Everything okay?" I asked, uninterested in what Nathan had to say apart from how it seemed to make her feel.

She waved her hand at me and grinned. "Just Nathan..."

Apparently that was supposed to communicate something.

Before I could respond, my phone buzzed in my pocket.

Karin.

"Excuse me," I mumbled to Savannah, as if I could step away to take the call. I wish I could have. Really, I wish I didn't have to answer it at all. "Hello?" I answered, clearing my throat.

"What the hell was that?" Karin's voice was just a peg below hysterical.

"What was what?"

"On the show just now."

"I—"

Karin cut me off. "You conveniently left out that you'd be playing with *Savannah Marshall*."

"I'm failing to see what difference it makes *who* I played with…" I trailed off, having forgotten for a second that I was sitting right next to Savannah in the car. I glanced over at her and she quickly looked to the floor.

"If it makes no difference, why didn't you tell me? You *knew* it would make a difference to me. You didn't even tell me she was part of the damn tour!" Karin sniffed and her tears on the other side of the country brewed fresh anxiety in me.

I hadn't told her. It was intentional and unconscious at the same time to leave Savannah's name out of the conversation. I knew it would cause another argument with Karin, and given all we were fighting about anyway, I didn't need to give her new material. But I grew agitated at the fact that being dishonest about Savannah said more about my feelings for *her* than my avoidance of a cross-country argument with my angry wife.

My wife.

"Karin, darling…" Unconsciously I looked at Savannah as I spoke those words. I caught her swallowing hard before she looked out the window. It speared through my emotions, and I couldn't piece together why. Until tonight we'd been anything but cordial to each other. Yet, here, in the car on the phone with my wife, I couldn't help but care more about the woman sitting next to me than the one I'd pledged eternity to three thousand miles away.

"What, Gregory? What? Are you about to apologize for basically making out with another woman on television?"

"*Excuse me?*" I snapped, catching Savannah jump out of the corner of my eye.

"It was all over your faces on that stage, Gregory. Don't *lie* to me about what's going on between you two on the road."

There it was. The accusation of an affair I'd tried to avoid since I first spotted Savannah one row back on our first day of rehearsal. The reason I'd been so cold to her for the last few weeks. I'd attempted to keep my distance from Savannah Marshall once, and it ended horribly for both of us. On this tour I knew I couldn't keep my physical distance, so I built an emotional wall to keep out someone who was mattering to me more each day.

Someone who could ruin things for me. For my life.

Again.

Thankfully, the car pulled up to the hotel and our driver opened my door.

"Listen, Karin. My car just got back to the hotel. Once I get settled into the room I'll call you back. I want to talk—"

"Don't bother, Gregory." With that, Karin ended the call, and I slammed my fist against the doorframe with a growl.

After mumbling an apology to our driver, and handing him twenty dollars, I rushed through the hotel doors, ignoring Savannah, trying to maneuver through the revolving door with my cello case in hand.

"Gregory!" She called after I made it into the lobby, moving rather quickly for wearing such high heels. I stopped but didn't turn to face her until she caught up. "Gregory," she said again, breathless as she put her hand on my shoulder.

"We can't do this, Savannah. Not again." I gritted my teeth as I faced her, shrugging my shoulder so she would drop her hand.

She did, scrunching up her forehead, shaking it slightly side to side. "Do what?"

"This...I...I--" I ran a hand through my hair and set it on my hip, barely able to look her in the eyes. I took a deep breath and continued. "Look, Savannah. I could very easily get hung up on you...swept up in you. Again. And, I can't. That would just be...disastrous to my life."

"Again," she said pointedly. Not really a question, but I sensed she wanted a response.

"Yes, again. Five years ago we—"

"Were in love, Gregory. At least that's what you said. That you were in love with me. Remember?" Her bottom teeth pinched her top lip before she continued. "But, if you were just swept up then...I guess...that's that." She crossed her arms and stared right through me.

I leaned in close, to avoid causing a scene. "Damn it, Savannah, I'm *married*."

"I know you're married," she hissed back. "I also know that I can't stop fucking thinking about you. That the anger I harbored toward you for the last five years was just wounded love. It never went away. The pain of you casting me aside on your front steps *and* the bottomless love I felt for you. None of it has gone away."

Her voice shook as she vocalized the identical feelings I'd felt off and on over the last five years. I was in love with her.

Still. Always.

And, once again, there was nothing I could do about it. This time, it was killing me.

I panicked and said something I never should have said.

Ever.

Still whispering, I said, "I suggest, Miss Marshall, that you find someone else's life to ruin. Mine is off limits."

Chapter 22

SAVANNAH

THE WORDS HADN'T even finished spilling from his lips before I landed my open palm across his cheek. He winced. I'd hit him with enough force he had to take a step backward.

Despite my refusal to cry, tears fell. He'd just told me I was a problem. A distraction that could ruin his life. I didn't care that he looked pained, anguished even, as he said it.

He said it. I heard it. It hurt.

"Jesus *Christ*, Savannah!" Gregory kept his voice low and measured. But I could see the red finger marks appearing across his face.

"Breaking my heart in front of your best friend once wasn't enough for you?"

I knew it wasn't fair to call his bluff on his emotions. Not now. Not when he was married. But, Christ, when you're in love with someone, you tell them.

You don't make them feel like dirt.

"It was for both of us—"

I put my hand up. "We've rehearsed this scene before, re-member? I know what comes next. I walk away." With a trem-bling voice I turned on my heels, ignoring the gaping stares from passers by.

Just put one foot in front of the other, Savannah. You've walked away from him once before, and you can do it again. Even if it kills you.

Straightening my shoulders, I took two even steps before Gregory's long, soft fingers tightly gripped my upper arm, stopping me in my tracks. I tried to tug it away without turning around, but in a second, I was spun around to face him. I only caught a glimpse of the fire in his eyes before his lips were on mine.

Instinctively, I wrapped my arms around his neck as he pressed one hand into the small of my back, the other hand cradling the back of my head. Our mouths were open and our tongues searching each other's before I had a chance to fight back.

I didn't want to fight back.

"I'm so sorry, Savannah," his voice was husky in the milliseconds our mouths separated. "I'm sorry."

The tears continued pouring from my eyes as I kissed back with equal force. "I'm sorry, too," I replied.

I didn't want to fight back. I was done fighting against my feelings for Gregory. Thoughts of Nathan's phone call from the car, accusing me of publicly flirting with Gregory on national television, thoughts of his wife on the other side of the country—they all fell easily by the wayside as I was wrapped up in the arms of the only man I'd ever loved.

"Come with me." The words were barely audible through his ragged breathing.

Discretion was the furthest thing from my mind as he took my hand and rushed me through the lobby toward the elevators. Everything was far from my mind. All I was doing was feeling. And it felt good. An elevator was ready right away, welcoming us inside before either of us could change our minds.

I wonder what would have happened if we'd been forced to wait.

As soon as the doors closed, Gregory pressed the 7 before taking both my hands in his, his tired eyes alive with passion I'd missed for several years. Gregory slowly glided his hand up my arm and over my shoulder before wrapping his hand around the back of my neck.

His lips were on my neck, and I threw my head back as I heard him rumble the words against my skin, "I've missed you, Savannah."

The elevator doors opened and we were moving, quickly, down the hall. The rational part of my brain screamed I was making a mistake. That Gregory would only break my heart again. That he wasn't even capable of real love, and that the one thing I'd never wanted was to be something he got on the side. That he was *married.*

And yet, I kept moving with him as he unlocked the door. He kissed me again when we entered the room, swollen lips on the side of my face, near my ear, murmuring words I couldn't understand as I ran my hands over the expanse of his back and shoulders. My lips slightly parted as I tried to catch my breath.

Without thought or volition my hands were under his jacket, yanking his black t-shirt out of his waistband and sliding up his back, my fingertips digging into his skin. Toned muscles that I'd seen move with the notes from his cello were now flexing beneath my touch.

"Gregory..." My voice was a husky whisper as I lifted his shirt.

He took a step backward and shook off his jacket. When he looked up I saw everything had changed. There was no orchestra, no tour. No classroom. No Karin.

Karin.

His wife.

The harder I tried to picture her, the fuzzier her face became in my mind. Now was the time to stop if I was going to. To slide the shoe back on that I'd just kicked off and leave the room with as much grace as I could.

As if he sensed my hesitation, Gregory took a step forward. I placed my hands on his shoulders and we both took a deep breath. As we exhaled in unison, his hands slid down my sides and over my hips. My eyes closed as I recalled Madeline's guest room five years ago. Dawn threatening as we recklessly tore off our clothes and gave in. The way his muscles flexed underneath me as he held my hips. The way his arms encircled me as he cried out my name. Watching his eyes as he told me he loved me. That's where I ended my trip down memory lane, choosing to push aside everything that happened in the moments that had followed.

"God, Savannah," he sighed as his hands slid down my backside. Now he was looking at me the same way. With the reverence I was certain he only held for his cello.

"I...we..."

I started to say it. I did. I started to say *I can't do this*, or maybe, *we shouldn't do this*. Or maybe what I started to say was *I love you* or *we belong together*. I don't know which. The emotion washing over me was too powerful, too confusing to reduce to a few simple words. The moment for reason passed as his lips touched mine again, as our bodies touched, as his hands ran down my back and he pulled me toward the bed.

Gregory

FROM THE MOMENT she slapped me, the moment I kissed her, I knew I was lost.

I stumbled through my apology because I'd been wrong to say what I said. I'd been wrong to blame her. I'd been the one to ruin my life. And I hardly thought as I grabbed her and pulled her into my arms, as I kissed her, but I *felt*. I felt so much, so much that I'd lost since the day I let her walk away.

And as I pulled her to the bed, even then, I was split, confused, my mind and emotions everywhere. It was as if I had a voice in my head, telling me *this was wrong*. But on a much bigger level it was so right, because I felt a passion for her that I'd never felt before in my life.

Not since the last time I had her in bed.

I closed my eyes as she dug her fingers into my back. It wasn't the physical sensations. It's that it was *her*. It was Savannah, the woman I loved, the woman I'd always loved, the woman I lost. And then it was too late for thought. I pulled her to the bed, laying her on her back, and she was pulling at my shirt, lifting it off of me, as my eyes and fingertips touched the delicate white skin below her breasts and our lips touched again.

My fingertips slid along the base of her breasts, just a feather touch, but neither of us could withstand the anticipation. She reached out and pulled me closer, so we were holding each other tightly, both of my arms wrapped around her as we lay on our sides, my right hand cradling the back of her neck, our lips together.

We were scrambling to make up for lost time.

Her eyes fluttered open, and I broke off our kiss for a few seconds and stared into them. Brown, beautiful. I'd always loved her eyes. They watered, just a little, and she whispered, "I've never wanted anyone else."

My whole body shook at the words, because I hadn't either. I brought my lips back to hers, and our mouths opened, tongues exploring. I was overwhelmed by the sensation of her body touching mine. Her breasts were warm and swollen against my bare chest, and as my left hand slid down to the curve of her back, she pressed her entire body hard against mine. My breath was ragged, and I was utterly overwhelmed by the emotion, the sensation, of having Savannah Marshall in bed again after all these years.

She let out a small groan as my hand slid down to cup her ass, and I pulled her tighter, the pressure of our bodies together almost too intense to bear. I wanted her clothes off right then and there. We had a crazy, confusing, frustrating moment where our bodies were too close to each other to manage getting clothes off, and I literally had to tear myself away from her to get up on my knees. I kissed her as I felt at her back, trying to find the zipper for her dress.

"Under my arm," she spoke through clenched teeth, lifting her arm slightly to expose the zipper.

I unzipped her dress, loosening it enough to slide the entire dress up and over her head, and then I found myself sitting back on my heels, staring at her, my heart beating even faster. Her skin looked almost porcelain. Incredibly smooth, flawless. Like her.

In that moment she stared up at me. Vulnerable, but strong. Here was someone who understood who I was on so many levels. Who I'd loved since I first laid eyes on her.

Here was the woman I'd hurt, badly. The woman I'd promised to walk away from, because of worry about my career. And her reputation. The woman who I lost, because I didn't fight for her. And even though she was right here in front of me, it didn't feel entirely real; everything had the texture of a dream.

But it wasn't a dream.

She reached for my belt, her hand pressing against me, and I groaned, closing my eyes for just a second. I eased out of my pants, and our bodies were back side-by-side again, and now I felt her skin against mine. I hooked a leg around hers, tangling our limbs, and slid my right arm underneath her shoulder.

She brought her lips to my neck, just below my ear, and I involuntarily sucked in a breath. She continued kissing, down my neck, then to my chest.

"I love you." As her lips formed her words against my skin, my back arched and I let out a groan.

The feeling of her breath and her teeth against my skin was almost unbearable. I couldn't take just being next to her any longer. Nudging her back slightly, she raised her knees, allowing me to settle between them as I stared down at her. With her hair scattered around her, I wanted to drink her in. To savor every essence that made her who she was. Shifting my gaze to her eyes, I found them slightly clouded with tears. But she looked happy. Content. Right.

"Are you okay?" I asked, taking a hand and brushing a strand from her face.

"Always," she whispered, sliding her hands to my buttocks, pressing her fingertips into my skin. Giving me unspoken permission.

I shook my head slightly as I leaned down to kiss her. "God, you're exquisite..."

With those words, Savannah let out a soft moan as I slowly slid inside her. She opened up her body for me and I was humbled by her trust, given everything we'd been through. Everything I'd put her through. Suddenly I wanted to touch her everywhere at once. I didn't want a single inch of my skin to be separated from hers.

"Oh..." She closed her eyes and rocked her head back on the pillow as her mouth formed around the word. My eyes traced along the smooth line of her neck, her jawline.

"Mmm," I moaned onto her breast as my tongue desperately circled her nipple, feeling it get harder under my touch.

I moved faster, pressing my forehead into her chest. Beads of sweat rolled down my cheek and onto her skin.

"Hey." Breathlessly, Savannah grabbed the sides of my face and hunted my eyes, perhaps looking for answers to five years of questions. "Go slow. I don't want this to end."

Slowly she lifted her hips, and lowered them again, teaching me how to move with her. I couldn't look away from her as I waited for her to close her eyes again. She didn't. I slid into her carefully, and backed out at the same cautious speed, watching her eyelids react to my motion. As I watched her reactions, my own body responded. Minute after minute I watched her as I felt every curve of her body move against mine. Making love to the only woman I'd ever loved.

As if sensing my need for more, she dug her fingernails into my shoulder blades and grazed her teeth against my earlobe. "Roll over." Intense authority carried through her whisper, and I complied.

My view of her was nearly paralyzing as we repositioned our bodies and Savannah straddled my hips. She ran a hand through her hair to move it out of her face, and it cascaded in careless waves over her breasts. Reaching up, I brushed her hair over her shoulder and let my hands slide down her arms, working their way to her calves. As she began to slowly rock, I arched my back in response. Trailing my fingers up her calves, her hips, her waist, soaking in every inch of her body. Committing every curve to memory.

My hands reached her breasts, cupping them, my thumbs grazing over her nipples as I stared at her in humble worship. Her head dipped to the left, as she moaned.

Biting her lip as she pushed harder against me, she commanded, "Harder."

I worked my fingers deeper against her breasts and she threw her head back for a moment, exposing her neck. I wanted more than anything to sit up and run my tongue from the base of it up to her ear, but feeling her hips circle against me kept me in place.

I dropped my hands to her hips as she moved faster, with urgency. Savannah lowered her head, her hair falling down over her shoulder again, curtaining around my face. I leaned up on my elbows and kissed her.

I wanted to tell her she was beyond compare. I wanted to beg her for more. Harder. My words failed me as I strung together a mess of inaudible gasps and groans. With a low growl escaping from the depths of my need for her, I grabbed her hips and rolled her back on her back.

"God, Gregory." She swallowed hard as she lifted her knees.

Sitting back for a second, I grabbed one of her ankles, then the other, and set them on my shoulders. She straightened her legs, bringing me even deeper as we cried out in unison at the raw intensity of the feeling.

Savannah's long fingers wrapped around the backs of my thighs, holding me in place, as I pushed harder and faster. The pitch of her cries climbed each time I thrust into her. Each time her nails dug harder into my skin.

"Yes...Savannah...ah..."

Her eyes closed tightly as she cried out one last time, every muscle in her body tensing underneath her glistening skin. She released her grip on my thighs, clawing at the sheets, balling the fabric in her hands as her back arched. Driving me insane. Watching, feeling her come undone overrode my sense of self, and I was completely lost in us. I curled my face against her neck, a moan escaping my lips, as I felt her entire body shuddering against mine. My eyes forced themselves to close as my mind went utterly blank. My body spasmed against hers once, twice, three times, before I collapsed onto her, my heart pounding in my chest, my breathing ragged.

Both of us lay there, gasping for breath. Our bodies were slick with sweat, and I leaned my head back and looked her in the eyes and said, "You are so fucking beautiful, Savannah."

"I love you, Gregory," she whispered for the second time since we'd been in my room. The words hurt this time. Because I did love her. I'd always loved her. But how did I reconcile that with my life?

I slowly and carefully rolled off of her, shifting so she could rest her head on my chest. Our breathing had finally slowed, but I could feel her heart beating against my chest. With one languorous arm stretched across my chest, her fingers curled up on my right side. My head leaned to the left, and if I leaned down, I could have kissed her forehead. I curled my left arm behind her and the fingers of my right hand intertwined with hers. Our legs were tangled, hooked around each other's, and goosebumps sprang up across her skin.

"Are you cold?" I asked.

"No," she whispered.

But I reached down with my right arm and pulled the blanket up anyway. Darkness had long since settled in the room, though very faint light shone around the curtains, just enough to illuminate the hair framing her face.

I was as relaxed, as calm, as happy as I'd ever been. Part of me wanted to drift off to sleep, right where we were. Which made no sense, because I didn't like touching anyone when I slept. I never, ever slept touching Karin.

That thought stopped me cold. *Karin.* A part of me asked, *what have I done?* But it was a small part. Because right then, where I was, here, with her, felt more right than anything I'd ever felt in my life. And I didn't want Karin, even thoughts of her, intruding into this space. This sacred, amazing space.

I blinked my eyes then squeezed them shut, because I was afraid if I kept them open, tears would spill over. Because...I could only ask myself...*why?* Why had I let her go? Why did I tell James those years ago that I'd cut off contact with Savannah? Why did I let her walk away? Because in all too many ways, I'd been living in hell since the day she walked away.

And now? Now I was married.

To someone else.

I breathed out, involuntarily whispering the words, "I love you, Savannah."

At those words she sucked in a quick breath. I squeezed my eyebrows together at an unfamiliar sensation. A tear, fallen from her eyes to my chest.

"I've loved you since the beginning," she whispered, her voice sounding fierce, desperate.

I slowly breathed in and swallowed. I started to answer, but before I did, she took a breath again and spoke.

"I loved you the first time I saw you play the cello. I loved how you caressed it, how you made the music alive."

I couldn't think. I couldn't answer. I just looked down, allowing her to finish.

"I love the way you look at me," she said.

I kissed her delicately on the forehead, a tiny wisp of her hair staying on my lips. I broke my right hand away from hers and brought it to my eyes, wiping them furiously. Because I'd never wanted to admit to anyone that when I'd married Karin, I'd always imagined I was really with Savannah.

I'd wished.

I'd wanted her so badly.

I opened my mouth to speak again, but she wasn't finished.

"I loved the way you looked at me when we played together. I loved that it was exactly the same as you looked when we were making love."

I swallowed. Tried to breathe in. I tried to say something. But I couldn't even think. And then she said the words. She said them in a quiet tone, her voice breathy, beautiful, as open and vulnerable as I'd ever heard anyone sound.

"I love us," she said.

I suppressed a sob. And I whispered, "I do too."

At that moment I knew this couldn't last. I couldn't have just part of her. I wanted Savannah in my life for good. I wanted her more than anything. I wanted her as my partner, as my lover, as my wife. For the first time in my adult life, I was...happy...overjoyed...to be touching someone, to have someone in my arms, and I never wanted to let that go. I never wanted to let *her* go.

And it broke me that I had pledged my life.

My eternity.

To someone else.

Chapter 23

SAVANNAH

IS COLOGNE WAS sweeter than I'd remembered. It was more intoxicating than I'd considered, but by then it didn't matter. I was fully his. Laying with my back to him, I was molded into his body as if we were crafted for each other. Still naked from last night, my bare skin touched almost every inch of him as one of his arms set snugly around my waist.

I cautiously opened one eye, not wanting to disturb him as I checked the time.

5:24 a.m.

We had to leave for the airport in three hours in order to meet back up with the tour in Lincoln, Nebraska for this evening's show. I'd never had a desire to go to Nebraska, but as I shifted to nuzzle my head back onto his shoulder, I submitted to the fact that I would follow wherever Gregory went in an instant.

I didn't know if he could follow me back.

I ignored that reality as I replayed the sight of his muscular shoulders towering over my body as we worked in slow rhythm with each other, expressing overwhelming emotions I hadn't realized I'd held onto for so long. Never had I ever felt so comfortable allowing someone in like that. Emotionally and physically. There were no questions, no awkward pauses as we transitioned easily from one measure to the next, our once silent song resonating between us.

I love you, Savannah.

We'd spoken those words to each other before. But to hear them again, after so much time and so much hurt, and to have them feel just like they had back then...no, they felt better. More sincere as we looked into each other's eyes, bared to one another under the soft moonlight sneaking admittance through the hotel room window.

Gregory shifted and tightened his arm around me, inhaling as he planted a soft kiss on my shoulder. I grinned, unmoving, reveling in the elegance of the moment. The allure of the next step was tantalizing as he pressed his hips into me, growing harder with each kiss he fixed down my spine. Involuntarily, my hips shifted back, pushing into him as I let out a small sigh.

His firm hand glided satisfyingly down my side. My muscles twitched as his fingers stumbled across the embarrassingly ticklish skin at the base of my ribs. I felt his grin on my shoulder blade as his hand rode over the curve of my hip and slid forward, slipping between my thighs.

"Mmm..." I rolled back slightly, parting my legs to allow his fingers full access.

His mouth moved quickly to my neck and his teeth gently nibbled at my skin as he sucked in a quick breath, his fingers sliding easily inside me. As his thumb worked over me in lazy circles, I shifted again, needing to see him.

To remind myself this was all real.

His crystal eyes brightened as I smiled, holding his face in my hands. Playfully, he bit his lip and grinned, leaning forward to kiss me.

"Good morning," he managed after prying his tongue from my mouth. His voice was sexy in the morning. Undisciplined roughness.

I had to close my eyes for a moment as his fingers worked faster, my hips shifting anxiously beneath him.

Suddenly, Vivaldi bellowed from the cell phone on his bedside stand, startling us both. The cold chill of reality settled like a lead ball in my stomach as he clumsily pulled his hand away from me and sat up on the edge of the bed. I lay there, unmoving, banishing truth from my daydream for a while longer.

Just one minute more. Please.

"Hello?" He cleared his throat and said it again.

I silently appealed to the universe to let it be someone from the tour. Joseph McIntosh, maybe, congratulating us on our job well done last night or confirming our arrival time in Lincoln later in the day. It was barely six o'clock, though.

It wasn't anyone else.

"Hi," he started again. "Mmm-hmm. Yes. I am, too." The flirtatious huskiness of his voice was gone. All the life was sucked from the room as I sat up, resting my back against the plush headboard and tucked my knees into my chest.

Gregory rested his elbows on his knees as he spoke, dangling his fingers through his hair as he let out a deep sigh. "Yes, my flight leaves in a couple of hours so I have to...yes. Of course. I will. You, too."

His phone slid from his fingers onto the bed next to him. He glanced over his shoulder, a grievous look on his face. He opened his mouth to speak, but I couldn't listen. I didn't know if he regretted what we'd done last night or that his wife interrupted our morning, but neither was appropriate. Neither acceptable. Neither better than the other.

"Don't," I said, wrapping the sheet around myself as I slid off the mattress.

"Savannah," he sighed.

Taking a deep breath, I walked to his side of the bed and squatted down, meeting his tortured gaze.

"Don't," I repeated, kissing him once. I didn't want an apology or an excuse for last night. It was incredible. So were we. I wanted to leave it as it was before we had to return to reality.

As I stepped away, he stood, grabbing my hand and pulling me toward him. He took my face in his hands as his expression softened. The stain of regret lingered, though.

It always does.

"I love you," he whispered as if we weren't alone in the room.

We weren't, really.

With tears stinging my eyes, I suddenly needed a shower more than I ever had in my life. I swallowed hard, nodding as I tried to find my voice.

"I know."

I shrugged and gave a timid smile as I pulled away from his grip and locked myself in the bathroom. Looking at my reflection, I watched two pathetic tears slip down my cheeks. Mocking tears. Tears that garnered no sympathy from me or my conscience.

I loved Gregory Fitzgerald with every fiber of my being. And I knew he loved me back. It was as undeniable as it'd always been. We were meant to be together.

But, for every breath I took, there would forever be the exhale to remind myself of what I'd just done.

I slept with another woman's husband.

And I could never take that back.

GREGORY

B Y THE TIME we stepped into a cab at the Lincoln Airport, my patience was shot.

Savannah left the hotel room in a hurry that morning. Such a hurry that I hardly knew what was happening, and by the time I got clothes on and followed her out the door, she was gone, and I didn't know what her room number was. She ended up meeting me in the lobby, where we took a car, in silence, back to the airport. Except for communicating the barest of information, such as which gate we were going to, she didn't speak to me at the airport, or boarding the plane.

When the plane reached altitude, she leaned her seat back, put in earbuds, and turned away from me, closing her eyes. I've never felt so conflicted and confused in my life. I understood confusion. I understood mixed feelings. I loved her so much. But the fact that I was married tangled everything in knots.

What I couldn't understand was why she was so angry that she shut me out?

The moment the in-flight service started, I ordered a gin and tonic, heavy on the gin, and tossed the first one back quickly. She slept through the entire flight. Or, pretended to sleep if my nights next to Karin taught me anything about acting. I dredged out my old notebook and began to write.

The notebook began as nothing more than a log. A place to record my thoughts about particular performances or practices that went well or badly. Lately, though, it had increasingly become an outlet, a method for me to compose my thoughts before I had to deal with Karin.

Finally, the excruciatingly long flight ended, and we were on the ground in Lincoln, Nebraska, of all places. I'd never been in Nebraska. I'd never planned to be in Nebraska. I didn't want to be in Nebraska. As the plane came in on its final approach, all I could see outside was flat ground, spreading out uninterrupted for a million miles in every direction.

Who voluntarily lived in such a place?

Savannah was awake enough that she stirred in her seat and put away her earbuds during the final approach. Thirty minutes later we were standing in the blasting sunlight of middle America, the smell of dust and car exhaust permeating everything as I carefully slid my cello into the back of a cab.

"Please talk to me," I said as we got in the back seat. "Why are you angry with me, Savannah?"

She looked at me, a puzzled expression on her face. "I'm not angry with you."

"Where to?" the cab driver asked.

Crap. I'd written down the hotel information somewhere, but I had no idea what I'd done with it. As I fumbled with my wallet and pockets, Savannah reached in her purse and read out an address for the Marriott Cornhusker. I could only hope that the hotel wouldn't match the name.

"Lot of construction over there," the driver said. "It may take a little while."

"Fine," I said, irritation flashing through me. "Let's just get going."

"There's no need to be rude, Gregory. It's not his fault you're married."

I muttered, "Damn it," under my breath. "Is that what this is about?"

She gave me a level stare as the cab pulled out. Then she took a deep breath and said, "What do you expect from me, Gregory?"

"I expect you to not shut me out."

She tilted her head, staring at me. Her brown eyes were huge. Seductive. Beautiful. And completely inscrutable. I hated that I had absolutely no idea what she was thinking.

Outside, the bright sunlight shone down on what might have been the most depressing sight of my life. Flat grass extended all the way to the horizon, interrupted by nothing but a few trees and buildings. It was oppressive. As the driver took us closer to the highway, my phone rang, and I froze. The odds were very good it was Karin.

The phone rang again.

Savannah raised an eyebrow. "Maybe you should answer your phone, Gregory."

I stared back at her. Then I slowly took out the phone. It was, of course, Karin.

"Hello?"

"Gregory? Are you alone?"

"No, I'm afraid not. I'm in a taxicab."

I leaned forward slightly, keeping my eyes averted from Savannah. We were headed into what appeared to be a more urban area, thank God for that. But the cab was slowing down, as traffic thickened.

"Are you with her?"

My entire body tensed. "What difference does that make? I don't really see how that's relevant, Karin."

"Of course you don't. That's because you're fucking heartless, Gregory. I don't know why I ever married you. And I don't understand why..."

Her voice trailed off a little as I held the phone away from my ear. I could still hear her talking. So could Savannah, and the cab driver, and probably the people in the other car next to us. I closed my eyes, trying to regain my equilibrium. Then I thumbed the red button, hanging up on her.

Savannah's eyes dropped to the floor. She blinked her eyes. I couldn't tell if she was trying to hold back tears or rage.

"I'm sorry you had to hear that," I said.

She shook her head, a tiny, constrained movement. "Why?"

"Why what?"

"Why are you sorry? It's reality. You're married."

The cab had come to a stop, and the driver laid on the horn. I leaned forward. Nothing but dozens of stopped cars in front of us. The sun beat down on the car, scorching heat coming through the glass of the windshield. At the sight of the wall of cars ahead of us, I felt immediate tension. I turned around. More cars were lining up behind us.

"What's going on?" I asked the driver.

He shrugged, holding out his hands. "Construction. I told you that when you got in."

"Are you in a hurry, Gregory?" Savannah had an ironic smile on her face. "I thought you wanted to talk."

"I want you to stop behaving like a child."

Her eyes flared open, and she replied, carefully enunciating each word. "I am not behaving like a child. I do, however, need some time to think."

"What is there to think about? We love each other." As I said the words, I wiped my arm across my forehead.

She leaned close and hissed, "We love each other. And you are married. To someone else."

"Do you expect that to change overnight?"

"I don't know what I expect." Her eyes were glazed over and she looked away from me.

I sighed and leaned back in my seat. The cab driver took out a phone and dialed, then began talking to someone. I leaned forward and said, "Can you turn on the air conditioning? It's roasting in here."

He shook his head and waved his hand as if to brush me off.

"Seriously," I said, trying to keep a lid on my anger.

"Gregory," Savannah said. "Relax."

"It's stifling in here!"

"Gregory!" she said in a sharp tone. "It's not about the heat. It's about us."

I turned back to her and said, "I don't know what to do, Savannah!"

She shook her head, violently, then said, "I don't know what I was thinking. Do you intend for that to be me someday?"

"What?"

She pointed at my pocket, where I'd put my phone. "Some day, you'll just be able to hang up. Like you did with her. And that will be that." Her voice had begun to shake, and she rolled her eyes up at the roof of the cab. "I don't know what I was thinking," she muttered.

"Savannah..."

Abruptly, she reached for the door of the cab and opened it. Immediately someone in a truck outside honked their horn. Before I could blink or catch a breath, she was out of the car, into the blistering heat.

I slid after her, but she slammed the door shut, hard, then turned and began to trot away, darting in front of another car and then to the curb. Her back was straight as she walked; her head flung back, her pride intact. But where was she going?

The trunk of the cab was full of our luggage. And my cello. My seven hundred fifty thousand dollar cello, which I was not leaving alone in the cab.

What was it she said yesterday? That this was the part where she walked away?

"You're paying her fare," the driver demanded. Because now he could interrupt his damn phone call.

Savannah was almost out of sight, walking along the curb. And then she was gone entirely, around the corner of a building. And then the phone rang. Again.

"What?" I snarled.

"Gregory? It's Joseph. Are you all right?"

I coughed. Joseph McIntosh, our conductor.

"I'm fine, Joseph. What's going on?"

"Where are you?"

"In a cab on the way from the airport."

"Oh good! I needed to talk with you and Savannah."

I closed my eyes. "I'm afraid she's not with me...she um... went separately. To take care of some errands."

"Damn," he muttered. "Anyway, I'll catch her later. Point is, reaction to last night's show is out of this world. You two were fantastic, and the tour is nearly sold out for our paid shows. Absolutely amazing performance. It was inspired, and I've got no idea when you even had time to practice the changes with her."

I didn't have a clue how to respond to that, so I didn't. They weren't my changes, and we hadn't practiced. I'd simply followed her lead.

"Anyway," he said, "we're adding your duet to the show for the rest of the tour. You two will replace the first act after the intermission."

"Joseph, I don't know if that's a good idea..."

"No false modesty, Gregory. It doesn't suit you. You're doing the duet. No arguments."

I was speechless. I looked ahead through the traffic but still couldn't see her.

She was gone.

"Fine, Joseph," I said. "Whatever you say."

What I wanted to say was fuck off, Joseph. But that wouldn't have gone over very well.

I hung up the phone and collapsed back into my seat.

Chapter 24

SAVANNAH

THE SHOULDER STRAP of my bag caught on the door handle as I tore into the hotel room. I growled my frustration and yanked the strap free from around the handle and sailed the bag across the room.

In the next second I was thankful that my roommate wasn't there. She must have been at dinner. Lizzy played the French horn and was extremely nice, but I didn't know her well enough to explain my outburst.

"Shit," I grumbled, collapsing onto my bed.

What the hell did I want from him? It's not like we made love and he told me by the way, I'm married. I knew. But he also knew, and he did it anyway.

He made me feel like I was his.

I wasn't.

Despite the sweltering, long walk I took from the cab to the hotel, I still wasn't able to coax my thoughts back from the edge. I picked up my phone, thumbing through to the only number that made any sense at the moment.

"Hey, babe, what's up? That was a hell of a performance the other night." Marcia's playful voice brought tears to my eyes.

"Hey." I barely squeaked out the word before tears tightened my vocal chords.

Marcia responded in a quick, urgent voice. "Savannah? Sweetie, what's wrong?"

"I...it..." I didn't know where to start. How could I express that my heart was breaking over the man I loved, because I couldn't say no to him. Neither of us stopped long enough to ask or think about what we were doing.

There was no question that what happened last night was the single most powerful experience in my life. And the most devastating.

Just as I was about to attempt an answer, my phone beeped. It was my mother.

I'd been avoiding her calls since our aborted lunch in Boston several weeks ago. Even my dad softly scolded me via text message over it. I couldn't put her off any longer.

"Shit, Marcia, it's my fucking mother. I...shit, I have to go."

"You call me back tonight, okay?"

I nodded in the empty room. "I will."

One long sigh later, I steadied my voice and pressed to accept her call.

"Hey, Mom."

"Savannah." If we were face to face she would have nodded as she spoke, raising a too-thin eyebrow. "Are you okay, darling?"

"I'm fine. What's up?" I sniffed as I made my way to the bathroom. When I flicked on the light, I still couldn't bear the broken eyes that stared back at me, so I darkened the room again and sat on the edge of the tub. I was covered in dust and sweat from the walk to the hotel. It was all so appropriate.

"You did a fine job on the show the other night, Savannah. I'm proud of you."

Proud of you.

Vita Carulli never doled out fluffy praise. In theory, this would have been the point that I would have hung up the phone, not wanting to hear whatever came next. To hear what she was priming me for with the verbal approval. This time, however, I was willing to let anything invade the space in my brain that was searching for escape from the emotions of last night.

"Thank you. Apparently we're going to do it at every show now."

Joseph's insistence on the addition of our duet to the regular program was aggravating at best.

"Don't sound so put upon, dear. It's a fabulous opportunity. You should think twice before squandering it."

Just like that she was back.

I sighed my response.

"Anyway," she continued, "that's not the reason I called."

"I suspected as much." I made my way to the minibar in my room, cracking open a tiny bottle of vodka that would probably cost me twenty dollars.

"You remember Malcolm Carroll," my mother stated, her voice turning a notch over his name.

"Mmm-hmm," I mumbled through the tiny plastic bottle dispensing the mid-shelf vodka into my mouth.

Malcolm was the conductor for the Boston Ballet Orchestra, and longtime friend of the family. My mother had tried to arrange an audition with them for me during my senior year of college. When I turned it down, she'd implied that my admission to the conservatory had less to do with my own skill at the audition and more to do with her influence, and it would be foolish of me to ignore the opportunity she was providing.

"He's leaving the Boston Ballet."

She seemed to choose her words carefully, but that didn't stop the vodka from burning my sinuses as it shot through my nose. "What?"

One doesn't simply leave a position like that unless they're headed to something better. I instantly searched my mental list of all the conductors of the major orchestras I knew, and couldn't come up with a single name of anyone leaving their current posts.

"He's accepted the conductor position for the Boston Lyric Opera."

"Okay, I'm not really sure what that has to do with m—"

"Where I've just earned lead role in A Midsummer's Night Dream."

I sat up. "You're performing again?" I can't say that I was surprised. After she left my dad and moved to Boston, I assumed it was only a matter of time.

Ten months on the nose, it turns out.

"Well, at least just for the run of this show. I'll see how things go afterward."

"That's great that you and Malcolm will get to work together. What are the odds?"

My mother cleared her throat. "Yes, it was quite fortuitous, but it complicates matters."

Once again I found myself shaking my head in my still empty hotel room, a nonverbal indication that the vodka in my hand was much stronger than the bottle promised, or maybe that my mother was speaking another language.

Maybe it was both.

"Mother, what's complicated?"

"I wanted to make sure I spoke with you tonight, before the Opera News story runs tomorrow." By the tone of her voice, which was quickly fading, I knew the news wasn't going to be about my mother's return to the stage.

I cleared my throat. "What is it, Mom?"

"The story tomorrow is going to say that Malcolm was growing restless with the Ballet and was looking to move on, dying to work in the opera." She spoke as if she were reading from a novel. The dramatic rise and fall of her voice had me picturing her on stage somewhere. "They're saying that once I landed the role of Hermia, I used my pull to get him the job currently filled by alternating conductors since Don Kimmel left the position last year."

"From what I recall, you're no stranger to tossing your name around as it suits those around you. What's the big deal now? You say everyone does it."

Talking about her attempt to sway the admissions committee in my favor at the conservatory got easier over the past few years.

Despite the fact I knew I got in on my own skill, doubt lingered. It always does.

"For one thing, young lady, that's not what I did." Her tone was clipped and defensive.

Growing tired of the conversation, I sighed heavily. "What's the point here, Mom?"

"The point is that the photo they're running with the story is one of Malcolm and I kissing in Venice."

I'd assumed she'd move on from my father at some point. But under a year seemed a bit hasty. Still, I remained unimpressed with the conversation I was locked in.

Trying to sound like an unwounded child, I pressed for more. "When did you and Malcolm go to Venice?"

Her long silence suddenly made it very clear it wasn't a recent excursion.

"Mom…" My heart raced, embarrassingly unprepared for what was coming.

"Coccolona..." she sighed, trailing off as her voice caught. Cuddly one.

My mother hadn't called me that in years. Years. We hardly spoke Italian on a regular basis anymore. She only slipped into Italian terms of endearment under times of great stress, like when my grandmother passed away.

"Seven years ago."

"Seven years ago?" I ran a hand through my hair just as there was a knock on the door.

Now? Really?

"Savannah, let me explain..." My mother's voice was uncharacteristically frazzled.

Opening the door, I found Nathan. He looked happy to see me, until he studied my face for a second. He quickly ushered himself into the room, shutting the door behind him. I mouthed to him that I was on the phone with my mother. He knew all the gritty details of my parents' falling out. He patiently waited, crossing his arms in front of his chest and leaning against the wall.

"I wish you would, because I'm dying to hear about how a seven-year affair is blowing up in your face as we speak."

Nathan's eyes widened.

The irony of the conversation brought me to my knees and I rested my back against the side of the bed. He sat next to me, resting his arms on his knees.

"Get ahold of yourself, Savannah, Malcolm and I haven't had an affair for seven years."

"You're lying. Are you two together now?" I stood, fuming with rage over what she'd done to my father.

"My private life, Savannah, is not any of your business. What you need to know is that Malcolm and I never had a relationship while your father and I were together. That's all I wanted you to know. Besides," she continued, rather distantly, "you know what it's like."

"I'm sorry, I know what what's like?" I couldn't even address her assertion that I should be happy about anything that was going on.

"To not be able to stop yourself from loving someone."

"I..." I trailed off, knowing full well what she was talking about, but unable to defend myself now that I had an audience. What I didn't know, however, was how she knew.

"I saw the performance, Savannah. Tread carefully. Whenever it happens it will be a mess, and I don't want it jeopardizing your career."

Hastily, I ended the call and turned off my phone. In a few short minutes my mom admitted to being in love with someone other than my father, all the while skirting the discussion of a possible seven-year affair and not appearing to give a shit about my feelings. Only my career.

Seven years.

Intermittently on the flight from LA to Lincoln, I considered what it would look like to try to be with Gregory, despite his marriage. Now knowing how that looked from the outside, I brought my hand to my mouth, stifling a sob. Nathan grabbed me into a hug in an instant.

"What's wrong?" he whispered, stepping back and holding me at arms' length.

Wiping tears from my eyes, I shrugged in defeat.

I had to tell him. I had to tell someone, and I was in no condition to call Marcia back.

"Nathan...I made a horrible mistake."

GREGORY

I FINISHED STRAPPING IN the cello, then lay down on the lower bunk and glanced at my watch. It was just past midnight, and the Amtrak California Zephyr would roll into Denver at 7 a.m. I sighed, staring up at the bunk above me. I didn't care for sleeper cars unless they were solo, and this one I cared for even less, because I would be sharing the car with Nathan Connors, who I really didn't want to see at the moment. I needed to have a talk with the production assistant who made the travel arrangements, because this was not acceptable. God knew Savannah had probably spoken with him, so I would be getting an earful of self-righteous yammering from a boy barely out of his teens.

Savannah and I had performed the duet together at the Pershing Center in Lincoln.

Despite our argument, despite her charging off by herself, she'd shown up for the performance on time, got up on the stage, and brought magic into that auditorium. Music that took my breath away. Not once during the four and a half minutes of our duet did her eyes leave mine. Until the end, when she turned away from me dismissively and bowed to the wildly applauding audience. Then she swept off the stage like a queen, leaving me to clumsily lumber behind her with my cello.

With a small lurch, the train moved forward, the car rocking back and forth, the thumping slowly accelerating as the train pulled out of the city. My phone rang. Probably Karin again. I shook my head and took out the phone and wrinkled my eyebrows in surprise. It wasn't Karin: the call was coming from Madeline.

"Hello?"

"Gregory, I'm not waking you am I?"

"No...actually, we just boarded the train in Lincoln."

"Good." She went silent.

I sat, waiting for her to speak, but she didn't, which was hardly normal, not to mention extremely uncomfortable.

Finally I said, "I trust your honeymoon went well? Is everything all right?"

She let out a small chuckle. "Yes, of course. I'm sorry...everything's fine. Actually...I was calling for two reasons. We didn't get a chance to talk before you left Boston, and I wanted to thank you for watching the flat. James and I really appreciated it."

"Of course, Madeline, after all, what are friends for?"

She let out a low chuckle, and said, "Well, that's what I'm calling about, now, isn't it?"

I stretched a little in the bunk. "Are you drinking? What time is it there?"

"I am, Gregory."

My reply was a little impatient. "What's going on, Madeline?"

She sighed. "I just got home from a particularly maudlin evening out. With your wife."

That caused me to sit up. Suddenly. And hit my head on the upper bunk. I cursed and dropped the phone, which I heard bouncing against the carpet to who knew where while I fumbled around in the darkness.

A sudden flash and horn racing by, then receding into the distance, marked a train going in the opposite direction. For a few moments our train was buffeted by wind and turbulence from the other one, and then it was gone.

I got on my knees and searched around until I found my phone. It was underneath the bed. Groaning, I put it to my ear and leaned back against the bunk, still sitting on the floor. "Madeline, you there?"

"I'm still here, Gregory. Did you fall, or jump out the window or something?"

"Hit my head on the upper bunk. What did dear Karin have to say?"

Madeline responded in an aggravated tone. "She's your wife, Gregory."

"I'm painfully aware of that, Madeline."

She sighed quite audibly. Then she said, "After your performance last night, she believes you're sleeping with Savannah."

I was silent. I couldn't tell anyone. I was married. But I couldn't lie either. Not to Madeline, who had been my friend for fifteen years, who had been Savannah's mentor. I couldn't lie. So I didn't say anything. Which would, unfortunately, tell Madeline all she needed to know.

"You love her, don't you?"

I closed my eyes and pressed my head against my knees.

"Gregory...how did you do this to yourself? You, of all people."

I just groaned. Then rode in silence for a few more seconds. Then I said, "What did you say to Karin?"

"Well...it was a long night. And...she's not having an easy time of it, Gregory. You know...I knew from the beginning you didn't love her. It really wasn't fair that you married her. And now...when she just found out she's infertile? You're my friend, and I love you, Gregory. I want the best for you. I want you to be happy. I want her to be happy. But your timing sucks. You're breaking her heart."

I leaned forward again, my mind focusing in on one single word in her monologue.

"She just found out what?"

Madeline didn't answer.

"Madeline. What the fuck did you just say? She just found out what?"

Her answer was so quiet I barely heard. "Gregory, she can't have children."

My thoughts exploded into a hundred different directions at once. If she couldn't have children, then why the hell was she hounding me about having children? What the hell? For that matter, what prompted this revelation? It's not as if we were trying to have children.

Were we?

"I don't understand," I said, my voice dry. "When...did she have a doctor appointment?"

"Gregory...are you saying...you didn't know?"

"Of course I didn't know," I hissed. "I've never wanted children. And she knew that." It didn't make any sense. Why would she go get testing without telling me? For that matter, why does anyone get fertility testing unless they'd been trying to have a baby? Had she? She was on the pill...that much I knew. It was one of the first questions I asked when we were dating. But now I was asking myself if she'd decided to stop taking them. If she'd decided to have a baby without discussing it with me. Had she only brought it up because it wasn't working?

What the hell is wrong with her? A wash of rage and guilt and confusion ran through me in a muddled mess, and I didn't have the first clue what to think or feel.

Madeline was silent at the other end of the call. So I sat, watching the occasional light flash by, listening to the tracks rumble underneath the car, and then the door to the sleeper opened up, hitting me in the side.

"God damn it!"

In the bright light from the train hallway stood Nathan. Who gave me a murderous look as he stared at me, sitting on the floor in the car.

"Madeline, I've got to go," I said, scrambling to my feet.

"Wait!" she called out.

"Seriously..."

"No," she replied, her voice firm. "You listen to me for a moment."

"Now is awkward," I replied.

Nathan was swaying in the doorway. He didn't look drunk. But he did look furious.

"Gregory," she said. "I'm not going to judge you. I've known you and Savannah for a long time. And...when she was a student I did my best to keep you apart. Because it was my responsibility. But...it's been obvious for a long time. But my support ends..." She paused, and I heard her sniff. "My support ends if you hurt that girl. Do you understand me?"

I closed my eyes. Then I said, "Yes, Madeline. I understand. I'll call you in the next day or so, all right?"

"Good night, Gregory."

We hung up. Just in time, because a pugnacious Nathan Connors pushed his way into the room and slung his bag onto the top bunk.

"Nathan," I said.

"I want to talk with you, Fitzgerald."

I raised an eyebrow. "Whatever for?"

"You screwing Savannah."

Something about his obnoxious little face, or the contemptuous wording he used, infuriated me. Not to mention the fact that she'd spoken to Nathan, of all people, about it. I'd have been happier if she'd picked just about anyone else on earth to confide in. Anyone else.

"Don't you dare speak about her that way," I said.

His cheeks were red, his eyes wide, aggressive. "That's a fucking laugh, Fitzgerald. You break my best friend's heart, and you tell me not to talk about her in a way that displeases you?"

I leveled my gaze at him and said, "Nathan, I really don't have time for this right now. You're standing in between me and the lounge car."

"You leave her alone," he said. "You don't talk to her. You don't touch her. You don't fucking hurt her."

I'd had enough. I'd awakened that morning in absolute bliss, with the love of my life beside me, only to have my wife destroy that moment. My wife, who was busy trying to get pregnant without asking me. I'd been yelled at, watched Savannah run off into traffic, I'd hit my head, been kept up on a train half the night, been forced to room with a too young and far too irritating member of this orchestra, and now I had to listen to this? I was done.

"Get out of my way. Now."

He stepped back. The menace in my tone was unmistakable. I held a finger up in his face. "The fact that we're colleagues does not make you my equal, Mr. Connors. You will never speak to me that way again. I care for that woman more than you can possibly imagine."

His eyes narrowed, and he took a breath to speak, and I pushed him back. "Don't cross me, Nathan."

He muttered, "If you hurt her, I'll ruin you, Fitzgerald. Your precious fucking career will never survive it. I guarantee you that."

I leaned close to him and said in a low tone, "Just remember when you make threats. I was sitting in my seat with the Boston Symphony before you were even old enough to care about girls and their feelings. I have enough pull to make your fucking career miserable. Now back the fuck off." Then I backed up, opened the door to the sleeper and walked out into the corridor.

I wasn't proud of myself. I wasn't happy. I wasn't anything but pissed off and sorely in need of a drink. Five minutes later I found my way to the lounge car. Two minutes after that I'd tossed back my first gin and tonic and ordered another. It was late, and I was tired, and we had a long day ahead of us tomorrow. I was regretting accepting a seat on this roving tour.

I was too old for this crap, and the last thing I needed to deal with was Nathan fucking Connors back in my room.

I shook my head. The hell of it was...if it was true? That Karin had just found out she was sterile, or infertile, or whatever the hell they call it? Then I was stuck with her, at least for the time being. Because what kind of bastard leaves his wife when heartbroken?

I stared at my drink. And tried not to think about it. Because one thing I'd always been was someone who could look in the mirror with pride. But twice now...both times with Savannah...I'd destroyed that. The first time, when I didn't risk it. When I didn't go after her. When I told James I'd cut off contact. It broke her heart, and it broke my soul.

The second time...hard to believe it was only twenty-four hours ago. Twenty-four hours to ruin my life. Twenty-four hours to break her heart. I loved Savannah, and I'd do anything, anything at all, to have her in my life.

And she was the one thing I couldn't have.

I tossed back my second drink then leaned my head on my hands for just a moment, rubbing my eyes. I kept them closed, leaning that way. Then I heard a voice.

Her voice.

She sounded exhausted, her voice rough, gravelly almost.

"Another gin and tonic for him. Red wine for me."

I lifted my face from my hands. And Savannah sat down across from me.

Chapter 25

GREGORY

EVERY FEW MINUTES a light flashed by, the railcar rocked periodically, and the wheels rattled with their own rhythmic beauty as the train sped through the darkness. I don't know how much further we travelled before we spoke. It could have been a hundred yards, or it could have been a hundred miles. I stared at her, rocking a little in my seat as the car moved.

She had dark circles under her eyes, which didn't suit her at all, and her face was even more pale than normal. She sat back and sipped her wine and seemed to study me.

"Does this mean we're speaking again?" I asked.

"We never stopped speaking. I just needed time to think." As she said the words, she looked almost drained of emotion. She let out a long sigh, and I must have mirrored it, because her mouth quirked up on one side in a tiny smile.

"Tired?" I asked.

"I didn't get much sleep last night," she replied, raising one eyebrow. Her tone was light, and she looked at me over her plastic wine glass as she said the words.

I swallowed, sudden tension in the air. Did this mean she was over her sudden anger? Or...what did it mean? Why did she joke about something so intense? So deeply personal between the two of us?

The hell of it was, the night we'd just had together? It was...everything. It meant everything. It was so much more than sex. So much more than anything I'd ever experienced, even more than our fumbling first night five years before. More than I'd even imagined.

I couldn't get a grip on my feelings, because every time I thought of her, I was overwhelmed. Every time I thought of *last night* I was overwhelmed.

Every time I thought of her whispering, *I love us.*

"Sometimes I don't understand you," I said.

She snorted, raising one eyebrow and looking at me with an expression that bordered on amusement. Then she took a long drink from her wine. "Did you seriously just say that, Gregory? You don't understand *me*?"

I shrugged. "I don't know what you want me to say."

"I want you to tell me what you're thinking."

I sighed, then leaned forward and took a sip of my gin. "What I'm thinking, Savannah, is that...last night...was the happiest I've ever been in my life."

She frowned and shook her head. "You didn't look so happy in the morning. When your wife called."

I shook my head impatiently. "That's not as simple a situation as you might think."

"What's complicated about it?"

I sighed. I didn't know how to answer, because it was a mess. I didn't love Karin. I should never have married her. I'd done it in a moment of heartbreak and loneliness, two years after Savannah left, knowing I'd lost her forever. Not even realizing that I'd condemned myself by doing so.

There was no right answer. There was no excuse. And no matter what happened with Savannah, no matter what happened with Karin, the fact of the matter was, I was the one who was wrong. Every single step of the way. I wanted Savannah so badly it was like a wound that wouldn't heal. I didn't know how to fix it. I didn't know how to make it right.

Then, before I could stop myself, I blurted out, "I can't promise you anything."

"You *what*?" she asked. Her tone of voice implied irritation. Disgust.

"Listen to me," I said. Fumbling. Confused. Unsure of myself.

"I'm listening," she said, "but you aren't making any sense."

I swallowed and closed my eyes. Then I opened them and met her eyes. She shifted in her seat, and as I spoke the next words, I had the feeling that I'd taken a headlong rush off a cliff.

"You're my heart, Savannah. Not in it. Not a part of it. I'm consumed by you. Obsessed by you. I need you in my life any way I can have you. Don't tell me you don't feel the same way."

She frowned then looked away. Her face seemed to tremble. She looked back and whispered, "I've always loved you."

I looked at the table. "Last night was undeniably the best night of my life."

She rolled her eyes and waved at the waiter, indicating another round. I was an unsteady mess as it was, but another drink would just be more of the same.

"Savannah, I need you to listen to me."

She shrugged. "I have been."

I swallowed. Then I plunged forward. "I never stopped loving you. I never stopped thinking of you."

She shook her head. "Inconvenient, isn't it, that you went and got married."

I winced. "Yeah. Well, I did. I was…lost. Lonely. I'd screwed up badly and knew it. I'd lost touch with you. I didn't know how to make it up to you. I didn't know how to fix it. And… she was there. It was just…easy."

"Easy?"

My tone dropped, and while I spoke the words, I couldn't possibly express the frustration, the disgust. "Easy and stupid. I married someone I didn't love."

She met my eyes. "What does that have to do with *me*, Gregory?"

I held her gaze. "I guess, what I'm trying to say is...I can't promise you anything. I can't ask for anything. But...I'm going to anyway. I want you, Savannah. I want you in my life... for...whatever happiness we can have, while we can have it."

She recoiled, confusion and sadness on her face. Then she started to stand, and I reached out and grabbed her hand.

"Please," I whispered. "Savannah...I need you. Desperately."

She shook her head, tiny movements, and I dove in and said, "We have this summer. We have...the next two months on the road. Savannah...don't turn me away. I love you."

"What are you asking me?" she cried.

"I want you to have an affair with me."

The words fell into the room, suddenly silencing everything around us. She stared at me, her lower lip barely trembling.

Then she stood, yanking her hand from mine, and ran out of the car.

SAVANNAH

YES.
    I got out of the lounge car as fast as I could, before I could utter the single most ridiculous word I'd ever considered saying. Gregory just asked me to spend the summer with him. *With him.* He loved me. Just me. There were things going on in his marriage that were complicated, but... he didn't love her.

He loved me.

I needed to talk to someone about this. I needed to tease out reality from fantasy, and love from choices. Because, really, whether or not Gregory loved Karin, he was married to her. He chose to marry her when I was thousands of miles away and not in his life at all.

What if I'd been around?

I'm consumed by you and need you in my life any way I can have you...

I couldn't tell him I didn't feel the same way. Because I did. I had been consumed by him from the moment he played at the end of our first class. Obsessed. Obsession makes people crazy.

Maybe crazy was okay if love was the reason.

Yes, I definitely needed to call someone.

Nathan listened to me cry about my mistake with Gregory after I'd gotten off the phone with my mother a few nights before. He yelled some colorful language about Gregory putting me in the position to get hurt. That I deserved better than that, and I was wise to stay away from him. The fact that I was considering graduating from *the other woman* to full *mistress* status for an entire summer, rather than a single night, was not a conversation I could have with the hot-headed flutist. No one needed a broken hand, and Nathan would be the last to consider the effect one could have on his career.

Marcia had texted me several times when I didn't call her back. I now had a hell of a lot more to tell her than I did after our initial call. Somehow I'd been fortunate enough to end up in a single sleeper room on the train. I have no idea who I'd have to thank for that, but they were getting thanked. A train is not typically a place that grants privacy, but I'd finally caught a sliver of a break.

Lying flat out on my bed, there was one person I had to call before my former roommate. I pressed *send* and spent a few seconds drumming up something to say.

"Hello?" His voice was groggy, unfocused.

"Dad. I know it's late...I'm sorry. I needed to...I needed to hear your voice. Can we talk?"

"Savannah! I'm glad you called. I never know when is a good time..."

"I know, Dad, it's fine. We're so busy all the time between playing and traveling, and figuring out which city we're in." I laughed for the first time in several days.

"How are things going?"

I chatted with him for a few minutes about the cities we'd been to, the various venues we'd played in, and how everyone was getting along. While the tour was mostly comprised of younger musicians, newer to their respective symphonies, there were some seasoned members amongst us. Some with long standing feuds with other musicians, which made for great storytelling during late night transit. Who would have guessed that trombonists could be so moody?

We never talked about my mom, apart from him telling me once in a while that I needed to call her back.

"Dad," I sighed, "I talked to Mom the other day. She told me about Malcolm."

"What...um, what did she tell you about Malcolm?" His voice had changed. He sounded slightly on edge. Not angry, though.

"About the story in *Opera News*."

"Uh-huh..."

"Did it go on for the whole seven years, Dad?"

"Savannah..." As he exhaled into the phone, I could almost see him pinching the bridge of his nose.

"Come on, Dad, I'm an adult. This is my life, too."

"Oh, sweetie, it's so complicated."

I chuckled half-heartedly, "Clearly. Did you know about him the whole time?"

My mother never admitted to a seven-year affair with Malcolm, but it was obvious. Given she was working in Italy and he was working in Boston, I gathered whatever relationship they had up until she moved back to the States was largely emotional.

"Malcolm was always a good friend to your mother. To the family. They have a lot in common and live in the same world."

"Yeah," I snapped, "a world you *left* for her." I felt my cheeks heating thinking about the career my dad walked away from to support hers.

"I didn't leave it for her, Savannah...it was for you."

"What?" Tears stung my eyes.

"It was for us. For our family. You mattered more to me than to try to raise you on the road. One of us had to make the choice. She was further in her career than I was. Making her give it all up wasn't something I could do."

"But you both *chose* to have a family. Why did *you* have to give it all up?"

"That's life, Savannah..." There seemed to be something he wasn't telling me in that silence.

"Was Malcolm around back then? Has it always been him?" I was whispering, disbelieving I was asking my dad something so personal.

"Your mother and I had a challenging relationship, Savannah. We wanted children together, but you came a little earlier than planned. That called for us to make some tough choices. It brought things out in us that...look, your mother is a good mother."

He didn't want to throw her under the bus, but it was clear that what went on—was now going on—between my mother and Malcolm was no secret.

"But you and Mom were *married*..."

"I don't have anything I can say to make this easier to understand. But, I do want to tell you something." His tone darkened to the stern set of notes he used when discussing drugs with me in high school. "Don't make things harder on yourself than they need to be. Love shouldn't be a fight, Savannah. It shouldn't be hard. It shouldn't tear people apart and leave everyone broken. If someone loves you, they give you all of themselves, not just parts. Do you hear me?"

My lips parted, startled by my father's bleeding honesty. "Yeah," I gasped, "I hear you. I have to go, okay? It's late."

"I love you. Check in again soon, okay? Even if it's 3:00 a.m."

"I will. Love you, Dad."

I didn't know before if my dad saw what my mom saw when watching my performance with Gregory, but that cleared it up. Of course he saw. He was wrong about one thing, though. You fight for what you love. Who you love. Giving up on Gregory six years ago left me empty. I had a chance to make that right, if even for a summer.

Spending a few weeks capturing what most people spend a lifetime searching for had to be better than nothing at all. Maybe Gregory and I had to grab whatever happiness was dangling in front of us. It was our window, and it was closing in a few weeks. I didn't know if it would ever open again. I didn't know what was going on in his marriage, and I didn't know what went on in my parents' marriage. All I knew was Gregory Fitzgerald was the only one who made me feel this way, and if this was the only chance we had to fully experience each other...I had to take it.

Even if it would break me in the end.

GREGORY

NATHAN VACATED OUR sleeping quarters early. The train arrived in Denver at 7:00 a.m., and he banged around the tiny cabin like a grumpy teenager before finally leaving. Frankly, I was relieved to have avoided a physical confrontation with him last night. I knew he cared deeply for Savannah, and despite the rage that bled from his pores, I felt less retaliatory and more ashamed of myself for hurting her.

Hurting her wasn't my intention. None of this was. I stepped out of the shower in my mid-grade hotel room and ran my hands through my hair, thankful my hangover was subsiding. When I'd started drinking in the lounge car, I didn't expect to leave there asking the woman I loved to engage in a relationship with me for the remainder of our tour.

I didn't regret asking her. If that was the only way I'd ever have happiness, then so be it. What bothered me was...I'd put her in a position where she had to make the decision. It was that I'd put my desires and needs onto *her*. The way her eyes widened as she swallowed when I asked. She went silent.

She's never silent.

She sat stoically and listened to my slurred reasoning. I meant every word. We needed to seize this time. We'd been given an opportunity to be together, even for a short time. It would be risky, and a lot of people could get hurt.

I didn't want her to get hurt. That was my bottom line. I would sacrifice just about anything to never again see the look she had on her face before bailing from the cab and walking down the busy road in Lincoln. Away from me.

It was approaching noon and I was anxious. I hadn't seen or heard from Savannah since our talk. It occurred to me that watching her stand and nimbly leave our table could have been the last time I saw her in any context other than the stage. I had to tell her, though. I had to tell her my feelings. My desires. I had nothing to lose, but her to gain.

Shit. What could she possibly think of me, a married man, asking her to willingly carry on with me this summer as if we were the only two people in our lives? As I paced back and forth, there was a weak knock at my door.

"Gregory, it's Savannah…"

I rushed to the door, swinging it open to find her standing with her arms loose at her sides, eyes cast down and looking swollen, as if she'd been crying. I wanted to take her into my arms in that instant, but I didn't know if she wanted me touching her anymore. She was wearing a short black skirt and a grey tank top. Her hair was piled on top of her head in a wild nest of curls. Still, she took my breath away. She always had.

"Come in." Instinctively I looked down the hall before closing the door behind her.

"No one's out there. I waited for them to clear out before I knocked." Her voice was flat as she sat on the edge of the bed.

Pulling my eyebrows together, I walked toward her and sat down next to her.

"That's how it'll be, you know," she said to the floor.

"That's how what will be?"

"Looking over our shoulders for the rest of the summer. Making sure no one sees you with your mistress." She stopped and looked at me as I gasped at her use of the word *mistress*. She started again, still not looking at me. "That's what this is, you know. I'd be your mistress."

I knew that's what it looked like. It was an affair in the sense that I was married, but Savannah was so much more to me than my *mistress*. I couldn't figure out how to say that to her, though, especially when she seemed to refuse to look at me.

I swallowed hard and tentatively placed my hand on her thigh. She didn't move it. "Savannah..."

"What? That's what you're asking of me, isn't it? To be your mistress?"

I clicked my tongue against my teeth and winced at the word. I wanted her to stop saying it. That's not what she was... who she was.

"You mean more than that to me, Savannah. You know that," I managed. Slowly.

"Then why..." She shook her head, looking at her manicured toes.

"Why what?" I asked, stroking my thumb back and forth across the top of her thigh.

She shrugged. "If I mean so much to you...I'm not saying leave your wife for me. But if I mean that much to you then why not wrap things up in your marriage and then come to me? Why an affair? Why now?"

I lifted my hand from her leg and ran it over my face. "My marriage...while it hasn't been a long one, has felt like it. There's...not a lot of love there, if any. I think it was convenient for both of us. Jesus, I don't want to sound like a bastard here—"

"You don't." She grinned slightly. "Trust me, I get it. I think."

I counted myself lucky that Savannah hadn't run from the room yet. That she was still sitting there listening to me, and asking questions, gave me some hope that she wouldn't disappear through that door forever.

I paused a moment before continuing, trying to consider how to talk about my *wife* with the woman I loved. "I was looking forward to this tour to have some space, some time to think. Honestly, some time to figure out how to make a clean break and not lose everything. Including my dignity. But something is going on with Karin right now. I don't have all the details. It's incredibly complicated, and I don't feel right talking to anyone about it right now."

"It's okay. I don't need to know." Since she'd sat on the edge of my bed she hadn't lifted her eyes once. They volleyed between her knotted fingers and her feet the entire time.

"Savannah," I sighed, "why won't you look at me?"

She hesitated before opening her mouth then tucked her lip behind her teeth and squeezed her eyes shut as several tears fell at once.

"Because if I look at you, I'll say yes." She lost it right then, taking a ragged breath as her head fell into her hands and she sobbed.

"Damn it," I whispered as I brought her shoulders to my chest, and she let me hold her as she cried. Resting my chin on top of her head, I breathed in the sweet smell of lilies for what I was certain would be the last time.

She silently cried for a few moments while I tried to string together a few coherent words. I didn't mean to make her cry. I'd never seen her cry like that before and knew I never wanted to again.

"Look," I whispered before clearing my throat. "I didn't mean to upset you, Savannah. If you want to forget about all of this, we can. We can continue the tour and play together, and be friends. I'd like to be friends with you if we can't be more. I *have* to be friends with you if we can't be anything more..." I trailed off, tears pricking my eyes, feeling the weight of what it would be like if Savannah Marshall vanished from my life, again.

She shook her head, as her forehead remained pressed against my chest. "I don't want to forget about it. I can't forget about it. I don't...I don't want to be friends with you, Gregory."

"Oh..."

Savannah lifted her head then and looked at me through a beautiful mess of tears. I was captured in her gaze, waiting for her to speak, praying she wouldn't leave. Not being able to blame her if she did. She slid her hands up the sides of my arms and across my shoulders, moving up my neck until they rested on each side of my face. Slowly gliding her thumbs across my cheeks as she steadied her breathing.

Carefully exhaling through her rose colored lips, she finally spoke. "I'm in love with you, Gregory." She smiled through still falling tears and I was at a loss on how to interpret her emotions.

"I'm in love with you, too, Savannah," I whispered.

"But," she continued, "I don't want you to say it anymore. I don't want us to say it to each other anymore. It will make me want more than I know we can have."

"Savannah..."

She tucked a loose strand of hair behind her ear as she sniffed. "Please, Gregory. You're already asking a lot of me. I need you to grant this. I *know* you love me...but I can't hear you say it."

With a heavy sigh, I nodded once. "Okay."

"I didn't sleep much last night, you know."

I chuckled nervously. "I didn't either."

"I'm afraid it'll break my heart, and yours, if I say *no*. But... I'm afraid you'll think less of me if I say *yes*."

I frowned, shaking my head in confusion. "Why would I think less of you?" I asked, bringing my hands to her face and tracing my thumb across her bottom lip.

"Willingly entering into a relationship with a married man is not a place I ever thought I'd find myself." She looked down again, shame sweeping over her face.

Jesus. In my own desire to have her in my arms, and in my bed, and in my heart, I hadn't considered what asking her might do to her sense of self. What it might do to her spirit—the very thing I fell in love with.

"No, I don't want you to feel bad about that," she entered, seeming to interpret the look on my face. "That's...my stuff. I could calmly get up and walk out of this room and smile and see you on stage every day."

I nodded. "You could."

"But then, no matter what else happened in the rest of our lives, I might look back on this moment and kick myself for not taking a chance with you. Even if our time is limited." Her voice trembled slightly over the last part, and it sank my stomach.

"I don't *want* there to be any limits with you. I just don't know..." I shook my head and looked away, internally at war with my own moral code.

"I know things are complicated with Karin. And, given the last few days I've had, I'm in no position to judge anyone anymore."

She gently grabbed my chin between her thumb and index finger, turning my face toward hers. "I'm saying yes."

I wanted to gasp, shocked by her answer. Three simple letters that changed everything. But, I couldn't breathe.

She said yes.

"You're saying yes," I whispered, unable to keep the shocked smile off my face.

She nodded. "I know we have a lot of details to work out, like how we're going to handle this without everyone finding out and it turning into a *thing*." Sometimes, when she rambled, her hands would wave in the air. It was adorable. "But... I'd rather have a few stolen moments with you over a short time than to live a lifetime wondering what it would have been like had I said *yes*, but chose to walk away instead."

Shaking with an intoxicating mix of nerves and relief, I pulled Savannah into a deep kiss. As her hands ran up the back of my neck and through my hair, I let out a small moan of gratitude.

She said yes.

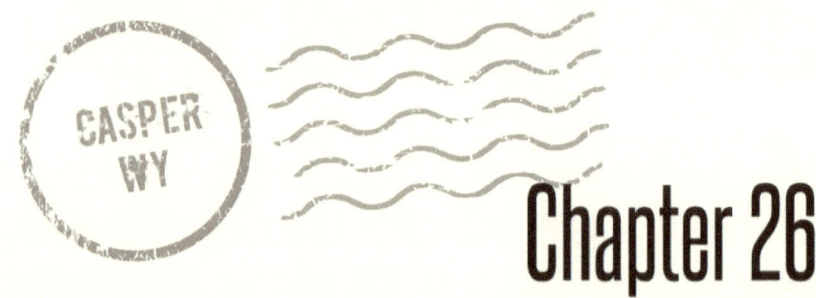

Chapter 26

GREGORY

D ENVER WAS UNSEASONABLY cool for July. In Colorado Springs I suffered from allergies. I don't remember what excuses I used in Fort Collins, or Casper, or Billings or Bozeman. But as we moved further west, mostly by bus and train, I continued to find myself giving excuses for long disappearances into my hotel room, excuses to not attend dinners, go out for drinks or any other social activities that came along with a tour of this nature.

Of course, given my reputation, hardly anyone blinked. Ironic. I'd spent my adult life pushing people away, keeping them at arms' length, never touching, or reaching out. Now all I could do, all I wanted to do, was touch.

At our stop in Fort Collins, we made love three times before finally collapsing into an exhausted, tangled sleep. When I woke in the morning, she was splayed across me, legs tangled around mine, her hair across my chest. I opened my eyes and watched her. She was...beautiful. Amazing. Mine. In her sleep, she looked so peaceful.

And then her eyes opened. She locked her eyes on mine, and I watched as her pupils slightly dilated. Her mouth opened, just a little, into a tiny smile.

"Hi," she whispered.

"Good morning," I replied.

Then we didn't speak.

Each stop was different, yet each was the same. We texted back and forth. Made secret arrangements to visit each other. Depending on whose room, one of us would make our way down the hall, or to a different floor. Check the hall for others from the orchestra. Knock, and then slip into the room.

The secrecy was maddening. And necessary. Because we could dress it up any way we wanted, the fact was we were having a secret affair. And it would remain a secret until I worked out whatever the hell was going on with Karin. Because *that* was a lingering question I didn't know how to resolve. It wasn't as if I could sit here and even pretend that what I was doing was morally right. And that sometimes devastated me, because I loved Savannah, I'd always loved her.

I'd asked her to be mine in secret, for just the summer.

But I wanted so much more.

And I didn't know if that was going to be possible. I didn't know what kind of future we could have when our beginning was founded in a lie. And that...was my fault. Sometimes I felt as if I'd completely taken leave of my senses. What could I have been thinking? Every time I looked at our situation, all I could see ahead was heartbreak.

But I couldn't stop. When I saw her, when I touched her, when I even thought of her, I was lost. And so, we kept on. It was beautiful. Exquisite. And sometimes it broke our hearts.

Generally, as one of the senior musicians on the tour, I had a room by myself. But not always...in Casper, Wyoming, neither of us had a room by ourselves. That night we snuck off together, reserving a room at the Sunburst Lodge, a bed and breakfast on the side of Casper Mountain. The drive up to the mountain in a rental car was fantastic, the sun shining through openings in the forest as we rode higher and higher into the mountains. Both of us had been tense, distracted. This chance to get away, to not hide for a few hours, was priceless.

The lodge was open pine construction, with a huge fireplace in a large open living room where all of the guests gathered in the evening. That evening, away from the pressures of the tour, the pressures of our lives, we both succumbed to the fantasy that we could be together. It was beautiful...and bittersweet. Sitting in overstuffed chairs next to each other by the fire, we drank wine and laughed and felt free. Because, for a few hours, we were out of cell phone range, out of touch, with no connection to our lives.

"Hey." Savannah gave my hand a slight squeeze, pulling my eyes away from the flames. The warm amber light reflected flecks of yellow dancing through her irises. It looked choreographed and made me catch my breath and ache to take her to bed.

"What is it?" I asked.

She tilted her head in a way that told me she was struggling to ask a question.

"What's going on? You've seemed distant." She leaned forward and placed her glass on the thick maple table in front of us. Resting back into the brown leather, she wrapped her arms around her legs as she pulled them to her chest.

I shrugged. "Why don't we just enjoy our time together?"

Her now sad eyes met mine. "I enjoy every second with you, Gregory. That's not an issue." A quick smile came and left before she continued. "I know that what we're doing *here* is...limited. I know that nights like this won't happen much more, if at all. But, I...I still care about you. I'll *still* care about you when this summer is over and...I care about what's going on in your life."

I considered her words with each rise and fall my thumb took over her knuckles. Instinctively, I'd been reluctant to ever discuss Karin with her. My wife occupied a separate part of my life, a distant and sad and lonely part of my life. I'd kept all of that closed off, walled away. But for the last few days the implications of what I'd learned from Madeline had been constantly running through my mind. And I'd discussed it with no one.

"You can trust me, Gregory." She misread my hesitation and cast her eyes to our locked fingers.

"Of course I trust you. That's not it." I took a deep breath. Closing my eyes, I said, "I'm just...reluctant to...taint our time together. With all of that."

"All of what?"

I swallowed. Then I said, "She wants to have children. My *wife*. I do not. I never have. And...it appears that she decided to take action on that without discussing it with me."

Savannah's eyebrows worked as she puzzled through my awkward wording. Then she said, "Are you saying she stopped taking birth control?"

I nodded. "Yes." I realized as I answered the question that my hand was shaking.

"Jesus," she mumbled under her breath, throwing her head back against the chair. "How did you find out?"

I snorted. "She got drunk and told Madeline she was seeing a fertility specialist. Apparently despite her desire to have children, she is not...she can't..." I rubbed my hand over my face, squeezing my eyes shut.

Savannah took her free hand and pulled mine away from my face. "I get it. I'm sorry...for her." Savannah's face softened and she looked conflicted. Hurt, almost. "What'd she say when you talked to her about it?"

"We've not discussed it. I refuse to have this conversation on the phone."

"Wow..."

"What?" I sat forward.

"You...you need to talk to her, Gregory. I mean, I know you *know* that, but..."

"But what?"

She ran a hand through her hair and left it resting on the back of her neck. Her head slowly shook side to side as she spoke. "I know this is going to make no sense at all, what does, really? But, I feel just...awful right now. There are reasons why you're hurting. Angry. And she has things going on, too. I know we're having an affair, but...you need to sort this out with her. Not for me. But for you."

I thought about her words. About the potential implications of the discussion with Karin. I'd considered it, imagined it, repeatedly. I couldn't see that conversation going anywhere good. I'd dreaded it, and perhaps that's why I'd put it off. Because it went to the core of what was wrong with us as a couple. The one thing I'd never wanted was a child. And she *knew* that. And despite the fact that I was, in fact, betraying her every day...I still felt...incredibly betrayed.

I took a deep breath and nodded. "Yes. I'll talk with her."

"Thank you for telling me about that. I didn't mean to pry, and I know that was insanely personal. Thank you for trusting me." Savannah brought her fingers to my cheek and traced her thumb just under my eye, that soft, genuine smile of hers lifting the heaviness from around us in an instant.

"Of course I trust you," I said again. "That's like saying *thank you* for breathing. Or...*thank you* for having two arms. You don't have to thank me. I *trust you*."

"I hate that she did that to you. That's not fair."

I shrugged. There was nothing to say. It wasn't fair. I hated it, too. One thing I did want was to not talk about it for the rest of the night. "Come here," I implored with a slight tug of her hand.

Savannah rose, slowly, and with a grace that I'm sure had people often mistaking her for a dancer, slid onto my lap and rested her head on my shoulder.

We spent the rest of the evening quietly talking near the fire, basking in anonymity. Breathing air free of potential judgment. A place where we could be anybody or nobody. *Together.* We made love that night until we both collapsed in exhaustion, and again when we awoke.

In the morning I drove the rental car down the side of the mountain, taking each switchback through the forest slowly, nearly coming to a stop at each magnificent vista. We were a third of the way down the mountainside when both of our cell phones began to chirp with missed calls, text messages, voicemails, which both of us, wordlessly, ignored. We didn't discuss it. We didn't agree to it. We said nothing. But I couldn't avoid seeing the tears that slowly rolled down her cheeks, the tears that reflected the slanting rays of the sun.

I started to say something, and she simply held out a hand, palm up, toward me. Telling me to *stop.* And so I shut up, took her hand in mine, and I drove, back toward the tour, back toward our lives. And she cried. And inside, I did the same.

We got back to the hotel at noon. I returned the rental car then finally checked my messages. I'd been trading voicemails and text messages with Karin for three days. It was Saturday, she wouldn't be working, and I wouldn't be able to put it off much longer.

We'd managed to keep our conversations short and businesslike for most of the last weeks. She knew, or suspected, about Savannah. I knew about her coming off the birth control pills and seeing a fertility doctor without my agreement. We were at a stalemate, and I absolutely refused to address the subject on the phone from thousands of miles away.

So that day, when I called from my room, I had more than a little tension and anxiety.

"Hello?"

I swallowed, and said, "Hey."

"Gregory? It's been a...couple days."

"Yeah," I said. "I've been busy." I felt a lump in my throat. Whatever else I was...I didn't like to think of myself as a liar. And yet, here I was, lying. Because I hadn't been *busy*. I'd been avoiding talking to her. Because I was sleeping with another woman. No matter how much of a gulf we had in our marriage, that wasn't right.

"How is the tour?"

I cleared my throat then said, "Okay."

"Okay?"

"It's going well."

"Gregory...what's going on? You don't sound like you."

A stab of irritation flashed through me. I wanted to say, *of course I don't. You tried to trap me into having children I didn't want.* I wanted to say, *I'm in love with another woman.* I wanted to say, *I'm leaving.*

I said nothing for a moment and simply took a breath because I didn't want to lose my temper. I didn't know who was at fault here more or less or what. I knew that I needed to tread very carefully. I knew that whatever *she* had done, I was the one who had been unfaithful. I was the one who had lied, systematically, for the entire summer.

So it didn't make sense that I was so angry with her.

But I was. I'd never been so angry in my life.

"I'm just not feeling well. The tour has been exhausting," I said. I was telling the truth. Just not all of it.

She didn't answer. And so we sat there, in an uncomfortable silence, for fifteen seconds or thirty or a minute or ten. I don't know how long it was. I only know it was excruciating. Finally she said, "Call me tomorrow?"

"Look...we need to talk. Can you fly out here? Tomorrow? Our next stop is in Billings, Montana."

She hesitated. "You want me to fly to Montana? Why?"

"Karin...please. I'll make the reservations. Get the time off work."

In a hesitant tone, she said, "All right. I love you."

I disconnected without answering, and then sat down, staring out the window. Wishing.

"I know it seems crazy. But I'll miss you," Savannah said.

I took a deep breath and said into the phone, "I'll miss you too."

I kept the phone to my ear, though for the next thirty seconds or so, neither of us spoke. My eyes scanned the signs for Domestic Arrivals as I turned into the airport.

"I love -"

"Don't say it," she interrupted.

I cleared my throat. "Fine. We'll talk...tomorrow or the next day then."

"Goodbye," she whispered. She sounded as if she was on the verge of tears, and I knew that I was.

I hung up the phone. I felt unaccountably angry, and I knew it wasn't fair. It's not as if it were Karin's fault. But the anger was there, and it sharpened when I pulled up to the curb and saw her coming out of the door of the terminal, dragging two suitcases.

The thought that ran through my head was this: *why does she need two suitcases for a single overnight trip?* Which led to wondering if she was planning on staying longer and just hadn't mentioned it?

Not logical. Not reasonable. But my anger pushed through regardless.

I pulled up to the curb and stepped out of the car, my eyes squinting from the intense summer glare. I'd left my sunglasses somewhere, and I already had a headache coming on. I left the emergency lights blinking, the car running, and walked across the concrete toward Karin.

She looked fatigued. Circles under her sad eyes. Her hair was tied up in a messy bun. She wore a canary sleeveless dress with matching heels. The dress was a familiar one... very familiar. She'd worn it three years ago, the day I proposed marriage. Irrationally, I felt angry. That dress, along with hair suddenly bleached to look like she'd had it years ago, felt like giant traps.

My stomach tightened as I approached her. She would expect a kiss. An embrace. Something. It had been a long time since we'd been very touchy. But now? After I'd had Savannah in my arms. After I'd felt that...warmth, that outpouring of love, or longing, of our souls touching? After that, the thought of touching Karin was ashes.

I reached out and took one of her suitcases, and she put her arms around me. I returned the embrace with one arm and kissed her on the cheek. Because anything less would be...cruel.

I was rigid, intensely stressed as I walked her to the car and opened the trunk, then lifted her bags in. By the time I closed the trunk she was inside the car, and I walked around, got in and cranked it up.

"How was your flight?" I asked. For the time being, neutral topics would be best.

She shrugged. "I've been through worse. You know I hate flying."

I swallowed. Of course I knew that. I hadn't considered it at all when I insisted on her coming out here. I creased my brows, wondering what that said about me. After all, on Tuesday we had a two-day break in the tour coming. I could have simply flown back to Boston then and had this conversation there.

Except...Savannah and I had made plans for those two days. We'd talked about them...breathlessly, because we were both planning to slip away from the tour, which would be stopped in Tacoma, Washington. We had reservations in Vancouver, where we could be assured of being away from everyone for two full days.

Two beautiful days.

I'd not even considered going home during those two days.

I'd not considered Karin at all.

I'd not even thought of her.

What kind of person did that make me? I didn't know the answer to that. Selfish? Self-absorbed? I didn't know how to reconcile the intense love I felt for Savannah with the fact that I was married to this woman. This obviously heartbroken woman who sat beside me in the car.

We barely spoke the rest of the way back to the hotel. Inconsequential things. I asked how her job was going. She spoke for a few minutes about the very substantial grant the conservatory had just received from the Rockefeller family fund, or Ford, or some other huge foundation.

I pulled the car into the valet parking lane at the hotel and popped the trunk. I checked my watch. It was 5:30 p.m. "Why don't we grab dinner?"

I passed a five-dollar bill to the porter and gave him my room number. "Please take the bags up," I said. Then I led Karin to the restaurant, my hand on the small of her back as I guided her.

Five minutes later we were seated in the restaurant at the edge of the seven-story atrium. Our table was off to the side, away from most of the other tables, and most importantly, away from the bar, where several members of the orchestra were currently tossing back drinks. We didn't have a performance until the next night, so apparently it was time for some hard drinking.

When the waitress approached, I ordered a margarita for Karin and a gin and tonic for me. Despite my occasional inattention to her feelings, I knew what she drank.

"So..." she said once the drink arrived. "You were insistent I fly out. Are we going to continue to dodge the subject? Or are you going to tell me what this is about?"

I leaned back, wincing a little, then rubbed the bridge of my nose between my thumb and forefinger. The throbbing in my head was growing louder by the minute.

She shook her head then took a drink from her margarita. "Spit it out, Gregory. It's not like you to dance around uncomfortable topics."

I grimaced and said, "Did you stop taking birth control pills?"

She stared at me over her drink and gave a soft, half laugh. "Why do you ask, Gregory?"

In a very quiet, even tone, I said, "Because we discussed this. We discussed it to the point of nausea. You know I don't want to have children."

She shook her head and rolled her eyes. "We didn't *discuss* it, Gregory. Every time I bring it up, you make pronouncements. That isn't a discussion...it's not a discussion when you refuse to compromise."

"Are you fucking kidding me? What compromise is there? Either we have kids or we don't. There's no meeting halfway on this topic. And I've been clear since well before we got married that I do not intend to have children!"

She leaned close, her face tense, and looked at the tables around us. "Can you please keep your voice down?"

I closed my eyes and took a deep breath, trying to calm myself. Then I took another one, because one breath just wasn't enough. Finally I opened my eyes. She was still there. I tried to think through when this had happened. There'd been a noticeable change in her behavior for almost a year. For several months our sex had taken on an almost frantic quality, and the more she pushed, the more I pulled away.

I hadn't realized then that it meant she was desperately trying to get pregnant. I only knew that the more she wanted to touch...the less I wanted to. I knew it and she knew it, but neither of us had actually spoken about it.

"When did you stop taking the pill?" I asked. My voice was ragged.

She avoided my eyes. That was a bad sign. I leaned close, reached out and grabbed her hand. "When?" I demanded.

"January," she whispered.

I sat back in my seat, feeling as if I'd been punched in the gut. *January?* She hadn't even brought up kids again until sometime in March.

I shook my head. "I don't understand. Why didn't you say anything?"

She shrugged, still looking away, and then wriggled her hand out of mine. "I didn't want to talk about it, Gregory. I knew you'd just get scared again. I thought...if I...if..."

"Scared? It's not about being scared, Karin. It's about wanting the same things out of life. I do not want to be a parent. That's a commitment I'm not willing to make."

She squeezed her eyes shut. Her next words came out in a whisper. "You're not willing to make that kind of commitment to me."

"It's not about you, Karin. We agreed before we got married. And then when you started talking about it this year, you...I thought we were *talking* about it. I didn't know you'd already decided to do it."

She shrugged. "Not that it mattered."

"How did this come about? Madeline said something about a fertility specialist? She wasn't aware that I didn't know."

Jesus Christ. As soon as I asked the question, her eyes went red and started to run with tears. Naturally that was when the waiter showed up with our food. Karin quickly wiped her eyes and face, and then made a comment about allergies which I'm sure fooled no one. The waiter put our food down in an awkward silence then politely asked if we needed anything else.

"Another round of drinks, please," I said.

So we sat in awkward silence for another ten minutes while our food and then drinks got situated. I toyed with my food and sloshed the ice in the bottom of my glass around. When the waiter finally returned with the second round of drinks, I tossed half my gin and tonic back in one gulp.

"Tell me about the fertility specialist."

She tossed back half of her own drink. Then she said, "I went to the doctor in March."

"That's why you finally talked to me?"

She nodded. "I knew you'd eventually see the bills. From the insurance company."

I can't imagine why she thought that. I never looked at them. She could have been seeing a hundred doctors and I would never have known it.

"So you went to the doctor. And what happened?"

She didn't look me in the eyes. At all. "As it turns out, I'm infertile. Completely. I cannot have children."

As she said the words, she stared at the floor somewhere to her right. And she began to shake. Violently. I leaned forward, utterly conflicted. What the fuck did I say to her? Was I sorry she'd been unable to trap me into being a parent? Did I express sympathy? I was sympathetic to her pain. I think? Actually I didn't think I'd ever been so confused and conflicted in my life. About anything.

When I didn't move to her, didn't move to comfort her, she buried her face in her hands and began to sob, silently. I sighed, furrowed my eyebrows, and thought. Hard. I was her husband. I should comfort her. But honestly I didn't want to. I didn't want to touch her. I didn't want to give her any out. I didn't want to give her any impression that I could forgive her for what she'd done.

But who was I to judge? Who was I to not forgive her? I'd spent the last several weeks committing adultery. And I had no intention of stopping. Whether she let me say the words or not...I was in love with Savannah Marshall. So I sat there, impassive, paralyzed, and unable to respond with a touch or any words of comfort or anything at all as my wife fell apart three feet away from me.

Right there, at that moment, is the closest I've ever come to hating myself.

In between sobs, she looked up at me, her expression desperate. "Can we go somewhere else? Please?"

I waved down the waiter, and said, "Can we get the check please, right away?"

Five minutes later we were standing at the doors to the elevator. Karin turned her back to me, arms folded across her chest, looking out toward the front door of the hotel. I stood there, waiting for the elevator to arrive, feeling exposed. The hotel was seven stories, a hollowed out rectangle with an interior atrium. From where I stood, Karin and I could be seen from the doors and windows of virtually every room in the hotel.

Savannah was on the sixth floor, and I could see her door from here. Could she see me? Was she wondering at this moment what was passing between Karin and me?

I didn't want to think about that. My life was segmented out, compartmentalized, and the part of me that performed in the tour, the part of me in love with Savannah, had nothing to do with Karin. Having them both in the same place was beyond disturbing...it set my entire body on edge with tension that I felt deep in my gut.

I jerked a little when the elevator arrived on the ground floor. We stepped into the elevator and stood on opposite sides like strangers. The door closed, the bell rang, and the elevator began to move.

Finally the excruciating, painful wait was over and I was unlocking my room. A room, which, thankfully, I'd not shared with Savannah. Because while I might be a complete bastard, an adulterer, a liar...I still couldn't conceive of them sleeping in the same bed. The idea of it, the secrecy, the lies... they made me ill.

The bellman had placed Karin's bags in the corner. I stood near the window, which overlooked the darkness outside, pacing, as she slipped into the bathroom to prepare herself for the night. My eyes darted around the room. Looking for anything incriminating. Condoms. Anything that belonged to Savannah. I knew there wasn't anything; we'd not shared this room.

But I couldn't slip my guilt into a drawer and hide it. I couldn't erase the stain of lies and manipulation. The rage I felt over her betrayal was real. But not as real as my own betrayal.

I sighed, staring out the window.

I thought it all through. What would happen if Karin and I divorced? Savannah and I could be together when that happened. But would she ever be able to trust me? After all...I'd cheated on my wife. Would she ever be able to trust that I wouldn't do it to her? Did a relationship founded in a lie stand any chance of surviving?

My heart told me yes. My heart told me that Savannah and I were meant to be together. But in the back of my mind, doubts screamed at me that I'd doomed our love from the start.

I jerked when Karin opened the door and stepped out of the restroom. She'd dispensed with her long t-shirt nightgown, instead wearing some sheer silky thing. *Crap.* I felt my mouth dry, instantly. There was no doubt what she had in mind as she walked toward me in her bare feet, eyes meeting mine.

I coughed and then muttered something about going to brush my teeth. Then I slipped by her, into the bathroom and closed the door. I turned on the water, all the way, and leaned on the counter. What the fuck was I doing? How did I end up in this place? In a hotel room with a woman I was married to, while the woman I loved was one floor, a thousand feet and a million miles away from me?

I closed my eyes, because I didn't like who I saw in the mirror. I didn't like it at all. Then, finally, I slipped out of my clothes, brushed my teeth, and slid on a heavy bathrobe.

When I opened the bathroom door, the lights in the room were off. I could hear her breathing. I walked toward the bed. She would be on the side closest to the window, so I slid off the bathrobe and got under the blanket.

Karin was three inches away from me and I wanted to flee.

As soon as I was under the cover, she slid over toward me.

"I missed you," she whispered.

Another stab of guilt. Because the truth was, I hadn't missed her at all. Then I froze, because she put her lips to my neck and a hand on my stomach.

"Gregory, why won't you touch me? You're my husband. I'm so sorry...I'm sorry I lied. Forgive me."

Jesus. Forgive *her?* If she only knew what she was saying.

"Kiss me," she said, and then her lips came into contact with mine. I responded because what the fuck else was I supposed to do? But it was the most uncomfortable kiss of my life.

She moved closer, and her right hand worked its way down my stomach until she was touching my penis, and God help me, but of course it responded instantly, even though the rest of my body was rigid, uncomfortable.

Her kisses became almost frantic, and the next thing I knew, she'd brought her lips to my neck again, as she raised to her knees, her fingernails raking lines in my ribs.

"I want you, Gregory. Please."

Her pleading made me want to run away and hide. To sneak under the bed. My stomach was in knots as she frantically pulled at my underwear. I winced and closed my eyes, because she touched me again, but I'd collapsed, flaccid, completely impotent.

My body had revolted, announcing in no uncertain terms what my confused mind hadn't made clear. *No. Fucking. Way.*

She froze. Then turned away, flinging herself to the far edge of the bed with her back to me.

I stared at the ceiling. Humiliated. Nauseous.

She shook with the beginning of a sob then whispered, "Do you really hate me that much?"

I couldn't answer. Instead, I lay there, silently, alone, as my wife cried herself to sleep.

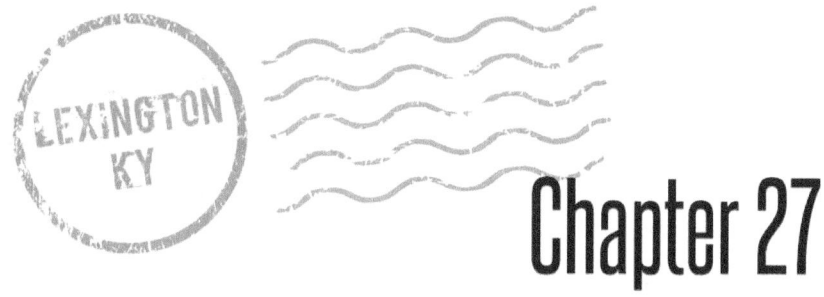

Chapter 27

SAVANNAH

"**S**AVANNAH, THAT'S AN **A-flat.**"

"Huh?" I whispered, turning to Nathan.

"It's an A-flat." He took his pencil and helpfully circled the offending note for me. "You've missed it like every other time we've gone over that line. There's a key change in measure thirty-six."

Sighing, I grabbed his pencil from his hand and put a star over the key change. "Well, what the hell? This is a march for Christ's sake, who writes this many key changes into a march?"

Tim elbowed me from the other side.

"What?" I snapped. He just nodded toward Joseph McIntosh, staring down at me from his conductor's stand expectantly.

"I said, Ms. Marshall, that I want the flutes to ease up on the staccato on that run of eight notes starting at thirty-six. The way he's written them is too choppy. Still accent them, just not so forcefully. And, in the correct key, please."

My cheeks heated as my eyes drifted over toward Gregory. I rarely messed up, and I was waiting for him to shoot me a condescending gaze, as if my messing up was somehow a billboard that the two of us were having sex in our private time. He just nodded and mouthed: *you're fine.*

The past few weeks had been a whirlwind. Gregory and I were granted the gift of privacy a few hours a week due to practicing our duet. We'd played the Assobio piece a few times and worked a few other pieces into the rotation. I savored the hours we spent practicing. Playing. Immersing ourselves in the craft that initially attracted us to each other.

It was a turn on to watch him practice. To work note runs over and over, studying them behind his furrowed brow. When he stopped, satisfied that he'd worked over the measures enough, he'd look in my eyes, and I could never stop myself from setting my flute down and grabbing him into a kiss. He always kissed me back with greater intensity than I'd seen him use to study the notes on the page. So much so that one time in Houston, we got so carried away in the practice room that we'd taken each other's clothes off before taking stock of our surroundings. Thankfully, no one caught us.

Caught.

I hated that what we were doing was something that someone could "catch." There would be no release from that.

We rarely talked about the future. Or even the present. Karin...his wife...had come out to visit him for two days. A visit that ended inconclusively for them. And left me hanging, twisting in the wind. He'd told me nothing of their discussion when she was here. But sometimes I could see it in his eyes. The stress and confusion and anger, and occasionally, deep melancholy.

At first, I'd been concerned that his desire to be with me for the summer was purely driven by physical need. The more time we spent together, however, the less that was a concern. He loved me. That was evident in the soft growl that came from his throat as he softly bit my earlobe, and the way he watched me as I moaned beneath him. It was the way he always stood at the end of the song and slid his fingers around the back of my neck before kissing me and telling me how beautifully I'd played, and how beautiful I was. It was the look in his eyes when he said it. They always widened slightly, as if he was trying to remind himself that this was real. We were there, in that space, just loving each other.

I still didn't let us say that to each other.

Love.

That was my limit. My singular request in this wildly irresponsible situation we found ourselves in. I loved him, madly. And I know he loved me, too. I just knew myself well enough to know that I couldn't hear him tell me that every time we were together and be able to keep my head on straight. He was married. And, at the end of this tour, he was going home to his life and I would go home to mine. We would always have the memories of the summer we toured together.

And that would be that.

"Where'd you go?" Nathan elbowed me as we stood by ourselves in the elevator of the Downtown Lexington Hilton.

"Huh?" I cleared my throat and glanced up at him, finding him scrutinizing my every move. I hesitated over the 7, which was Gregory's floor. Nathan knew I was on the ninth floor. Reluctantly, I tapped the 9 with my knuckle and leaned against the wall of the elevator car.

"Today. That shit with the key change."

"It was just one key change, Nathan. Jesus. Sorry." I rolled my eyes and stared at the descending numbers on top of the elevator doors.

"It's not just today, Savannah. You've been wicked focused in performances, but it's like during rehearsals you're somewhere else. You're off. Something's going on. What is it?"

Shit.

I'd taken Nathan's possession of a Y-chromosome for granted in hopes that he'd never find out about Gregory and me. Certainly, I'd thought, as long as I showed up and did my job, no one would notice that what I was really doing was barely holding on to reality. Tightly.

"It's nothing, really." I shrugged and offered a half-assed smile.

"Is this about that article on your mom?"

"How'd you know about that?" I hadn't mentioned it to Nathan, or anyone. Not even Gregory. Somehow, I cynically thought bringing up an affair my mother had would sour ours.

Nathan shrugged as the elevator dinged and the doors opened to the ninth floor, where Nathan's room was, too. He followed me off and continued. "Everyone knows, Savannah. Cynthia Reynolds plays for the Boston Lyric Opera. She knew about the alleged *scandal*." Nathan playfully mimed air quotes as his eyes bulged mockingly.

"So, what, she ran around and told everyone about my mom and Malcolm?"

Nathan had followed me to my room and as I slid my key into the slot, he shook his head.

"No...not about your mom and Malcolm. About the stuff about you."

Ignoring the green light by the handle telling me I could enter, I dropped my hand and looked at him. "What the hell are you talking about? That article was about my mom and Malcolm and their—"

Nathan grabbed my key from me and opened my door. "Did you read it? The whole thing?"

I shook my head, my pulse picking up speed. "I skimmed the thing, saw their picture, I know the rest."

"You have a copy?" he asked as the hotel room door locked loudly behind us.

"Unfortunately." I reached into my suitcase and pulled out the Opera News magazine, which was rolled into a tight tube. I don't know why I kept it.

Nathan took it from my hands and flipped through to the article, turning the page once more before handing it back to me, his finger on a section of the story I hadn't read. Watching his eyes, which seemed to darken slightly, I took the worn periodical from his hand and looked to the section he'd pointed out.

An anonymous source reports to Opera News that Carulli's daughter, Savannah Marshall, was admitted to the New England Conservatory after Vita Carulli gave a substantial gift to the school's endowment. According to school records Marshall did not complete her studies at the conservatory. Marshall currently plays for the Bolshoi Ballet.

My cheeks were a thousand degrees as my nerves buzzed with rage. "Why didn't you tell me about this?" I yelled.

He seemed startled. "Jesus, Savannah, I thought you read the whole thing. I know things with your mom have been shitty, and I figured this was why."

"It *is* why...I...shit, I'm sorry," I said, my eyes filling with tears. "I have to...just...I have to go." Clutching the magazine in my fist, I headed out of the room and back to the elevators.

"Where are you going?"

"I just need a minute, Nathan. To call *her*." The lie came more easily than I was comfortable with, but it came all the same.

"Sorry, I thought that was the reason you were so..." Nathan trailed off and ran a hand through his hair.

"What," I snapped. "Focused? You thought I was out there every night trying to *prove* myself? Wait...do you believe that's why I got in?"

"Jesus, no. You're better than I am. You know that. I'd never think anything like that about you, Savannah, you know that."

Just then the elevator doors opened and I rushed inside.

"We'll talk later," I mumbled as the doors closed. I didn't want to fight with Nathan. I knew he didn't believe those things that were written. What I didn't know, however, was who might.

But I did know who I could start with.

I gripped the magazine tighter as I knocked on the door to room 744, causing the glossy pages to squeak against my fingers. Gregory opened with a sexy grin on his face, which quickly disappeared.

"What's the matter?" he asked, stepping back to grant me entrance.

I smacked the magazine against his chest. *"This."*

The door closed slowly as Gregory stared between me and *Opera News.*

"Page ten." I paced back and forth across the window, resisting the urge to throw something.

A few seconds in, Gregory looked up. "Your parents are divorced?" he whispered. I hadn't told him.

I nodded. "That's not why I'm here. Read on."

Within the span of sixty seconds, his jaw dropped and his eyes shot to me.

"Why didn't you tell me?" I shouted as I snatched the magazine out of his hand.

"What are you talking about?"

"That you were all apparently bribed to let me into the conservatory."

Gregory's nostrils flared as he took a rough breath. "First of all, Savannah, I've never been bribed in my life. I'd never participate in such a thing. And if that's what you came in here to accuse me of, then you can leave and come back when you have your head on."

"Explain it, then. Explain who would say something like that."

"Have you talked to your mother? Seems she should be the one you smack with that magazine."

"So she did it, then?" My head was spinning as I thought of that day. The day I received my acceptance letter. Everything I'd spent my life working toward was wrapped up in one word: Congratulations. Now, it was about to be destroyed by one word: Donation.

"I have no way of knowing who gave what money to where. Nor do I care."

"*I care,*" I snapped as I walked toward him, meeting him toe-to-toe as my vision blurred with tears. "I care, Gregory. I care that everything I worked for means shit if this is true. You were at my audition. Just tell me. Did you even score me or was it already determined that I was a shoo-in because of *this?* Is that why you were such a dick to me when I had you in class? Because I was the spoiled brat whose mother bought her way into the conservatory?" I was speaking so fast I had to stop and catch my breath, just as Gregory caught my shoulders.

"*Listen.*" He leaned down slightly so we were eye-to-eye. "I wasn't a dick to you, Savannah. And, if I was, it was unconscious because I was trying to avoid dealing with my feelings for you. I'm sorry for that. I've been sorry for that. That aside, you're not a spoiled brat and you were *not* a shoo-in. Any time I've heard rumors of things like that happening have been after we've already declined someone's admission. You were in before you walked off the stage, but not because of some *bribe.*"

"What?" I wiped under my eyes but didn't try to pull away. His grip on my shoulders calmed me.

His voice softened significantly. "Until that point it had been years since I'd heard a high school student of *any* instrument play with such skill. You were in before the last note from your flute silenced in the auditorium that day. I didn't care what the others had to say. And, I had no idea who your mother was. I didn't know if you had the money to come, but I was prepared to do anything to make sure that you got into that school. Because of your talent, Savannah. Because you deserved it. Because you *earned* it."

My lip involuntarily quivered as I took in the sincerity of his eyes. The truth. I opened my mouth to say something, but he stopped me.

"Why didn't you tell me about your parents?"

"It's not important. It's not part of the deal here, Gregory. We don't...share things like that." I'd wanted to tell him. Badly. But relying on him for emotional support seemed risky given the rest of the summer was likely to fly by and I'd be left with open wounds he was unable to tend to.

"Sit," Gregory commanded as he led me to the bed. I silently obeyed. He took my hands in his and continued. "It is important. *You're* important. I know our time together is limited, but your thoughts and feelings still matter. They happen, and they matter. I want to know what's going on with you."

I sighed, and with a sinking feeling in my stomach, I looked him in the eyes. "You understand, though, why I might not want to discuss my parents' marriage breaking up because of an affair?"

His lips parted but he had no words. What could he say? He just nodded and swallowed hard.

I grazed my thumb across his knuckles and tried to change the subject. "Who would say that stuff about me, then? Even if my mom did try to *get* me in, and believe me, we'll have the discussion, who would say something to the magazine?"

"I don't know," he replied. "But I can try to find out. I have my suspicions."

"You'd do that for me?" I looked away from his strong hands and met his eyes. I knew there was no way he'd be able to find out, but his allegiance to me meant more. But then my mind ran to the question of his suspicions. Did he think Karin had something to do with this? And why hadn't he talked about what happened when she flew out?

"Savannah," he sighed, stroking his fingers down the side of my face. "You know I'd do absolutely anything for you. I'm so madly in l–"

"Don't." I stopped him by putting my finger over his lips. "Don't say it."

His lips opened again and, for a second, I thought he was going to argue with me. To say that he loved me. I would have come apart then. Demanded things I had no business demanding. Instead he closed them again around the tip of my finger and quickly traced it with the tip of his tongue. His eyes closed as he moaned softly.

I caught my breath at the intensity of the swift movement and brought my hand to his chest as I rested my forehead against his. His lips searched for mine immediately, as if whenever they were an inch apart they *had* to be together. Gregory's bottom lip skimmed the hyperaware skin of my top lip. Normally I'd playfully tease him. Turn my head to the side or duck my chin in the cat-and-mouse game our mouths liked to play.

Not this time.

Clenching the cotton of his shirt I sucked his bottom lip into my mouth as he took in a sharp, quick breath. In one movement his mouth was open and our tongues were working together as feverishly as my hands worked to undress him. Gregory shifted up the bed and grabbed onto my hips as I straddled him, pulling off my shirt as he looked on approvingly.

Leaning forward with my hands on the bed, I let my hair skim across his chest and shoulders.

"I'd do anything for you, too, Gregory," I whispered as I brushed my lips along his jawline. "Absolutely anything."

GREGORY

Savannah's cheek rested on the hot skin of my chest, her warm breath circling my skin and making me feel like I was home. With one arm tucked under my head, I let the fingers on my other hand trail through her hair and down her back. Her hair had grown several more inches in the years since I'd last seen her. Lying here now, her blonde waves were scattered across my chest and over her shoulders, damp with the sweat we'd just worked up. She'd been quiet for almost two minutes before I spoke.

"Hey." I kissed the top of her head as she lifted it to look at me. "I need some water. Do you want some?"

She nodded as she lifted her head and shoulders so I could unwrap myself from her. I hated doing that. Everything was colder when I wasn't touching her. I quickly pulled two bottles of water from the mini-fridge and slid back into bed.

"Thanks," she whispered, opening the bottle and taking a sip before screwing the cap back on and setting it on the bed next to her.

Sitting with my back against the headboard, I opened my arm so she could curl up against me again. As she lowered her head to my shoulder, she let out a slow sigh.

"You okay?"

She nodded, but didn't look up. I'd have believed her if I didn't feel the slight shrug of her shoulders.

"What's wrong?" I pressed.

Still silent, she shook her head. I didn't want to push, but I knew she had a lot of things that she needed to talk about. I wished she had told me about her parents' divorce, and the look on her face when she told me why she felt she couldn't say anything to me was devastating. She deserved better.

"Nathan knows something's going on with me," she finally blurted out. My muscles tensed as I tried to decipher what she meant by *something*. She must have felt it, because she continued speaking. "Not about us, I don't think. But, something. He thought it was about the article. He knew about my parents' divorce, and my mother's relationship with Malcolm...and he thought that the stuff about my admission to the conservatory was what was making me distant from everyone."

Flames of irritation rushed over me at the thought that she'd confided in Nathan Connors. I was well aware they'd known each other for years. But I still hated that she felt I couldn't provide an emotional shelter for her. I *knew* realistically that I couldn't, but that didn't stop the pain of pushing my pride aside as she kissed my neck once.

"Have you been distant?"

"I guess. I just...don't want to waste any time with you." Her voice was uncomfortably distant.

I pulled my eyebrows together and looked back over the last couple of weeks. Savannah and I spent so much time together rehearsing, and even our spare time was spent in whoever's room was lacking a roommate, that I hadn't taken a step back to look at her other relationships. Everyone knew how I was. I didn't spend a lot of time socializing, especially on the road. Travel exhausted me, and I was often shuffling between practicing and sleeping. But Savannah was significantly more social than me, and I quickly calculated that she was spending nearly all of her free time with me.

"I don't want you to pull away from your friends, Savannah."

"I'm not pulling away, but there's a big chunk of my life
that I can't talk to them about...I think I need to talk about
us with someone. Just...to process what's going on. I won't
broadcast it, but—"

"Anyone but Nathan," I spit out without regard to the del-
icacy of my tone.

Savannah sat up and pulled back slightly, looking me in
the eyes. "What?"

"I get that this is a really emotional and conflicting situation, Savannah, I really do. And I appreciate the need you
have to talk to a friend, but...anyone but Nathan."

"Gregory...I..." She drew her knees up to her chest, wrapping her arms around her legs.

My pulse kicked up, but not the way it did when her legs
were wrapped around me. "Were you considering telling him
about us? The boy detests me, Savannah, and I can't say the
feeling isn't mutual. He'd take great pleasure in ruining my
reputation."

Savannah bit her lip as her face melted in what looked like
disappointment. She cleared her throat. "This isn't about *you*,
Gregory. He's *my* friend and wouldn't do that to me. But, I get
it. I don't want to...cause a problem. That's why I haven't said
anything."

Relieved, I sat back and held out my arm, seeking the
comfort of her skin against mine. "Thank you," I said as she
moved into my side.

"I said I'd do anything for you, Gregory. I meant that." Her
muscles stayed tense as she draped her arm across my torso.

I'd told her earlier that I'd do anything for her. As we sat
in the quiet hotel room, surrounded by rough cotton sheets,
I added up the cost of *anything*. As Savannah's breathing

evened out and she fell asleep against my shoulder, the cost mattered less and her heart mattered more.

I ran a hand down my face, stopping briefly to pinch the bridge of my nose. The thought of parting ways with Savannah at the end of the tour was absurd. And painful. But it was reality. *Anything* ended as soon as that hotel door opened and we were on stage. *Anything* would slip away when I got home and faced my wife.

For the next hour, as Savannah slept, breathing softly against my skin, I ran through every scenario possible to allow me to stand up to my words to her. To stand up to *anything*. Because I meant it— I would do anything.

Because she was becoming my everything.

Chapter 28

SAVANNAH

"We're almost at the end." Nathan yawned and stretched his arms overhead as we wrapped up what would be one of our final rehearsals. Our show that evening in Hartford was to be our last before the finale performance in Boston.

"Yeah," I laughed, "thank *God*. And, just in time for me to stop screwing up that key change in the march." I chuckled, feigning relief. Really, I was heartbroken.

The end of the tour meant the end of me and Gregory. The only "me and Gregory" there could ever be. I'd caught a few ends to some tense-sounding conversations between him and Karin, but I rarely asked about them. Talking about them would have invited her in between us. She was ever present in my mind as it was. I couldn't imagine how it was for him. And I didn't want to. I just wanted to enjoy *us*.

"Did you ever end up talking to your mom?"

"No." I stood and slid my bag over my shoulder. "I just let it go for now. She'll be in Boston when I get back. That conversation needs to happen face-to-face."

"I'm glad. You've been in a better mood the last two weeks." Nathan gave me a quick side hug.

"Yeah, I've been feeling a lot better about that whole situation. My mother is who she is, and I can't let her get in my head anymore."

Turns out, I was more like my mother than I cared to admit. An incredible actress. I hadn't wanted to draw too much scrutiny to my distant state, so I dialed up the charm when I was in group settings. It slowly ate away at me all summer to lie to Nathan. That would be over soon. Like everything else. Then, I could get back to normal. Whatever that would be.

Nathan and I headed backstage and he met up with Christine. He wrapped his arms around her petite waist and bent down to kiss her on the lips. She was a lot shorter than Nathan, with a cute blonde pixie cut.

"You guys are sweet." I smiled as I searched through folders of music, looking for a replacement for a sheet I'd dumped coffee on earlier in the week.

"You know," Tim Flannigan bellowed behind me, "you should come audition for Chicago. You could watch this sweetness all the time."

Tim had been less and less guarded about flirting with me in front of everyone. He was incredibly attractive and had the talent to match. I skillfully shrugged off his advances, though, despite the possibilities presented by getting involved with someone who *wasn't* married.

"Ha." I shook my head and set the folders down once I found what I was looking for.

"I'm serious, Savannah," Tim said. "Grace Callahan is leaving. Just got word this morning, actually. She's taken a job in Atlanta and the spot is available immediately. You should consider it. Do you really want to hunker down through another Russian winter?"

"Right, like Chicago's any better?" I snickered to push through the uncertainty rising in my throat.

The thought of returning to Moscow for the start of the new season in a few weeks was too much to consider. And, Gregory and I hadn't talked about it.

"Maybe I will." I shrugged and gave a half smile, hoping to appease the three sets of eyes trained on me.

"Hell yes, you will!" Nathan held up his hand, requesting a high five. Rolling my eyes, I appeased him.

"We're headed to dinner, you want to join us?" Christine laced her fingers with Nathan's and smiled sweetly at me.

"No, thanks. I need to get together with Gregory to go over our final performance."

"Don't let that grumpy bastard work you too hard." Tim gave my shoulder a quick squeeze, laughing at his own joke.

"Come on, Tim," I sighed, "he's not that grumpy."

Nathan eyed me for a second longer than the other two before the trio left and headed to dinner.

Chicago was a fantastic opportunity, but I had a secure position at Bolshoi, and I wasn't sure if playing with an American symphony was what I wanted. I had to start mentally preparing to head back to Moscow, leaving my heart here. Kneeling down to slide the sheet music into my bag, I sighed in the thick silence of the dark space.

"Are you okay?" Gregory's smoky whisper startled me, causing me to jump. "Sorry." He laughed softly as he knelt down next to me.

Instinctively, I leaned my head onto his arm. I was missing him already and I had to keep my tears in check. "I'm fine. Just getting some music. Ready to go rehearse?"

Gregory stood with elongated grace, leading me up by my hand. He didn't let go when I was up on my feet, and I didn't either. "Come to dinner with me."

"What? We can't..." I shook my head in confusion.

"Look. We can brush up the pieces later. You know them. I know them. We're good. But," he took my other hand and arrested my gaze, "the tour ends at the end of the week and we won't get a chance for who knows how long to dine together in public, and—"

"Wait...what are you talking about, in public? You mean ever, right? The tour will be over and you've got to..." I trailed off, looking down, not wanting to address his need to get back to his life. Or, me getting back to mine.

Gregory slid his fingers between mine and squeezed, forcing me to look back up. His lips were in a hard line and his forehead creased against whatever he was about to say.

"I..." He sighed and ran his free hand through his hair, looking to the ceiling briefly.

"What, Gregory?"

"I can't do it."

"Do what?" I tried to pull my hand away, but he gripped mine tighter.

"I can't simply walk away from you when this tour is over. I can't stop seeing you. I don't want to stop seeing you."

The force with which the air left my body could only be measured in the volume of the gasp that escaped my lips. "No."

I shook my hand free and reached for my bag. While we were still standing in a darkened backstage area, I felt heat as if stadium lights had just been turned on. My thoughts made no sense as I tried to put them in order. As I tried to form a sentence.

"Savannah." Gregory tugged gently on my arm.

"You're *married*," I hissed, my eyes automatically flicking around us to make sure no one had slipped uninvited to the conversation.

"I'm aware. I just need some time to work that out." The indifference in his tone forced me to take a step back.

"*Work that out?* It's not a business proposition, Gregory, it's your *marriage.*"

"You know my marriage is a disaster. I need to sort that out...there are things...just hear me out." He brought his other hand to my other shoulder, tilting his head to the side.

I took a long, slow breath and tilted my chin up, straightening my shoulders. "No, hear *me* out. When the *hell* do I get a say here?"

His eyebrows scrunched in apparent confusion, but I didn't let him speak.

"*You* were the one who stopped our relationship five years ago—"

He cut me off, "Savannah—"

"Stop. *You* walked away from us then, Gregory. Then *you* asked me to have an affair with you. You outlined the parameters of that affair, too. I realize you are the only married one here, but we were *both* involved and you were the only one making the rules. I followed because I had no choice. It was either follow along with your wants and needs because I'm insanely in love with you, or be alone. You knew that, too. You knew I'd say yes."

I hadn't realized how much anger and insecurity I'd been pushing down about my role in our relationship. Blindly and mutely following behind a man is not how I'd intended things to end up with me. My breath was short as the anger rose.

"I didn't know you'd say yes. I'd hoped, of course, but I didn't—"

"You wouldn't have asked if you didn't know, Gregory. You don't take risks."

He grabbed my shoulders and his eyes seared me with intensity. "You don't call *this* a risk?" he said gruffly.

"Of *course* it is, but not one to your marriage. That was dead a long time ago. If I'd said *no* you would have certainly found someone else to take my place." I was so angry and lost that I wanted to hurt him. Even if it was with a lie.

It worked.

Air flew from his lungs as though he'd been punched in the stomach. "You don't honestly believe that, do you?" He let his hands slide down my arms until they found my hands.

I shook my head reluctantly. Ashamed to admit I'd hurt him on purpose. "I don't think so...no...I don't..." I pressed my lips together tightly, as if they had any control over the tears forming in my eyes.

"I'm sorry, Savannah. I thought I'd made my feelings clear. This wasn't just about sex..." he trailed off, letting go of me and running both hands through his hair as he took a step back.

I couldn't bear the look on his face as his eyes surveyed the space around us, as if he'd just awoken from a nightmare and he was trying to grasp onto something real. I met him in the middle of our emotional mess and put my hands on the sides of his face.

"Look," I whispered. "I don't want to ruin our last week together. Please. I'm sorry for lashing out. I don't want to screw things up for you personally or professionally. We practiced when and where you said to all summer, I didn't talk to Nathan about us, as you requested...and...I haven't really talked to any of my friends, for that matter."

"I never asked you to isolate yourself, Savannah." Gregory put his trembling hands over mine.

"You did. But, I agreed. It was for a short time, and I knew that. A short time that I got to have you, and only you. To be an *us*. I was willing to give everything else up for this summer. But, it's over now. And...I just don't know how people do this all the time. Affairs. For years. I don't know how my mother did it." My voice gave up at the end of my sentence.

In an instant Gregory's arms were around my shoulders and his hand was holding my head against his chest. "Shit, Savannah, you're nothing like her. That's not what this is. I lo—"

"Don't!" I yelped into his chest.

Gregory gripped my shoulders again and held me at arms' length, looking me directly in the eyes. "No. I'm going to tell you. I love you, Savannah. I *love* you. I know you're hurt by what happened with your mother and father, but you are *nothing* like her."

"If we keep going, Gregory, I'll be fucking up a marriage. Whatever is left to fuck up, I guess."

"Savannah, my marriage has issues that go back much longer than this summer."

"Can't we just wait until you divorce her...if that's what you're going to do?" I couldn't believe I was actually discussing Gregory divorcing his wife. I didn't know if I was asking him to leave her for me. Or if I was just asking him to leave her because he was so miserable in their relationship.

Gregory nodded. "It'll take time, though. And, something is going on with her, as I've said. It's personal and private and I can't just walk away from her until we get it sorted. I just don't have all of the facts right now because it's not really a conversation appropriate for the phone."

"Are you asking me to wait for you?" My whisper kicked up an octave, soaking in the possibility of his request.

"I want you, Savannah. Desperately. I'm in love with you. But, being in love with you means that I need to place your needs above mine. Your heart before mine. I *want* to ask you to wait for me, but I know how unfair that is. If someone comes along that can give you what I can't..." He squeezed his eyes shut briefly, turning his head away, as if trying to avoid the thought.

"You mean someone who can be there for me?"

Gregory stared silently for a few moments before shaking his head. "I'll be there for you, Savannah. I'll always be there for you."

"The season at Bolshoi starts when your season does. Long distance is just messy."

Gregory paled, eyes looking startled. "You're going back?"

I scrunched my eyebrows. "It's my job, Gregory."

He looked to the floor, running a hand through his ragged hair as I panicked, my fingers tingling, and my throat running dry, wondering if he was preparing to ask me to give it up for him. I didn't have an answer to that unasked question.

"But," I continued before he had the chance. "*yes* on dinner." I needed a drink, and a breath.

Gregory pulled me back into the hug, kissing the top of his head. "I don't want to lose you, Savannah. Not again. It hurt enough for the both of us the first time. There can't be a second."

I just nodded against his chest, unsure how else to respond.

Then, someone cleared their throat behind me, and I felt my knees go weak with fear.

Gregory dropped his hands. I studied his face, gauging his expression. It went from surprised to annoyed quickly.

Nathan. Great.

I turned to find Nathan standing cross-armed, nearly seething with tension. I didn't have time for his shit.

"Hey you," I said, heading for the door with Gregory slightly behind me.

"What the hell was that?" Nathan asked.

"Gregory and I are heading to grab a quick bite before we practice."

Nathan stopped short as I wiggled by him, out the door. He turned to Gregory and stood straight. I rolled my eyes at the pre-historic posturing. "What gives, Fitzgerald? I thought you and I talked about this already." Nathan's voice was moving on a less than discreet crescendo.

My mouth opened as I turned to face the men. "You *what?* Nathan!"

"What?" Nathan shrugged. "I had a little talk with him on the train from Lincoln."

"I told you not to say anything!" I screeched.

Gregory stepped in front of Nathan and addressed me in a panic. "You *told* him?"

"Don't talk to her that way, asshole. She told me about your little romp after the TV performance." Nathan tried to push past Gregory, but they ended up standing shoulder-to-shoulder facing me. Gregory's face relaxed just slightly, perhaps recognizing I hadn't told Nathan about the affair. Just as he asked.

"You should have seen her," Nathan continued. "She was a mess. Savannah doesn't cry a lot, Fitzgerald, but she seems to a lot more now that you're in her life."

Gregory's lips parted as his eyes softened, looking at me desperately.

"Both of you shut up." I put up my hand and took a breath. "Look. Yes, Gregory and I slept together. We're also performing together in every city so we have to work together. We're ending this week and are happy that we've had such a successful run. That's what the hug was about, Nathan. And, Gregory, yeah, I cried. But…it's fine now. So, if you'll both excuse me, I'm going to the bar."

"I'll come with you," they said nearly in unison.

Oh for fuck's sake.

I shook my head. "Alone, please. *Please.*"

Turning quickly on my heels, I left two of the most important men in my life, and the lies I just told them, behind.

GREGORY

I T TOOK A few seconds after Savannah disappeared through the heavy metal doors for me to register that I was still standing shoulder-to-shoulder with Nathan Connors, who also appeared to be watching Savannah's exit. Rolling my eyes, I turned and made my way back through the door to collect my cello backstage. The hot-headed bastard had the audacity to grab my arm.

"Not so fast, Fitzgerald," he nearly growled.

I'd had it with him. I spun around and pointed my finger a half-inch from his face. "Listen here, you little *shit*. I allowed your little tantrum on the train from Lincoln, but you're not about to get away with another one."

"Excuse me? That girl is my friend and you're screwing with her emotions, and I don't fucking appreciate it."

"You don't know what the hell you're talking about, Connors."

"Oh, I don't?" Nathan condescendingly tilted his head. "Then tell me this, you spineless fuck. If I don't know *what the hell* I'm talking about, then why is it she's had the same lost look in her eyes over the last week as she did when she quit school and showed up at my apartment in Chicago? The day after you tossed her aside like a used toy."

"She went to Europe," was the first thing out of my mouth.

"Yeah," he chuckled moronically, "she went to Europe after she cried on my couch for a few days." He arched his eyebrow and clenched his jaw in unison. I didn't care for his implications.

"I don't need to take this shit from you," I grumbled, walking away again.

"Yes, you do, Gregory. She deserves better than whatever second rate relationship you're offering her."

I stopped in my tracks and turned around. "What the hell are you talking about?"

"Everyone sees it, man. We all know *something* is going on. Those glances you think you're each stealing? You're caught. Every time. How you stare at her when she has a solo? I don't miss it. And," he took a long breath, "how she looks at you any time you show up? I don't know what fucking game you're playing with her, but I will tell you what I do know. You're married, she's in love with you, and the only way this can end is badly. I've said it to you before, and I'll say it again. *Don't* fucking hurt her."

I clenched my fist against my side, letting his words swirl through my brain. He knew. If he knew, certainly more people knew. I wouldn't let her go just based on that, though. I'd done that once and it only made things worse. What I didn't like was his possessiveness over her. The fuck of it was, he had more of a right to be protective of her. At least openly. He was her best friend. What was I?

"I'm not going to waste a punch on you, Connors, but I've got some words for you, too." I leaned in close so he'd get the point. "Don't you *dare* threaten me. You don't know the first thing about me, and it would be a huge mistake for you to assume you do. What goes on between me and Savannah is just that. Between *me* and Savannah."

He snorted. And in that instant I really *did* want to punch him. "Okay, Fitzgerald. Until the end of the tour you can think what you want. Then, that's it." He shrugged.

What did he know about the end of the tour? Savannah hadn't told him about our...agreement. Had she?

"What the hell are you talking about?"

Nathan grinned almost menacingly. "You can play your game with her for another week. Then she'll be in Chicago and far away from your bullshit." My pulse raced and Nathan must have seen the change on my face. "Oh, she didn't tell you? There's a flute opening that Tim and I told her about. Come September you'll have to find someone else to mind-fuck. You and I both know she'll get in." With one more mock-ing grin, the pretentious little shit shook his head and left me alone in the dark.

Where I'd been spending far too much time.

I'd left Savannah alone at the bar that afternoon, as she asked. That didn't stop me from leaning against the entryway for several minutes, staring at her back. She was drinking a glass of white wine. Sipping slowly for more than a half hour, she randomly ran a finger around the rim of the glass every few minutes. She never checked her cell phone, and she didn't talk to anyone else around her, save for the passing *hello* when someone tapped her on the shoulder. I couldn't see her face, but her slumped posture told me enough.

I didn't want to make her sad.

I kicked myself for even suggesting that she continue the affair with me. There was nothing I could do to take it back now that I'd spoken the words. Nothing except hope that may-be she would actually wait for me while I got my life sorted out. Still, *Chicago*. She was slipping away and I'd started to panic. Panic makes people do desperate things, so I slipped away to my hotel room before I did something that would make things worse for both of us.

She deserved so much damn better than this. *Shit*. I asked her to *wait* for me. For an undetermined amount of time, I asked her to sit back and wait for things that I could only promise her. Nothing I could show her.

As we stepped on stage that night, though, she exuded professionalism. I waited for a tell, for a moment within the notes that she'd look at me like I was hers, and she was mine. That she was considering it. She stuck to the script, though, and maintained our secrecy. Even on stage.

Just as I'd asked of her.

As we took our seats after our duet, I searched for her eyes. Finally, at the last second before we started our final piece of the night with the orchestra, she looked back. A smile flickered across her lips but never made it all the way to her eyes. Nathan was watching me, too, and I could only wonder what conversations they'd had in my absence. Conversations that might lead her to discuss everything. That might lead her to say *no*.

I was uncharacteristically slow at getting everything put away after the show that night. Thankfully, she was, too. In hushed, but harsh tones I heard her tell Nathan to leave her alone. That she was fine and could *handle it*. Shortly after he sulked away, shaking his head in apparent disappointment, she mouthed *nine thirteen*. Her room number.

I waited for her to get on the elevator, then for another carload of people to go, before I got on. There were moments over the past few weeks that we could sneak an elevator ride together, alone. Moments when the door closed that I could take her hand and press into her for a kiss before the *ding* separated us. That wasn't often enough, though. Too many eyes. Too many mouths.

"Hey," she smiled and backed up so I could enter her room. "You never use your key. Why?" She always gave me a copy of her room key when she had a room to herself. I always knocked, though.

I shrugged. "Just being polite, I guess." I grinned and pulled her into a deep kiss. "Are you okay? You've seemed off since this afternoon."

"Oh, you mean since you and my only friend on this tour almost got into a fistfight? Yeah, I'm fine. I just...needed a minute." She walked over to the bed and sat up by the headboard, patting the space next to her.

"So, tomorrow night is it, huh?" I decided against asking her about Chicago, unsure if she was considering that over

Moscow. I couldn't be sure Nathan was ever telling the truth when it came to Savannah, and I wasn't in a place where I was prepared to lose her to either city.

"Yep. That's it," she whispered.

I was aching with the need to ask her if she'd thought more about waiting for me. Or if she'd thought of it at all.

"Savannah," I started.

But, she stopped me. Wordlessly. Extending her hand palm up and resting her head on my shoulder, she said all she needed to. Swallowing back tears I didn't know I had, I wove my fingers between hers and closed my eyes, leaning my head back against the headboard.

She was saying goodbye.

Chapter 29

SAVANNAH

N O MATTER HOW many times I'd heard it performed, or played it, Brahms' Symphony No. 3 in F gave me chills. The melancholy crescendos and diminuendos were punctuated with an airy dance that left a smile on your face and a longing in your heart.

Irony is one of music's cruelest weapons.

I couldn't look at him. Not knowing if we were about to play on stage together for the last time. I had to keep it together because I knew my mother was in the audience. Despite how I felt about her or her personal life at the moment, I still wanted to make her proud. To make myself proud.

As the nearly fourteen-minute piece came to an end, I closed my eyes and took a deep breath, reaching for my sheet music. Tonight we were playing "Clair De Lune." No one knew. We'd spent a couple of weeks with the pianist to work on turning the piano accompaniment into a flute harmony to compliment the cello. By the time we were through, we no longer needed the piano.

It was just us. And it would be beautiful.

"Knock 'em dead," Nathan whispered, patting me on the back as I stood. He knew the plans for our song and, while he had no use for Gregory, he was excited about me doing what I do best. Pushing boundaries and breaking rules.

How those parts of my personality manifested in my relationship with Gregory over the summer still left me heavily conflicted. But, I'd process all of that later. For now, I had to meet him at center stage and tune.

Middle C.

While that was the note we'd always tuned on, we typically mouthed it to each other beforehand out of habit. Not tonight. I simply looked at his hands and checked that they were resting on the correct strings. I hadn't the faintest knowledge of how to play a stringed instrument, but I knew exactly how Gregory's hands looked while they played. The position of his fingers for each note, and the way his hand would tremble in solemn vibrato at the end of the piece...always the same. Always perfect.

I'd spent most of last night and this morning in silence. Gregory and I were afforded the grace of being able to spend the night together the night before. We didn't make love. We didn't tumble breathlessly through hotel sheets. I'd spent the night with my cheek against his chest, listening to him breathe, never sleeping. His breathing never evened out fully the way it always did when he was in a deep sleep. He was awake, too, but we stayed in that position until the sun rose and we both pretended to wake up.

As a matter of practicality, I allowed my eyes to connect with his for the brief moment we needed to start the piece. He nodded once, we took a breath together, and then...

Piano.

I whipped my head to the right, finding the pianist in her seat, playing along with Gregory. But, it wasn't to "Clair De Lune." This wasn't the right piece. It was...it was a piece we'd played only a few times. Rather, one *he* played sometimes at the end of our practices and I would sit and watch. And, try to breathe as he played the agonizing melody of "Nocturne" from *The Lady Caliph*.

We hadn't put together any arrangement for this piece, and I had no idea what I was supposed to do. He'd gone off the course of our program. His eyes didn't move from mine as he played. He was begging me to say *yes*. To agree to a life with him that had no certainty, no clear future. Gregory stripped himself bare to me on that stage, going against his musical boundaries, pushing his personal limits, and he was asking me, again...

Say yes.

I did all I could do in that moment. I brought my flute to my lips, closed my eyes, and started playing. Gregory had no way of knowing that I'd spent many solitary hours working on a complimentary melody and harmony for that piece. I wanted to feel the way he looked while he'd played that piece, so I made it my own. And, I felt it. I don't know if I'd ever intended to show it to him, but, now wasn't the time to sort through intentions.

I couldn't possibly stand to see his reaction, though, so I left my eyes closed until I turned toward the audience. An audience which was stirring, because many of them recognized that the music being played wasn't on the program, and the ones closest to the stage had likely seen the confused look on my face.

During a long rest of mine that allowed for the cello solo to shine through, my eyes scanned the crowd inside Symphony Hall Auditorium and fell instantly on my mother. She was in the VIP section near the front of the stage, naturally. What was unnatural to me was that she was seated next to Malcolm. It hadn't occurred to me that she'd be brazen enough to bring him along. Not because of the Opera News article, they *were* in a relationship and had no reason to hide it. But because she had no idea who I was as a person, and that seeing him with her in a place my dad should have been sitting would make me uncomfortable. And sad. My grandmother was sick, and my dad couldn't make it to the concert. I hadn't seen him in months and longed to find his bright eyes smiling back at me as I played. Watching Malcolm nod along almost approvingly to the song was enough to make my stomach churn. His smile turned up the corners of his mouth in a way that was neither genuine, nor calming. Screw him. And her.

The desire to please Vita left me like a swift kick, and I hastily brought my flute to my lips and played the last long, slow section of "Nocturne." The last notes I'd ever play with Gregory Fitzgerald.

Inside of a few seconds I was shattered.

I couldn't continue any sort of relationship with Gregory. Not with things the way they were. I didn't make eye contact with him through the rest of the song, knowing the conversation I'd have to have with him once we got backstage.

Amidst the roaring applause, I bowed a poorly contrived bow toward Gregory, and he returned the gesture. I kept a well-practiced stage smile until I was securely in my seat between Nathan and Tim.

"That was…" Nathan's wide eyes looked for answers.

I didn't have any.

"Thank you."

I looked to Nathan and watched him take me in for a few seconds. He opened his mouth twice, but never said anything. After a deep breath, he shook his head and readied his sheet music for the next piece.

There were no more words.

GREGORY

I'D BEEN PERFORMING in the Symphony Hall Auditorium for more than ten years...night after night during the season, often twice a day. I knew this hall. Front and back stage. I knew the acoustics. I knew the moods of the crowds. I knew the way being inside this hall, playing inside this hall, lifted my mood and sometimes brought me close to a spiritual state of focus and clarity.

That only made it all the more disturbing now. Disturbing that from the moment I walked in, I was off balance. Despite my efforts, Savannah and I hadn't been able to talk, and the one chance we might have had was disrupted by Joseph, when he insisted on talking with me before the performance.

I watched her as I started "Nocturne." As I played my soul out for her without much planning other than handing Grace Daniels the piano sheet music a few minutes before I went on stage. She'd reacted the way I'd anticipated...initially. She scrunched her eyebrows together and raised one all at the same time, the way she always did when something seemed completely preposterous. But, despite reason, which had left us long ago, she took a breath, closed her eyes like I'd watched her do at her conservatory audition several years before, and played.

Damn it, she played right along with me. A perfect accompaniment.

She was *my* perfect accompaniment and I feared, as she seemed to refuse to look at me, that I'd ruined that chance forever.

It was so clear, the second she made her decision. Her posture, the pain in the notes, the look in her eyes when she'd finally opened them. Savannah was done with me. And as we played our final duet together, it broke my heart.

I wasn't ready to say goodbye. Not tonight. Not tomorrow. Not ever. So I watched her for the remainder of the concert. She never looked at me again, her eyes occasionally moving to the audience, to Joseph, to the music on her stand, but never once to me.

Nathan saw me, however. He watched the entire time.

I slumped in my seat when the final crescendo was completed and the curtain closed for the last time.

But not for long...I breathed for maybe twenty seconds, four or five breaths, then I was on my feet. Walking the twenty-five feet across the stage floor to Savannah. She saw me. Her shoulders jerked as she caught her breath, and spots of color appeared on her cheeks.

Her eyes widened as I approached her in front of the entire orchestra.

"I need to speak with you."

She darted her eyes toward Joseph, who raised his eyebrows much as he often raised his baton. The entire orchestra gathered in closer as Joseph began his end of tour congratulatory speech. Except for Nathan, who glared at me, and Savannah, who cut her eyes away.

I slipped a hand around her arm. "I mean it."

"Can't it *wait?*" Her voice was uneven, agitated.

Nathan began to push his way around her, toward me, and she elbowed him in the side. Joseph paused in his speech, and I straightened, standing next to Savannah and unfortunately practically on top of Olivia Mason, who had to scramble out of the way. Joseph gave me an odd look, uncomfortable in its intensity, but at that point in time, I really didn't much care anymore. Because the one thing I was *not* willing to do was give up Savannah without us even talking. Without us having a chance to hash this out. Without at least *trying* to convince her to wait for me before she went and auditioned for Chicago.

I knew she deserved better than me. I knew she needed more than I had to offer.

But I wanted her anyway.

So Joseph continued. Platitudes about our fantastic teamwork, how we'd done more to raise the profile of classical music in the United States, a parade of unnecessary and simple-minded bullshit which might have seemed inspiring to the twenty-four-year-old set but had passed its time with me.

As he continued I leaned close and whispered, "When can we talk?"

She glanced at me with hooded eyes and replied, "Your wife is here, Gregory. Call me some other time."

I frowned. She was right. As Joseph poured on more thanks and praise to the group, I noticed that some of the VIPs from the front row were now back stage. James and Madeline stood awkwardly next to Vita Carulli. All three of them were staring...uncomfortably...gazes alternating between Joseph, Savannah, and myself. Karin stood a little bit apart from them in a yellow skirt suit and matching heels.

"She can wait."

A stab of...sadness...sympathy...ran through me. Because Karin's face was twisted, grief showing in her eyes. Savannah saw it too. Everyone in the entire orchestra saw it. And in that moment I felt as if we'd been transparent. As if everyone in the room had known all along what was going on, as my actions here and now declared that Savannah, not my wife, was who mattered to me. It was a bitter choice, knowing I was hurting her and going forward regardless.

And in that moment I knew I had no choice. Whatever happened, someone's heart was getting broken. Probably more than one. Probably mine. But I did the calculation of hurting Karin, who had lied to me just as I'd lied to her, or hurting Savannah, who meant everything to me, and there was never any choice, was there?

"Gregory..." Savannah shook her head and took a step back.

My whisper was failing, but I tried again. "She can wait, Savannah. You...I need to talk to *you*. *Now.*"

Nathan, still standing next to her, audibly gasped. "You motherfucker," he said. His face went red, and he approached me. "I've fucking had it with you."

Joseph stopped pretending to give his speech and stared, shocked.

"Nathan, *stop it!*" Savannah said through clenched teeth.

At that, I saw Vita and Karin meet each other's eyes. At this point I'd made a hash of everything. I'd destroyed whatever speech our conductor was going to give, I'd likely destroyed what was left of my marriage, and, unless I did something about it now, I'd probably wrecked whatever chance I had with Savannah.

I turned to Joseph and said, "Forgive me, Joseph. But it's urgent I speak with Miss Marshall *right now.*"

Nathan puffed himself up angrily. "You aren't talking with any—"

Without thinking, I balled my right hand up into a fist and hit Nathan Connors in the face.

Savannah and several others in the orchestra screamed as Nathan went flying back from me, stumbling over a music stand and landing on his ass, one hand suddenly cupping his nose.

I took half a step forward and Savannah shouted, "Gregory, stop!"

That's when I felt the pain shooting through my right hand, and I cradled it against my chest. Half in a panic, because an injured hand could be a disaster for a musician. That thought ended quickly as Nathan let out a yell and charged me.

Two of the other musicians grabbed him.

"Motherfucker!" he shouted again, his face red from my fist. "Why can't you just leave her alone? Every fucking stop on this tour you've been screwing her...and breaking her heart."

Half the orchestra gasped, as if they didn't know already, and I saw Karin's face pale. Rage impelled me forward, but James grabbed my arms.

"Don't!" he said. "You've already done too much."

Everything went silent, however, with the sound of Savannah's open palm slapping Nathan's face. "Nathan, shut up!"

I stood there, part of a frozen tableau, with the orchestra ringed around me, and James holding my arms. And then the silence was broken as my wife burst into loud sobs.

His tone bitter, angry, Joseph said, "Thank you all for an amazing tour. Good night." Then he turned and marched away, quickly.

"Let me go," I said to James, my voice quiet. "I'm done with him."

I was too late, though. Savannah had already run to her mother.

I sighed, then turned toward Karin. "Let's go."

She stared at me, her face a mixture of grief and complete disbelief.

"Let's go," I repeated. "We need to talk."

Chapter 30

GREGORY

KARIN AND I walked out of the hall in silence. Because what was there to say, after all? She walked quickly, slightly ahead of me, her back straight, tense, angry. I'd quickly packed the Montagnana and now carried it in my right hand.

An after party was scheduled in one of the ballrooms upstairs. I would not be attending, nor, I suspected, would Savannah.

I had to talk to her. Somehow, I had to convince her not to go to Chicago, or back to Russia, or anywhere else. To stay here with me. I had to...I had to make her understand that she'd become so important to my life that to lose her would destroy everything

But first, I had to deal with Karin.

Her heels echoed off the marble floor as we walked to the parking reserved for members of the orchestra. Most of the audience had already cleared the hall, but traffic exiting onto the streets of Boston would be snarled for another half hour or longer. Delightful.

We reached the car in silence. I quickly put the cello into the back then automatically walked to the passenger side to open her door for her. She gave me an aggrieved look as I closed the door and walked around to the driver's side.

I started the car, and in the silence that followed, she said, "Just tell me the truth, Gregory."

My stomach was twisted—my entire body flooded with dread and nausea, sharp pain pounding a crescendo between my eyes.

I stared straight ahead and gripped the steering wheel with both hands. "I want a divorce."

She flinched.

I put the car in reverse and backed out of the spot. This end of the parking lot had few cars, but I'd been through this before. There would be hundreds trying to leave at the same time. I wished I'd taken a cab tonight. I wished I'd left Karin at home. I wished I was in Colorado or Idaho or Montana or any of the dozens of cities I'd been in over the last few weeks. I wished I was anywhere but here.

I wished I was with *her*...

"Do you love her?" she asked.

I paused. It was so much more complicated than that. Yes, I loved Savannah. But that wasn't the reason I wanted a divorce, even though that was what Karin was trying to assert. It was all tied together, though. Because I *didn't* love Karin. And our marriage had simply gotten worse as the last couple of years went by. And much worse when she decided she wanted to have children, whether or not I wanted them. But I couldn't absolve myself of blame. Because...I'd been a complete shit and there was no way around that.

But Savannah...

Savannah had shown me what I didn't know I was missing. What I never realized I'd been craving. Connection. Understanding. No matter what was going to happen between us, she'd shown me what true love was. What it felt like. And, what it felt like when it was gone.

Finally, I settled on the one answer that I knew was the wrong answer, the one that I knew would hurt the worst, but the simplest one, the only answer I could give.

"Do you love her?" Karin repeated as I tumbled through my thoughts. Her voice was angry, but tight with tears.

I nodded once, closing my eyes briefly. "Yes."

I put the car in park on the ground level near the exit as we came to a stop behind a dozen or more other cars.

"I hate you," she whispered.

I swallowed. Then I said, "I know."

"You never loved me. It was always her. Always."

I couldn't answer that. Because it was true. Even if it wasn't the cause of our marriage falling apart, Karin wouldn't be able to separate it all out in this tiny Lexus as we sat traffic. What exactly was I supposed to say? My instinct was to temporize, to tell her it wasn't true, to comfort her. But that would be wrong. It would simply drag this out and make it so much worse. And it was going to be bad enough as is.

She stared out the window at the parking lot. Someone behind us honked, because honking their horn was going to make us all go faster. Idiots.

"Is what Nathan said true? Have you been sleeping with her this summer? On the tour?"

I squeezed the wheel and said, "I don't think it's necessary to get into that."

She slapped her hand on the dashboard with a loud crack. "It is! Tell me truth, Gregory! You're still my husband."

I sighed, and said, "Yes. It's true." I couldn't help it. As I spoke the words, I knew I sounded...defeated. Ashamed.

Most of the cars ahead of us had cleared out. But the one ahead of us was just sitting there, the couple inside seemingly texting or something as they sat thirty feet from the gate. Not moving. No cars in front of them. Brake lights on. I felt my irritation rising rapidly, and I finally muttered, "Could they possibly drive any slower?" I laid on the horn, the sound echoing through the parking lot.

"Gregory," Karin said.

I hit the horn again. The brake lights on the car ahead of me turned off, the driver apparently waking up. But then they turned on *again*.

For Christ's sake. Now I hit the horn continuously.

"Gregory! Stop it!"

Finally, the car moved up to the gate and whoever was driving pulled out. I drove forward, and felt in my tuxedo for the parking ticket. Of course I didn't have it. Karin had driven.

"Do you have the parking ticket?"

"No, I gave it to you."

"Are you fucking kidding me?" I shouted.

She recoiled, her face suddenly reflecting...intense sadness. Fear. And I deflated, the anger rushing out of me.

"Shit," I muttered. "I'm sorry."

"If you don't have your ticket it's thirty-two dollars," the attendant said.

"Fine." I passed over two twenties and drove on.

We were silent as I pulled into the slow, lifeless traffic around Symphony Hall. We weren't going anywhere any time soon.

It was 1.9 miles home. I could walk it in twenty minutes, up Huntington to Saint James, across the Common to Beacon Hill and I was home. It looked like the drive was likely to take an hour tonight, and this was one night when I didn't need that. But there was nothing I could do.

We made it a block, ten precious quiet minutes, before she spoke again.

"How long have you been sleeping with her?" she asked.

I frowned. "It doesn't matter."

She shuddered. "Yes. It does. Did...did you sleep with me? After?"

I shook my head. "No."

"I hate you. You took my life." It showed in the empty inflection of her voice.

I sighed. "If you must. If it makes it easier for you."

"What the *fuck* is that supposed to mean?"

"Karin," I replied. "I...I'm sorry. I wish I'd done it differently. I wish..."

"What do you wish?" she asked, her voice laden with disgust. "That we'd never married?"

I shrugged. "It would have been wiser."

"Because now I'm a big fucking inconvenience for you, aren't I?"

Traffic stopped again. Huntington ran under a bridge near the front entrance to Symphony Hall. I leaned my head against the steering wheel, frustrated and angry and wishing I could be anywhere else on earth.

"It's not a matter of convenience," I said to the steering wheel. "We haven't been happy. We don't want the same things."

"Married couples compromise, Gregory. That's what it's all about."

I straightened up. "Compromise, yes. But you don't give up who you are. You don't give up everything about you."

She shook her head and turned away. "And you think she'll be any different? That she won't expect you to be a husband? Instead of a robot who plays the cello and sleeps and looks at me like I'm not even here?"

I winced. Because the first thought that ran through my head was, *Savannah* would be worth that change. I didn't have any problem envisioning changing my schedule, giving up eighteen-hour practice days. In fact, when I thought of Savannah, I thought of us...improvising...live in front of an audience. I saw us laughing. I saw her hair, splayed out on my pillow. I saw...love.

I glanced away from Karin, twisting my grip on the wheel again, and looking at the traffic ahead, which wasn't moving at all. And my eyes trended upward, up to the overpass.

I tried not to gasp. I tried to hide my reaction. But standing on the overpass, looking...lost...was Savannah. No more than fifty feet away, but it might as well have been ten miles. Her eyes were sad, her face lined with grief.

She turned away and faded into the crowd like the beautiful mirage she was.

If I'd known then it would be the last time I saw her? I'd have gotten out of the car, leaving Karin behind, and chased her down. But as it was, I saw her turn her back and disappear, and my heart broke as she walked away. But I knew I had every intention of finding her, the next day or the day after that. But first, I had to deal with Karin.

"It's not about her, Karin. It's about us."

"*Bullshit!*" she screamed. "If you hadn't spent the summer sleeping with her, you wouldn't be asking me for a divorce! You are so full of shit!"

"You want to fucking lay money on that, Karin? You *lied* to me about trying to get pregnant. What were you going to say if it worked! *Oops?*" My voice came out in a roar that filled the car, and I immediately recoiled, even as part of me took immense satisfaction in letting out all of the rage I'd felt.

Another car behind us honked their horn, and I heard a voice with a thick Boston accent shouting obscenities from up ahead. Then we inched forward five feet, and everyone came to a stop again, and Karin said, "If you weren't such a selfish coward...I gave up *everything* for you."

"What the fuck are you talking about?" I shouted. "You gave up exactly nothing."

"I gave up children!" she shouted.

I didn't answer, just slammed my fist into the door. And then my phone rang.

SAVANNAH

OST OF THE VIPs... and Gregory and Karin, left in a hurry, leaving all remaining eyes on me. I quickly made my way to Joseph, who was still staring at the space vacated by Gregory, confusion rippling across his face.

"I'm sorry that happened, Joseph..." I trailed off, shaking my head. "Thank you for the opportunity this summer. I'm... I'm sorry," I said again, giving him a quick hug.

"No worries, Savannah." His reaction surprised me. He grinned and shrugged. "Musicians can be quite...passionate, you know."

I did. I gave him another hug before turning to Nathan, who, thankfully, didn't seem to be bleeding. I just needed to get out of there. Brushing past him, he grabbed onto my wrist.

"Savannah."

"*No,*" I cracked sharply.

"I'm sorry." He looked up at Christine as he sat, holding a bag of ice to his swollen cheek. She sighed and shook her head with a mix of emotions playing across her face.

"You're sorry? Sorry? I can't deal with this shit right now, my fucking mother is here."

I shook free from his grasp and purposefully configured my posture to hide every emotion possible from my mother.

In truth, my pulse never quieted after my song with Gregory. Seeing my mother standing cross-armed next to Malcolm did little to help that. The judgmental look on her face was enough to make me want to slap her, but there had been enough violence in Symphony Hall for one evening.

"That was quite a show, Savannah." Her expertly manicured eyebrow judged me as it arched its way skyward. Malcolm shifted uncomfortably at her side.

Suddenly I had no interest in giving her any of my time. I was desperate to process what had just happened and to discuss the summer. But I couldn't. Not with her. I turned to leave.

"Where are you going?" she asked, sounding rather annoyed.

"Cab. Home." I shoved my flute case into my shoulder bag and made my way down the long hall, knowing full well she was following closely behind. I made it all the way outside before acknowledging her. "Leave me alone."

"Hardly, darling. Not when you're in the middle of destroying your career." Whenever she said *darling* it took on a haughty British air, which annoyed me even further given Italian was her first language. And she was an American citizen.

Turning around, I sized Malcolm up quickly before speaking. *"Vai."* I commanded her to *go* in a language she might understand, since her English seemed to be failing her.

"Calmati." She tilted her head to the side mockingly, suggesting I actually *calm down*. "There's no need to hide this conversation, Savannah."

"We're not having a conversation. I'm leaving." Turning without a second glance at her silent boyfriend, I made it down one stair.

"And where is it that you're going? Home? You don't have one here, remember? Or, were you planning to run to the house of your lover...who appears to be married?"

"Wow," I turned around and took three measured steps toward her, "those are some serious accusations coming from someone like you."

My mother swallowed once, sneaking a sideways glance at Malcolm, who looked as though he was about to speak. She stopped him by putting her hand up. "You seem to have your facts mixed up, Savannah. I never slept with a married man."

"That's where you're mistaken, *Vita*." I leaned in so only she could hear me. "Dad. Dad was a married man. To you. Or, is it that your marriage vows meant so little, you conveniently forgot about them while you were in bed with *him*?" I tilted my chin toward Malcolm who wisely looked away from me.

Without missing a beat or stumbling over her composure, she straightened her shoulders. "It's funny, hearing you discuss the sanctity of marriage vows as you've apparently spent the summer destroying someone else's. Grow up, Savannah. Let's go, Malcolm." My mother held out her arm, linking it with Malcolm's as they descended the grand stairs of Symphony Hall, leaving a trail of emotional carnage up and down Massachusetts Avenue.

Feeling faint, I sat down on the stairs, leaning my back against one of the gargantuan white pillars that signified the greatness that was held inside the hall. Right now, it shouldered my shame.

It's different. It was different with us, I thought, cradling my head in my hands as I tried to regulate my breathing. Gregory's marriage was dead in the water long before I showed back up in his life. At least that's what he'd told me.

Shit.

A few words from my mother regarding the condition of my morals and I was hyperventilating on the steps of Symphony Hall, looking for an escape. I'd chosen to lead my mother out this way specifically to avoid the exit of the other orchestra members, knowing they'd leave out the back. I was thoroughly regretting that decision as I longed to find someone I knew. Anyone. I thought about wandering back down the maze of halls to the area where I knew some members of the orchestra would be lingering, but I had no excuse. My luggage wouldn't be back there, it was in a truck being hauled to Marcia's house in Andover, which was an unfortunate 40-minute drive away. I could call Marcia to come get me, but Nathan and Christine would be with her and I just...couldn't yet.

Damn it, Nathan.

Oddly enough, I wasn't angry with him. He'd always been undisciplined in the passion of his emotions, which is why we'd hit it off as friends in the first place. He was trying to protect me from the emotional monster he'd long labeled Gregory. He didn't get it. No one did. We were different. *This* was different.

Slinging my flute bag over my shoulder, I carefully descended the stairs and made my way to the overpass across from the hall, leaning against the railing for a moment to steady myself. My emotions. I needed to call him. Panic rose as I considered the painful possibility that we were no different at all. No different from my mother and Malcolm. No different from every cliché and Lifetime movie I'd ever seen. I'd call him and it would be okay. I'd hear his voice and it would assure me. He loved me. I never let him say it, but I needed to hear it from him now.

I hailed a cab, pulling out my phone as I slid into the back seat.

"Where to?" the middle-aged man asked, eyeing me through the rearview mirror. "Ma'am?" he requested my attention again as my thumb trembled over Gregory's name.

"Huh? Oh, sorry. I don't care." I waved my hand dismissively, smirking at having picked up that habit on tour.

"Come on, I don't have time for this." I could only see his eyes in the rearview mirror, but that was enough.

Knowing better than to piss off a cabbie on a busy Saturday night, I looked up. "Sorry. Uh...the bar around the corner."

"Which one?"

"*That* really doesn't matter." I shrugged, pressing *call* and bringing my phone to my ear as the driver grumbled something unflattering and took off into traffic.

Ring.

He'd left with Karin. I saw that. But given the look on her face, I didn't know how long their conversation would be. Either way, he said he'd always be there for me.

I needed him.

He needed to tell me I wasn't the morally bankrupt shrew my mother implied with a soft click of her tongue and an arched eyebrow.

"You've reached Gregory Fitzgerald…"

"Shit, come on," I hissed at the phone when I was greeted with his voicemail. I pressed *end*, waited a second, and called again.

"Here ya go," the cab driver said passively as he pulled up to a bar I'd never been to.

"Thank you so much." I gave him far too much money and slammed the door shut, desperate to get Gregory live on the phone.

After hearing his voicemail greeting two more times, I leaned against the cool brick of the exterior of the bar, deciding to call one more time. All he had to do was answer, and assure me. It rang only once before a brief silence. I knew he'd picked up because I could hear the sounds of traffic.

"*What?*" he spit out. His tone was toxic.

I hesitated for a moment, convinced he wasn't speaking to *me*, that maybe he'd answered the phone without checking the caller ID.

"*Hello?*" His tone hadn't changed.

My voice took on an ungraceful tremor. "Hi. I…um…"

"I can't do this right now," he snapped as he ended the call.

I pulled the phone away as the timer blinked *:15,* mocking the time it took for Gregory to prove I was no different. That we were no different.

The last fifteen seconds I'd ever speak with him.

Chapter 31

SAVANNAH

I CHECKED THE TIME on the departures display. It was 9 a.m., which meant I still had three hours. I'd spent a small fortune to move my departure up a week, especially given it was a non-stop flight once we got to New York. Sticking around in the purgatory that had become Boston, though, wasn't a healthy option.

My phone rang again, and I breathed a sigh of relief as I checked the caller ID. It was Nathan, who was hopefully on his way. Gregory had called half a dozen times this morning, and I'd sent him straight to voicemail. I knew he was probably calling to apologize. To tell me he was sorry. He didn't really have anything to *apologize* for. Well, maybe both of us did. After all, he was in the car with his wife, undoubtedly arguing. About me. And that was the point really. She was his wife.

I wasn't.

No matter how much I wanted it, no matter how much I might fantasize, no matter how much it might seem right, the fact was, he was married to someone else. And that was an insurmountable obstacle.

I answered the phone. "Hello?"

"Am I too late?" Nathan asked.

"No...I've got an hour or so before I go through security."

"Good...I'm just looking for parking. Where are you?"

I looked around then gave him my location in the terminal.

After saying goodbye, I sank down on my heels, holding onto my flute bag with one hand and stifling a cry with the other.

I was relieved I'd had the good sense to throw jeans and a t-shirt into my flute bag before the performance last night. I'd intended to change into them before the after party, but I changed in the dirty bathroom of a dive bar at 3 a.m., cramming my green satin dress into the garbage can on my way out the door. It was Gregory's favorite; I'd worn it when I saw my mother perform on my birthday in 2001. It was the first time I caught Gregory eyeing me in a way that tightened my belly and made my neck hot. Surveying my curves as I'd introduced him to my mother, his eyes barely left my body as he shook her hand.

This was it. This was how my perfect summer with Gregory was ending. Not just my summer. Our story. Over like this—me, alone in Logan on zero hours of sleep, waiting for my 16-hour flight back to Moscow. I hadn't said goodbye when I should have. I hadn't been clear with him about going back to Bolshoi, but he hadn't asked, either.

Honesty.

I shook my head, lamenting over the muddled intentions of that word. Lofty promises and dreams on the horizon. We believed them, though. I believed him when he said he would do anything for me, because I'd meant it when I said it to him. As odd as it seems, I had no reason not to believe him. Gregory had always been honest with me, even in the beginning. Even when I was just his student. He'd always shown me a side of him he never let anyone else see. Who he really was. No matter what truths we'd bent over the years, we were always pure in our interactions with each other.

I can't do this right now.

He couldn't do the one thing I needed. In the moment when I held onto his honesty, his word, the tightest, he failed me. I knew he was in the car with his wife, but I didn't need him to say anything to me other than *It's going to be okay* or *I'll call you as soon as I can*. Something other than the annoyed and angry dismissal I received. How people behave under intense stress shows a lot about who they are.

And he couldn't be bothered.

I felt my body shudder, another suppressed sob trying to force its way out of my body.

Nathan's voice. "Christ, Savannah. You look like shit."

"I haven't slept," I said. I started to cry again.

Nathan sighed. "Ahh, shit." He slumped down to the floor next to me and pulled me into his arms. And that was all it took to reduce me to a sniveling mess.

"Marcia told me you called her."

I nodded. "Is she pissed at me for not coming home?"

I felt Nathan's chin moving back and forth across the top of my head. "No. We were all concerned, though. You just kind of disappeared. Did you talk to him?"

"He wouldn't talk to me...or couldn't..." My tears came harder as I grasped at the fabric of his shirt.

"Fuck," he whispered.

"I'm so sorry, Nathan." My voice was louder than I'd intended, given I was trying to speak over my tears.

"No, I'm sorry." He kissed my forehead and pulled me tighter. I sat up and started my rebuttal, but he cut me off at the pass. "It's really important that I get this out."

"Okay," I muttered, pulling the collar of my t-shirt up and wiping my eyes and nose.

"I didn't mean to let things get so out of hand last night." Nathan had let his hair grow out a little over the summer, and his curls were a mess.

"It got intense, Nathan—"

"Savannah, stop. Let me finish, okay?" I nodded, and he continued. "I knew something was going on between the two of you, but that didn't give me the right to scream it out in front of *everyone*, let alone your mother...and his wife." Nathan's eyes fell away from me for half a second, as he seemed to consider Karin's title.

"Everything okay, Miss?" A security guard with stern tenderness in his eyes stood over Nathan and me.

"Oh, yeah, sorry. I'm just a total wreck." I sent him on his way with a weak smile and tied my hair into a pathetic ponytail to try to look a little less destitute.

"Anyway," Nathan picked up where he left off, "you deserved better from me than to have a secret like that broadcasted. You did an awesome job this summer, and those duets you two did were so incredible. I feel like I took all of that away, and now that's all people will remember..." he trailed off, wringing his hands.

I reached for his hand and he gave it up, letting me wrap my fingers around his. "That's all the orchestra will remember, maybe. But not me, not you, and not anyone in the audience. I'm not worried about that, though. I'm worried about what a shitty friend I've been all summer."

Nathan cracked his neck and looked at me like I'd gone insane.

"I'm serious. I knew that you realized something was going on, and I should have either been totally honest with you, or kept it a complete secret. The limbo I put you in was an unfair position. I was so excited to spend the summer with you and...I blew it."

He shrugged and smiled, wiping the last tear from my cheek. "You were in love, Savannah. It happens."

I could feel my cheeks heat up as I looked to the floor, my actions of this summer flashing through my head.

"Don't look so uncomfortable, Savannah. I've known you a long time. I caught onto the look in your eyes after a few days."

I furrowed my brow. "So, why are you so pissed at Gregory?"

"Because he led you on. Let you fall in love with him when he wasn't able to give it back. You deserve all of someone, Savannah. Not what's left over after they've dealt with the rest of their life." Nathan's hazel eyes faded a little and my chin quivered.

"I really do love him, Nathan."

He put his arm around me again, pulling me so my head rested on his shoulder. "I know you do. None of the rest of us ever stood a chance as soon as he showed up." He let out a tired laugh.

"So now what the hell do I do?"

"You *sure* you don't want to consider Chicago?" he asked with weak hope.

"I'm sure. I love you, but it's never been my city."

"Well," he sighed, "in that case...you go back to Moscow. Learn Russian or whatever the hell it is you do in your spare time, and you play. You've been so happy the last year with the ballet."

"I hate that it's so far away from you, though."

"I'll come visit. Christine wants to come, too."

"Oh Christ, doesn't she think I'm a complete whore?" I sank my forehead into my hands.

Nathan grabbed my shoulders and turned me to face him, a look of fight in his eyes. "*No*. No one thinks that, Savannah. And fuck them if they do. That's not what you are. Don't ever talk about yourself that way. Jesus, I hate that he made you feel that way."

"He didn't make me feel that way. I did. I slept with a married man." I thought, maybe, the more times I said it, the less it would hurt that I was leaving him behind. And my heart. It didn't work.

"Well," Nathan snorted, "if he didn't intend for you to feel that way then I guess he shouldn't have put you in that position."

"Don't hunt him down and beat him up or anything crazy like that." The grip Nathan had on my shoulders had me worried about his plans for the rest of the day.

"Hardly. I go back to Chicago in two days and plan to spend exactly none of them in jail."

I checked the time on my cell phone and let out a defeated sigh. Time, and timing, hadn't been on my side for years.

Nathan stood and held out his hand. "I'll walk you as far as I can."

Nathan and I walked through the airport, and he told me that he and Christine would be shopping for an apartment together as soon as they returned to Chicago. I was happy for them and the effortless dreams most couples take for granted. It ached when I tried to let myself go to a place in my head where Gregory and I were living together, practicing together...loving together. So, I pushed those thoughts out of my head and focused on my best friend and his happiness.

Thankfully, the security line wasn't long so I wasn't likely to miss my flight, but that meant Nathan and I had to say our goodbyes immediately.

"I'll miss you, Nathan. I loved spending time with you this summer. I wish it could have been more..."

"No regrets, okay? We all grew up a little, I think. Be happy, Savannah. Find someone who takes your breath away and supports you and nurtures you."

"I did." I could barely get the words out without more tears. But I managed.

"You know what I mean." Nathan sighed and shagged a hand through his hair.

"Please tell Marcia that I'll call her as soon as I get settled in."

"Love you," Nathan said, swallowing me into his long arms for a sad hug.

After several seconds I pulled back and held Nathan at arms' length. "Love you, too. Now, go back to Marcia's, get Christine, and go be happy."

Nathan shot me a sad smile as I turned and made my way through the maze to the belt, praying my luggage would end up where it was supposed to, since all I had on me was my flute and my cell phone. Once I was settled into a chair by my gate, I texted my father. I know I should have called him, but his silence last night told me that he hadn't spoken with my mother. I was too tired to get into it at the moment and told him I had a change of flight plans and I'd call him when I got settled back into my apartment in Moscow.

A couple of hours later I was finally boarding my final flight to Moscow from JFK. The layover wasn't a bad as I thought it'd be. I busied myself reading over some new music for the upcoming season that had been FedExed to me while I was on tour.

As we taxied away from the gate, I leaned my head against the window and exhaled long and slow.

"Nervous?" a woman in her fifties sitting next to me asked.

"No. Just...tired."

"You look sad." Her thick Russian accent sent a wave of emotions through me. It sounded like home, the new home I was returning to. But...it reminded me how far away I was going. As I wiped a tear away she took my hand. "I saw you looking at music. Do you play over there?"

"Yes. Bolshoi. Flute." The sounds of the engines hauling us down the runway did their best to silence the screaming in my heart.

Her eyes lit up. Russians are, of course, serious about their ballet. Remembering the story I'd told Tim and Nathan on the road let a small grin escape. "Impressive. So, you're sad about leaving the States?"

"No." I shook my head and met her eyes. She looked sincere, and comforting. I'd picked up a fair bit of Russian by that point, mainly emotive words since they were often written onto our music by composers and spoken to us by conductors to direct our playing. "I just...I'm going back...*s razbitym serdtsem...*"

She swallowed hard, this kind stranger, and didn't let go of my hand. She gripped it tighter as we cruised above the clouds and tears formed in her eyes. She seemed to have appointed herself to escort me back to Moscow.

With a broken heart.

GREGORY

"CHRIST, GREGORY. YOU look like shit."

I grumbled a little at James as I poured hot water over a tea bag and sat down at his kitchen table. My head was splitting, and I had a vague memory of switching from gin to something else deep into our conversation. Tequila, maybe?

I shook my head, which was a mistake, because it caused the entire room to tilt to the left. "Leave me alone."

James poured coffee for himself and sat down across from me as I tried to piece together what had happened the night before. The show, followed by Nathan's outburst, and my own. The argument with Karin, which had resulted in me dropping her off, then me peeling off in the car, tires screeching. I'd ended up with James. Drinking. Pouring out the story of Savannah and our love affair.

That was no affair...it was...like a safe place in a storm, a quiet, purposeful, beautiful duet in a silent theater.

I don't know what James said.

I don't know how he responded.

Because for the first time in my adult life, I'd drunk so much I blacked out.

James slid several Tylenol across the table to me. "Take these," he said. "And get a drink of water."

I took the Tylenol without comment, just staring at the table. I rubbed my forehead and looked up. "What exactly did I say to you last night?"

James snorted a little and shook his head. "The question is what *didn't* you say, Gregory. I've never seen you such a mess before."

"She won't answer my calls," I replied.

James winced.

I leaned forward and stared at my tea, then said, "I screwed up. Badly."

He shrugged. "We all screw up. Though I'll admit, adultery..."

I shook my head, then looked up at him, irritated. "That's not what I meant."

"What *did* you mean?"

"I screwed up five years ago. When I told you I'd drop her. I screwed up when I didn't put her first. And...I'm pretty sure she got that message when she called last night. I couldn't have said it any clearer. *God*, I'm such an asshole."

I leaned my head in my hand. The Tylenol wasn't helping. My head was pounding, and worse, I...I felt empty inside. Empty like I hadn't felt since that day five years ago when I learned she'd left the conservatory. Just...empty.

I stared miserably into my cup. Then I took out my cell phone and dialed again.

Straight to voicemail. Again. I tapped out a text message.

I'm sorry. Please call me.

Then I hit send and looked up at my oldest friend. "I don't know what to do," I said. "I just don't know what the fuck to do."

That's when I heard Madeline's voice, behind me. "You go to her," she said. "You tell her how much she means to you. You do whatever it takes."

James frowned. "Madeline," he said, an edge in his tone.

"Oh, shut up, James. You know they're in love."

I twisted around in my seat. "And if she won't take my calls? I don't even know where the hell she is."

Madeline grinned. "I can help you with that. She's staying with one of your former students, Marcia Taylor. In Andover."

I shot out of my seat, which was added to the list of my poor decisions for the last 24 hours. My head pounded. "You know the address?"

Madeline nodded.

Ten minutes later I'd had the shortest shower of my life and was in the car on my way to Andover, wearing clothes borrowed from James with too short arms and legs and a waist I could fit two of me through. As I drove, I glanced in the back seat and froze.

My cello was still in the back seat.

I'd left a seven hundred thousand dollar cello in the back-seat of my car, parked on the street in Boston, overnight.

I frowned and kept driving. Right now I had more important things to worry about. I tried to call her as I drove, but the phone went straight to voicemail. Again.

Thankfully, I didn't have to deal with much in the way of traffic. It was still relatively early on Sunday morning, the summer light still faint as I drove north out of Boston. The grey sky suited my mood. But I had one thing going for me.

I had hope.

It took forty minutes before I pulled up to the address on Chestnut Street Madeline had scrawled on a sheet of paper.

I parked in front of the house and took a breath, suddenly terrified. A white two-story home, with three dormer windows cut into the attic. A small structure, originally separate, must have once housed a kitchen or garage. A low stone wall bordered the edge of the property, and a slow wind blew the leaves off several old trees towering over the house. Somewhere inside, Savannah had lived, briefly, after returning from Moscow and before we went on tour.

I opened the car door and got out, then slowly walked up the front walk. My upper body was tense, my throat tight. Something told me this was my only chance to make it right. Because I'd been so fucking cold on the phone. I'd been so angry. It wasn't her fault. It wasn't anything she'd said or done. It was just the timing. And my own carelessness.

I don't have time for this is not something you say to the love of your life.

I found myself wondering what death row inmates feel like when they are walking toward their execution. Was it this tension? This fear deep in your gut? I swallowed my fear, reached up and knocked on the door.

Nothing.

After a full minute, I hit the knocker again. This time, from deep in the bowels of the house, I heard a female voice calling out, "Just a minute."

And so I waited.

Almost a full minute later, the door opened, and I stood there dumbly confused for a moment. I'd so anticipated Savannah being there that I was confused when Nathan Connors' girlfriend, the harpist, answered the door. A moment later Marcia, my former student and Savannah's roommate, approached the door.

"What are you doing here?" Marcia's voice wasn't hostile, but it wasn't exactly friendly either.

I coughed. Then I said, "I need to speak with Savannah."

Marcia's eyebrows drew together. And then she burst out the front door, standing in front of me, and poked me in the chest hard with her index finger. "What the fuck did you say to her last night, Gregory?"

I staggered back. I had nothing I could say. No defense. Because her reaction was confirmation of what I'd already known...that my flippant, angry response on the phone last night had destroyed what little trust Savannah had in me.

I closed my eyes and looked at the ground and said, "Please...just let me talk to her." And I was horrified. Because for the first time in my adult life, my voice cracked.

Marcia's eyes widened. She whispered, "What the hell happened between you two?"

I looked away, ground my teeth, and said, "I lost her. And...just...please..."

She shook her head, looking terribly sad. "She's gone."

"What do you mean, gone? Where did she go?"

"Back to Russia. She...didn't come home last night...called early this morning to let me know she's going straight to the airport."

I staggered back. "Back to *Russia?*"

Without transition I found myself sitting on the edge of a flower planter next to the front walk. Potting soil and water soaked into the back of my pants as I shook my head. "Why?" I asked, my voice at a whisper.

Marcia shook her head. "You tell me. I've never heard her sounding so distraught in my life. Whatever you said to her Gregory...you hurt her. Badly."

"Fuck," I groaned. I leaned forward, resting my elbows on my knees and my head in my hands.

"Can you get off my flowers?" she asked, her voice edging toward annoyed.

I sighed and stood. "Sorry for...wasting your time."

My shoulders slumped; I walked back toward my car. And just to cap the morning, as I unlocked my car, Nathan fucking Connors drove up and parked behind me. I almost got in and drove off before he could get out of his car, but something told me to wait.

As he got out of his car, his expression told me he wasn't thrilled to see me either.

"Fitzgerald."

"Connors."

"What are you doing here?" He closed his door and leaned against it.

I shrugged. "I came...to see her. But I was too late."

He shook his head and walked toward me, then leaned back against *my* car. Presumptuous as usual, but I didn't say anything. "I just saw her off at the airport."

"She's going back to the Bolshoi."

He nodded.

"She's done with me. For good."

He nodded again.

I leaned against the car, next to him, and said, "I didn't mean to break her heart. I'd do anything to take it back."

"Little late for that," Nathan said. "Twice, Fitzgerald. Twice, I've had to put my friend back together after you tore her to shreds. Just...stay away from her. Let her heal and get her life together and don't...don't hurt her again, all right? She deserves a whole man. You understand what I'm saying? The one thing you couldn't ever do—put her first."

I closed my eyes and groaned. He was right. Everything he was saying was right. I never had. It has always been... the conservatory. My career. The music. Karin. It was always something else, anything else, when it should have been her.

No fucking wonder she felt the way she did. I had the arrogance to ask her to wait for me, to ask her to set aside her career, her entire life, to stay in Boston while I fumbled through whatever the hell was going on with my marriage.

And I couldn't even take her phone call.

I gasped. "Don't you ever say anything to anyone. But... nothing else will ever matter again. Not after losing her."

Nathan made a disgusted sound and shook his head. "I've spent my whole morning dealing with the fallout from your carelessness, Fitzgerald. Don't ask me to feel sorry for you on top of it."

I grimaced. The *last* fucking thing I wanted was Nathan's sympathy. I glared at him and said, "Just tell me she's going to be okay."

He looked away from me, his mouth twisting up in a parody of a smile. "I don't have a clue. This was...much worse than when you dumped her five years ago." He looked at the ground, and whispered, "I don't know if she'll ever be over you. And I hate that for her. She's better than this."

I closed my eyes. "When you talk to her. Please...tell her I'm sorry." I turned and opened the door, getting in my car as Nathan stepped back.

Then I drove away, with nothing but ashes in my soul.

Chapter 32

SAVANNAH

O NE WINTER IN Russia is enough to remind you, forever, to always carry your scarf. That day was particularly glacial, though. The wind whooshed through my hair with such cruel rawness I was certain my brain would freeze.

"Bella!" Aldo called from behind me as I crossed the street to head for my apartment after rehearsal.

"Ciao, Al." I smiled as he caught up to me. He was a short Italian cellist who had been at Bolshoi a year before me. All last year he'd walk me to my apartment after rehearsal, especially in the winter when the sun left long before we did. Given the incidence of street crime in Moscow these days, I was grateful for the escort.

"You always call me Al. Why Al?" His broken English cracked me up. He knew I could speak fluent Italian, but also knew I longed to speak English whenever I could. My roommate was from Moscow and I spoke more Russian than she spoke English.

Our apartment was a quiet place.

I shrugged. "No reason. It's cute."

"Ah, like you."

Poor Al...he'd been courting me from the minute my plane landed in Moscow in August. I haven't a clue what gave him the urge to seek me out, but I was his target. He had no way of knowing I had little time or desire for Italians...or cellists.

As we approached the stairs to my fourth floor apartment, Aldo spoke faster.

"Savannah, you...do you want to come over for tea?" A nice request on the surface, but his hand had slid to my lower back over the course of our short walk.

I hated to let him down, but I wanted to be fair. "Maybe another time? We should get everyone together to go to the teahouse down the road tomorrow after rehearsal, or on break or something."

He nodded, pulling his lips back in a sweet smile. He was only capable of sweet. "Another time. *Essere sicura.*" He gave my shoulders a tight squeeze as he told me to be safe.

Despite our silence-inducing language barrier, I was still grateful that Sasha was part of a brass ensemble that kept her out late most nights. With a sigh, I made my way to the front window, where I saw Aldo Marietta heading down the road to his apartment two blocks away. Turning back to the front table, I sorted through the mail I'd picked up the day before but hadn't gone through yet.

Christmas cards from my friends in the States were starting to decorate the bare walls in my tiny bedroom. Christmas in Russia wasn't celebrated until January 7th, so it was always a topic of conversation among friends that visited our apartment. They'd point at cards illustrated with a very fat and cartoonish looking Santa Claus and laugh, highlighting our deep cultural differences that went far beyond our celebration of this particular holiday.

Settling back into Moscow and the orchestra was seamless. Some of my friends had kept tabs on the tour and congratulated me on the performances but, luckily, no one had heard about the end. How that never ended up in the artsy tabloids was beyond me, but I was grateful. After what I learned on tour about how people spread lies more than truths, I'm sure someone spent a lot of money to keep the backstage scuffle between Nathan and Gregory a secret, affair revelation and all.

I felt comfortable with my position at the Bolshoi and was being groomed for the principal chair in the coming years, but I wasn't sure that I wanted to get to the top of my career at the Bolshoi. The atmosphere at the highest levels was cutthroat, and a level of bitter intensity that I never wanted to associate with a professional career. I'd been keeping my eyes and ears open throughout Europe for auditions. In truth, I had my eyes set on the London Symphony Orchestra. While the BSO had filled every musical aspiration I'd had since I started playing, it was no longer an emotional possibility. I didn't resent him for it, but I knew that the tethers of Boston's Symphony Hall still had a grip on my heart, and I needed time and distance for them to wither away.

I paused briefly as I got to the large manila envelope that came once a month from my dad. He'd collect news clippings from friends of mine from high school, or any he came across about Nathan or my other friends from the conservatory. I was relieved each month that he dutifully ignored my insistence that I could locate such information on the Internet. He said it just wasn't the same as having a piece of it with me. He was right.

Still, I set the envelope aside for the time being and wandered over to my laptop, pulling up Spotify's Adele station and the Boston Globe's website as I sat down. Automatically I clicked on "Arts" and scrolled until I reached the *Theater and Art* section.

I hadn't spoken to my mother since watching her walk down the steps of Symphony Hall four months ago with Malcolm by her side. My dad encouraged me to reach out to her any chance he got. I told him I would when I was ready, and he said he understood. His understanding lasted until the next phone call or email, where we'd have the same conversation. My promise. His understanding. The end.

News on my mother had died down since opening night at the end of September, but I still scrolled through, peeking for glimpses of the life she chose. Maybe looking for reasons why. Before I had a chance to click on the "Theater and Art" tab to take me to the full list of stories, the headline smacked me in the face.

Carroll and Carulli To Wed.

...Proposal during an after-show party earlier in the month.

...Wedding this summer at Symphony Hall.

...That's right. Symphony Hall. An affair that will cost well over fifty-thousand dollars and host the most prominent...

Seeing it in print held a different weight than reading it in my father's email last week. *Things with them are getting serious quickly,* he'd said. It was only quick for someone who refused to, or couldn't, acknowledge a prior seven-year affair.

"Well, there *that* is." I sighed and worked my way out of the *Theater and Art* section, scrolling past the *Music* link I'd grown to avoid out of habit.

Until this time.

Prized Antique Cello Fetches $1 Million at Auction.

My shoulders tensed as I hovered the cursor over the link. It had to be him. It was him. I knew it was him. But...*what?* So, I clicked.

At the annual New England Center for the Arts Gala, sponsored by Sotheby's, Gregory Fitzgerald auctioned his nearly 300 year-old Montagnana cello, netting $1 million dollars on the nose.

Shit, it really was him. The article continued and, despite myself, so did I.

The donation was sent, upon request by Mr. Fitzgerald, to the New England Conservatory. Fitzgerald is earmarking the funds to be used for a new program he's helping to develop for music education students to be trained in specializing in working with children with disabilities.

I pressed the heels of my hands into my forehead as I rested my elbows on the table. Months ago he'd confessed to me how thoroughly unprepared he'd been to take on the young blind cellist, Robert. This was for him.

The rabbit hole wasn't quite finished with me as I read and reread the last line of the article.

Gregory Fitzgerald was the principal cellist of the Boston Symphony Orchestra until his resignation earlier this month.

"*What?*" I shouted into the empty air of my apartment. "That's it?" I scrolled up and down and clicked back and forth, but that was it.

He stayed with Karin...and they're having babies.

That was the only reasonable explanation for such preposterous news.

I didn't know which to address first, the bile rising rapidly through my throat, or my dizziness. I was already sitting, but not, unfortunately, near a toilet. I only had time to make it to the kitchen sink, so my painted blue teacup from the morning's breakfast bore the brunt of my resurgent heartache.

After rinsing my mouth out, I cautiously returned to the Globe's web page to find the answer.

There was none. The article just...ended there.

Gregory had left the BSO.

And auctioned his cello.

And suddenly nothing made any sense.

"Oh shut up, Adele, what the hell do you know." I clicked off her instructions to have me make someone feel my love and picked up my phone, scrolling to Nathan's number. He'd know something.

"No," I said, only mildly concerned about my increased talking to myself. I set my phone down and took a breath. "Just...leave it alone."

GREGORY

"OH, HELLO," KARIN said. She looked as surprised as I felt to see each other.

I coughed lightly, then said, "Hello, Karin."

She gave me a sardonic smile, then said, "Don't look so uncomfortable, Gregory. It's all over."

"Indeed." I wasn't sure how I felt about seeing her. The New Year's party at Joseph McIntosh's house was in full swing, at twenty minutes to midnight. I'd had three drinks and had a warm glow going that even the sight of my ex-wife couldn't kill.

"You received the final check?" I asked. The sale of our house, which I'd mortgaged all those years ago to buy the Montagnana, had finally gone through. The tiny amount of cash left over from the sale was split between us, but the lawyers had handled that end of things.

"I did," she said. "And I'm all settled in my new place."

"Oh, good." The words felt stiff.

In the end, our divorce had been amicable, uncontested. All the same, I felt uncomfortable in conversation with her, unsure of what to say, especially in a social environment like this. We'd only been married three short years, but it was long enough to create an immense, complicated tie. I had my own plans, but part of me wanted to know that she was ready to move on with her life without me. But, of course, we didn't talk about such things.

She put a hand on my arm. "I heard about what you did. With your cello."

I nodded. That was something I didn't feel comfortable at all talking about.

"It was a good thing to do, Gregory."

I shrugged, unsure about how to engage in "normal" conversation with her.

A tall man, in his early forties approached, sliding his arm around her waist. Surprisingly comfortably.

She smiled, blushing a little. "Gregory, meet Richard Hightower. Richard, this is my ex-husband, Gregory Fitzgerald."

Richard—apparently her new boyfriend—reached out to shake my hand. I gritted my teeth for a second, then let it go. He looked like one of those guys who liked to test his manhood by squeezing the life out of opponents during handshakes. But I was surprised. His grip was surprisingly limp.

"Pleased to meet ya, Greg."

Karin winced when she heard him shorten my name. His false familiarity was both grating and somehow gratifying. On the one hand, anyone who shortened my name and spoke to me in such a casual manner was extremely irritating. On the other hand? I was happy to see she'd found someone, especially someone so unlike me.

Two could play that game. "Nice to meet you, Dick."

Karin actually looked amused as she said, "Richard is associate director of the endowment at Harvard."

"I see...so you share a line of work. How nice."

My eyes were starting to glaze over. So it was a blessing when I heard Madeline's voice across the room. "Gregory!"

"Please excuse me," I said. "Karin, a delight to see you. Dick."

We exchanged pleasantries and I escaped as quickly as I could, joining Madeline and James at the opposite corner of the large room. They were part of a small circle of men and women, mostly musicians, who stood near Joseph, our host. Madeline was drinking soda water. She wasn't showing yet, but by August, they were expecting a baby.

Madeline leaned close and whispered in my ear. "I saw you cornered over there."

I shrugged. "It was really all right. Though her new boyfriend Bob is a little insufferable."

"I think his name is Richard?" Madeline said.

I shrugged. At that moment I froze in place. Vita Carulli and her fiancé Malcolm Carroll had approached the crowd.

I'd once admired Vita. She was a remarkable performer, a remarkable musician.

She was also Savannah's mother...the mother who had hurt and abandoned her.

"Gregory," Vita said, nodded. One star of the music world to another.

I turned away from her, taking a sip of my drink. I had an established reputation as an arrogant bastard; might as well monopolize on that by snubbing a world class opera singer. Her career was on a downturn anyway.

James clapped me on the shoulder. "It's time you moved on. I meant to tell you, I met a lovely young cellist the other day..."

Madeline rolled her eyes. "James, really..."

"Seriously. He needs to go out and—"

"Don't say it." Madeline raised a disapproving eyebrow as he spoke.

I chuckled. "I think you can let it go," I said.

"So...what *are* your plans?" she asked.

I shrugged. I didn't have an easy answer to that.

"Whatever it is," James said, "you look...relaxed. Happier than I've ever seen you."

"I am happy," I replied. And in truth, I was. I had a cello still, but somehow giving up the Montagnana had freed me.

Freed me of the kind of expectations that I'd put on myself. The house was gone. My divorce was final. I no longer had a million dollar instrument weighing me down, like a chain around my neck. "I'm very happy, in fact..."

As I began to expand on that, someone in the crowd began to shout, counting down the seconds until midnight. I trailed off. They didn't really need to know where I was headed, anyway. But as everyone shouted *Happy New Year!* and began to kiss and toss down drinks, my thoughts turned, far off to the east, to a woman I'd loved and lost.

And hoped to win again.

Chapter 33

SAVANNAH

ONE OF THE lovely things about attending the Bolshoi Christmas Ball is the dancers; several of whom were twirling in circles in extravagant ball gowns as I stood on the sidelines watching. I'd always been a confident dancer, but in front of these women? Hardly. I sipped my champagne and let my eyes scan the crowd.

It was a lavish setting without a hint of pretense. It was a celebration. Polished white marble columns that climbed to forty foot ceilings. Four hundred or more people were in attendance. Musicians, dancers, businessmen and women, politicians, and diplomats. A small contingent of soldiers were led in a dance by the beautifully gowned dancers of the Bolshoi.

Like many of the women in the crowd, I wore a ball gown and felt unabashedly like a princess. The dress was a soft gold, all the way from the fitted silk bodice, down to the tulle-covered oversized skirt. Gold rhinestones covered the bodice and trickled down throughout the skirt, creating a dazzling effect under the lights. I chose black opera length gloves to compliment my mask. *Ah, the mask.* It was a deeper gold than my dress and adorned with scrolls of black music notes and black, silver, and gold feathers along the outer edge. Thick jewels circled my eyes. While it paled slightly in comparison to the rich opulence around me, I felt like I was in the middle of a fairytale. The vodka, the music, the dancing... it was choreographed with breathtaking precision.

My evening had begun by playing for an hour with a small ensemble, but others had taken over, and I had the rest of the night to avoid the politics and infighting and enjoy my evening.

As I watched a group of dancers make coordinated turns across the room from me, Aldo approached. He wore a black mask that bore a long nose. I hated those, but his tuxedo was far more elegant than the one he typically wore for shows.

"Good evening, Savannah," he said, taking my gloved hand and bending over it, brushing it with his lips.

"Good evening, Al." I couldn't help but smile.

"You will dance with me," he stated. I think he intended it as a question or an invitation, but his garbled English came out as an imperative.

I thought about it for just a moment and then said, "I'd be delighted." Although I didn't particularly want to make a fool of myself in front of the most advanced dancers in the world, I wasn't a bad dancer. And not a single one of them was a world class musician. So I took Aldo's hand and allowed him to lead me out to the floor.

I tried to ignore the undercurrents as we began to dance. Sergei Danshov, the ballet director, held court at one end of the hallway, surrounded by many of the younger and more aggressive dancers and cast members in a raucous circle.

At the opposite end of the room, Nikolai Timoshenko stood with his own smaller and slightly older group. Last year, when the previous director retired, probably due to the stress of all the politics and vicious infighting, Nikolai had been a candidate for ballet director. He lost out to Sergei after a vicious competition that I sometimes thought probably wasn't over.

In between the two camps, the rest of us watched and enjoyed the spectacle of the evening. Of course, I'd spent much of my life around musicians, the symphony and opera. But the Bolshoi operated like no other outfit, and put on balls like nothing I'd ever seen. In the dead of the Russian winter, this was a night filled with exuberance.

Aldo spun me around in a circle as we danced, and I felt lightheaded from too much vodka and champagne. After my third twirl, I stopped in place at the sight of a man who had his back to me. Even among the sea of black tuxedos, I would recognize him anywhere.

Aldo stumbled and said, "Are you thriving?"

"Excuse me?"

He smiled and said, "Um...are you well?"

Aldo had been studying his vocabulary, apparently. "I'm thriving," I replied. "Excuse me."

There was no question it was him. He didn't see me yet, so I slowed my pace as I crossed the floor. And watched him.

He wore a simple tuxedo, and his shoulders were pulled back and tense. His head was moving fractionally back and forth, as if he were scanning the crowd. Gregory's hair had grown enough to reveal a slight wave that I didn't know existed. He bore a relaxed look I'd never seen before.

As I stood in what felt like the center of the room, but was far off to one side, he turned around. He was twenty feet from me, but from the emotion that passed between us, he might as well have been touching me. Unlike most of the men at the ball, he wore no mask. His eyes, startling blue in this light, arrested me.

And I froze.

Impervious to the ballerinas, their dates, and people who thought they ought to be ballerinas circling around me in vodka-sponsored jubilance, I fought to hang onto some sense of composure.

Gregory took a deep breath, his shoulders rising, then lifted his chin slightly and walked directly toward me. I felt fixated by his eyes, afraid that if I looked away even for an instant he would disappear.

"Savannah." He reached out with a confident hand and ran the tips of his fingers along the jewels of my mask.

I nodded and then shook my head. Yes. No. Contradictory actions mirroring my emotions. "What...how...why?"

Slowly, his other hand came to the other side of my mask and with painful deliberation he lifted it until it rested on top of my head. He slid his hands down the sides of my face, stopping when he reached my jaw where he held them there. Held me there.

"What are you doing here? Don't you have shows this week?" I continued, as his eyes fell on my lips.

"There are no more shows for me. I resigned, Savannah."

Of course. I knew that, but it still didn't explain what he was doing *here*, holding my face. Or tracing my bottom lip with his thumb.

Snapping back to reality for a moment, I was again aware of the party surrounding us. I reached up to my face and grabbed his hand and led him out the nearest door, which spilled us out onto a narrow balcony. I barely noticed the icy wind that blew along the outside wall of the building. "You *left*? What the hell do you mean you left?"

"It was time for me to make some changes in my life."

I stopped my unattractive pacing and held out my hands. "And the cello?"

"I have another cello...one that isn't so priceless that it becomes more valuable than the people in my life. I sold the Montagnana—"

"Auctioned it," I cut him off, "and gave the money to the conservatory. For the new program you're funding. I read the article in the Globe. You can't leave the BSO, Gregory."

He shrugged. "I've already left."

"It makes no sense." I was breathing faster, sending small white clouds of frozen breath into the space around us. A chill ran through me and I wrapped my arms around my body."

"It makes perfect sense, Savannah." He shrugged off his tuxedo coat and wrapped it around my shoulders, leaving his hands on my upper arms. "I can play the cello anywhere."

I didn't want to bring it up, but for once I had to. "But, your wife..." I swallowed the pain of that phrase and stared straight ahead.

"We divorced. It was final a few days before Christmas." He shoved his hands in his pockets and took a step back.

"So...you didn't leave because you stayed with Karin and decided to have children?" I'd intended that to be more of an internal, rhetorical thought, but it spilled out anyway. Gregory's eyes bulged as he leaned his head forward as if he hadn't heard me properly.

"Children? Savannah—"

"I know," I cut him off, "I know you said you don't want kids, but there was no reason for you to leave the BSO, or to sell your cello...or to come here."

I sniffed as the wind bit at my eyes and nose. Finally directing my eyes back to him, I said, "What *are* you doing here?" My teeth chattered in the pause before his answer.

"I came here...to ask for your forgiveness. And because we never had the chance to say goodbye."

My *forgiveness?* "I don't...forgive what?"

He stepped closer to me...an inch? More? I have no idea how close. Then he said, "I wasn't there when you needed me. I couldn't put you first. I had...too much...weight in my life. The cello, the career, Karin...all of it. I...I'm asking you to forgive me for not doing what I should have done five years ago. Because...I love you."

"You—" I wasn't given the opportunity to finish my thought as he pulled me to his body.

For months I tried to forget the feel of his shoulders and chest, but they felt the same. Just as I'd remembered. He smelled the same, felt the same, and, most disturbing of all, made me feel the same as he always had. Not only could I not look away, not fight him. I didn't *want* to. One of his hands slipped around the back of my neck, causing me to lean my head to the side.

"No...*you*." His hand gently led me forward, and as I watched his lips part, mine did, too. Then our lips were touching, tentatively at first, and then he pulled me tight against him, his lips insatiable against mine.

I couldn't have fought it even if I wanted to. My lips molded with his so effortlessly, it was like they hadn't missed a day. Only, they had. They'd missed the last four months and most of the five years before that. Just as the tip of his tongue grazed my bottom lip, I pulled away.

"Wait." I pulled away, planting my palms against his shoulders and keeping him at arms' length. "You can't leave because of me. You'll resent me for it. I've seen it happen, Gregory, and I can't let you do that to yourself. Or me."

"I'd never resent you. I didn't leave *because* of you, Savannah. I left because of me. Because of the person I'd become, and the one I want to be. I'm no longer willing to spend my life walled away with just my music. You've taught me that life can mean so much more than that." He leaned in to begin kissing me again, but I turned my head.

"I live *here*, Gregory. I have an apartment, and a job that fulfills me, and a life that's mine. I don't know," I paused and looked to my left and right before whispering the rest of my sentence, "I don't know if I'm going to stay with the Bolshoi, but I plan on staying in Europe for a while."

He gently grabbed my chin between his thumb and fore-finger and turned my head so I'd look at him. "Savannah, haven't you listened? I'm...I want to be with *you*. I can play anywhere. Or not. Even if I never join another symphony I've had a career I can be damn proud of. I want to support you and love you and...be with you."

"That's what my dad said."

"Jesus," he sighed, pulling me into a hug once more and resting his lips against my neck. "This isn't the same thing. You know that. There's nothing else I can say to...hey, dance with me?"

"What?" I wiped a stubborn, and slightly frozen, tear from my cheek.

"Come dance with me. Inside." Gregory stepped toward the door and held out his arm, saying no more.

Wiggling out of his tuxedo coat, I said, "You're going to need this."

After fastening the button and adjusting his cufflinks, he placed his hand on the door handle, but paused and took my hand in his. "Before we go in, I want you to know how absolutely stunning you look this evening, Savannah. Now and every other evening since I've known you. I never said it enough, because you struck me speechless more than I care to admit."

My cheeks welcomed the blush overcoming them, and I kissed him softly before opening the door myself. "Thank you."

Inside he took my hand, pulling me toward the still crowd-ed dance floor. My chest tightened a little as I followed him. Despite his words, the fear of ending the night, once again, with a broken heart, pulled me back. I would dance with him. But I needed more. I needed to know I could depend on him. I needed to know that this was actually going somewhere.

My trepidation ceased as he took my right hand in his left, and put his other hand on my waist. Seconds later we were dancing, and it was as seamless as it had ever been. He stayed quiet, but his eyes said everything. He still loved me, but I wasn't sure that was enough.

Neither of us really led, because we didn't need to. Just as we responded to each other without words on the stage, communicating with the notes, the tempo, the harmony, so we communicated on the dance floor with our bodies. Our feet and legs and bodies moving together in unfaltering rhythm, and the longer I looked at him, the longer I felt his body against mine, the longer I smelled him, the less I could imagine letting him leave when the song ended.

As the band played its final note, he leaned close, his lips near my ear, and he whispered, "Savannah, I want you to be mine."

I sucked in a breath at his words. I couldn't think. I couldn't even see. My emotions were overwhelmed. I was overwhelmed.

"You can't leave your life..."

He kept one hand firmly at the small of my back and said, "I already did. I want you to be my new life."

I felt my pulse in my neck as my hands slid down his shoulders onto his chest. "But...where will you work?"

He chuckled softly. "I was principal cellist for the Boston Symphony Orchestra. I can work anywhere I want."

I shivered, because I knew he was right. And I could not get my mind around the idea that he'd walked away from it.

"I...live in Moscow. I'm not planning to be here for long, but I'm not going back to the States."

He shrugged then whispered in my ear, "We can go anywhere we want, Savannah. Anywhere. Just...let it be together." His voice dropped to a low growl, the same early-morning voice, which sent shivers down my spine every single time during our months together. "Savannah...I'm begging you."

I pulled him tighter, and his arms tightened on me as I whispered, "I'm afraid, Gregory."

"Don't be afraid. Because I'll always be there. I belong to you now. And forever."

My chin quivered as I briefly examined what my life would look like without him. Always wondering. Wishing. Regretting. My lips twitched into a smile as I let out a small chuckle, my eyes filling with tears.

"Forever," I whispered, pulling back so I could kiss him the way I'd wanted to since I spotted him across the ballroom.

The room had emptied, the call for dinner had come and gone, but Gregory and I held onto each other, and our promise, until the musicians took their places once more. A waltz closed out the last portion of the evening, and Gregory led me. The music sounded different, even though the same group was on the stage.

Music always sounded better with him.

With us.

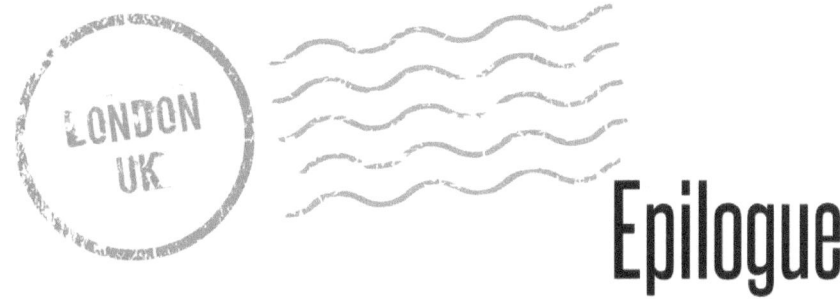

Epilogue

GREGORY

THE COOL SEPTEMBER breeze blew off the River Thames to the fifth floor balcony where I sat, drinking a cup of tea. Our flat on Chicheley Street, right in the heart of London, was little more than six hundred square feet. Six hundred square feet of joy that we'd rented not long after Savannah was offered first chair with the London Symphony.

I'd never forget the day she got the call. The pride in her glistening eyes as tears ran down her face. The pure joy I felt for her at the realization of her dreams.

"Are you sure you don't mind?" she'd asked.

As if I could possibly mind. Savannah was at the top of her career. Every single day I was stunned by her talent, her beauty, her love. Every day.

Today I was nursing a little bit of a hangover, but that would clear soon enough. I took out my phone and scanned through the various congratulatory emails and messages. Some of them, such as those from former students and friends like Joseph McIntosh, were genuine. The others mattered little to me. I'd spent so many years pushing people away I could hardly be disappointed when they responded in kind.

But the last two years had changed that in so many ways. And *that* made me grateful for the friends, like James and Madeline, who had stuck it out with me, who had stayed friends, who had brought their own wisdom and love and care to my life.

The door opened, and James stepped out on the balcony. He set his coffee down and took a seat. He was already dressed. I slid the letter across to him. It was from the National Children's Orchestras of Great Britain, offering me the position of Principal Director of Music. It would be a change. Instead of being a professional musician, I'd be a mentor, a conductor. I'd be nurturing children who sought careers in music.

James scanned the letter then looked up at me, folding it back into thirds.

"Not what I expected," he said. "You'll be teaching only... not playing."

I nodded. "I'll always play. But...I've been there, James. I spent ten years as principal chair at the BSO. I feel like it's time to give something back."

He nodded. "I get it, Gregory. I'm just...surprised. And very happy for you. Can I tell you, I almost didn't recognize you. You're so happy it's almost frightening."

I chuckled. "You expect me to be tortured? Closeted somewhere with my cello?"

James laughed. "Yes. Generally that's exactly what I expect of you." He shook his head and took another drink of his coffee. "Does Savannah know yet?"

"About the job? No. Rather, she knows I've been talking with them. The offer came yesterday and I wanted today to be...about us. Not about the job."

He smiled. "I'm incredibly happy for you. Madeline is too."

I leaned forward, took another sip of my tea. "Speaking of Madeline, she's pretty far along. Do you know if this one's a boy a girl?" Pretty far along was an understatement. Even though she wasn't due for another three months, Madeline was as big as an upright bass.

He shook his head. "Not yet. She doesn't want to know in advance."

"And how is little Delaney?"

"She took her first steps two weeks ago." The pride on his face was transparent and beautiful. He said, "What about you two? Any plans for kids?"

I shook my head. "Neither of us is really thinking along those lines. I don't know what the future may hold, but for now, it's the two of us."

Oddly enough, I really *didn't* know what the future held. I'd never planned on kids, and Savannah hadn't either. But neither of us was as opposed to the idea as we'd been a year ago. So for the time being, we simply moved forward, and made sure we talked, a lot, about what we wanted.

This much I knew. Savannah and I were meant for each other. Now and forever.

James and I finished up our drinks. He looked at me and said, "Time to get ready, friend."

I gave him a serious nod, then stepped inside and prepared myself. Freshly shaved and dressed, I rode the elevator down with my oldest friend and we got in the hired car, headed to Wilton's Music Hall on Graces Alley in the East End.

Steeped in London's history, Wilton's was one of the most important and oldest music halls in London. A nineteenth century concert hall was joined by a terrace to the Mahogany Bar. Three houses made a unique, fascinating setting. Savannah and I had agreed almost immediately on the concert hall here for our wedding, because it echoed with the melodies of three hundred years of musicians. And, it was us. It was our life together past, present, and future.

It was a small wedding, but the hall was filled with people we both loved, and who loved us. Taking one last look over the crowd, my eyes rested for a minute on Vita and Malcolm. While Savannah hadn't attended their wedding, their relationship was finally on the mend. I doubted it would ever return to whatever it was each of them thought it once was, but it worked for Savannah, and that's what mattered.

Vita gave me a polite smile, and I returned it before watching her eyes move to the memory candle at the base of the stage. Stephen, Savannah's father, had passed away the year before, after an aggressive battle with brain cancer. Savannah was there at the end, and I was next to her, holding her as she cried for weeks. Getting through that together in one piece gave us a strength neither of us realized we possessed together.

The string ensemble took a long pause at the end of their number, and I knew this was it. At their next cue, the doors would open and my future wife would be walking toward me. As the violin led, the doors opened, and I had to stop myself from racing down the aisle to get her myself.

God, she was exquisite. The simple long white dress highlighted nothing but her beauty. I watched her chest rise in a deep breath before she leaned in and gave Nathan a kiss on the cheek. Her eyes never left mine as he led her down the aisle. After a million years she finally got to me, and Nathan held her hand out to mine.

Leaning in, he said, "Take care of her." He was serious, but not threateningly so.

I gave him a pat on the shoulder. "I promise I will."

With that, he gave her another hug and kiss before he stepped back and left me with Savannah at the altar. I took her hands in mine and she squeezed them tight.

Breaking convention, as she did best, Savannah kissed me once and whispered, "I love you."

"I love you, too," I whispered back, ignoring the *Awws* from the guests.

She rested her forehead on mine for a beat and said, "Marry me?"

I kissed her once more. "Absolutely."

And so I took her hand and we faced the minister. The music from the ensemble in the back of the hall had stopped.

But for us, the music was only beginning.

the end

www.ingramcontent.com/pod-product-compliance
Lightning Source LLC
Chambersburg PA
CBHW051541250626
47157CB00001B/133